THE
BARTENDER'S
CURE

THE BARTENDER'S CURE

Wesley Straton

FLATIRON
BOOKS
NEW YORK

THE BARTENDER'S CURE. Copyright © 2022 by Wesley Straton. All rights reserved. Printed in the United States of America. For information, address Flatiron Books, 120 Broadway, New York, NY 10271.

www.flatironbooks.com

Designed by Donna Sinisgalli Noetzel

Illustration of barspoon © Prokhorovich/Shutterstock.com

Library of Congress Cataloging-in-Publication Data

Names: Straton, Wesley, author.
Title: The Bartender's Cure / Wesley Straton.
Description: First edition. | New York : Flatiron Books, 2022.
Identifiers: LCCN 2021055565 | ISBN 9781250809070 (hardcover) |
    ISBN 9781250809094 (ebook)
Subjects: LCSH: Bartending—Fiction. | LCGFT: Novels.
Classification: LCC PS3619.T742558 B37 2022 | DDC 813/.6—dc23
LC record available at https://lccn.loc.gov/2021055565

Our books may be purchased in bulk for promotional, educational, or business use. Please contact your local bookseller or the Macmillan Corporate and Premium Sales Department at 1-800-221-7945, extension 5442, or by email at MacmillanSpecialMarkets@macmillan.com.

First Edition: 2022

10 9 8 7 6 5 4 3 2 1

For Nicole & Marissa & Kevin & Steph

& Tony & Thomas & Tyson & Jarred

& Priscilla & Pita & Adam & Dan

& Duncan & Casey & Jen

& all the other bartenders who got me here

Most bartender's guides can tell you—along with a few pertinent remarks on mixing drinks, chilling and serving wines, and a thousand or so recipes for drinks that no sane person would ever drink—the signs of the zodiac, how to take spots off your suits, remedies for curing hiccoughs and removing warts, what hour the sun comes up, the rise and fall of the tides, some after-dinner magic—and end up with a full chapter on horse racing.

Just to make this book unique, I'm going to try to stick to bartending.

—*Trader Vic's Bartender's Guide*

THE
BARTENDER'S
CURE

FIRST WORD

You've seen bars like this. It's New York City, the center of the universe, and you've seen everything. Speakeasies, dives, pubs, wine bars, beer bars, tiki bars, bars in restaurants and hotels, in breweries and distilleries, in cafés, in grocery stores, in basements, on rooftops, on boats. Bars with twelve seats and two hundred. Bars that serve nothing but cocktails, bars with no liquor license at all.

Joe's Apothecary is one of many, and yet, there is nowhere else like Joe's. It's small, with white walls and exposed brick, big windows looking out onto the street, a scattering of high-tops in the front, a handful of tables in the back. The bar itself a golden gleam in a dim room, a ten-seater "L" built out of wood and brass, lit by Edison bulbs and candlelight. A cocktail bar, at its core, though not pushy about it, though there are regulars who come in for top-shelf Scotch and Narragansett alike. It's a true neighborhood bar, the kind of place that is harder to find by the year in this city, the kind of place that could only possibly exist on this block, in this neighborhood, in this borough, under these exact unlikely circumstances.

It's June in New York and the city is awash with kids in robes, blue and black and purple, the class of 2018 on the streets and the subways, double-parked in front of dorms and apartment buildings, and if I close my eyes I can pretend to be one of them, pretend the last two years never happened and I'm twenty-two again, fresh out of Columbia, a Bachelor of the Art of English literature, *cum laude*, thankyouverymuch. The world my oyster, waiting to be plucked and shucked and swallowed. Pretending I'm not flat broke and sleeping on my best friend's couch and painfully single and so far jobless, although this last is about to change, I'm hoping, standing outside this lovely bar, ten minutes early for a trial shift, peering in through those front windows with a wine key in my pocket and my hair tied back in a ponytail and my stomach tied up in knots. Brooklyn is still dusky rather than dark, but I can see the flicker of candles inside, a dim warm glow. I crack my knuckles, try to remember the feel of a cocktail shaker, the heft of a tray. I have, as you can probably tell, some reservations.

How do any of us end up working in bars? Some become bartenders on purpose—Han, Gina, Scott the Scot. But more often we stumble into it, in moments like these. Because our shiny degrees have not delivered the futures we were promised. Because we are night owls in a world that prizes early birds. Because we are tired of staring at screens, of sitting in unending meetings, of working for companies that do and make nothing. Because something marked us in our lives, or we marked ourselves, as somehow unfit for the office, for the classroom, for the nine-to-five. Because we descended, and found that once we had drunk the nectar of this particular netherworld, we could never go home.

· · ·

But I'm getting ahead of myself. For now, like so many before me, I am just looking for a job. Something temporary, just enough for rent money, just to get me off Hayley's couch, just to keep me in the city until next year, when I'll be going back to school myself. I open the door. I walk inside.

FRENCH 75

1 ounce gin
3/4 ounce lemon juice
3/4 ounce simple syrup
Sparkling wine

Short shake the first three ingredients with ice. Strain into
a champagne flute and top with sparkling wine.

Go to Joe's, Gina said. Gina, the beautiful, heavyset, heavily
tattooed owner of Hayley's favorite bar, a thirty-something angel who
took pity on me, who, she would insist later, saw something in me, and
sent me to the other bar she owned, which is to say, this one. Carver's
short-staffed, she said, and I'm tired of helping them out every weekend.
And I wasn't looking for a bar job—I am not looking for a bar job—but
I was in no position to say no, especially not in front of Hayley, and so
here I am, and I walk in, and Dan Olsen is behind the bar, and I am
tempted to walk right back out again.

A bar story. Once upon a time, a twenty-year-old virgin had a big dumb
crush on a tall blond bartender. The bartender worked at a sticky Irish
pub that didn't card, or at least that didn't card the virgin and her beautiful

best friend. The bartender smiled and made jokes and gave the virgin free whiskey-gingers when she came in after work, and she would recycle her tips into his tips. One thing, as they say, led to another.

The virgin never told the bartender that it was her first time, assuming that he would be a weirdo about it. Unfortunately, he was a weirdo about it anyway: grew awkward, distant, unavailable. And while the virgin was never in love with the bartender, she did like him, and he was a real dick about the whole thing, and after four more ill-advised hookups, she and the best friend had to stop going to that bar. But four years later, the bartender greets her with a smile and a hug, calls her unexpected appearance *a pleasant surprise* in a tone that is more or less convincing.

A pleasant surprise. The pleasantness is the surprise; he may have been a dick to me, but I know him, and this grounds me. I am in need of grounding; the bar is busy already, no time for a tour or any further orientation, just quick handshakes with the other men behind the bar— Carver, the manager and Gina's *protégé* (her word), a classic Brooklyn bartender type, stocky and tattooed and sporting a dark beard best described as luxuriant; and Han, a lanky East Asian guy with a man-bun and a grin so wide you think it'll break his face open.

You're just in time, Han says, as if I have wandered in by coincidence and not at exactly the hour appointed. You can make the Snaiquiris.

Excuse me?

Baby daiquiris, Han says, brandishing a bottle of rum at me. It's a Friday night tradition.

We don't really have time, Carver says, and I can understand why; the place is packed, every table taken, no seats free at the bar, dirty glasses for days back by the glasswasher. Han pulls a face at him and drags me over to one of the bar stations. You know how to make a daiquiri?

It's a question that's not a question. The daiquiri is one of the basics, the bare necessities of cocktail bartending, the simplest of simple sours: light rum, lime juice, simple syrup. If I don't know that, I don't know anything.

There's a shaker already sitting on the bar-top, and I lift up the rum first, and go to pour.

Oh, no, Carver says. Not like that.

He takes the shaker back, dumps it out. No free-pouring at Joe's, he says. And he nudges me out of the way and makes the drinks himself.

And so, our first bartending lesson. In spite of everything you may have been told at your last bartending job, you must measure your ingredients. Take your jigger. That's the funny metal measuring tool, two cones with their points stuck together. Most decent bars will have these in two different sizes, and you want the larger one. The big half holds a full two ounces, the smaller holds one, with a line at the three-quarter mark. You'll hold this upright in your nondominant hand and you'll take the bottle of, in this case, rum, with your dominant one. When you pour, a Scottish bartender once told me, hold the bottle like you'd hold somebody else's penis. Scott the Scot, the bartender at my second-ever New York job, begun the summer after sophomore year. He was straight and I was a virgin at the time, so I'm not sure how meaningful the advice was to either of us, but it's stuck with me. More directly useful was the instruction to keep a thumb pressed against the speed pourer—that's the rubber and metal beak that goes into the mouth of a bottle to control the flow of liquor—because one day you won't, and the speed pourer will fall out, and you'll get booze fucking everywhere.

When you pour, fill that jigger all the way up, and then some. Experiment with the magic of surface tension. If you don't have a nice domed meniscus, just about to burst, you're under-pouring.

Scott the Scot taught me to do this by touch, by taste, by sight. Count to four, that's two ounces, a standard pour. That goes up to *here* in a Collins glass, *there* in a rocks glass. A quarter ounce of simple syrup feels like *this*; an ounce of citrus pours like *that*. You can do good work free-pouring; you can certainly save time. Great debates have arisen out of this, schisms in the cocktail scene; bartenders have come to blows; families have been torn asunder. The world of bartending, you will learn, is a world of strong opinions. But Carver says no free-pouring at Joe's, and so, we won't.

When everything has been measured and shaken, Carver pours the drink, cloudy and faintly green, into four elegant little glasses, and mine is heavy in my hand as I lift it up. To Sam, Han says, who I'm sure had better things to do with her Friday night.

I didn't, but I let them toast me anyway. It tastes like summer.

Having failed my first test, then, I am relegated to the glasswasher. Han and Carver resume their roles behind the bar, and Olsen—they call him Olsen here, because by some strange coincidence or a small, dumb joke of fate, everyone but me has the same first name—Olsen is out on the floor. The glasswasher is a noisy, scuffed steel contraption that cleans and sanitizes and expels tray after tray of hot, gleaming glasses, which I am supposed to polish and put away. Joe's is the sort of place that polishes everything—wineglasses, of course, but also coupe glasses and rocks glasses and water glasses and Collins glasses and even the beer glasses, although those need only the most cursory of wipes. I use brightly colored cloths and I am thorough, if not as quick as I would like to be. Scott the Scot never made me polish anything.

The washer is in a corner behind the bar, the back corner, far away from Olsen as he works the floor, far from Han as he works the point, near only to Carver, who keeps his back to me as he bangs out drink after drink after drink. I watch the Dans as I work, their rhythm behind the narrow bar, the quickness and ease of movement, the economy. Olsen's speed and agility on the floor. I'm not an asshole; I know that working in the service industry requires certain skills. I can tell that everyone here is good at what they do, that I am the odd one out and not only because I have the wrong name and the wrong gender and not only because I'm younger and less experienced. None of this surprises me. What surprises me is that I feel a small pang of envy.

Mine is not a glamorous job; it is dull, repetitive work, and not at all what I expected, although I will admit that for long, pleasant stretches it becomes meditative, even soothing. A couple hours in, Carver comes over with a pair of coupes, and he sets these down to the right of the washer with the rest of the dirties, and then he puts a hand on my arm and he shakes his head.

Not like that, he says. I have a wineglass in my hands, stem in the left, bowl and polishing cloth in the right. I can't tell you how many bartenders I know who have sliced their wrists open like that. You snap the stem and next minute we're rushing you to the emergency room.

He shows me how to do it properly, carefully, but it takes longer and the glasses don't get as clean and I'm getting further and further behind, when I was keeping up just fine before, without injuring myself, and Carver leaves his bar station and comes back and starts polishing again. I'm sorry, I say. I'm just not used to doing it like this. I'll get quicker.

Just let me do the stemware for now, he says, and then he doesn't say anything and I polish everything that doesn't have a stem as quickly as I possibly can. I'm not sorry. I'm annoyed. I'm wondering if this is what working here is like, being micromanaged by this unfriendly stuck-up hipster who treats me like I'm stupid. My chest feels tight and I feel hot all over and the silence is stretching on and on and thicker and thicker but I don't know how to break it. And then after fifteen minutes or so I'm caught up, and Carver walks away again without a word.

At a normal job, like, say, the gig your best friend's mom gets you at her law firm, you have a résumé. You have references; you have an interview, maybe a couple. In the service industry all of these things are true, too, sometimes, but then nine times out of ten you have an extra step, a trial shift, which means you work for free in an attempt to prove that you're not a total idiot. There is an innate awkwardness to this; you don't know anything about the bar's policies or practices, you don't know that they use jiggers or that the manager has some kind of stick up his ass about how to polish glasses. It's like walking into a stranger's apartment and using their kitchen—you've cooked before, I hope, but you don't know where they keep all the pots and pans or how sharp their knives are or what they have in the pantry. Plus it has been a long time since I last worked in a bar, and that bar was much less nice than this one, and I am flushed and raw and nervous and I am also desperate to succeed, and not sure how likely that is. I am so broke that I walked the hour to get here rather than taking the subway, trekked in the ninety-something heat and the ninety-something humidity from Hayley's apartment down through the Disneyland sheen of Williamsburg, through the Orthodox neighborhoods with the women in wigs and the school buses painted in Hebrew, past the projects, down into Bed-Stuy. Showed up drenched in sweat and so thirsty, and my feet are sore already, and I need this job, because I need to be able to afford the subway, and new shoes, and eventually my own apartment, too. Did I mention you don't get paid for trial shifts? I polish another wineglass and I wonder if it might be a better idea to cut my arm open just how Carver said and sue.

And then it's eleven and Joe's Apothecary is all but empty. Funny, these service industry tides; the bar will be busy again before the night is over, though the biggest wave is behind us. Our daywalkers are gone, either home or to rowdier places, and our nightwalkers are yet to arrive. We reset the bar: Carver and Han wipe down wet and sticky surfaces, clean the sinks, replenish the stacks of square black bev-naps on the bar-top; Olsen and I restock beer and liquor and wine from the stores down in the basement.

So how have you been? he asks me, and I don't know how to answer. The walk-in is cold and dark and entirely too intimate, and I stand a careful arm's length away as he fills a bus tub with cans of beer and bottles of wine, all of it pretty and expensive, the hipster beers with their names like nail polish colors, the wine in every imaginable shade of white and pink and orange. Artsy minimalist labels and dark glass. Fine, I say; I've been fine. Brief stint back home, newly back in the city.

Olsen nods, crouching down to reach for something on a far back shelf, his white tee riding up to reveal a band of pale skin and a stripe of dark elastic. I suppress a shiver. California, right? he asks, and I say yes, and I remember that he's a California native as well, and that there is perhaps common ground to be found there, but I do not want to talk about California. He straightens up, leads the way out of the walk-in, and I turn the question back. How have you been, Olsen? How's The Bright Brigade?

These last words spoken with feigned hesitation, as if I were not quite sure I had the name right, as if I had not lost hours and perhaps days of my life listening to Olsen's band, stalking Olsen through their Sound-Cloud or whatever, utterly in the thrall of his voice, striking and urgent like he was singing to survive.

Olsen sets the bus tub down, starts adding more bottles, well whiskey, two different gins, mezcal. Broken up, he says, and when I say I'm sorry he looks at me with his sharp blue eyes and his face twists into a mirthless smile. All those guys are back in California now, he says, working in *tech*. This last spit out like the four-letter word it is. He hefts up the bus tub, and I watch him, my hands empty and useless at my sides. You think you know someone, he says, shaking his head, and I think of my techie ex-boyfriend, and I tell him I know what he means.

Fuck 'em, he says. He nods to another shelf and tells me to grab two pinots and meet him back upstairs.

Upstairs, Carver has disappeared, and Han is the very image of relaxed, leaning against one of the ice wells with a glass of water in one hand and his phone in the other, though he puts the latter away now, and straightens, and says, All right, Samantha. Let's make a cocktail.

He waves me over to his side. He smells like sweat and ethanol and he is a good half foot taller than me and he looks down with deep brown eyes and the same toothy grin as before, and he asks me, What do you drink?

I guess my go-to is a martini, I say, and I hear Olsen laugh. Last time I saw Sam she was more of a Jamo and ginger kind of gal, he says, and I want to defend myself, first of all because there is nothing wrong with Jameson and ginger ale, it is a perfectly reasonable order, especially in an Irish pub in the East Village, and also because I was twenty and new to drinking in general, and also because, if memory serves, the Jameson and gingers were Olsen's suggestion to begin with. But I understand that this is only good-natured ribbing, and best not argued with. I laugh, too.

Han stands half a step behind me as I work, looking down over my shoulder, and I hope I'm not blushing, but I probably am. I've made martinis before, of course, but he talks me through it like I haven't, and I let him. The first thing, he says, is to keep everything cold. That's easy enough: the mixing glasses are kept in a freezer under the bar, and the coupes are, too, and I pull out one of the former, setting it gently on the bar mat. The second thing, Han says, is vermouth.

There's a famous quote from Hitchcock, or Churchill, depending on who you ask, about how much vermouth to put in a martini: to paraphrase, a dry martini should consist of gin stirred over ice while looking at a bottle of vermouth. This, Han says, is bullshit. It's a two-ingredient cocktail, he says. If you leave out the vermouth, it's just gin in a cup.

Nothing wrong with gin in a cup, Olsen says, and Han shrugs.

Sure, I guess. But don't call it a fucking martini.

Vermouth first, because it's cheaper, and you use less of it, and as a general cocktail-making rule, Han says, you should start with the cheaper ingredients and the smaller pours, so that if you fuck up the drink early on, you're not throwing out the expensive stuff. It's all booze in this case, so the order matters less, but still. Vermouth first, then gin, a hefty pour of, in this case, Plymouth, which Han has already selected from the back bar, and then a big scoop of ice.

The next lesson: stirring. You want that mixing glass to be full up with ice, and if you are using big cubes, like they have at Joe's, you'll want to crack some of them to fill the gaps. There is a tool for this called, cleverly enough, a tap-icer, a plastic, lollipop-looking device that will break up ice nicely, if you know how to use it, which I don't, and the first time I hit my hand and the second time I crack the ice only to immediately drop the shards back into the well, and now I know I'm blushing, but Han doesn't say anything about it, just waits beside me as I try yet another time and manage the great feat of cracking a couple cubes, and now all I have to do is slide a long, spiraled barspoon into the glass and stir until everything is cold and diluted just the right amount.

Ideally the ice should stir as one, almost silent, but mine clatters around horribly and I'm thinking of Scott the Scot, who never said anything about *filling the glass all the way* or *tap-icers* or *stirring silently*, who used the small, chipped ice from the old machine in the kitchen, the technical term for which, I will soon learn, is *bodega ice* if you're polite or *shitty ice* if you're not. On top of this he shook his martinis most of the time anyway, and nobody ever complained.

I wish I were working with him again.

I know better than to say any of this out loud.

How long do I stir? I ask. How many times?

You get a feel for it pretty quick, Han says, but that's not an answer. What do I do until then? He tells me that when he started, he always just counted to twenty-three and then tasted.

Twenty-three, Olsen scoffs. What kind of arbitrary hipster nonsense is that?

It was Michael Jordan's number, you philistine, Han says, and Olsen is surprised into laughter. I finish stirring and Han leans in close, and he straw-tests, which is to say he dips a long steel straw into the drink, covers the top opening with a finger so that through the joy of science, the straw holds a sample of the drink steady as he lifts the business end from glass to mouth, releases the finger, tastes.

Just a couple more, he says, and I do it, and he tastes again. Perfect, he says, and I strain it out into a coupe, garnish with an olive from one of the jars on the bar-top, and then I hear Carver's voice and I jump a little, I wonder how long he's been watching, realize belatedly that this is another test, that everything about tonight is a test, and not the kind I'm good at.

Let's talk, he says, and he tells me to wait for him in the back room, and I'm so nervous I feel sick.

I sink into a wine-red banquette, exposed brick behind me, more Edison bulbs and tea lights and a couple old Art Deco liquor advertisements framed on the walls. Cliché, I think, and I want to be cynical, but like many clichés, it works. The music is quieter back here, the light dimmer, and I can't hear well enough to eavesdrop properly, and I feel generally like I'm in the world's sexiest oubliette. I trace my finger along the dark grain of the table and then I weave my fingers together and then I make a circle around one of my wrists with my thumb and middle finger, measure my slender bones, see how far down my forearm the loop will go.

I drop my wrist when Carver reappears. He sits down across from me, his expression unreadable as ever, and he says, Tell me about your experience.

I run through it with him, start to finish, more or less honestly. It doesn't take long. My first service industry job, a high school summer in Palo Alto, clearing tables at a café run by a friend of Hayley's mother— easy enough, high margin for error, nothing fresh or hot to be carried out, just detritus to be taken away. Later, technically an adult, acne mostly gone, people skills slightly improved, fresh-faced at the host stand at an upscale Thai-fusion joint in Midtown Manhattan. Then there was the pub, with the aforementioned Scott the Scot, just a runner at first, clumsy with three plates but young and cute enough to get away with it, mostly, plus even if you're not great at your job, you can get pretty far on a good attitude and an anathema for being late. Promoted to server, clumsy again with trays full of beers and cocktails, at which point Scott the Scot got me behind the bar on quiet nights, which is on my résumé as, simply, *bartending.*

I'm not a total neophyte, I say.

Neophyte, Carver echoes. He looks down at my résumé then, back up at me. What about the last two years?

I had an office job, I say. I say nothing about the months in the Arizona desert after that. I say nothing about the specter of grad school looming on the horizon, fifteen months away, not that I'm counting. Carver's eyes are gray and grave, crow's-feet gathering at the corners. I realize with a rush of cold blood that he does not want to hire me; that I am not good enough; that this, too, will be added to my lengthening list of missed and squandered opportunities. That I will have to go back to Hayley and say, Still no.

Plus I can tell Carver doesn't like me, and that irks me. It's not that I don't believe anyone could dislike me—I left San Francisco pretty universally reviled. But Carver doesn't know about any of that. He's only just met me. So why doesn't he like me?

How do you make your Manhattan?

It takes me a second to realize he's talking about the drink and not the borough, to realize that I am being quizzed. Manhattan, though, that's easy; Scott the Scot taught me that ages ago. Whiskey, sweet vermouth, Angostura bitters. Cherry garnish.

Can you name a tequila cocktail that isn't a margarita? he asks, and that's harder, but I remember one from my favorite bar back in San Francisco, something sweet that Greg liked, an El Diablo, and when I say the name Carver looks surprised and almost impressed.

What's in a French 75? he asks, and this one stumps me. I have never heard of a French 75. Um, I say. Cognac?

Maybe, Carver says, which I think is him being a dick, though I will later learn that there is some disagreement as to whether a French 75 calls for gin or brandy and so, yes, maybe cognac.

Carver is quiet for a moment, staring down at my résumé as if there were anything illuminating on it. Look, I say. I'm not a rock star mixolo-gist or whatever. But I'd like to learn. I'm a quick study. And I'm nice, and I'm always on time, and I'm a good, hard worker. And Gina—

Fucking Gina, Carver says, which shuts me up. He sighs and rubs the back of his neck with his fingers and he says, Well. Olsen likes you. And Han says you make a great martini. His eyes meet mine again. He looks tired. Defeated, even. What's the rest of your week look like? he asks, and I tell him it's open.

Let's get you training with Han and Olsen on Sunday, he says. And we'll go from there.

Great, I say, and he smiles, but it doesn't reach his eyes. He stands up, shakes my hand.

Oh, he says. And don't say *mixologist*. And then he's gone.

I walk back out to the bar like an astronaut readjusting to gravity, and I wonder if I should just go home, if it's weird for me to hang out here, but Olsen is pulling out a stool for me and Han is grinning from behind the bar and I sit down, and they make me a drink. French 75, Han says. Carver's orders.

French 75: a classic, pre-Prohibition drink enjoyed by the likes of Er-nest Hemingway, named after a specific French field gun used in World War I. Drink and weapon alike known for efficacy and strength. Some argument, as we mentioned, about whether it was, originally, made with gin or cognac, but the other ingredients are consistent: sugar, lemon, champagne.

Our next bar lesson, then. As a general rule, anything with citrus gets shaken, and the French 75 is no exception. At Joe's they use tin-on-tin shakers, two stainless steel cups in different sizes. Scott the Scot used Bostons—same general idea, but you replace the larger of the tins with a pint glass—but Han says the tin-on-tin is pretty much industry standard these days.

Build your drink in the smaller of the tins, cheaper ingredients first again—simple syrup first, then lemon juice, gin last. Don't shake the champagne; that will end badly for you. Fill the whole tin with ice—again, all the way up. Seal it with the bigger tin, at a nice angle, the outside edges flush on one side, like a wide-based obtuse triangle. Shake it hard, harder, see how the tin is frosting over. How long you do this depends on the size of your ice, and on how the drink is served—you can pour it a little stronger if it's going on ice, whereas if it's going up it should be diluted to precisely where you want it. A French 75 gets a *short shake*: just enough to chill and mix.

There are all kinds of different fancy shakes out there, Han says, but as long as you're getting the drink cold and aerated and mixed together, the form of your motion is really just a matter of aesthetics and ergonomics. He says this, and yet I can't help but admire the sharp fierce form of his shake, the forceful elegance of it.

Hit the base of the triangle, crack it open. Strain the drink through a Hawthorne strainer—that's the funny-looking one with the spring around the edge—and if you're serving it up, which we are, a mesh one, too. This gets the ice chips out. Before Joe's I never considered ice chips in a cocktail offensive, but Han assures me that they are. Aesthetics again, but also because they will further dilute the drink, and you have, presumably, diluted it perfectly already.

Top with champagne, pass to your eagerly awaiting guest.

This is the most delicious thing I've ever tasted, I say, and Han bows.

I hear we get you on Sunday, he says, and I like the way he says it, as if this were a privilege and not a pain in the ass. I nod. Come in at eight again, Han says. I'll run you through closing.

The door opens then, a group of noisy women descending on one of the high-tops, Olsen hurrying over with menus and water. The late-night wave beginning, me alone with my French 75 and a feeling like a fever breaking. The bar-top before me is cool, dark brass, dulled and stained with rings from past glassware, splashes of Angostura bitters, streaks of green. Every bar-top has its scars: warped wood, scuffed marble, scratched plastic. Part of the charm, Scott the Scot used to say; you want your bar to feel lived-in.

Even tarnished, I find this one particularly lovely.

How you doing there, kiddo?

It's Han again, leaning over to refill my water, gesturing to my French 75, which I am surprised to realize I've finished. Can I get you another?

But I shake my head. I have to go, I say. The commute to Williamsburg is a real bitch.

You're living in *Williamsburg*? He looks horrified. Why, did you lose a bet?

Just crashing there for now, I say. While I look for my own place. True and not true: I have not yet started looking because, until now, I have not had any source of income, have not had any indication that my return to New York would be anything more than a brief, ill-starred visit.

So no, I will not have another drink, and I get up to go, and Han holds up a finger. Calls out to Carver, Olsen. Team meeting, he says, and I'm worried for a second, but by *team meeting* Han just means shots, whiskey all around, and I choke mine down and I say my good nights and then I walk the long walk to the G and wait the long wait for the L and I'm tired and I'm hungry and I have to pee but I am so relieved that it doesn't matter. I have a job. I can stay.

NEGRONI

1 1/4 ounces gin
1 ounce Campari
1 ounce sweet vermouth

Stir in a mixing glass over ice. Strain into a rocks glass over ice; garnish with an orange twist.

The couch I am sleeping on is not uncomfortable, but Hayley's apartment is small, and most mornings I am awoken entirely too early by my hosts or my roommates or whatever you want to call them, and I have to pretend not to be groggy and annoyed. I have been on this couch for the better part of a month; I am the one person in this apartment with no right to irritation, no right to be anything but blithely grateful. Hayley has told me a dozen times that I can stay as long as I want, and on some level she means it, but on a level closer to the surface I know she's itching to have the place to herself again. Tyler, the boyfriend, is much more open with his impatience, but then, he always liked Greg more than he liked me, and I guess I can't blame him. I did, too.

Obviously this makes my living situation tense, on top of everything else. Obviously it's not sustainable. Me and Tyler staring daggers at each other every time we cross paths, speaking in monosyllables. Tyler banging around unnecessarily loudly in the mornings, even though he gets up at 6:00 A.M. to go to the gym like a fucking lunatic. If it weren't for Hayley, we would have murdered each other already; even with Hayley, you get the sense it's only a matter of time.

There is no passive-aggressive banging this morning, though; it's a Saturday, and even Tyler sleeps in on the weekends. In fact, I'm the first one up, and I've already finished my first cup of coffee when Hayley emerges from her bedroom. Hayley, my oldest, truest, closest friend, smiling at me with her blond hair haloed around her face, glowing as always, even though she's just woken up, whereas I've been awake for forty-five minutes now and I still look like a fucking gargoyle.

How was it? she asks.

Good, I say. She fills a mug and comes to sit with me on the couch. I'm going in for training tomorrow.

She knocks her coffee against mine like we're doing a toast. Perfect, she says. This is the perfect thing for you right now. She does not say, *plus it will get you off my couch*, but it's implied. She does not say that she has been worried about me, although I know that she has been. She says, Bartending. It sounds fun.

When Hayley and I were younger we used to tell people we were twins, and people used to believe us. Two little blond Californian girls, utterly inseparable. The happy accident of meeting that first year of elementary school, and then we were off, spending the afternoons and weekends and summers of our childhoods together, playdates and summer camps, Girl Scout troops and birthday parties, soccer teams and swim lessons. I would go to her house most days after school, the place enormous and clean, her nanny sweeter and more welcoming than my mercurial mother, *her* mother imposing when she came home in her sharp suits and her high heels. Jackie Kane, who went to Harvard Law School and whose life has always seemed more or less perfect. Even my mother envied and admired her, used to take an hour to pick me up from a playdate, the two of them chatting away in Hayley's family's beautiful kitchen, my mother in a long hippie dress with her fingers stained with paint, Jackie pristine and elegant as ever. Pristine and elegant and viva-cious and *happy*, with a good job and a doting husband and beautiful children and a sort of self-possession that I have come to recognize as rare.

A self-possession that Hayley has inherited, along with most of Jackie's best qualities, although it is best not to say this to Hayley, because us girls always hate being compared to our mothers.

Tyler appears then, goes straight for the coffee. Sam got the job, Hayley tells him, and he leans back against the kitchen counter, and he says, Does this mean I get my couch back?

Tyler says he's happy for you, Hayley says.

As soon as humanly possible, I tell him.

Could we focus on the good news, please? Hayley asks, and Tyler tosses me an unconvincing *congratulations* and retreats into the bed-room. Sorry, Hayley says, and she leaves her mug on the coffee table and goes after him, and I go after the both of them and listen with my ear to the thin door like a nosy child.

Could you give her a break?

Hayley sounds genuinely angry, which shouldn't make me happy, but it does. If the apartment were on fire and she could save only one of us, I have to believe it would be me. I can't tell you why this is so important, but it is.

She's *had* a break.

Arizona was really more of a *breakdown*, Hayley says.

And the month she's been living rent-free in our living room? That's not a break either?

She doesn't have anywhere else to go.

And whose fault is that?

I take my ear away. Tyler can hate me all he wants. I'll still hate me more.

I leave them in the bedroom, grab my bag and my phone and let myself out, and walk south. It's just shy of noon and it's hot already and I should have put on sunscreen but I didn't and I don't want to buy another bottle, and so I walk to the library, figuring I can kill a few hours there, avail my-self of the books and the air-conditioning. This has been a staple of my return to the city so far—I have been here so many times the librarians all know me, by face if not by name, and still every time I come I'm im-pressed by it all over again, that a building that looks like this is open to the public. It's beautiful. Every Californian I know is a sucker for a nice old brick building, despite ourselves. Charmed by a chimney. Smitten with anything built in the 1800s that wasn't thrown together ramshackle and burned to the ground half a dozen times, that isn't earthquake-proof and doesn't have to be.

I wave to the woman behind the circulation desk, and I head for the fiction section, my customary stomping grounds, despite my new and alarming inability to get through a novel. For all the time I spend here, the truth is I haven't been reading much, and yet I keep coming back, be-cause there is a stubborn part of me that is still a great believer in books as the solution to my problems.

After fiction I try self-help, but there are too many diet books here, and I am too drawn to them, and so I turn away, and I catch sight of the sign for cookbooks. Which no doubt will also be blighted with diet books, and which is generally useless to me because I am too nervous to cook anything more involved than instant noodles or toast in Hayley's kitchen, but which I suspect might have something about bartending.

I find a modest selection: a couple battered recipe books, a sleek new hardcover from a bar somewhere in Manhattan, a couple fat tomes about cocktail history. I gather them all up in my arms and I take the first free chair I find, at a table full of teenagers on laptops. The first couple are a bust, but one of the histories hooks me, and I'm forty pages in before I remember I haven't eaten yet today, a potentially dangerous slip, and so I check out three of the books and I walk back to Hayley's and I am lucky enough to have the place to myself.

What I learn is: once upon a time, the word "cocktail" had a specific definition. A more specific definition, I mean. Liquor, bitters, sugar, water. Once upon a time there were cocktails and toddies and slings and smashes and bucks and daisies and fixes and, well, you get the idea. Somewhere along the line, the other names got discarded, or at least pushed aside, bowled over by the inexplicable, undeniable catchiness of the C-word. The origins of which are unknowable, the origins of the word, I mean. Is it an old term for *a woman of easy virtue*? A bastardization of the French word for *egg-cup*? A piece of ginger shoved up the ass of a lackluster old horse to make it seem peppier at market?

Don't laugh. That last one might be the most likely.

What I learn is: the Old Testament of mixology, the first in the long, ongoing line of bartenders' guides and recipe compendia, the foundation of the art and business, is a slim and otherwise unremarkable volume published in 1862 by a man named Jerry Thomas, a New Yorker (of course a New Yorker) who traveled the world over, who worked as a sailor, a gold prospector, and many other things before settling upon the noble profession of slinging drinks. He was, at the height of his powers, extraordinarily famous. Things he was known for: a solid silver bar kit, tame white rats that would crawl on his shoulders during service, and his cocktail book. Things he was not known for: modesty. Jerry Thomas was a showman—a flamboyant dresser, plus those rats, plus he was also effectively the father of the dying art of flair: that juggling of bottles, that throwing of drinks, that tossing of blue flaming alcohol from one vessel to the other.

What I learn is: bartending and storytelling are inextricably linked, and I love the stories. I love the breathless enthusiasm of these writers, I love their love. I devour the books one after the other, hungry as always, and still unsated after.

And when I go back to Joe's Apothecary on Sunday, my first paid shift, I bring that hunger with me. I want to learn everything. This is how I've always been: incapable of half-assing anything. Greg used to call me a *garden-variety perfectionist*, first affectionately, later with the icy addition of the word *insufferable*. He wasn't wrong. As a general rule, I do things very well, or I quit.

I am aware that I did not invent this breed of intensity. I come from Palo Alto, and in Palo Alto, people who are not perfect jump in front of trains. It's quick, unless it isn't, and after each sacrifice, vigils are briefly held, support groups briefly formed, crossing guards briefly employed to counter the copycats. Parents who do not wish to think that they are

part of the problem donate scads of money to various suicide preven-
tion organizations. Reporters circle, psychologists and sociologists con-
fer. The same conversations unfold, worn as old maps: How can we take
this pressure off our children? How can we teach them both to strive
for greatness and to accept goodness? Or even, god forbid, mediocrity?

How can we wash the blood from our hands without rescinding the
prizes they cling to? The fancy degrees, the good jobs, the handsome
partners, the well-compensated domestic help, the new electric cars, the
publication credits, the profiles in *Forbes* and *Wired* and *Better Homes &
Gardens*?

May one be pardoned and retain the offense?

It's eight o'clock and Joe's is quiet, empty except for the back room where
I had my interview, which has been overtaken by young parents, half-
feral toddlers running up to me as I pass through to use the bathroom.
Joe's Day Care, Olsen says when I go to join him and Han at the bar. He
rolls his eyes. I fucking hate Sundays.

Somebody's a little hungover, Han tells me in a stage whisper. Olsen
flips him off and takes off his apron. I'm out, he says. I think the two of
you can handle this.

Olsen thinks Sundays should be a one-man shift, Han explains, and
Olsen shrugs and nods and swings around to the customer side of the
bar.

He wants a gin and tonic and Han has me make it for him: two ounces
of gin, jigger filled up to the meniscus, into a Collins glass—that's the tall
skinny one. As much ice as will fit, then tonic not from a soda gun like
we had at Scott the Scot's, but from a small glass bottle, in the interest
of freshness and bubbliness and quality in general. You don't want to
stir, exactly; this is a good way to water down a drink and flatten out the
tonic, not to mention a waste of time on a busy night, not that this is a
concern at the moment. Han shows me how to do it, takes one of those
long bar spoons and just slides it gently up and down along the inside of
the glass to blend. A lime wedge perched on the side of the glass, which
Olsen squeezes and drops into his drink.

·　　·　　·

This used to be my drink, too. I have Greg to blame for this; his love of gin and tonics, when we first started dating in college, seemed so classy and adult, and so I adopted them as my drink of choice as well, until I shifted to gin martinis, which I would like to say was a matter of palate but was, at least in part, a matter of calories. There is a lot of sugar in tonic water. And there are calories in gin, too, but fortunately/unfortunately nobody really understands how alcoholic calories get processed. This is a thing I learned during my brief but memorable career as a calorie counter: there are many, many things about the human body that we do not understand. When skinny bitches and internet trolls say things like, *it's a simple equation*, when they insist that everybody and their fat mom could land in that sweet middle spot of the BMI spectrum if only they ate less, or differently, or more often, or less often, if only they walked more, or did HIIT or heavy lifting or hot yoga or just cardio, lots of cardio—they are wrong. I used to spend hours on health websites, late at night when I should have been asleep or on dull afternoons when I should have been working, scouring forums and studies and articles, and all I learned was that nobody knows anything for sure.

At any rate. *Gin*: a neutral grain spirit infused or distilled with aromatics, with the primary flavor being juniper. The name, Han tells me, comes from "genever," which is Old English for "juniper," and also Dutch for "juniper," and also the name of the Dutch liquor from which modern gin derives: a malty spirit that they, the Dutch, introduced to the English way back during the Thirty Years War. Another name for gin is Dutch Courage.

After the juniper you can put pretty much whatever you want in it: herbs, spices, citrus. Han pours us a series to demonstrate the range, little sips of pine and lemon lined up behind the bar. It's always best to taste things side by side, he says; you get much more out of it when you have some basis of comparison.

Careful, Sam, Olsen says. Han's trying to get you drunk.

To taste a liquor, start with your eyes. Everything before us is clear, which is what any liquor looks like straight out of the still; color comes from time spent in barrels or from ingredients added after distilling. Gin, generally, is unaged, and so, clear. Next you smell, holding the glass close but not too close—it's straight liquor in there. Imagine a tennis ball balanced on the top of your glass, and your nose on the other side of it. That much distance. Try with both nostrils together, then one at a time, because they do smell differently. So much of taste is olfactory, so this is a very important step. And then, finally, take a sip. Hold it in your mouth; spread it around as much as you can. Scott the Scot taught me the Kentucky Chew, which sounds like a brand of chewing tobacco but which is in fact a method for tasting that involves getting some liquor in your mouth, closing your lips, and moving your jaw as if you were chewing. You're looking not only for flavor here, but also for mouthfeel, heat. And then you swallow, and come to the finish.

Another name for gin is Mother's Ruin. Because back in the English Gin Craze, in the eighteenth century, gin was used both to prevent pregnancy—taken like the pill—and to terminate it: gin and a hot bath, supposedly, would induce miscarriage. I have to assume it was not terribly effective in either role, although I suppose an obstetrician would not *prescribe* drinking gin in a hot bath for a pregnant woman. But it was also ruinous for those who were already mothers: because women drunk on gin would neglect the children they did have. Nothing special about gin there; they could have been drinking anything. In fact they might have been; "gin," back then, was a sort of blanket term for any grain spirit. Used to be the English drank more than two gallons apiece of the stuff a year. A calculation that includes English people of all ages: men, women, children. Assuming a relatively low number of child alcoholics, this means the mother's consumption might be very high indeed.

My mother did not drink gin and she could never have stepped in front of a train. In Palo Alto she was something of an outlier: an artist who spent hours of my childhood sculpting and painting in the spare room once slated for a sibling who never came. Before Palo Alto she had lived in a co-op in Berkeley, a big old house in a shitty neighborhood, grimy kitchen, dim living room stinking of patchouli and what I would later identify as weed. A world of artists and misfits, strangers whom my mother called my aunts and uncles. She took me there often when I was little, and I remember loving it. She'd pick me up from school and we'd race to beat the traffic, John Prine or Bob Dylan blasting as we drove north and north, my mother brightening with each mile, practically skipping from the car when we arrived, whaling on the doorbell like a kid on Halloween. Both of us greeted with grins and cries and welcoming arms, ushered into the hippie wonderland within. A house full of strange, lovely people: the designer who would let me play dress-up with her clothes, the handsome queen with a gorgeous collection of vintage Barbies, the professional tie-dye artist. This is where I lived when I met your father, my mother told me; it was almost unimaginable.

Then once when we were there my mother's car got stolen, and my father had to drive up to get us, and he did not like what he saw. They had an argument I didn't understand, but looking back I presume it had to do with the seediness of the neighborhood and the co-op's copious marijuana use. And so I stopped going to Berkeley with her, and soon after she stopped going herself, and I didn't see any of those people again until the funeral.

What I learn is: I like working with Han. He's a good teacher. He's patient and generous, does rounds on the floor so I can practice making drinks, talks me through the cocktails on the menu, gently corrects my missteps. He introduces me to the regulars, their names disappearing immediately as I smile and shake hands, my hands always clean but wet, the bartender's curse. Even on a quiet night there are so many regulars, far too many to learn all at once. A hierarchy there: at the bottom tier, the ones Han bitches about after, the needy guests and bad tippers; then there are the superficial friendships, nice people but no one he would hang out with outside of work; and then there is the top tier, the real friends, the Joe's extended family.

Just below this, the other service industry folks. The chefs arrive at eleven, a cavalcade of ragged T-shirts and baseball caps and bright tattoos and Negronis. Maybe there are rules about this, some sort of pirates' code, or chefs' law, that dictates what postshift cocktail one drinks. Some of them work at a fancy Italian place down the road, which might explain it, the Negronis, but then there are chefs from the New American restaurant six blocks away, or from more distant corners of the borough or even early Manhattan, and they all seem to drink Negronis, too. It's the busiest we've been all night, and Han has me making the drinks four at a time—two per mixing glass, one mixing glass per hand—which is a real struggle for me, because if I am still clumsy with my right hand, I am shockingly bad with my left. Han lets me labor through anyway, pretending not to notice, chatting away with a woman named Paula until I am ready for him to taste and tell me whether or not I can start pouring the drinks.

Fantastico, he says, and I raise my eyebrows at him, and he says, It's Italian. For "fantastic."

Once upon a time, he tells me, there was a badass Italian duke named Camillo Negroni.

Count, Paula says. She's a tall brunette with a deep tan, her breasts enormous under a Megadeath T-shirt, her eyes brown and bright. The other chefs call her Chef as often as they call her Paula; another hierarchy, and she's right at the top. She says, I'm pretty sure he was a count.

Okay, fine, not a duke, still a badass. Count Camillo Negroni. Now, Count Cam liked to drink Americanos—the cocktail, not the coffee. Maybe he liked the coffee, too; I'm clearly not an expert. Anyway, he liked Americanos, but one day he was feeling particularly feisty and he thought to himself, there is too much water in this drink. Too much water and too many bubbles.

You're losing me, Han, I say, but he waves his hand dismissively. There's club soda in an Americano, he says. Seltzer. Pellegrino. Whatever. And so my man Count Cam says to his barkeep, Hey, *amico mio*, whaddayasay we get some gin in this bitch?

I believe those were his exact words, yes, Paula says.

Well obviously he said it in *Italian*, Han says. He continues. *Absurdo!* thinks the bartender, but he's a pro, so he does it anyway, a nice big glug of gin, and whaddayaknow? It's the most delicious thing anyone has ever tasted, and we're still drinking it today, three hundred years later.

This is what I want to learn. Storytelling.

The chefs don't stay long, not tonight; they filter out to their homes or to their lovers or to other bars, and then it's twelve thirty and empty and

Han and I close together, Han a little tipsy after one too many farewell shots, and yet even slightly intoxicated, a good coworker, a team player, more than happy to clean the toilets and take out the trash, just the right level of neurotic, vehement about the importance of leaving the bar clean and dry. *Bone dry*, he says to me as I clean the ice well, and I think of the Arizona desert, I think of Georgia O'Keeffe's skulls, I can taste it in the back of my mouth where the Campari in a Negroni hits me. Like licking a stone. Like it hasn't rained in years.

Thanks, I say.

For what?

For helping, I say. And for letting me practice.

Han shrugs. He's on the other side of the bar now, scrubbing down the brass with soapy water. It's great for me, he says. This was the easiest shift of my life.

But he is being too nice to me. I think I'm a little out of my depth here, I say, and he looks at me and says, That sounds like Carver talking.

Did he say that to you?

Han ignores the question. Here's the thing about Carver, he says. Carver is a raging misanthrope. You can't take it personally.

He likes you okay, I say, and Han cracks a smile and says, Yeah, just *okay*. He has to. We've been working together for like three years, it's basically Stockholm syndrome.

He dumps the water and goes downstairs for a dry cloth and when he reappears he says, There are two types of bartenders: service and point. Technician and personality. Introvert and extrovert. Nerd and—

Yeah, Han, I get it. Two types of bartenders.

Obviously I'm a point bartender, Han says. He comes back behind the bar, which is all but clean now, just needs to be swept and mopped. So is Olsen, he says. But Carver's service.

What does that have to do with him not liking me?

It's not that he doesn't like you, Han says. It's just that he's not really a people person. Give it a couple of months and you guys will be getting along great.

The bar-top is still dull when he finishes with it, and he shakes his head, mutters something under his breath about Brasso. Looks back up at me. Most of this stuff is just a matter of practice anyway, he says.

What about the recipes? I ask, and Han tells me that even those get more intuitive with time. In the meantime, there are books for that, he says, gesturing to the modest selection of hardcovers on the point side of the back bar.

I have some of the books already, I tell him, and he smiles. You're going to do great here, he says, and I want it to be true.

When everything is clean and dry and restocked and covered, when the fly strips are out and the money is done, Han pours us shots, whiskey again. I am not much of a whiskey girl myself, those Jamo and gingers more a means to an end than something I actually enjoyed, but I'm not about to argue. It's not like we can do shots of gin. I remember I asked Olsen for one once, in the early days, and he made a face like he'd just bitten into something rotten, and he said, No.

I had never had a bartender say no to me before. This may have been the origin of my crush on him, if we're all honest with each other. Shots of gin are for teenagers who don't know what they're doing, he said, or for old alcoholics who know *exactly* what they're doing.

And so, whiskey. I accept my shot without protest. I'm heading to Casey's for a nightcap, Han says. If you want to come.

Later I will understand that this is an honest offer, that he has no agenda, that he will guide me into this world—kindly, gently, with no ulterior motives—if I will only allow myself to be led. But in this moment I'm nervous, and I say no. Rain check, I say.

We gotta get you out of Williamsburg, Han says. He picks up his shot glass, stares down into the nut-brown liquor. I'll ask around, he says. Somebody always has a room going.

I pick up my glass, inhale. Butterscotch, I say. Vanilla. Maybe peach? It's not a test, Sam, he says, but isn't it always?

MARTINI

2 ounces gin (or, if you must, vodka)
3/4 ounce dry vermouth
optional: olive brine, orange bitters, etc.

Stir over ice and strain into a chilled coupe or a martini
glass. Garnish according to preference—generally with
olives or a twist of lemon.

I train on the open next, this time with Olsen, a Tuesday
afternoon, the air sticky and thick with the threat of thunderstorms,
power walking the whole way there in the hope of beating the rain,
which I do, just barely. Olsen sitting at the bar when I walk in, staring
down at his phone, something flipping in my stomach when I see him,
some trace of my younger self creeping back in, now that we're alone
together, full of admiration and longing and the pleasant, tingling sort
of anxiety.

My therapist thinks I need to get laid, and she's not wrong. I have
not had sex since leaving San Francisco, this being an impossibility in
Arizona and an impracticality here in New York, but I have not lost my
appetite. But I don't want to sleep with Olsen, not again, not really. Not
after last time. Besides, the rule of the service industry is: *don't screw the
crew.* Everybody knows that.

.   .   .

I mean, obviously not everybody knows that. Certainly nobody worried about it at that first New York job of mine, at the fancy Thai place. There seems to be, in my limited experience, an inverse proportional relationship between how nice a place is and how well behaved the staff is behind the scenes, and the staff at that place got into a hell of a lot more trouble than anyone I've worked with since: stealing bottles of wine during service, cocaine in the staff room, fucking in the bathrooms after hours. There was a private dining room in the back, and when the manager was on one of his binges the whole staff might stay there until three, four o'clock in the morning, stumbling out past the porter into the Manhattan predawn. I never did. I was afraid to, and besides, as the hostess I was never quite one of them on any level—not part of the tip pool, not on the floor, just the same uncool lonely teenager as ever. How I even got the job I have no idea. Now I hear stories about Mario Batali and Ken Friedman and all the rest of them and I think maybe I dodged a bullet, even if at the time it was horrible: walking home by myself four hours before anybody else left, a splash of wine in a Styrofoam cup because one of the older, nicer servers felt sorry for me, bone-tired and thinking that if I wasn't having fun now, eighteen years old and unsupervised in New York City, I might as well give up because I was clearly never going to have fun anywhere ever in my life.

I've gone off track here. They were screwing the crew, is my point. The whole place was incestuous, the relationships between servers and bartenders and chefs and managers impossible to map, ever shifting, drug addled and messy, and somehow it did hold together. But nonetheless. Conventional wisdom is that you're better off keeping it out of the workplace.

And so I push my younger self down, and I get to work. Joe's is quiet and bright and clean, and I trail behind Olsen as we unravel last night's close—put away the fly strips, drag in the rubber bar mats, put fresh trash bags in the empty bins. This is all easy, familiar, no different from any open I've done with Scott the Scot until we get to the bar stations, and I get nervous all over again.

Han calls the bar stations *cockpits*, and I can understand why he likes the term. The setup of each is precise and consistent, everything organized for maximum efficiency: tins placed just so on the bar-top, jiggers beside them, a jar full of bar tools to the right, strainers on little hooks over the ice well. Two rows of speed racks set up already—those are the steel boxes hanging off the sides of the ice wells and the sinks, packed full of the most-used spirits, plastic caps over the speed pourers (*bottle condoms*, Olsen calls them, and I feel myself blushing) at night to keep bugs out.

Olsen goes for ice, which comes in chunky one-inch cubes from a temperamental machine in the basement, and I open one of the lowboys and start pulling out big bottles of juice and vermouth and syrup, which will sit in plastic holders along the sides of the ice well, to keep them cold. Small bottles of bitters, which go on the bar-top, and cheater bottles to follow them.

Cheater bottle: a small vessel for an oft-used cocktail ingredient. Useful, Han has explained to me, for something you don't have space for in the speed well, a liqueur you only need a quarter-ounce of, for example, and won't go through too quickly. Or a mix of two or three ingredients for one of the house cocktails, so you can pour one ounce of that instead of measuring three different liquors or whatever, thereby shaving precious seconds off the time it takes to put a drink together. Each of these is labeled, but they also go in a specific order on the bar-top.

Mise en place: everything in its place. Watching the Dans work you can see how they don't even look at the labels, don't hesitate, pull juices and cheaters without looking to pump out a round of drinks as quickly as possible. The magic of muscle memory. The body remembers.

I do juice next, fill a bus tub with lemons and limes and a handful of grapefruits and retreat to the prep kitchen. In a cocktail bar you go through a lot of citrus, so if you are smart about what you're doing, you batch-juice: squeeze and strain out a quart or two at a time, rather than frantically squeezing lemons to order. Lemon and lime will last a couple of days in the fridge; grapefruit and orange, about a week.

Then comes simple syrup, as easy as it sounds, equal parts sugar and hot water, and then we top up all the cheater bottles, and we're ready to open well before five. Extraordinarily ready, Olsen says. Outside, it has started to thunder.

He sits down on one of the barstools. May as well get comfortable, he says. It's going to be a slow start.

But I can't get comfortable. Because I'm the new kid, and I have to feel helpful. Because I don't know what to say to Olsen, and the thought of sitting down beside him and making conversation until our first guests arrive is unthinkable. Shouldn't we do more prep?

Prep for what? he asks. It's a stormy Tuesday. We're not going to get busy tonight.

And yet. And yet. There is a saying in the service industry: *If you have time to lean, you have time to clean.* It is inane and snotty and true, or at least, I have internalized it despite myself, used to spend quiet nights at Scott the Scot's scrubbing out fridges, taking out all the speed pourers from the bottles to soak them in sanitizer and bleach, wiping the legs of the chairs and barstools. Polishing the bottles on the back bar, which was always my favorite task, the most satisfying, the way you could step back and see them gleaming up there when you were done. And so this is what I do now, dig up a couple of bar cloths and a bottle of Windex and get started.

You're insane, Olsen says, but it sounds more or less affectionate.

I am just finishing up the gins when the door swings open, and Olsen leaps to his feet, shoves his phone into his pocket, turns his winning smile toward our first visitor of the evening, a middle-aged, stocky white guy, bald pate, shrugging out of a dripping rain jacket and wiping his shoes before he ventures farther inside. This is Joe Himself, Olsen tells me. This is his bar.

This is, I will learn, an old joke, the shared name purely coincidental. Joe looks pleased and abashed, sidles up to the empty bar and claims what I will later recognize as his customary seat, Joe Himself being regular enough to have a favorite place at the bar, and for the Dans to make a decent effort to keep it open for him whenever they can. Olsen doesn't bother to give him a menu, just gestures at the back bar and asks Himself what he's drinking.

I leave Olsen to it, feeling awkward. I'm not great at small talk at the best of times, at my most comfortable; I am forever finding myself on the curb of a conversation, looking for a way in, wondering, *what do people talk about?* As if I weren't people. Joe Himself, it seems, is similarly afflicted. I listen to the stuttering start of a conversation between him and Olsen and then they fall silent, and when I risk a glance back over, Himself has pulled out a book, and Olsen is back on his phone.

This is the beauty of having a local bar, really—it can be whatever you need it to be. *Sometimes you want to go where everybody knows your name.* Where you know you'll be taken care of, you'll be welcome, you'll be known. To have somewhere cozy and quiet to read on a Tuesday afternoon, or somewhere loud and joyous to spend a Friday night, or somewhere to give you the home field advantage on a first date. A symbiotic relationship, at its best: it's nice for the bartender, too, to have guaranteed business, consistent tippers, familiar faces.

I had a local back in San Francisco, a sweet little spot I shared, at least at first, with Greg. It was a block from our apartment and the bartender there made the best martini I have ever had—technically a Gibson, that is, a martini garnished with a pickled onion, which sounds crazy until you try it and realize that it's perfect. My Martini Soul Mate, I called him, and I would order my Gibsons as sexily as possible, turning my longing into a joke—*wet and a little dirty* or *slightly soiled* or *delicately defiled* or whatever thesaurus-inspired version I could think of for my rather more innocent request for *a little dirty, not too dry*. Neutralizing the threat of my crush, certain that I was no longer the sort of girl who fucked the bartender, that I had grown up, calmed down, become sweet and smart and stable. The sort of girl who lived with her boyfriend and drank martinis and pretty much had her shit together.

I put the last of the gin back on the shelf, and I shake away the thought of him.

I clean the entirety of the backbar and then Olsen cuts me at eight, pours me a glass of wine, and goes back to his phone, and I take a cue from Joe Himself and grab a book from behind the bar, sit in silence and continue my bartending education. Lose myself in the old recipes and the stories behind them for the duration of a glass of wine, until Olsen comes to check on me and I'm brought back to the present.

What are you doing here, Sam? Olsen asks. I look up from my book, start to say something about wanting to learn, wanting to do a good job, about, perhaps more importantly, wanting to give Hayley and Tyler some space, seeing as I told them I'd be out all night. But Olsen shakes his head; this is not what he means. Obviously it's nice having you around, he says. But I sure wouldn't be working here if I'd gone to Columbia.

I raise my wineglass to my lips, but it's empty. I'm going red. I'm always going red. I just needed a job, I say, and Olsen laughs.

Fine, he says. Don't tell me.

It's almost ten by the time I get to Williamsburg, and I'm hungry enough to go for a slice of pizza, which is not even an indulgence, not really, not when I've been on my feet for six of the past eight hours, and I haven't eaten since two, and well anyway, I don't have to defend myself to you, it's just a fucking slice. I wolf it down as I walk up Bedford, dodging puddles as I trace the familiar path to Gina's bar.

New York City is glutted with speakeasies, or with places that are at any rate gamely pretending to be speakeasies, the word, technically, denoting something illegal, clandestine, best spoken about only softly. There are, I know, real speakeasies in the city, figuratively and perhaps literally underground, but I have never been the sort of girl who gets invited to places like that, and instead I am familiar only with the imitation speakeasies, with their artfully concealed doorways and their dark, sexy interiors and their bartenders dressed up like it's the 1920s. That whole thing. And Gina's bar is one of these imitations, a fairly convincing one, tiny and hidden away in a building near Hayley's place, disguised as an apartment, door labeled only 1L.

The room itself is cozy and candlelit, white walls and dark tables, the shelves behind the bar heavy with glittering bottles, the bar-top with the expected array of shakers, mixing glasses, steel straws, cheater bottles, jars of dried fruit and fresh lime slices. Scent of liquor and palo santo in the air, the latter smoking now beneath a framed photograph of Anthony

Bourdain, recently departed patron saint of the New York service industry, whom Gina refers to, sadly, lovingly, as *Tony*, and whom she toasts at every opportunity.

Hayley and Tyler are at the bar, both a little worse for wear, a little loud, a little flushed. Hayley jumps up to hug me, and Tyler gives me the usual tight smile. The bar is beginning to empty itself, checks down on a couple of the tables, free seats on either side of Hayley and Tyler. I take the one beside her, and Gina greets me with a glass of water and a smile, starts mixing me a martini, asks me how I'm doing. How's Joe's? she asks. How are the Dans treating you?

The Dans are nice, I say, and it's pretty much true.

Han says you're looking for a place.

I turn to look and am surprised to see Paula, the chef, two seats away from me. I hadn't noticed her. Do you live around here? I ask, and she mimes gagging. Oh, god no, she says.

You know, Gina says, setting my drink down before me, you don't *have* to come here.

Sorry, Paula says, but when Gina turns away to take another order, Paula leans close to me and says, I'm not sorry.

She says, We have a room opening up soon. If you're interested.

In Bed-Stuy?

Like four blocks from Joe's.

I think this over as Gina begins to build a round of drinks. Han has told me the system for this, the order of operations so you can put three or five or, god forbid, eight different drinks together without anything getting watered down or warm or otherwise compromised. Cocktail ingredients and liquor first, into tins and glasses respectively, then ready your garnishes, then pop open the bottle of beer from the fridge, then the red wine, then the white. Ice last, always; cocktails poured just before you're ready to carry the drinks out. Every move precise and economical. Gina is quick and even graceful, and I watch her as she stirs with her left hand and shakes with the right, a challenge akin to patting your head while rubbing your stomach. Her ice silent as she stirs, of course. The round ready before I have even processed what all the drinks are. As if it were easy.

Do I want to live that close to Joe's? The answer is, maybe.

Gina catches my eye and winks, and I'm embarrassed to be caught staring. I tear my gaze away, and it lands on Hayley, whose boyfriend is hugging her from behind, kissing her neck, and I want to vomit.

I'm interested, I tell Paula, and she grins and gives me her number.

And then it is last call and neither Hayley nor I nor, certainly, Tyler, needs another drink, and Gina gives us our comically small bill, which I insist on taking care of, because I finally have a little money and I owe both of them many more drinks than this. And also because I want to make sure to leave enough of a tip.

To leave an aggressive tip, if we're honest. Tipping between bartenders tends to be competitive often to the point of silliness: 50 percent on the bill, 100 percent, sometimes more. Sometimes you won't get charged at all, and you will just have to hope you have an appropriate quantity of cash in your wallet, leave ten or twenty or thirty on the bar, which, if we're talking percentages, the number is infinite.

But yes, it's excessive. Let's say you are not a bartender, just a drinker, a polite one, one who would like to do right by your servers and bartenders. First: whoever came up with the dollar-a-drink rule was drinking in dives twenty years ago, and if I make you a cocktail and you tip me a dollar, you're tipping me less than 10 percent and also I'm assuming you're a monster, which is mostly my problem and not yours except that going forward you will be the last person at the bar I serve, every single time. But let's say you know this. Let's say you are a polite drinker who defaults to roughly 20 percent already. On behalf of servers and bartenders everywhere, you are seen and appreciated. Let's say you're also a fun and charming patron, maybe even a regular customer, and your bartender wants to show her appreciation of you by buying back a drink. Suddenly your bill goes from, say, $36 to $24. You can throw a ten down, knowing that you have still saved a few dollars, and earning gratitude and guaranteed future buybacks and maybe a shot for the road, too. If you leave seven dollars, 20 percent pre-buyback, you are still behaving well. If, however, you see that $24 on your bill and default to your 20 percent tip, which, again, is normally very good behavior, and you leave four or five dollars for your server or bartender, you will not get buybacks in the future. If I know you're going to tip 20 percent on whatever I charge you, I'm going to charge you full price. It does not make financial sense for me to give you a discount, because doing so is costing me money. This is, after all, my job. No matter how much I like you, and I might genuinely like you, I still have bills to pay.

It's a lot of math, I know; I'm sorry. I did not invent tipping culture, am not wholly sold on the idea, but this is the way our society functions.

Anyway, Gina has taken good care of us, and I leave her a good tip, and I reiterate my promise to call Paula, and then I walk home with Hayley and Tyler, the two of them meandering a little as we go, me trailing behind, more sober, less affectionate, and when we get home I put on the big donut headphones I really should have given back to Greg months ago to block out the noise of whatever they're doing in their bedroom, and I pull out my phone to cue up an episode of something or another but the whole time I'm watching I'm hearing Olsen's voice in my head, asking me, *What are you doing here?*

Once upon a time, there was a little girl who wanted to be an astronaut. It was the sort of thing you expect your child to grow out of, like when she was six and wanted to be an Olympic gymnast even though she couldn't do the splits, or when she was four and wanted to be a mermaid even though she couldn't breathe underwater. But our little girl didn't, not for years. It began with *Star Wars* and glow-in-the-dark constellations on her bedroom ceiling, progressed to birthdays at the planetarium, culminated, at the age of twelve, puberty just around the corner and her mind turned more heavenward by the day, with a week at Space Camp. A week of mock missions and astronaut ice cream, simulators and movies, the little girl surrounded by little nerds from all over California and some from even farther afield, having basically the time of her life.

It was not so wild a dream, you understand. She was doing well in school, in the upper lane for math and science already, the most important subjects for an astronaut. Had things continued as they were for her, our little girl might well have found her way to NASA in the end.

But tragedy struck, as tragedy is wont to do. A July afternoon in a Moffett Field warehouse, the little girl on the multi-axis spinner, whirling wildly in all directions but, as the counselor explained, her center did not move, and she felt no nausea. She was giddy, as joyful as she'd been all year, still laughing when the camp director came and made it stop, took her away, sent her to her newly widowed father.

She loved you very, very much, everybody told her. Over and over and over.

But no, I've gone too far back. How did I get here from Columbia? This is an easier question to answer. Back in San Francisco, I worked in an entertainment law firm, which, at first, I liked. Hayley's mother was a partner there, and if most of my tasks were menial—fetching files and coffee, data entry, transcription—at least I felt like I would be getting something in return, something besides my paltry entry-level pay. Experience, guidance, mentorship. I had always liked Jackie, and she had always been kind to me, taken an extra interest after my mother's death that summer, welcomed me into the Kane family as the Fisher family fell apart. The plan was, I would get some work experience at her firm, take a break from academia, and then go to law school, and then my life would be perfect.

It was a solid plan, and in those early San Francisco days, it seemed like everything was coming together for me. Greg and I were happy playing house in our Pac Heights apartment, IKEA furniture, Target kitchenware, the biggest TV I'd ever owned a housewarming gift from his parents. Greg was a Palo Alto native, too; in fact we'd gone to high school together, though we hadn't really known each other then, Palo Alto High being a large school, Greg being much more popular than me—varsity track, rich parents, hot girlfriend. Me being the awkward nerd with the dead mother and only one friend. But now that we were dating, I was welcomed into his social circle—his childhood friends who had ended up in San Francisco, too, all of them working in tech now, and what we called the Girlfriends Club, which was exactly what it sounds like, and which adopted me as one of their own. Me feeling like a cool kid for the first time in my entire life. A cool kid with a good job and a steady boyfriend and a clear, straight path into her future.

But the job soured soon enough; I loved Jackie, but she didn't have much time for me, and without her, I was only a paralegal, the hierarchy sharp and unforgiving, and I began to retreat into myself, drinking my burnt office coffee and avoiding eye contact and listening to *London Calling* over and over again on those same donut headphones, so bored and frustrated and lonely that if it were not for the sweet guitar work of the great Mick Jones I would surely have hurled myself from one of the enormous windows. Listening to "Koka Kola" like being a cynic about the corporate world made me somehow less complicit, as if I could remove myself through the sheer force of my disdain.

And after that soured, it was only a matter of time before everything else did, too. What am I doing here? I'm here because I have to be. Hayley was right: I have nowhere else to go.

PALOMA

2 ounces tequila (blanco)
1/2 ounce Aperol
1 ounce grapefruit juice
1/4 ounce lime juice
1/4 ounce simple syrup
Seltzer

Build in a Collins glass with ice, top with seltzer, and
garnish with a lime wheel.

I move to Bed-Stuy in the middle of July, dripping sweat,
everything I own in the trunk of an Uber. Like so many of the places we
have begun to live (*we*: the poor young fools who still believe in the New
York City dream), my new home was not built to be livable but has been
adapted in ways both innovative and absurd. Look how many of us have
piled in here, a building designed as a catering hall, as a theater, no one
can agree. Four red-brick stories, divvied up into apartments described
on the website with words like *split-level* and *open-plan* and *modern*, and
not inaccurately, although better terms would be *privacy-free, creatively
deranged.*

You can tell it was not built to be livable, because only some kind of
architectural sadist would have designed a residential space like this.
There's a certain charm in all that exposed brick, in those very high

ceilings, and if the kitchen were cleaner I might appreciate the newish appliances and the plentiful counter space. A front door into a kitchen that bleeds into a dining room that becomes a living room and out of all this primordial soup, three narrow wooden staircases, unvarnished like something hastily completed in high school woodshop or in an earlier round of a home makeover show, leading up to bedrooms that offer a change in altitude in place of a door. A total of three doors in the whole place: the first accounted for, the second for the bathroom (large, granted, though dirtier even than the kitchen), the third mine, thank god, though this luxury I pay for in space: no closet, forget about a dresser, and get used to sleeping in a twin bed, like you're back in college.

And then there are the roommates, a mixed bag. Paula is great, of course, though she's hardly in the apartment at all, working those long chef hours, staying with Gina a couple nights a week. Toni's boyfriend has a studio in Crown Heights, and she spends most of her time there, coming home only, she says, when they're fighting or when she needs to shit in peace. The third room belongs to a pair of server-cum-musicians who are always having noisy sex despite the aforementioned dearth of closing doors. Part of you has to respect the chutzpah, the self-confidence. Part of you would like to applaud when the shrieks become particularly loud and then end, abruptly and with what seems like great satisfaction.

On top of this, one of the smoke detectors has started chirping in the week between my last visit and my move. It's begging for a new battery, but it's so high up on the ceiling that there is nothing to be done but email our unresponsive super to have him come take care of it.

Do you ever read old Soviet literature and feel the creeping certitude that this is the direction we're headed, that we are all doomed to a life of powdered milk and filthy Primus stoves, and arguing over who finished whose vodka? Grandmothers and strangers in communal apartments, everybody gray and shrieking and essentially miserable?

No? Me neither.

At any rate my room is cheap, by the frankly offensive standards of Brooklyn life in the twenty-first century. And there is another undeniable advantage: proximity to Joe's. Now that my training is done, I have been awarded four regular shifts a week—Sunday and Monday with Olsen, Thursday with Han, Friday with everybody—which in the service industry world is considered full-time, which after nearly six months of unemployment is a blessing. And now my walk is a mere ten minutes door to door, almost too easy, me always fifteen minutes early, and today's no different, quarter to one on the first Friday in August. We don't open for another two hours, and my shift doesn't start 'til six, but Carver's called a bar meeting, and so here I am.

Joe's is lovely in the preopen hours, bright with daylight, perfectly clean. Carver's notebook is sitting on the bar, and I put my things down several seats away. I am still wary of Carver. I will always be wary of Carver.

I'm heading to the bathroom when I hear voices, Carver's first, and then, unmistakably, Gina's. I'm not trying to eavesdrop, it's just that they're in the back room, blocking my path, and they're loud, and I'm frozen there, and Gina's saying, You know you only have a three point nine on Yelp?

You're throwing *Yelp* at me?

You think people staying in Airbnbs in Bed-Stuy aren't looking at reviews when they decide where to go out? You think you're not losing customers?

I don't want those customers.

Um, yes, Carver, you do. Those are the assholes who will spend a hundred dollars without batting an eye, which lets *you* give free whiskey to Joe Himself and keep stocking that ridiculous pinot for Teresa.

So what, I need better reviews?

For one. Maybe update your social media every once in a while. Host some events. Throw a launch party for your new menu and invite a bunch of industry people. Stop having two bartenders on every night of the week. Whatever. I'm not going to tell you how to run your bar. I just need you to start turning a profit, or we are going to have to have a serious conversation about whether we're going to renew our lease next year.

I feel like you're telling me how to run my bar.

Carver.

Is that why you made me hire the greenest bartender in Brooklyn?

I don't pretend to think I can *make you* do anything.

She's cute, but she is *useless*.

That snaps me out of it, and I creep away as slowly and softly as possible. Carver's saying something about late-stage capitalism and neighborhood loyalty and I don't hear what Gina says but I can tell she's exasperated, and then I'm back in the safety of the empty front room, and I feel sick not just to my stomach but all over, and I sit down at the bar and take deep, careful breaths, and I wonder if I should just leave now and forever, except I can't, because now I fucking live here.

And also because, fuck Carver. I have no argument with *green*, but *useless*? What I said in my interview was true: I am a quick learner and a good hard worker. Everything else can be taught, given the right teacher. He just hasn't given me a chance.

I am still stewing when Han and Olsen show up, but I push that down deep, force a smile. Olsen's visibly hungover, quiet and clutching a cold brew like a lifeline, but Han's bubbly and excited. He has a bag with him full of rosemary and sage and apples and pears and cranberries and one sad, off-season pomegranate, and he spreads these across the bar-top. Inspiration, he says. For the new menu.

Which is what we're here to discuss. Most cocktail bars, like most good restaurants, adjust their menus for the season: swap out the berries and gin of summer for pumpkin spice and whiskey, that sort of thing. There's some debate, in craft cocktail circles, about how this should be done, and how often—is four menus a year too many? Should you leave some of your house classics on all year and just rotate through some seasonal specials? Should you, as Joe's does, change twice a year, fall/winter and summer/spring, same as the fashion houses?

Wherever you land, the goal is always the same: a well-balanced list, a spread of spirits and styles, so that no matter your guest's tastes, they can, in theory, find something they love.

And so here we are at the height of summer, mapping things out. I say *we*; all I'm really doing is sitting there listening to the Dans, feeling, well, useless. We sit there with our various coffees steaming or sweating in front of us, the Dans pouring themselves little glasses of beer, talking about flavor profiles and base spirits and glassware and specs.

Why do we use the words *flavor profile* and not just *flavor*? Why *specs* and not just *recipe*? When I ask Han, later, he'll think about it for a minute, and then shrug, and then say, Because those are the words that we use.

Both Han and Carver have already been working on drinks—rye, bitter and stirred, on the rocks; gin, fruity and shaken, tiki-style. So that's one gin and one whiskey, Carver says, but there's room for at least one more of each, especially whiskey, this being the season. We'll need agave and rum for sure, he says. A hot drink, if anyone has any ideas for that. I assume Han will be doing some sort of flip, as usual—

Brandy, probably, Han says, nodding. Carver makes a note.

I want shaken and whiskey, Olsen says, and Carver nods. He doesn't ask me if I want to claim anything. We'll meet again in a month, he says. In the meantime, you're all welcome to hang out and do some R and D until we're open. Just no getting wasted before your shifts, please.

You're no fun anymore, Han says, but he's already swinging around the bar, getting to work.

R and D: research and development. In this case, specifically, the creation of new cocktails. There are many paths to a new drink: you can start with a base spirit, or a title, or a flavor profile. You can start with a liqueur you really like, or a fruit that's in season, or an old recipe you want to riff on. Whatever inspires you, Han says, which is easy for him to say, because he seems to be constantly inspired, forever trying things out. Whereas I'm sitting there staring at the bottles behind him with absolutely nothing in my head.

I get up, finally, to go to the bathroom like I meant to before the meeting started, and Gina is sitting there at one of the tables in the back, hunched over a laptop. I had forgotten she was here, and I jump a little, and she laughs, kindly, and takes out her earbuds.

So what are you putting on the menu? she asks.

Oh, no. I'm not ready for that.

Don't let the Dans intimidate you, she says. They're all idiots. And I smile then, almost despite myself, which seems to satisfy her, because she turns back to her laptop and I leave her to it.

Still. I'm not ready. I might never be ready. And that's fine, because in just over a year I will be in law school, and three years after that I will have a real job, and this entire ridiculous period in my life will fade from my memory like a bad dream.

Not just law school, either. *Harvard Law School.* I am supposed to be there this year, but life got in the way and I was forced to defer, for health reasons, even though I'm fine now, really, and I would love to start next month instead of treading water for another year. But it's too late; that decision was made in March, during the worst of times, and there's nothing to be done now.

It's an old dream, Harvard. My mother used to say *Harvard* as if it were synonymous with college. As if it were synonymous with success. As if that Iviest of Ivies would solve all my problems.

Imagine Hayley and me at seventeen, desperate to get out of Palo Alto, looking at colleges as far away as we could get. I wanted Harvard, but Hayley wanted Columbia, and I wanted to stay close to her. We both applied to both. Harvard was a bust; the only Paly kid to get in that year was some legacy on the baseball team. A devastating blow, for me, although I at least made the cut at Columbia, which was a devastating blow for Hayley. Hard to say whether she would have felt better or worse if I had gone somewhere else, but a moot point, because when Hayley picked NYU, I had no other option. I didn't do it to be cruel. I did it to be nearby.

A second chance, now, for graduate school. If I can just keep myself afloat for a little while longer.

So I go home without doing any R and D, kill a couple hours back in my apartment, come back at six for my shift. Joe's is busy by then, and packed by the time Olsen returns at eight. With all four of us there, I am assigned to the floor, Olsen in the back on glasses. The hope being, I suppose, that I will prove a better waitress than a barback.

But this is a foolish hope. I have never been mistaken for a great waitress. I'm too clumsy and not quick enough, although my memory is good, and I smile a lot, and I can generally fake my way through. But I'm off my game tonight, Carver's disdain a difficult fog to see through, and I can feel him getting frustrated with me all over again, barking at me to hurry up, saying, I have drinks dying up here, Sam, which only makes me shakier, more nervous, and generally less capable. Guests trying to flag me down to place orders, to ask for checks. Dirty glasses accumulating on tables. I can't keep up.

At one point Carver snatches a cocktail from my hand and dumps it out, saying, It's been there too long, I'll make it again, go and come back. Adding, as I walk away with the rest of the round, *Quickly*. As if that weren't implied.

At one point I knock over a glass of Malbec on the bar, deep red going everywhere, narrowly missing the nearest guests, and on top of this the glass breaks, and I'm worried Carver is going to kill me. No, my fear is more real than that. I'm worried he's going to take back my apron and send me out into the night, never to return. He doesn't, obviously he doesn't; he pours another glass and waves my apologies away.

At one point the door opens and a group of four pushes in and I think *maybe if I throw myself down on the ground now and start crying, maybe then people will stop asking me for things.* My whole body is so taut it feels like something might snap.

In the weeds: behind and unable to catch up. I am so deep in the weeds that I have lost sight of the garden.

I smile extra wide and tell them I'll be with them in just a minute.

When things are under control again, finally, Han waves me over to his section, and when I get there, he has shot glasses in his hands. You look like you need it, he says, handing me one. The liquor in there is clear and unmistakable, smelling like citrus and bad decisions. Oh, no, I say, but Han just laughs at me and knocks our glasses together. Drink up, kiddo, he says, and I obey, and it goes down like lighter fluid.

Hayley won't drink tequila to this day, cites a bad experience at a college party, and she's not the only one. Han says this is stupid, but understandable, but mostly stupid. Shitty tequila, he says. *Mixto*: tequila blended from at least 51 percent agave spirit and up to 49 percent whatever the hell else the manufacturer wants to put in it. Sugar and grain alcohol and bullshit, he says. Of course it does horrible things to you. But as long as you stick with 100 percent agave, you'll be okay.

Agave: a spiny, flowering succulent native to the American desert. There are different types; tequila must be made from Weber Blue, whereas mezcal can employ several different varietals. There are other spirits, too, to be made from the plant, but mezcal and tequila are the most popular, and the only ones we have at Joe's. Tequila smooth, floral, and bright; mezcal smoky, rich, lightly spiced. The smoke, I remember from one of my books, because mezcal producers roast their agave hearts in underground ovens, whereas tequila producers tend to steam or cook the hearts aboveground.

But Han has selected tequila for more than just the taste. The other thing about agave is, agave is magic. People will tell you things that are scientific nonsense about how different spirits affect them: gin makes you cry, whiskey makes you angry, rum is your night-ender. Placebo effect. It's all, ultimately, just ethanol. And yet every bartender you will ever meet will tell you that there is something different about agave. All logic aside. And I feel it all through my body, now, like a sugar rush, like a caffeine high, and almost immediately. Placebo effect? Maybe, or maybe there are just things about the body that we still don't understand, and this is one of them.

And so I am carried through another hour, less miserable, more competent, although it is not a surprise that I am cut first, the minute things quiet down. I take a seat in Han's section, and he pours me a big glass of water—hydrate or die, kiddo, he says; hydrate or die—and he asks me what I want to drink. Before I can answer he shakes his head, puts up a finger. Paloma, he says.

Excuse me?

You're drinking a Paloma, he says, and he starts making it, and I don't think I could stop him if I wanted to.

.   .   .

A bar lesson: the Paloma, in its purest form, is very simple: a highball of tequila and grapefruit soda with a splash of lime. It is, Han tells me, the most popular cocktail in Mexico; more so even than its salt-rimmed cousin, the margarita.

Han, unsurprisingly, has made it a bit more complicated. We don't have grapefruit soda in Joe's, for one; don't use it often enough to justify the storage space. Instead I watch him pour fresh grapefruit juice and a little simple syrup and a little lime and, to my surprise, Aperol into a Collins glass. Generous two ounces of blanco tequila, ice, seltzer. It's perfect, I tell him, and he says, Of course it is.

Once upon a time in Mexico, Han says, the owner of a tavern fell in love with a young girl. A very young girl, a child in fact, but anyway he was obsessed with her and he named this highball after her, *la Paloma*, the dove. But another man took credit for the drink, publishing it in a pamphlet entitled Popular Cocktails of the Rio Grande. When the tavern owner read this, he was furious; not only at the other man, but at the child as well. She must have given away the recipe, he thought. She must have been going to other bars, ordering his drink from other men. This was unacceptable. The tavern owner spiraled. This small betrayal hinted, to his fevered mind, at other betrayals, and he felt the girl slipping through his fingers. She was newly fifteen, a woman now, and he was losing her to some enterprising pamphleteer. He did what anyone would do. He rushed to her family home, where her quinceañera was underway, and he shot her and himself in front of everybody.

Never happened, Carver says, and Han looks horrified. Carver laughs, and elaborates. Back in the early days of the cocktail renaissance, when hardly anyone was paying attention to things like, say, the Wikipedia page for a classic Mexican highball, you could pretty much write whatever you wanted, and some Bostonian prankster wrote that. The Wikipedia entry's been cleaned up now, but it was cited enough times that you'll still see its echoes on other websites, maybe even in poorly fact-checked books.

As our parents used to tell us, you can't believe everything you read on the internet.

It's a bit sad, I think, hanging out at my work when I have a Friday evening free, but Paula is at her restaurant and the Dans are all still working and Hayley is out with her boyfriend at some club in the West Village that I know I will hate and Greg doesn't love me anymore and my father is out west and my mother is dead and I have no interest in being alone in my stifling new apartment and I have truly nothing better to do, and so I sit there and I take out my phone like any other lonely barfly might, and I open an app, and I'm sitting there doing the thing, swipe left, swipe right, right, right, left, left by mistake, right on purpose. You know what it's like.

Han glides over, takes away the watery remains of my cocktail, stretches out his neck to see what I'm up to. Han has the cheekbones of Clark Kent and demeanor of an Animaniacs character. He is the best specimen of extrovert I have ever encountered. They should study him in a lab.

He takes the phone from my hand and starts prodding it. Hey, I say. Don't go swiping for me. You don't know my taste.

Sure I do, he says, but he passes the phone back. Sam, he says, shaking his head. Sam, Sam, Sam, Sam, Sam. You meet single people all the time. If you need Tinder, you're not a very good bartender.

I go red, and I close the app, and I tell him to go fuck himself, and he gives me a saccharine smile and pours me a glass of wine. And I know he's right.

And yet, is he right? Is it possible to just meet people anymore? I've been broken up with Greg for the better part of a year, and I have not found anyone I like even a fraction of a percent of how much I liked him. Hayley says this is ridiculous. Greg, she says; what a complete and utter asshole. And I appreciate her loyalty, her unwavering allegiance to my heartbreak, undeserved though it may be. She says to take my time, she says maybe I'm just not ready to date again. But I am ready. I am ready for someone who is exactly like Greg, but a Greg who doesn't hate me.

In the meantime, I lie awake nights with itchy feet and sweaty sheets and a bone-deep, lead-heavy sort of unhappiness.

And yet, Han is right, because the second Ben walks in I know what's going to happen. Ben is a top-tier regular, although I haven't met him yet, because I would have remembered. He's a friend of Carver's, a stupidly handsome dark-skinned Black guy with a muscular build and a smile that I feel in my entire body when he turns it on me. This is the new girl, Han says, and Ben shakes my hand, introduces himself, takes the barstool to my left. He's coming back from a concert in the city, a band Hayley and I saw once in college, and I tell him this, and I tell him I wouldn't have pegged him for a Belle & Sebastian fan, and he accepts his Negroni and he looks at me and says, Did you think I would listen to rap?

And I stammer out something about how that's not what I meant, it's just that they're so twee and kind of a throwback at this point and I'm always surprised when I meet people who like them, especially dudes, and he laughs and he stops me with a hand on my arm. I'm fucking with you, he says. Also, I do listen to rap. I just also listen to early-aughts indie pop. I contain multitudes, he says, loftily, and I want to stick my tongue down his throat.

We sit there together as the night comes slowly to a close, the bar contracting around us. The chefs come and then the chefs go, and we have a round of shots to see them off, whiskey I don't need burning through me, and the music swells, Carver's pick, Johnny Cash, and Ben and Han are teasing him about it, calling it dad music, college coffeehouse music. "The Man Comes Around" starts, and Ben, at the tail end of his second Negroni, starts singing along, a rich baritone, making up new lyrics, *when the Dan comes around*, demonstrating an unexpected gift for rhyme— *when he says last call just order one more round/have another beer and drink your whiskey down/make like the Vikings, throw your glasses to the ground*—and Han is laughing so hard there are tears running down his face. I'm laughing, too, but I feel as if I am looking down upon the scene from a distance. This is someone else's bar, someone else's life.

I finish my wine, and the Dans begin to clean, and I stand up, and I say my goodbyes, and Ben says he'll walk me home, it's late, we're going the same direction. Throws cash down on the bar, takes his leave with a mock-grave salute. Han grins, but Carver's face remains unreadable, and I'm not sober but I'm not past the point of wondering how he feels about me hitting it off with his friend, if this will make things worse or better or if we will all just pretend nothing has happened. I wave awkwardly, ignore Han's lascivious wink, step out into the sticky night. Tell myself not to get ahead of myself. Maybe nothing is going to happen. Maybe Ben is just being nice.

Ha. His apartment is wonderful: garden level in the old family brownstone, enormous, real art framed on the walls, and packed wooden bookshelves, a big kitchen island that digs into my sacrum as he kisses me, a neatly made king bed that we fall into after. His body a delight: a surety to it, a solidity that mine lacks even at its largest, a confidence knit in there with the muscles, a man and not a boy. His breath hot against my skin, Campari kisses, white teeth.

TOM COLLINS

2 ounces gin (ideally Old Tom)
1 ounce lemon juice
3/4 ounce simple syrup
Seltzer

Short shake the first three ingredients, then strain into a
Collins glass over ice and add seltzer to top. Garnish with a
lemon wheel.

What did I tell you, Han says. You don't need Tinder.

I don't know what you're talking about, I say. I can feel myself blushing. Han leans back against the bar and says, I met Meg like that.

What, I say, not on Tinder?

He rolls his eyes, mutters something about how Tindering while
Chinese is a waste of time and energy. At a bar, he says. I was maybe a
little drunk, the place was packed, I couldn't find my friends. I'd gone
up to buy a round and ended up stuck at the bar with four beers and no
idea where to go with them. And there she was, looking bored, she was
friends with one of the bartenders but they were too busy to talk, and
so I sat next to her and explained the situation. Why she humored me I
have no idea, but we drank the four beers, and then the DJ played a song
she liked—Meg loves to dance—and suddenly it's two weeks later and we
haven't spent a night apart.

He says, That was four years ago.

It's a nice story, but I don't think it's my story, cannot envision a night with Ben as the start to a long and glorious love story. Yeah, Han says; Ben doesn't seem like your type.

How so?

Han makes a face as he thinks it over. Well, you're *you*, he says, and Ben's just . . . a square.

I don't really know what he means by his *you*, and I have a feeling it is not entirely a good thing, but I don't press him on it. I like squares, I say, and Han makes a retching noise, and I punch him in the arm. I do like squares. Exhibit A: Greg. Reliable, straightforward, contented. A good influence. Someone to help me find my way to the life I wanted.

I met Greg junior year, at a party. I mean, like I said, I had met him before, the two of us the only two Paly kids in our year at Columbia, but we'd never hung out, plus he'd been dating Angie Walker forever, even after graduation, even though he was in New York and she was all the way out at UCLA.

And then he'd stopped dating Angie Walker, and there we were at this party. I didn't go to many parties at Columbia, spent most of my college years hanging out in the Village with Hayley and her NYU friends, but that was the spring Hayley studied abroad, leaving me suddenly friendless, which is the danger of putting all your emotional eggs in one basket. And so when the nice girls across the hall had a party, I went for once, and there was Greg, tan and blond and wearing a Ramones T-shirt, and I complimented him on it, and he asked me if I liked the band, and I told him I was more of a Clash girl myself, which is just a statement of fact but it made him laugh and we got to talking and, well, that was kind of it for me.

The thing about Greg is—all else aside, Greg was a nice person. *Is* a nice person. A good person, even. Smart, obviously, but not condescending like so many of our peers, even though he was in the hard sciences and I was a failed mathematician and a reluctant English major and I know for a fact many of his friends thought I was stupid. Whatever. Greg was sweet. He didn't want to keep our hookup a secret, was happy from pretty much the get-go to hold my hand as we walked across campus, to kiss me in public. He believed in the person I wanted to be, the sort of person who deserved him. For a brief, beautiful time, I was that person. I was golden next to him: happy, well-adjusted, whole.

It's quiet when I get in, and it stays quiet. *August:* the dead month, the real doldrums of summer, the slowest month for bars in New York City, or at least, bars in New York City without rooftops or backyards. Everyone who can afford it leaves the city for the weekends, goes camping or upstate or out to the Hamptons, and everyone else is at a park or a barbecue or an outdoor establishment. I remember this from my summers with Scott the Scot, the way everything would move slow as molasses until Labor Day. I had thought, seeing the bar on Friday, that perhaps Joe's was some kind of exception to the rule. It is, Han says. On Friday nights.

So it's quiet, an easy Thursday night, and Han has me make every single order, standing a few feet away, straw-testing everything before it goes out. Reminding me to pour up to the meniscus, to fill the mixing glass all the way with ice, to prepare my garnishes before I start making my drinks. Telling me when the sour I've made needs another shake—A little hot, he says; *hot:* too boozy, not diluted enough. The opposite of hot is *bruised:* too watery, overstirred, nothing to be done but pour it out and start over.

Even watching him with customers is a lesson. For one: don't call them customers, call them *guests.* Acknowledge them the second they walk in: even if you're busy, a *hello* and a promise to be with them in a minute goes a long way. People will wait, Han says. If you ask them to.

But it's not just time management. If they are guests, you are their host, and it is your job, perhaps your most important job, to make sure they are made welcome. We're a neighborhood bar first, Han says. Anybody who walks through that door should feel comfortable here. No matter who you are or what you look like or what you drink.

A brief catalog of our Thursday night guests: when I arrive, a group of schoolteachers enjoying the last dregs of their summer vacation, sharing their second bottle of chardonnay. Joe Himself, with a book and a glass of Eagle Rare. Kay, one of our most regular regulars, a thirty-something midwesterner, drinking a gimlet and working on their laptop over by the window. As the evening deepens, the modest crowd shifts, people returning from their jobs in the city, stopping in on date night. There's a couple Patrick Bateman types (Han's words, but it takes me a minute to get the reference, and he's not wrong) having Vieux Carrés and Scotch, one woman with them, drinking them under the table. Raj, the South Asian stoner who drinks beer and talks to Han about video games. Lacey and Tonya, the older Black couple who have known Carver since he was a child, whose cocktails Han comps almost entirely.

A shift again, into Tinder dates and serious drinkers: an adorable duo who must be *just* twenty-one, sitting at the bar as a delighted Han introduces them to the wonderful world of cocktails. A trio of comics, one of whom I vaguely recognize, drinking menu drinks in the back room and talking about somebody's undeserved big break. A rheumy-eyed old neighborhood character whom Han calls the Mayor, and who drinks two glasses of our cheapest white in quick succession and lurches out into the night.

No matter who they are, Han says, simple steps of service. Bring them waters and menus first, chat a little if you have time, tell them you'll be back in a minute for orders. Check in after their third sip of a drink, so if there's something wrong you can fix it before it's too late. Circle around refilling waters, so you can be continuously checking in on your tables without seeming to hover. Bring back a menu when they're in the bottom third of their drinks, before they have time to talk themselves out of another round.

You're good at this, I say, and Han preens. You'll soon learn that I'm good at everything, he says.

We polish glasses together as our ten o'clock pop dies down and there are lessons here, too. There are seven types of glass in Joe's: shot glass, rocks glass, shorty, beer mug, wineglass, coupe, and Collins. Why is it called a Collins? you may wonder. To which Han will answer that a Collins is a type of drink, somewhere between a sour and a highball; a sort of spiked lemonade, not in the style of the prebottled sugar bombs I drank once or twice in my underage years, but made fresh, a splash of liquor, lemon, sugar, seltzer. Is it too simple? Certainly it's simple, but that doesn't have to be a bad thing. There is a time and a place for an eight-ingredient cocktail, but there is an elegance to confining yourself to three or four. Like a good punk song. If you pick the right three chords, you don't need any more than that.

And a Collins is refreshing as all hell. Invented in the nineteenth century, made originally with gin—Old Tom gin—thus the name Tom Collins, the best known of the Collins family. Old Tom gin being a softer, sweeter style of gin than the now standard London Dry, a style lost for many years, brought back this century, sometimes made with added sugar, sometimes simply taking on caramel notes in the barreling, or by the use of corn in the mash bill, or any number of other techniques being explored by curious and eccentric liquor enthusiasts the world over.

So all right, the glass is named after the drink, but what is the drink named after? Once upon a time in New York, Han says, a great number of pranksters began, for reasons long since forgotten, to play a particular joke on their unsuspecting associates. The prankster would come across a friend or acquaintance, and tell him, Friend (or Acquaintance), you will not believe what they are saying about you. You will not believe what I have just heard about your mother's virtue, or your honor, or your habits, or perhaps something so simple as your physical appearance. They have been insulting you criminally, and I have said that it is not true, because I am your friend (or acquaintance), but they have gone on saying it.

The horrified listener, the victim, would demand, quite naturally, to know who had been slandering them so prodigiously, and where, in order to make things right; and the prankster, perhaps eagerly, perhaps with some great phony show of reluctance, would say, It was Tom Collins, and he is just around the corner now, he is in that tavern across the street, he is holding court in that café down the road. And off the victim would run, and the prankster would go along his merry way, delighted with himself.

This became known as the Great Tom Collins Hoax, and has been somewhat obliquely attributed as the namesake of the drink. However, the Hoax occurred five years after the first appearance of the Tom Collins in print, and so this, too, is a fake bar story.

And *coupe*? Isn't that a kind of car? Like in that Beach Boys song.

You'll have to take that up with the French, Han says. He holds up the glass in question, the stemmed and rounded vessel for all of our up drinks. Here's another fake bar story for you: the original coupe glass was modeled on Marie Antoinette's left breast.

A snort of laughter from the bar. The aforementioned Meg has joined us, Han's wife, a pretty, petite Black woman with long braids and clear plastic hipster glasses drinking one of Han's creations from a menu two years ago, tequila and lime and mint. Wow, she says, when we turn to look at her. You finally found someone who's as big a nerd as you.

I know, Han says, beaming. Isn't she the best?

Glasses done, Han's focus turns to the new menu. Quiet moments like this are ideal for R and D, he says, and that makes sense, that's the other side of *time to lean, time to clean*. And I watch him as he lines up bottles of liquor on the bar-top, you can see the cogs turning in there, and I think about Gina, asking what I was putting on the new menu, and I say, Should I be working on something?

He brightens. Do you want to? And I say something about not knowing where to start, and he says, Pick a liquor.

I had not necessarily wanted to create a drink right this second, but of course I go along with him. Gin, I say, and he pulls the bottle of gin out of the speed rack and sets it heavy on the bar.

Citrusy or boozy? he asks, and I say, I guess boozy.

So now we just pick modifiers, Han says. A syrup, maybe, if you want to go a kind of old-fashioned route. Liqueurs, maybe. Amaro. Vermouth? He's turned away from me now, going through the backbar. You could split the base, he says, throw some whiskey in with it, or even some tequila. Applejack, that's nice for fall. Or you could do some kind of Negroni-ish thing? Aperol? Cynar? With each option he holds up a bottle, and I watch him, and I feel smaller and smaller, overwhelmed, dizzy. I am so unbearably out of my depth here.

What do you think? Han asks, turning back to me, a bottle of Suze in his hand, and I don't trust myself to speak, and I shake my head, and he says, No, you're right, not Suze. Gin and Suze has been done to death.

I am rescued by the arrival of dinner, burritos from someplace on Nostrand, inevitably a disappointment after California, but Han insisted and I'm trying not to skip meals. We hide out in the prep kitchen with a weather eye on the bar as I take slow nervous bites and Han does his damnedest to swallow his whole. I am looking for a way to articulate my concern. With the R and D, I mean. My concern about the burrito I'll keep to myself.

The thing is, I'm just not a creative person. You'd think I might have inherited some aptitude from my mother, wouldn't you? But you would be wrong. When I was small I would beg to be allowed into her studio, loved to sit on the floor with acrylic paints and thick paper, imagining myself growing up just like her. Another parent would have encouraged this. Would have at least been flattered. My mother would say, No. No, Samantha, you can't grow up like me. She would soften this with, You are much smarter than me. She would tell me how I would go to college—to Harvard—and I would have better things available to me than paints and canvases. Looking back, I understand what she meant: economic freedom, emotional stability, general quality of life. Things that being an unknown artist in Palo Alto did not afford her. Looking back I understand that she was trying to protect me. Looking back I understand, objectively, that she did love me, that she wanted the best things for me. At the time, it just felt like a dismissal.

A moot point, because, again, I was never very good. The older I got, the more the blank page felt insurmountable; I had no ideas, no skills, no calling. I tried a different tack, briefly, in high school, with a photography class. I liked the chemical side of it, the way light could burn away silver, the way the developer made it visible and the fixer made it stick. But I never knew what to take pictures of. I would go out with my cheap old Nikon and I'd walk for an hour before I even took off the lens cap. Ended the semester with a portfolio of nothing—empty playgrounds, the pedestrian overpass over the predawn freeway, an empty lot near Hayley's house where the owner had torn down a handful of town houses but left their chimneys standing. A study in isolation and grief, the teacher said, in front of the entire class, me feeling like I'd been caught doing something unspeakable, my classmates mortified on my behalf. The teacher knowing nothing about my mother, being new to Palo Alto and averse to town gossip.

He gave me a B, and I never took another class with him. I couldn't apply to colleges with a bunch of Bs in *art classes*. That would be ridiculous. That would be an extremely stupid reason not to get into Harvard.

How about this, Han says. He sweeps back behind the bar, pulls a long ribbon of receipt paper from the printer, starts writing. I do a round on the floor, my dinner a brick in my stomach, my smile perhaps less than convincing. Take a couple orders, top up waters, go to get checks. Han is still scribbling away, so I make the drinks, too, two menu cocktails and a Manhattan, a glass of Riesling, an IPA from the tap. This part, at least, is starting to feel manageable. As long as Carver's not yelling at me.

Okay, Han says, fifteen minutes later. He hands me the paper, a numbered list in his cramped, crooked handwriting. Fifty classic cocktails every bartender should know, he says. Well. Fifty-ish. Look 'em over, pick one, and we'll work from there.

When Han cuts me, I take my notebook and one of the newer books from behind the bar, a hefty volume from some bar in Manhattan whose recipes I trust, and I sit down at the bar one seat away from Meg and I start going through Han's list. I have heard of many of these, which is something of a relief, and Han makes me one of the gin entries, a minty gin sour called a Southside, bright and refreshing and entirely too easy to drink, and I sip at this as I copy down specs. Han lets me get away with this for about ten minutes, and then he slaps a long-fingered hand down in the middle of the page and tells me to stop.

This is sad, he says. You're making me sad. Go out and have fun, you weirdo, he says, and I tell him I am having fun, and he says, Not nearly enough.

Later, in the privacy of my shoe box bedroom, I will make flash cards. I've never been the best at memorizing things: I can learn vocabulary, equations, I can be made to understand, but I have trouble learning by rote. School plays, history tests, the names of phyla and species in biology: these were all anathema to me. But I am nothing if not stubborn. And so I'll write down every drink on Han's list, and a few others that sound promising or have good stories behind them or good names, and I'll stick these up on my plain white walls, and the first time Ben stays over he will tell me it looks like the den of a serial killer, which is not entirely unfair, and yet. And yet it's a good system, because when I'm bored in the afternoons or at night when I'm sleepless and alone, I can peel the cards off at random and read the specs, repeat ounce measurements aloud to myself in my suffocating windowless bedroom, and begin to remember.

But for now, Han takes the book away. Consider this part of your bartender training, he says: stop taking notes and go introduce yourself to Casey.

Casey again. Her name keeps coming up, the Dans talking about her like she's some kind of local celebrity, the chefs always leaving for her bar when we start to close. But I don't understand what I'm going to learn from a dive that I can't learn from the books or the list or, well, Joe's. But Han is insistent. Meg, he says. Make her go.

Meg downs the last of her drink and turns to me. Come on, she says. You'll like it.

I do like it. Casey's is an entirely different school of bar from Joe's, one big open room full of low wooden tables, a pinball machine glowing in the back, old paintings and posters on the walls, these impossible to make out because the space is so dark. A long Formica bar with twelve taps behind it and a modest liquor selection, the menus handwritten on chalkboards hanging on the wall behind. It's the platonic ideal of a bar, I think, and Meg drags me over to a couple empty seats and introduces me to the bartender.

Casey is a tall white woman, short black hair streaked with silver, glasses thick and enormous on her face. She takes both of my hands in her own and smiles down at me and her hands are warm and her smile is unbearable and I feel an overwhelming wave of peace and satisfaction break over me. It is like being blessed by a saint. And it's not because she's beautiful, although I don't mean to insinuate that she's ugly, I only mean to say that her pull is more mysterious than that, and deeper. Sam just started at Joe's, Meg says, and Casey says, Welcome.

Casey has a cocktail list, but you can tell by looking that this is not that kind of bar. This is a beer and liquor place, and I don't drink beer, which is partially about the taste, but mostly, if we're being honest with each other, about the calories. I'm already feeling bloated and gross from dinner and even a gin and tonic seems excessive, and I am almost tempted to order a vodka-soda, which my Martini Soul Mate used to call the Skinny Bitch and which I drank for a spell back in San Francisco, with my friends or at any rate the people in my life there who passed as friends, the aforementioned Girlfriends Club, skinny bitches drinking Skinny Bitches.

Once upon a time there was a nervous girl in a new city. She had come there for her one true love, and her one true love was doing his best to make her feel welcome, and so it was that the nervous girl fell in with a group of slender, gorgeous women, women who were never nervous, but who were, to their credit, kind to her, and gentle. The slender women took the girl out, to fancy lounge bars and self-conscious imitation dives and wildly overpriced nightclubs, to all the places you were supposed to go when you were young and well paid in the big city. And at these places, the slender women drank clear, nothing highballs, the lowest-calorie and least-flavored way to intoxicate themselves, and the nervous girl began to drink them, too.

And as these nights wore on, these long, loud nights in these dull, loud places, the slender women would enact their sacred nightly ritual. One would make the call, would find herself tripping over her words and declare it time to *pull the trigger*, and her cohort would follow her into the bathroom, would hold her hair as she stuck a couple fingers down her throat, coughed up a rush of stomach acid and liquor into some grimy toilet, would await their own turns to come up clean.

And the nervous girl would watch with envy, an outsider always, wishing she could wring herself out so easily. Of course, she learned.

Vodka: a spirit with no distinctive smell, flavor, or color. Bartenders, you will learn, have a thing about vodka. My Martini Soul Mate didn't even stock the stuff. This is partially a backlash thing, against all the terrible faux-martinis of the 1980s and 1990s, but then also, it's a liquor designed to taste like nothing. So what, bartenders will ask you, is the *point*?

And so I can't order a vodka-soda, not here, not now, not when I want to make a good impression. So I get the gin and tonic, and Meg doesn't order at all, because she's a regular here, and Casey already knows what she wants. The bar is still pretty busy; it's open 'til four, won't be winding down for another couple of hours. Casey leaves us with our drinks and Meg turns to me. Not bad, right? she asks.

I've met Meg a few times now; she's in Joe's pretty often, and she's always so friendly, clearly all the Dans love her, but it's different now, being on the same side of the bar, just the two of us. A first date, that's what it feels like, and we behave accordingly, making nervous small talk at a clip. Meg is from DC, a middle child, a graduate of one of the Seven Sisters, twin degrees in art history and sociology. She works for the Brooklyn Museum in a capacity I don't entirely understand but that has something to do with accessibility and diversity. Something good for the world. Something impressive.

I feel bad, though this is clearly not Meg's intent, and I wonder how Han feels, with his less-conventionally impressive career path. I wonder how *she* feels about it, if she feels like she's dating down, which I know is how Greg felt, a toxic feeling that I tried to kill with the promise of law school, leaving my LSAT prep books lying around the apartment to remind him that I was doing something with my life, or at least, moving in the direction of doing something. But Meg and Han seem solid. I mean, they're *married*.

I want to tell her about my law school plans, to explain to her that I am not *just a bartender*, but something stops me. The thing is, I'm enjoying my training with Han, and I worry that if he knows I'm going to leave and go to grad school, he won't want to train me anymore. I worry that Carver will hire someone else, someone permanent, someone he likes more. And I know that if I tell Meg, soon enough everyone will know. What's the old saying? *Three men can keep a secret if two of them are dead?*

And so when Meg asks what brought me to New York, what I came here to do, I tell her that I'm still figuring it out. Which is not really a lie; just because I know what comes after, doesn't mean I know what comes *next*. And then there is a hand on my shoulder and I turn around and it's Paula and Gina, smiling down at us. They've been sitting in the back, Paula explains; she's not surprised we didn't see them.

Casey, Paula says. Fuck, marry, kill. Prince, Bowie, Mick Jagger.

You're a monster, Casey says.

For a pack of lesbians, you all talk about fucking a lot of men, Meg says. Gina rolls her eyes at me. Don't mind her, she says. She's still mad that she married a dude.

I dated one guy, Meg says, *one guy* my entire time in New York.

I guess I'd marry David Bowie, Casey says. I mean, you'd have to.

Han's great, though, I say. Right?

I think I'd marry Prince, Paula says.

Han is an angel, Meg says. But I feel like a bisexual cautionary tale.

Casey, meanwhile, has decided to kill Mick Jagger. I'm not happy about it, she says. Especially since he's the only one who's still actually alive.

But you couldn't kill Prince, Paula says. It would be like killing a unicorn.

A cursed life, Casey intones. *A half-life.*

What the hell are you talking about? Gina asks, turning away from me, and Casey and I answer in unison, *Harry Potter*. She high-fives me over the bar.

And here with these women, I don't feel like such an outsider. I feel like I am exactly where I'm supposed to be.

PIÑA COLADA

2 ounces aged Spanish-style rum
1 1/2 ounces coconut cream (Coco Lopez, traditionally)
1 1/2 ounces pineapple juice

Shake with ice and strain over crushed ice, or blend with
ice. Garnish with a pineapple wedge or a sprig of mint,
maybe a little umbrella if you have one.

I pay my rent for September, and I have money left over, and
for the first time this year, I feel like I can actually start settling in. I have
my apartment and my four shifts and my flash cards; I have a café I like
and a local bar and a favorite Laundromat. There is a library three blocks
away, pretty as the Williamsburg one, albeit smaller, albeit louder, albeit
with a cop sitting at the door all day. But I like it. In Bed-Stuy everyone
seems to know each other, the women at circulation laughing and gos-
siping with visitors, the groups of men talking over borrowed laptops at
the big tables, the kids' area full of chatter and off-key song.

(It's not that everyone knows each other, Ben says. It's that everyone
talks to each other.)

I go for long walks and slow, slow runs through central Brooklyn—
tree-lined streets and brownstones, the inexplicable castle on Marcus Garvey and Jefferson, the big public housing blocks peppered throughout,

the restaurants and shops and bars, so many bars. The green spaces: the small Herbert Von King near my apartment, Fort Greene farther on, the sprawling and unlikely Prospect Park. I'm learning my way around. I'm getting comfortable.

I tell my father this on one of our increasingly infrequent phone calls and he's quiet, chewing on this information for a minute. When I told him I was moving to Bed-Stuy he was skeptical, had certain preconceived notions about this notorious neighborhood, when arguably it's safer than where I lived in San Francisco. When I told him about the bar job he had no opinion whatsoever.

I speak again, too nervous to let the silence stretch any further. Anyway, I say. It's a good stopgap until law school. And my father asks, Will law school make you happy?

This, I think, is the Arizona effect. Back in Palo Alto my father was just fine with my laser focus on school, with my Ivy League dreams. He would never have told me to sacrifice work ethic or ambition for something so esoteric and intangible as *happiness*. But then he was not exactly up for fatherhood in those first years after my mother's death. Not really. Not buried, as he was, in grief and guilt and regret.

My father was my favorite, growing up. I know you're not supposed to have favorites between your parents, and you can bet I felt like an asshole when my mother died, but she's dead now, so let me be honest: my father was my favorite. I was an only child and he was devoted to me: taught me to swim, taught me my first chords on my first child-size guitar, played with me endlessly in our backyard. If it weren't for the influence of Hayley and her family, I would have been an inveterate tomboy. As it was I was a sort of part-timer: at home I could climb trees and get dirty and watch *Star Wars* and then I could go to Hayley's house to dress up like princesses and play with Barbies.

My mother was around, but also, my mother was not really around. Officially she was a stay-at-home mom, I guess, but she spent so much of that time at home shut up in her studio, smoking cigarettes, the foulness of her moods seeping out under the door. And after she died that gray misery lingered. Our house was not haunted, but it was not *not* haunted. My mother watched us from her paintings, from our family photos, from the studio we never cleaned out, where my father would sit for hours, hours that in my younger years would have been spent with me, and in this way he and I began to drift apart. I poured myself into my studies, the one thing in life that felt wholly under my control, manageable, comprehensible. And the better I did in school, the less adults seemed to worry about me: my father, for one, and Hayley's mother, but also the school counselors and teachers and administrators who knew the sad, sad story of my mother.

By the end of high school my father and I were more like roommates than family, and he was dating the woman who would soon become his second wife, and by my sophomore year at Columbia the Palo Alto house was gone and my father was in Arizona, starting his life over.

My father asks, Will law school make you happy? And I say, Law school will make me a lawyer.

And that will make you happy.

It's better than what I'm doing now, I say. Do you know how demoralizing it is to keep getting passed up for jobs I don't even want? But if I'm a lawyer, I'll be actually qualified to do something that doesn't totally suck.

What about the bar? he asks, and I say, That's something to worry about later, and I'm sure Harvard will get me nice and ready, and I've always tested well.

No, he says. The bar you're working at.

Joe's Apothecary.

Right, he says. How's that going?

I look around my shoe box bedroom, at the piles of bar books and the flash cards all over the walls. This is the room of a bartender. It's fine, I say.

My father says, I just don't want you rushing into anything, as if I hadn't already wasted two years on my ass in San Francisco, as if I weren't wasting another, now, with my stupid deferral. As if I were by any stretch of the imagination *rushing* into anything. But I don't say any of this, and my father continues. He tells me things I already know about how my first months after my treatment are the most precarious, are when I am in the most danger of relapse. He tells me, You're still so young, and objectively I guess I know that's true, but I feel like all of my doors are beginning to creak shut already.

After another painful silence he asks if I'm still meeting with my therapist, and I say yes. I am still meeting with my therapist and I have been eating salads and having healthy breakfasts and drinking water and going for the aforementioned runs and generally more or less taking care of myself. I tell my father I'm doing fine, and he lets it lie.

After we hang up I cradle my phone in my hand and I bring up Greg's number. There is a part of me that thinks if I do everything right—if I keep going to therapy and taking care of myself and getting better at my job and showering regularly and flossing my teeth and shaving my legs and all the rest of it—if I do everything right and then I go to Harvard next year and I get my degree and I get a good job and I move back to the Bay Area, and Greg sees me with my shit together, he will want me back. My therapist says this is the wrong reason to want to do anything, but what does she know about it?

But I don't call him, obviously I don't call him. I put my phone away and I go out into the living room, which is empty and silent but for the smoke detector, and I do my sad, lazy approximation of a Sun Salutation, yoga being, according to my therapist, one of my *resources*, and then I lie down on the floor in Corpse Pose, flat on my back, trying to meditate, trying to let go of my thoughts like so many balloons.

There was a yoga teacher I liked in Arizona, a woman named Blue who came in once a week to do the gentlest of gentle classes with us. Blue was pretty but not skinny, a stocky Scandinavian who wore basketball shorts over her yoga pants and nothing over her sports bras. She was a recovered anorexic, her bulk now enough to move some of the girls to tears, but I found it comforting, which I guess was probably intentional. She had grown larger, but stronger. Happier. Better. I would roll out my mat at the front of the room, the same teacher's pet as ever, seeking to impress Blue with my elastic hamstrings, my open hips. Looking, my therapist would say, for love.

There was a book my parents used to read to me when I was little, a picture book in which a baby bird goes around asking all manner of creature and machine, *Are you my mother?* Blue was nothing like my mother. She would end our classes with Legs-up-the-Wall, which is just what it sounds like, and we would lie there with her, holding our stomachs, that universal problem area. I named mine, Blue told us once. You know, like you're not supposed to do with farm animals. We laughed, but also what she said made sense. I am many things, but I am not cruel. I strive to be kind to people and to animals, I do not even eat meat, just oysters and only because Greg insisted it was ridiculous not to, because they are biologically incapable of experiencing pain. I am only unkind to myself.

The blood pooling in my hips, my pelvis, the belly that I knew was not really enormous pooling, too. My feet tingling. I asked Blue, Does that help?

Oh, yeah, she said. His name is George. I like him. I didn't use to.

Your Buddha Belly, that was what Greg used to call it when I complained, a similar strategy—make it cute and you won't hate it. Privately I have named him Sid, like Siddhartha, you know, the original Buddha. But also like Sid Vicious, sometimes: an undeniable fuckup and maybe an asshole, but mostly just a sweet, lost kid.

In the absence of my perfect ex-boyfriend, I go to see Ben. It's a Saturday, mid-afternoon, early September, and I meet him at a tiki bar in Crown Heights, small and bright and lovely, lots of turquoise and neon and flowers and, of course, rum. *Rum*: a liquor distilled from fermented sugarcane juice, syrup, or molasses. Redheaded stepchild of the North American bar, for the most part, although tiki is having a real moment now. Han says this is a pendulum-swinging thing: fancy cocktail bars emerged out of a distaste for sloppy drinking culture, but now people are tiring of the pretension and the silly vintage outfits and the self-seriousness, and swinging back, to dives, yes, but also to tiki: kitschy, goofy, colorful tiki. If the ethos of craft cocktails is generally *less is more*, the ethos of tiki is *more is more*: more ingredients, more garnishes, more color. Noisy and bright. Drinking, after all, should be fun.

.   .   .

Once upon a time there was an enterprising Californian barkeep in Oakland. He had been a sickly child, losing a leg to tuberculosis at an early age, and he bounced around odd jobs and periods of ill health until opening a small restaurant in the early days of the Great Depression. A terrible idea, you might reasonably think. Doomed to fail. And yet. And yet our barkeep was very good at what he did, and he kept the place going and even had to expand the building to make room for his devoted patrons. With some surprise, he found himself making money on his cocktails, and so he took a drinking reconnaissance trip to New Orleans and the Caribbean and Los Angeles. And soon after, his little restaurant was reborn as a tiki bar. Rum drinks and Chinese food and all of the kitsch required by the culture. In the early days, our barkeep was known for giving drinks and food to his guests in exchange for more Polynesian artifacts and decorations for his establishment, earning him his moniker, Trader Vic.

At its height, the Trader Vic empire spanned the entire country. Queen Elizabeth II herself once dined at his San Francisco outpost—the first meal of her life not prepared by palace chefs, if Han's stories are true. There was one in Manhattan for decades, in the basement of the Plaza Hotel, until the late 1980s when the hotel's new owner declared the place *tacky* and it was shuttered. The hotel's new owner, bastion of taste and sophistication, Donald J. Trump.

I like the place at first glance, take a free seat at the bar as I wait for Ben to arrive, me chronically early as ever, and the bartender comes over to greet me, and suddenly I like the place a lot less.

At Joe's we are blessed with good regulars, by and large; on all tiers they tend to be friendly and patient and welcoming and I feel lucky to have them. But there is one whom I have already learned to hate, and here he is, grinning at me, reaching over the bar to shake my hand. I smile and try desperately to remember his name. It is a generic white-boy name like Will or Kevin or Montgomery, and when I met him a couple of weeks ago, at Joe's, our roles reversed, he made a big show of exchanging it with my own generic white-boy name, explaining that he, too, was a bartender, although I don't think he mentioned this bar, because I think I would have remembered. You'll be seeing a lot of me, he had said. This is my favorite bar in Brooklyn.

So far so good, you're saying. Why do you hate him? He seems nice enough. And he is nice, enough, if condescending, and I could probably get past that, too, but there are two unforgivable offenses. The first is that, despite having made a big show of exchanging names with me, he calls me nothing but *Darling* forever. The second is that he gives me the Daiquiri Test.

As you have no doubt noticed already, bartenders have a fascination with daiquiris. The Snaiquiris we take at the beginning of our shift are a common practice at bars all over the city, and that makes sense—fruity and bright but not too strong, not when you're splitting one full cocktail among four people. But there is another side to this, which is that in addition to its role as the universal start-of-shift drink, the daiquiri has become the universal bartender test, the drink you order to determine whether or not the person serving you knows what they're doing. There is some logic to this, I can admit: the daiquiri is a three-ingredient cocktail, so balance is essential, and it's served up, so proper dilution is essential, too; there is, in short, nothing to hide behind. Not even a garnish.

And it's fine, because I make a good daiquiri, but I find the exercise ridiculous. This little baby bartender, calling me *Darling*, judging me by my ability to make a simple goddamn sour, as if that were some great accomplishment. This part of a larger pattern of the aforementioned cocktail bartender self-seriousness, as if he and I and everyone like us were out here saving lives and not just pouring booze into cups. Talking about willfully obscure drinks as if this knowledge made him better than anybody else. Talking about the higher-ups of the New York bartending scene as if they were real celebrities: famous actors, rock stars, household names. It's the sort of wide-eyed enthusiasm that we ruthlessly mock in teenage girls, but apparently encourage in good-looking white men in their early twenties.

Carver, to his credit, doesn't like this kid either. After the bartender left, that first time I met him, Carver poured us shots and said, *Darling.* I thought you were going to kill him. He said nothing about the Daiquiri Test, being, no doubt, the type of bartender who relies upon it when he goes out. Still, I appreciated the support, and from Carver of all people. It was almost a nice moment. And then he began referring to the bartender as *Darling*, which made me feel better still, except now I am in his bar and I cannot for the life of me remember his real name.

For our purposes, then, let us do as Carver does and call him Darling. Darling is in the middle of building a round, a bottle of beer sitting open already, two shaken drinks to be poured into coupes, and then he goes to a machine at the far corner of the bar and returns with something thick and bright and blended. Piña colada, he tells me, and I must make a face, because he laughs, and he delivers the drinks and when he comes back he pours me a little shot of the mixture and he says, The piña colada is criminally underrated.

Criminally? I echo, and he says, Yes; somebody should go to jail. Probably the guy who wrote that goddamn song.

I take a sip. Damn, I say, and he laughs, and he tells me a story.

Once upon a time, Darling says, there was a young Puerto Rican nobleman named Roberto Cofresí. His family, like much of the archipelago, had fallen upon hard times, and he found work as a sailor in his youth before eventually going rogue. El Pirata Cofresí was a great scourge of the Spanish Empire—and the British, and the Danish, and no doubt others besides. This was the early 1800s, back when everybody had an empire, and every empire had a fleet, and Cofresí stole from all of them, a kind of maritime Puerto Rican Robin Hood.

But a pirate's life is hard, full of long boring stretches at sea, months of wormy rations and doldrums, hard work and dreary routine. Back then, it was standard for sailors to have a rum ration; less standard was what el Pirata Cofresí famously did with that ration, which was to mix it with coconut and pineapple, to bring joy and courage to his crew. An invention of his own, they say, and with his early death (piracy not being a career with a long life expectancy), the recipe was lost. Only to be reinvented a hundred years later, still in Puerto Rico, at a luxury hotel, where Joan Crawford declared it better than slapping Bette Davis in the face, which you have to figure was just about the highest praise she could give.

I want desperately to be annoyed, but the truth is he sounds just like Han.

Ben saves me then, shakes Darling's hand over the bar, touches my back as he takes the seat next to me, and his heat lingers on my back, in my chest, all through the rest of me. We have slept together, now, three times, but this is our first real date, and so we're doing the new sex thing, where everyone around you can smell the pheromones but you are cordial with each other in public, make no acknowledgment or indication that you have seen one another naked, that you are intimately acquainted with parts otherwise unknown, that you have slept tangled up together, that you have sneaked out of each other's apartments at indecent hours in last night's clothes. That thing. If it were a Victorian novel we would be calling each other Mr. Jackson, Miss Fisher, and talking about the weather.

Han calls Ben *a square*, and I get it. Ben is good-looking and mild mannered and his main hobby seems to be going to the gym, and he wears nice, boring suits and he has a nice, boring job, something I don't entirely understand for a big, national corporation, MBA attained through said company, where he has worked since he was twenty-one. You must like it, I say, and he shrugs. It's fine, he says, in a tone that implies the opposite, and when Darling comes back to take our order Ben goes for the booziest drink on the menu.

Darling turns to me, and the thing is I actually do want a daiquiri, and if there were ever a place to order one it would be here, from him, but I don't want him to take this as tacit approval of his Daiquiri Testing ways. I guess I'll have a piña colada, I say, and he grins.

I just feel like I've plateaued, Ben says. I missed out on a promotion last week. Some twenty-five-year-old Murray Hill Yalie asshole. The word *white* not used but heavily implied. Makes me wonder if I need to start looking for a new job, he says. Somewhere I can actually grow.

That's how I felt in San Francisco. Plateaued. Treading water. You want to feel useful, but nobody gives you the chance. A dangerous place to be, stagnation; this is what leads to bad haircuts and poor financial decisions and extramarital affairs. This is the sort of thing that can fester and mutate until it is big enough and ugly enough to devour everything good about your life and leave you with nothing. I tell Ben I know what he means. I tell him, The job market is fucking *grim* these days, and he raises his eyebrows and I say, I've been trying to find a real job since I got to the city.

A frown shadows Ben's face and I know I have misspoken. You don't like Joe's? he asks, but this of course is not what I mean. It's just that I didn't come to New York to bartend.

You know, it used to drive me nuts, he says. When Carver first started talking about opening a bar. He was in his last year at this great art school, and he was so talented, and so brilliant, and he'd spent so much money, and I just—I couldn't understand why he would throw that away to work in the service industry.

It seems crazy, I say.

Yeah, but Carver's *happy*.

I am unable to suppress a laugh, and Ben smiles, nods. Yeah, he's a fucking curmudgeon, he says. But he loves what he does. And honestly the older I get, the more it makes sense to me. You know what I do all day?

I shake my head. Me neither, he says. I send emails, and I wait for emails, and I go to meetings, and I schedule more meetings. None of it means anything. None of it is useful.

No less useful than bartending, I say, but he disagrees.

First of all, he says, lifting the enormous tiki mug before him, this is delicious. And it makes me feel better about how much I hate my job. And I'm out of the house, and I'm not looking at a damn screen for once in my life. And I get to spend time with you.

He kisses me then, just briefly, and I melt a little.

My therapist, for the record, agrees with him. Anything that pays your bills is a real job, she says, as if she didn't have an advanced degree, as if I didn't know she were charging my father's insurance a cool three hundred dollars a session.

I say, But I went to *Columbia*.

She chooses to ignore this. You don't have to do it forever, she says. Something we have talked about a lot in these past few months is the importance of *taking it one day at a time*, because looking at the great span of life is horrifying; because it is easy to get derailed when you start thinking about how you must always and forever foreswear your bad habits and your bad thoughts, but if you just think, *today I won't*, that feels attainable. The word my therapist uses for this is *apeirophobia*, the fear of the infinite, although it is not the sort of word that appears in, say, *Merriam-Webster* or the *Encyclopedia Britannica* or the *DSM-V*. When I point this out to her, she says we should talk about my need to be the smartest person in the room. Which I suppose is fair enough.

Once upon a time, there were two little misfits, a fat one and a skinny one. The first day of kindergarten, the skinny one went up to the fat one and asked if he wanted to be friends. The fat misfit didn't, not with some scrawny white boy, not at first, but when he went to play with the kids he *did* want to be friends with they laughed at his wobbly run on the playground and they tripped him during Duck Duck Goose and they called him names and soon enough he retreated to the equally athletic-adverse skinny misfit, and they formed an alliance.

Their parents were delighted; it turned out that the misfits lived just down the block from each other, and they began to spend all their time together, playing video games in the fat misfit's family brownstone, doing their homework in the skinny misfit's tiny living room. Grew up more or less into nerds, but were saved from the worst of the school bullies by the fat misfit's older brother, who had something of a reputation.

The skinny one's parents lost their apartment in his senior year, moved to Jersey. He finished the year in the fat one's apartment, which might have been a tight fit except that by this point the fat one (no longer fat, having already by then developed his gym habit) was in the garden apartment, which he has never since vacated. The skinny one applied somewhat against his parents' wishes to a myriad of art schools. The fat one went with CUNY, graduated in three years, straight into business. The skinny one went to Pratt, first for undergrad and then for his master's in design, bartending to support himself, bouncing between Bed-Stuy and Clinton Hill, from dorm to shitty apartment to the fat one's couch to another shitty apartment, before eventually falling in love with a beautiful bartender and moving in with her. They opened Joe's Apothecary together and the rest, as they say, is history.

·   ·   ·

I put my drink down. I'm sorry, I say, he fell in love with *Gina*? And Ben nods. No accounting for taste, he says, and he's smiling, but it doesn't sit well with me.

I like Gina, I say, feeling strangely childish. I know she's been hounding Carver lately, but I like her.

That's not—hmm. What do you mean, hounding him?

Isn't that why you don't like her?

I don't like her because she's a bitch, he says, and I'm shocked by the vitriol, and he apologizes. Squeezes my knee, and leaves his hand there, and I feel it through my entire body, stronger than the rum, and I am not ready to fall in love again, not yet, but I am heavily in like and lust, and that is enough for now. That is, in fact, ideal, because there is an expiration date on this, because this time next year, I'll be in Boston.

It's just, she broke Carver's heart, Ben says, and I say I get it. *Bros before hoes* and all that. He asks again: What do you mean, hounding him?

I just heard them arguing the other day, I say. I didn't hear about what. I feel my stupid, unfaithful cheeks going pink, but I can't tell Ben what I heard. I say, I bet they argue all the time. I imagine what it would be like to have to maintain a business relationship with Greg, after everything. It would kill me. Why are they still working together?

Ask Carver, Ben says, and I say, I can't *ask Carver*. He's not exactly an open book.

Ben laughs. One might go so far as to call him a closed book.

Closed and locked.

Closed, locked, and buried.

MANHATTAN

2 ounces rye whiskey
3/4 ounce sweet vermouth
2 dashes Angostura bitters

Stir over ice and strain into a coupe. Garnish with a cherry
or an orange twist.

I am newly curious, too, about Gina. She's there when I wake
up on Friday morning, drinking coffee with Paula in the kitchen, Paula
dressed for her workout already. The chef's life is a notoriously unhealthy
one: those endless, breakless shifts; late nights, early mornings. Not to
mention the laissez-faire attitude toward drinking and drug abuse. And
life is all about balance, and so Paula has a religious dedication to her
health while not at work: rides her bike everywhere, goes to the gym two
or three times a week, goes for regular runs in the park. I have gone on
a couple of these runs with her, but when she invites me today I say no,
no thanks.

Coffee? Gina asks, and this I say yes to. She pours me a cup and I walk
over to get it, but when I reach out, she doesn't let go.

Christ, Sam, she says, looking me up and down. You've gotten very
skinny.

My first impulse is to thank her, but there is something in her expression that tells me she doesn't mean this as a compliment. That it is something closer to a question. I can feel Paula looking at me, too, and I wish I were wearing more than a baggy T-shirt and granny panties. The truth is, I have lost weight. But I haven't purged at all. I've just been eating less, and walking more. It's nothing to be worried about. I'm all right, I say. You know how it is, I say. Working on the floor all night, going up and down those stairs.

Gina releases the mug, and I step back. The boys are putting you on the floor all night? she asks, and I feel like I've betrayed the Dans by mistake and I say something about how I'm still the new girl, it's only fair, and Gina says, No, it's that classic bullshit thing where dudes are bartenders and chicks are waitresses.

I don't know what to say to that; I understand that she is on my side, but I also think that she is wrong, that it is not only my gender, that it is because I am not very good at my job. Not ready to be behind the bar. A little useless.

The coffee is too hot and too bitter, and I set it down. I bartend a little, I say. On Thursdays and Sundays. I'm working on a drink.

Gina is not placated, but Paula puts a hand on her back. Come on, G, she says. You can agonize about Joe's later.

Don't think I won't, Gina says, and Paula laughs, and I take my coffee cup with me back into my room.

I hear Paula tell Gina not to scare me. I'm trying to help, Gina says, and then I shut the door and I don't hear any more.

There is a mirror on the inside of my door, left by my predecessor, and I stand there before it and I lift up my shirt, look at my stomach, reach down to draw out a love handle. It's not much of one, which is encouraging, and I can admit that it's possible that Gina is right, that I am indeed looking skinny.

Body dysmorphia: an obsessive idea that your body is severely flawed, and/or a perception of your body's flaws as much more severe than they are.

Fatphobia: prejudice against people with bodies larger than an arbitrarily determined norm. Fear of becoming one of them yourself.

I wonder about Ben, *the fat misfit*, no longer fat. That kind of thing leaves its scars—the stretch marks on your skin, sure, but the memories of those kids, their teasing and their laughing and their unbridled prepubescent cruelty. I was a twig of a kid. All my trouble came later.

I turn to the side; there is still a belly there, undeniable, the front line of my profile not parallel with the curve of my spine, and I push it out until I look grotesque and then I suck it all the way back in until I look emaciated and then I drop my shirt and I back away and I fall onto my bed.

I have the second start, arrive at Joe's with the fading daylight to a quiet bar, the usual group of schoolteachers at their usual high-top and Joe Himself at the bar with his usual paperback, nobody behind the bar, although this mystery is quickly solved when Han pokes his head out from the back room, waves to me, vanishes again.

I put on my apron and go to investigate. He's at one of the tables with a camera slung around his neck, something stirred in a coupe glass on the table before him. Carver wants to work on the bar's Instagram, Han explains, rolling his eyes, as if this were a ridiculous proposition and not the literal bare minimum of running a business in the twenty-first century. He holds the camera up for me, clicking through the pictures he's taken. I think maybe this one, he says, pausing, and I'm still searching for something nice to say when he looks at me and bursts out laughing. All right, he says, and he slips the camera strap off his neck and places it around mine. *You* do it.

I pick the drink up and carry it out into the front room. Daylight's going fast, but there's enough to work with, and I take over one of the free high-tops. My brief foray into photography in high school has left me with a solid understanding of aperture and depth of field, although what little expertise I offer now is thanks mostly to Vanessa Garfield, the ringleader of the Girlfriends Club.

Vanessa Garfield was an influencer—continues to be an influencer—and over the course of our time together I picked up a couple tricks. Obviously most of those tricks were for selfies, but there are some universals. Get rid of visual noise, that's one; your subject should have the viewer's full attention. Use natural light, unless you have one of those fancy ring light setups, which she did, but obviously we don't. Overcast days are actually best, because on a sunny day your contrast will get blown out. Watch the angles, always, and take twenty more photos than you think you have to. Color correct but don't use a filter; it's not 2014 anymore. Hashtag your posts to death, and post between eleven and one, when people are bored at work and looking at their phones.

Han's looking at me like I've just started talking about string theory. I shrug and try to swallow my smile. I'm a twenty-four-year-old girl, I remind him, handing the camera back. This is my wheelhouse.

The bar begins to fill up, the customary first wave of shift workers and freelancers, people who don't have to work until six thirty or commute back from Manhattan, service workers on a night off trying to beat the crowds. Han leaves me behind the bar, as he often does, prowling the floor and letting me mix drinks, a welcome change for both of us, I think. Soon enough our roles will be reversed. In the meantime, I'm left with Joe Himself and his book and his whiskey.

I ask him how he is and he says he can't complain, Brooklyn thick in his voice as ever, and he asks me how I am and I say Yeah, I'm fine, and then he glances down at his book and I feel this great, awful wave of empathy for him. I see myself, this time last year, visiting my Martini Soul Mate as things with Greg began to fall apart, as everything began to fall apart, seeking refuge. Isn't that what a bar is for? To be a safe space for the lonely and the unhappy, for those who don't want to go home to their empty houses or their chirping smoke alarms or their disinterested boyfriends or their loud children or their sick parents or their shitty roommates or themselves, worst of all themselves?

I wonder how things might have been different if my mother had had a place like that. If this was the role her co-op filled, before my father and I ripped her away from it. But my mother had *us*, her family, and yet we were apparently not enough. My therapist says that this is not a useful line of thinking, and she's right; nothing I could have done as a child would have saved her. And yet. Why did we let her spend so much time alone?

And so I dedicate myself to Joe Himself. I give him my full attention, and I dig for common ground, and the truth is it's not actually hard to find. A bar lesson: people who love their liquor generally love to talk about their liquor, and as long as you don't mind some meandering odes to something you don't care about and possibly some light mansplaining, it's a great icebreaker. And so, I ask Joe Himself what he's drinking, nodding to the glass on the bar in front of him, and he tells me.

Whiskey: spirits distilled from a fermented mash of grain at less than 95 percent alcohol by volume (190 proof) having the taste, aroma, and characteristics generally attributed to whiskey and bottled at not less than 40 percent alcohol by volume (80 proof). That is the American legal definition, and as you can see, it is almost meaningless. You can use any grain you want to make whiskey, technically speaking, and there are some odd varietals kicking around—oat, millet, blue corn, rice, quinoa—and then you can age it as little or as much as you like, however you like. The rules are stricter when you start breaking it down into types: for bourbon, for example, you have to use at least 51 percent corn, and then you have to age the product you distill in new, charred American oak barrels. There are different levels of charring: 1, 2, 3, and alligator. I think that's one of Han's bullshit stories at first, but it's true; that's really what they call it.

There is some confusion/debate around the spelling of the word, specifically around the "E." In the United States, we say "whiskey;" so, too, in Ireland. In Scotland, Canada, and Japan, however, it's "whisky" instead. This is the type of pedantic and utterly trivial concern that bartenders and devotees tend to be freaks about, and you can tell by looking at the Joe's menu that Carver is a freak about it, too, and so for our purposes, we will vary our spelling accordingly.

Joe Himself is drinking Scotch, a nice honeyed single malt, twelve years old, which is, for Scotch, on the younger side. *Single malt Scotch*: whisky (no "E") made only from malted barley, in Scotland, and then aged in oak at least three years. It doesn't all have to come from the same barrel, in fact it rarely does, but it does all have to come from the same distillery. Himself lays out what he knows as simply as he can, has Han and me line up bottles with exotic and unfamiliar names, one or two that I recognize, six in all, and he talks us through the terroir. Lowlands, light and delicate, aperitif style. Highlands, larger, more diverse—younger whiskies light and floral, older ones richer, fruitier. Within the Highlands is Speyside, cradle of one third of all single malts on the market. Good starter whiskies, Himself calls them, and it's true that the only Scotch I've ever had before was a Speyside, Glenfiddich 12 at the behest of Scott the Scot, who went through a bottle a month easy, mostly by himself.

Then the Coastal Highlands, which are similar but begin to pick up coastal characteristics: saline and seaweed, minerality. Islands, even more oceanic. Peatier. *Peat*: a substance somewhere between live plant and coal, an ugly, rotted, fossilizing thing used to cook barley, used especially on the islands, and most especially on Islay, where there are no trees to burn and peat is essential. Ardbeg, Laphroaig, Bruichladdich, I like the names, I like the taste of smoke and salt, a meaty, barbecue sort of flavor, or the echo of a beach campfire, the kind that clings to your clothes for days afterward, the kind we used to have in my childhood, before the fire danger grew too severe, before the Californian outdoors became too fragile. A measurement of smokiness: phenol, a quantification of flavor. I find this information useful in the way that I find knowing about the regions useful: broad strokes within which I can begin to understand something so esoteric and ethereal as taste.

Han says I have a good palate, and I want to believe him. Tasting whisky, I think, I can taste sugar and wood. Himself will say *red apple*, and I will taste for it, and it will be there, but that's the difference between doing karaoke and singing an aria. I can chase this to some scary places. Sit there with nothing but saliva on my tongue and wonder, what does *red apple* taste like? Can I summon these sensations, cold, like having perfect pitch? Do I know what anything tastes like? Have I ruined my taste buds through the years of disordered eating and self-hatred?

Still, I thrill to hear him say it. *A good palate.*

When we have run through all the basics and I am developing a pleasant buzz from all my little tastes and the first of our nine-to-five guests have begun to filter in, we put the bottles back on the shelves, and I thank Joe Himself. He shrugs it off, though I can tell he's pleased. People think Scotch is so intimidating, he says, but once someone explains it to you, it's easy.

I am just finishing my last taster—Caol Ila, an Islay twelve-year-old, bell pepper and vanilla, smoke and oak—when Carver arrives. I'm worried I'm going to be in trouble, that he's going to be upset that I've been drinking whisky with Himself instead of cleaning or prepping or whatever else I no doubt should have been doing with the slow start, and my stomach twists as his eyes flick to the glass in my hand. Are you getting my staff drunk, Joe? he asks, and there is an edge to his tone but it's playful, too, and I give him my best attempt at a smile.

We're having a little training session, I tell him. Learning about Scotch.

And how's that going?

I'm converted, I say, lifting up the Caol Ila. I'm a whisky drinker now.

This has exactly the effect I'm hoping for. Carver's face lights up, a real smile breaking over his features. The predictable man's reaction to a woman with a palate that is, by some arbitrary and senseless rubric, *masculine*. It's bullshit, and it's sexist, and I know better, or at least I should know better, but this is a tack that works, and I have to win Carver over somehow.

Well done, Joe, Carver says, and Himself beams.

The masculine palate. The gendering of taste is scientific nonsense, but still I relied heavily upon it during the brief period of time I spent attempting to ingratiate myself to Greg's coworkers; gave up my effete martini for its butch cousin the Manhattan—rye whiskey instead of gin, sweet vermouth instead of dry, hefty doses of Angostura bitters—even though at the time I didn't like whiskey at all, choked it down purely for effect. I would go meet them after work, uncomfortable as they made vague and inconsequential attempts to include me, happier when they left me to sit on the sidelines, on the curb of the conversation, though I would not say I was *happy*. Ended up talking to the bartender nine times out of ten, the bartender or some friendly solo patron, usually a man, usually visibly put out when it became clear that I was not looking to hook up. Or I would go to their parties and spend the night poring over their bookshelves, playing with their pets. I told myself that this was enough; I was there, showing face, drinking my boy's drink with my boy's boys.

It was obviously not enough. I remember one night in particular, leaving a get-together at Greg's coworker's house, the two of us walking the mile home, buoyed by large quantities of conspicuously nice whiskey—a good whiskey, these days, as much a status symbol as a name-brand watch or a Tesla. Mostly Greg and his friends were bourbon drinkers, but the star of that night had been a bottle of Japanese whisky, the Yamazaki 12 Year Old, trendy and expensive and increasingly hard to find. The thing about a twelve-year-old whisky is, it's generally been blended from a number of different barrels. The *youngest* of which has to be twelve years old. And so if you are a newly popular Japanese whisky distillery, and your twelve-year-old bottling is globally coveted, but your whisky wasn't popular at all twelve, fifteen, twenty years ago, you're not going to have the stock to keep up.

Yamazaki 12, we sell it for $35 a pour at Joe's, so expensive your hands shake to pour it, you're torn between the fear of spilling even one drop and the desire to pour a good meniscus, to give the drinker their money's worth. Han will tell you not to be so precious about it, will pour you a big taste, almost an ounce, honeysuckle, orange, a hint of coconut. I can see the appeal, now; but back then in San Francisco it tasted the same as anything else, which is to say, I didn't like it.

And this, in my inebriated state, was what I was talking about. I made a joke that was not really a joke about our host's dangerous proximity to the classic techbro stereotype, the white guy with the weird fetish for all things Japanese. And Greg was silent at first, and then he said, I wish you would be a little less cynical. And I felt the guilt in my bones, the bad thing inside of me, the thing that, if I were honest with myself, was unhappy now, might always be unhappy, might always need to devour everything and everyone in its path. The thing I had fed, that night, with the excellent catered dinner that I had just thrown up in the fancy (Japanese, for the record) toilet in his coworker's upstairs bathroom. The thing I would attempt to feed when Greg and I got home and I arranged myself on the bed in the sexy underwear I had worn for the occasion, certain that if he would just fuck me, everything would be okay.

I can't, he said. He peeled off his shirt, kicked off his jeans. I could see his hard-on through his boxers, and said so. I'm too tired, he said.

I offered to be on top; he wasn't interested. I offered him a blow job; still no. I got up, went to sit beside him. I was desperate. He had never not wanted me before. And if he didn't want me, what was I even doing here?

I said his name, put my hand on his thigh, kissed his shoulder.

He pushed me away. Don't, he said, and he went to sleep on the couch, and I retreated into the bathroom for the saddest solo session of all time, crying in the shower, digging for an orgasm that wouldn't come, anything to make the night feel like less of a disaster.

How would it have been different if I'd known to talk about, say, the difference between Japanese and American oak? The flavor of barley versus that of corn, rye, wheat? Would they have folded me into their world? Would Greg have wanted me more, for longer? The answer, I suspect, is yes.

Joe Himself is nursing what he claims will be his final drink, Caol Ila, same as me, and I am lingering across the bar from him, leaving the floor to Han for the time being, letting Carver mix drinks, just standing there with my whisky and listening because for once, Joe Himself is actually talking.

What I learn is: Joe Himself grew up just down the street, not far from Carver and Ben, though some twenty years earlier. The youngest child of three, an Italian family in a building long since razed for luxury housing, in a Brooklyn I can only just imagine, the Bed-Stuy of Spike Lee and early Jay-Z, my only cultural touchstones from the era, and Himself speaks of it with a fond, conflicted pride: the violence of it but the sweetness, too, the tightness of the community that has been driven out by (he does not say) people like me, gunshots and cookouts, home. His parents, kind but often absent, his brothers out of the house by the time he hit puberty, his schoolboy days pockmarked with fights and school-yard bullies and mediocre grades, but never enough to get him in too much trouble. Rocketing up to six foot three at sixteen, at which point his classmates mostly left him alone, him gliding through the rest of high school, straight into a good government job, one that he liked. He liked the trains, had begun to work with them in the days of the subway renaissance, the brief golden decade or two between the subway you see in *The Warriors* and the subway you see today, where people disappear into stations in Greenpoint and turn up weeks later in Flushing, in Canarsie, on the Upper West Side, dazed and hungry, changed, haunted.

I could talk to him for another hour, happily, but this is all I get tonight. Himself finishes his Caol Ila and leaves too much cash on the bar, refusing change, and he stands up and shakes my hand. Always a pleasure, he says. Never a chore.

What are you doing now? I ask, and he shrugs. Thumps on the neglected Patterson paperback on the bar-top. Go home, finish reading, go to bed. Do it all again tomorrow.

When he goes, Carver and Han turn on me. What did you *do*? Han asks.

I've been trying to get him to talk to me for literally years, Carver says.

I'm uncomfortable under their scrutiny, but of course I'm pleased with myself. I'm sure you laid all the groundwork, I say, and Carver shakes his head. Well then, I say, picking up the stack of bills. I guess I'm just a better bartender than you thought.

The night picks up speed. Any concerns about Joe's viability as a bar tend to vanish on a Friday night, when all the seats are full and all four of us are in constant motion for hours on end. The music turned up loud, the conversations louder, laughter and clinking glasses. The lights low and candles flickering on all the tables, on the shiny bar-top. Black tray in my left hand, heavy with as many empties as will fit on my way back to the bar, heavy with the next round of drinks on my way back to the floor. *Full hands in, full hands out*: the service industry golden rule. Any time you return from the floor, you do it carrying something.

When Hayley and I were in high school we used to go to concerts in San Francisco, take the train up to see willfully obscure indie rock outfits at tiny venues all over the city. If we were looking to escape Palo Alto—and we were always looking to escape Palo Alto—this was as good as it got: the anonymity of San Francisco, the dark crush of a crowd, dancing and wild in a way we so rarely were. Screaming along to our favorite songs, staring up at these boys with guitars and skinny jeans, losing our minds. At a good show I could really let go of everything and let joy in. It took me out of myself. Or, no, perhaps that's not right. Perhaps it was the only time I was really fully inside of myself.

A good bar shift does the same thing. Once I've found my rhythm, I ride it, high on the job well done, laughing with guests and coworkers, efficient and beloved. Becoming a vessel for something, some communal spirit of the night. It's hard work, sure, me sweating through my T-shirt as I ferry drinks and orders, empties and checks, back and forth and back and forth, nothing to sustain me but a Snaiquiri at eight and the occasional shot of tequila, a slice of the pizza Han orders wolfed down so fast I barely taste it, no time to catch my breath, forget about a bathroom break. So maybe it is less like attending a concert, and more like performing in one.

Olsen says this is ridiculous. There is *nothing* like being onstage, he says. Bartending doesn't even scratch the itch.

It's midnight and starting to quiet down, the chefs settling in at the bar, Ben, too, Han taking off his apron and picking up the last piece of pizza, Carver pouring a round of shots. I don't know what to say to Olsen; obviously he would know better than me. Maybe I haven't articulated myself well enough. I down a glass of water to buy myself time, looking for the words, but I'm not finding them, and anyway Olsen is unlikely to be convinced.

Carver presses a shot glass into my hand. I know exactly what you mean, he says, and I try not to look too pleased.

I stay on for another hour as we get restocked and reset, and then I sit down and Carver pours me one of the fancy whiskeys, a twelve-year-old rye, apricot and spice, and it fills me up with something I don't have a name for, and then I'm leaving and Ben holds my hand as we walk home, to his home, and I lean in close to him, and I'm so tired, and I'm so happy.

SIDECAR

2 ounces cognac
3/4 ounce Cointreau
1 ounce lemon juice
1 dash simple syrup

Shake with ice and strain into a chilled coupe (with an
optional sugar rim). No garnish.

He sounds great, Hayley says.

He's okay, I say, but I can't stop the stupid grin spreading across my
face, and Hayley grins, too. You deserve it, she says. After Greg. And I
accept this, even though we both know I was not the girlfriend I should
have been, that I am far from blameless for the way things ended. Still.
That's what best friends are for.

It's early Saturday afternoon and we're in my apartment, Hayley's first
visit, her walking in with a massive blue IKEA bag and her cheeks pink
from the crisp fall air, hugging me tight and stepping back to take in the
glorious absurdity of my new home, gratefully accepting a cup of coffee
as I give her the briefest of tours, visibly alarmed by the size of my room,

or perhaps it's not the size but the serial killer flash cards that are upsetting her. Whatever it is, she keeps it to herself. Cute, she says.

What's in the bag? I ask, and she grins. Presents, she says; she has been doing another one of her closet cleanses, these cleanses traditionally the source of all my nice clothes, of most of my clothes, period, because I find shopping unbearable—standing in the shrill, ugly light of a dressing room, looking at my clogged pores and my doughy body in the mirror, the unfathomable horror of having to ask for a size up, the aspirational nonsense of buying something that doesn't fit right out of a misplaced loyalty to the number four.

I dig through the bag as Hayley goes to the bathroom. I could have a wardrobe like this, I think. I could pay $3,000 a month for an apartment and buy designer and eat organic and get my hair cut in TriBeCa and go out three nights a week and not have to worry about any of it. I mean, I'm still mostly broke now. But I could do it, if I stopped bartending and actually started making money.

I imagine it, for a minute. Imagine working for a firm in Midtown, commuting to and from an apartment in a building like Hayley's, no beeping smoke detectors, no noisy roommates, just someone like Tyler or Greg or Ben and a fridge stocked with fresh, healthy produce or at least a favorite neighborhood salad bar and the money to justify eating out every day of my life. In this vision, I'm happy. I'm healthy. I'm almost unrecognizable.

But, of course, money is not the reason to do anything. If you will allow me to borrow a concept from the Japanese: *ikigai*. Something Greg used to talk about, Greg and all his Japanophile coworkers. To understand *ikigai*, imagine a Venn diagram with four overlapping circles: what you're good at, what the world needs, what you love, and what will make you money. If you can find something that sits right in the middle, you will be successful and fulfilled. Hayley has almost all of it, working for her gender-equality nonprofit, making life better for girls and women in New York City and beyond, although I am pretty sure her parents are still paying her rent. But Hayley is not a lawyer. The average starting salary for a Harvard Law graduate is $150,000.

Greg, on the other hand, was a great believer in inventing your own job. This is why tech was so appealing to him, although he is, to my knowledge, still working for somebody else, a cog in a larger machine. But his long-term plan was always to start his own company, to find both his *ikigai* and his independence. There are a thousand ways to make a living, if you're a little creative and a little daring and a little lucky. And it doesn't hurt to be a straight white man with a good education and a trust fund.

I have no interest in inventing my own job; I am certain I can find my *ikigai* within existing channels. I'll go to Harvard, and I'll get into environmental law, become an advocate for the planet, a defender of the sky and the water and the trees, like some kind of gainfully employed, overeducated Lorax. I will be good at it, I think. It will be good for the world; it will not be the most lucrative of law careers, but it will nevertheless make me money. I am not sure about the love, but I'm cautiously optimistic. And at any rate, of the four circles, that one seems the most like a luxury.

I try on one of the dresses, blue brushed cotton, an unfamiliar designer's name on the tag. I've seen Hayley wear this before, dozens of times, admired it on her, the way her boobs look in it, the boobs I've envied since she got them in middle school. Even at my heaviest I never broke a B cup.

It hangs off me in a way I don't want to like and I stare at myself in the mirror on the back of my door. Hayley may be richer and prettier than I am, more accomplished and more fashionable, but I'm still thinner.

Oh, you have to take that, she says, and I jump a little, and I feel like an asshole. You love this dress, I say.

It makes me look chunky, she says, wrinkling her nose, and now I *really* feel like an asshole. Hayley has always been so comfortable in her own body, from her admirable lack of shame in the locker rooms of our youth to her lengthy teenage crop-top phase to her decision, in college, to stop wearing bras entirely and forever. I've thought about her a lot this year, attempted to channel her self-confidence and her unflappability. I am still trying to channel it; forgoing pants in my apartment at all hours of the day and night, wearing the least on the days I feel the fattest.

And Hayley knows this. I'm sorry, she says. I shouldn't say that to you.

I'm fine, I say, but I wish you wouldn't talk that way about my friend Hayley.

I look back at my reflection, run my hands over the soft, smooth fabric. If you're sure you don't want it anymore, I say, and she says she is.

We leave the stagnant air of my apartment, leave the bag of clothes that make Hayley feel bad about her body, and we step out into Bed-Stuy. I am still new to this neighborhood, but Ben has been the consummate tour guide, taking me to the best bars and restaurants, introducing me to everyone he knows, me like an endless debutante, nervous but excited. So obvious how much people like him, and he has chosen to spend his time with me.

He's a good boy, a bartender said to me the other week, Ben in the bathroom, me twisting my fingers together in my lap trying not to look too uncomfortable in his absence. We were in a Caribbean place eating jerk tofu (me) and chicken (him) and drinking rum punch, me not the only white woman in the place but very much in the minority, and the bartender was older, a butch Black woman with a gap-toothed grin, and she looked at me across the bar and she was telling me I was lucky, and I knew she was right. He's the best, I said, and the bruise of my ex-boyfriend was not gone, but it was fading, it is still fading, it will continue to fade.

Hayley and I walk down my quiet street, and I wave to the old lady on the sidewalk sweeping up leaves and rubbish, to the women deep in conversation on neighboring stoops, to the man with the small dog who is always sitting outside the bodega on the corner. In Palo Alto people don't acknowledge each other, would never greet someone they didn't know by name. In San Francisco, forget it. It's nice, Hayley says, and I can tell she means it.

We turn onto the avenue, pass some kids on skateboards, a group of Black women on their way to brunch, a white hipster dad pushing a stroller and talking loudly on his phone. One of the churches is having some kind of fall festival, the smell of burgers and charcoal, the sound of laughter. The man Han calls the Mayor is holding court on the sidewalk, and I catch his eye and stop to talk. Mr. Mayor, I say, and he claps me on the shoulder, smiles wide enough for me to see a gold tooth blinking in the back. Miss Bartender, he says; I can tell he doesn't remember my name. He turns to his friends. This is my favorite barkeep, he says, and they ask where I work, and I tell them, smiling awkwardly around at this group of older men, and I tell the Mayor to take care, Always a pleasure, I say, never a chore, and I keep going before I have to make conversation. A regular, I tell Hayley, and she nods. Seems like you're settling in, she says, and yeah, I guess I am.

I take her to the café I like, buzzing and loud, the two of us squeezing in at a wobbly table in the back, going to the counter for drip coffees and pastries, both of us watching each other eat, pretending not to watch each other eat, pretending not to notice. Cute, she says, and I agree.

And then she wants to see Joe's, and I'm happy to show it to her; I know how much she likes Gina's bar in Williamsburg, and I know she will like this one.

But. There's something I have to tell you first, I say as we wait at a corner for the light. I'm nervous saying it, though I know I'm being silly. Remember that bar we used to go to in college? Of course she does. Remember that bartender?

The one you—

Yes, the one I. Dan Olsen. He actually works at Joe's, I tell her. He's working today.

For a moment I think she's going to be angry, but then she laughs, long and hard. New York is such a small town sometimes, she says.

The light changes. It was surreal, I tell her as we cross. Walking into my trial shift and having *him* behind the bar.

You should have told me, she says.

I thought you'd be mad. You *hated* him.

Look, she says. He was a real dick to you, and I would still love to punch him in his stupid face, but. When you were hanging out with him you—you *unclenched*, you know? You weren't so serious. You stopped being this flawless, shiny humanoid and became a normal person like the rest of us. It was kinda nice.

I do know. I know exactly.

.   .   .

In the Olsen era, I was wild. I had been so buttoned up for so long that I went, admittedly, a little crazy. I embraced the work-hard-play-hard ethos of Columbia with new vigor; the working hard I was used to, but the playing hard! You could party any night of the week in New York; there was this whole enormous, exuberant world and I had only just arrived. The first time I slept with Olsen was a real five-alarm of a night; the bar where he worked sticky and slammed, Hayley and me both shit-faced, and I will never know how Olsen and I ended up back at his apartment, but I know I was happy to be there, and that I pretended it wasn't the first time, that I wasn't frightened. I mean, I wasn't really frightened. I wanted to have sex with him so badly. I wanted, perhaps even more, to not be a virgin anymore. The act itself a blur, but not an unpleasant one, repeated in the morning, repeated a handful of times after until Olsen stopped returning my texts and I stopped going to his bar.

After that I calmed down a little. I went home after my shifts instead of spending all my tip money at dive bars. I brought my sagging grades back up, I lost the whiskey-ginger weight I hadn't realized I'd gained. And I didn't have sex again until Greg, but then it was only with Greg, and Greg was many things, but he was never wild. He was, as Han would say, a square. Han would mean this as an insult, but Greg kept me grounded. He tethered me to the life I wanted.

But no, *tether* is not quite right. It was a rope, and it held me only as long as I held on to it. And when I loosened my grip I fell back into chaos, into binges and mood swings and getting wasted by myself at my Martini Soul Mate's bar and throwing up two or three times a day. I fell and I fell and I fell and if Greg hadn't caught me, pulling me back to safety even as he cut me out of his life, I would have kept falling until I ended up just like my mother.

We sit at the bar and Hayley does not punch Olsen, although she is not nice to him. Dan, she says. It's been a while.

He looks wary. Which makes sense; last time the three of us were together, Hayley had called him a string of nasty things—a complete and utter asshole, a washed-up wannabe rock star, a predatory creep. I'm not going to yell at you, she says. I'm told you have grown up to be less of a douchenozzle.

It's true, he says. I've retired. Douchenozzling is really a young man's game.

He makes us Snaiquiris, a peace offering of sorts, and he lays a menu in front of Hayley, who dives in. So how is everything? he asks, and Hayley looks up with one of her signature icy stares, her poison smile. I said I'm not going to yell at you, she says. I still think you're a cunt.

I feel myself go red, and Olsen, wisely, retreats, and Han makes himself available. You, he says to Hayley. I like you. Let me make you something.

Hayley gets a menu cocktail, a shaken invention of Carver's, and I continue my cocktail education with a sidecar, which is basically the French cousin to the margarita: cognac, citrus, Cointreau. Invented in Paris, during World War I, and named for its most devoted fan, a captain of forgotten nationality who used to ride up to the bar every day in a motorcycle sidecar.

But wait. Sixty years earlier still, in New Orleans: the Brandy Crusta, an almost identical drink, though fussier. Served in a little port glass, with a rim of sugar on the outside and the inside lined with a long peel of lemon, curled to sit just inside the glass.

Stealing? Inspiration? Coincidence? Proof that we are all just drawing from the same universal well of ideas and creativity, that as Virginia Woolf says, There is no Shakespeare, there is only *Hamlet* and the lucky sod who put the words to paper?

Perhaps it is more scientific than that. A Cocktailian Law of Conservation: drinks can be neither invented nor destroyed, only changed from one form to another.

When I think of brandy I think of old white men with cigars, globes of brown liquor in their fat hands. A world in which I am not included. It's not an entirely misplaced impression, especially considering how expensive a nice cognac can get, but it's not entirely fair, either.

Brandy: any liquor made from fruit (as opposed to grain or sugar). Cognac and its ilk are made from grapes, or, basically, distilled wine. Cognac strictly defined, an appellation. The French, as you may already know, have a lot of strict rules about their food and drink, and their brandies are no exception. Cognac comes from a specific region, and can only be made from specific types of grapes, which must in turn be fermented in a specific way, which must then be distilled, twice, in traditional copper alembic stills of specific, legally regulated dimensions, which must then be aged in Limousin oak barrels for at least two years. Which is then blended and bottled and labeled with (you guessed it!) specific, legally regulated designations according to age.

We sell a surprising amount of it at Joe's, in fact; specifically, we sell a lot of Hennessy. Never underestimate the power of brand recognition, Han says. That's why we keep Jack Daniel's behind the bar, Grey Goose, Tanqueray. Not through any specific personal fondness—they're all fine, I guess, but rarely the most interesting option and never the cheapest—but because people can be relied upon to order them, and to happily pay an extra couple bucks for the privilege. Hennessy, at least, Han will tell you, has earned this—put real money and effort into courting the Black community, long before any other big liquor brands thought to bother, and are still reaping the benefits today.

On the American side of things, apples. *Applejack*: an American liquor made from a blend of apple brandy and neutral grain spirits. Once upon a time, Han says, there was a young American man in a wild northwestern region where settlers were given free land, provided that they planted orchards on it to prove their intention to stay for the long haul. The young American traveled the land with his bag full of apple seeds, so that when the settlers arrived the orchards would be waiting for them. In our national consciousness, he was sowing sustenance, nutrition, wholesome good health.

Not so. First of all, he was making good money off those orchards. Second, his faith (Swedenborgianism, whatever that is) forbade grafting (though not, apparently, capitalizing on the desperation of frontiersmen). As such the apples he planted were all but inedible by themselves—but perfect for hard cider, which in those times was safer to drink than water.

No doubt made those grueling early frontier years easier on the soul, too. And then from the cider, it was easy enough to leap to brandy: to freeze off the water from the cider in the winter, and then eventually to build stills, and anyway one way or another to end up with what became known as applejack, at which point any claims of health benefits had to be begrudgingly abandoned.

It's interesting, being here as a guest, sitting at the bar with a friend on a Saturday afternoon like any normal person might. Watching Han and Olsen work together. Olsen ceding the bar to Han, sweeping around the floor with a bottle of water, with a tray full of glasses. Joe's is quiet, too quiet, perhaps bar-closing quiet. A trio of beer drinkers at a high-top, a couple with a double-wide stroller in the back room, two strangers on a date in the window. Not enough. It's September now; we should be busy.

What if Joe's doesn't start making money? What if it *does* have to close? What will I do then? Law school is still a year away, and I have this new apartment and these new friends and this new boy, and Joe's Apothecary is at the center of all of it.

And the fact is, most bars and restaurants fail. The margins are so slim; there are so many reasons things can fall apart. Even a busy place can go under—that Thai place closed at the end of my first summer, gave us all a whopping forty-eight hours' notice. There were signs, I guess, not that I knew how to read them at the time: closing Mondays, introducing lunch and happy hour, putting an inexplicable burger on the menu in hopes of drawing in hipsters. Of course fine and fine-adjacent dining is the hardest to make work, but even a barebones dive is subject to the whims and weather of the city, of the economy, of the climate. There are endless stories of bars that went under post 9/11, after the crash in '08, after Hurricane Sandy.

So what do you do? What can you do?

The door swings open and Han brightens and greets the newcomers. I sneak a look as they sidle up to the other end of the bar: no one I've seen before, two old white men in suits despite the weather, ignoring Han's greeting as they settle in. They are rude and unfriendly people, we are not going to learn their names: let's call them Short and Bald. Professors, it turns out: they order expensive Scotch from Han and then immediately begin to bitch about their latest batch of students, who are lazy, entitled, and unmotivated, and I eavesdrop for a little while, remembering all my least favorite teachers.

Like how in high school, I was this star of STEM, top of my Calc class, entering Columbia as a math major, dreams of working for NASA abandoned but my love of numbers unrelenting. With the exception of a mediocre geometry teacher in tenth grade, every math teacher I'd had so far had been excellent, generous, engaging. And then suddenly there I was at Columbia with a professor I hated, me dog-paddling through the semester, passing, but at great cost to my emotional well-being and sleep hygiene and other classes. A real shock after high school, as you might imagine. Still, I passed, in fact I scraped a B, but by the end of the semester I was done, I came back after winter break and I made it a week into Linear Algebra before I dropped it and switched over to the Humanities.

I hadn't realized how angry I still was about that.

But I push that anger down and I force myself to stop eavesdropping and turn my attention back to Han and Hayley.

So you came out here for school, he's saying, and never looked back. Why would I?

Well, Sam did, he says, and they both look at me, and I make a face. Temporary insanity, I say.

And now she's never allowed to leave me again, Hayley says. She slings an arm over my shoulders. Right, Sam?

Sure, I say, but she doesn't let it go that easy. I'm serious, she says. I'll even move to Boston with you.

Why on earth would Sam move to Boston? Han asks, and before Hayley can say anything incriminating, I'm forcing a laugh, saying, I know, right? As if the idea were some absurd invention of Hayley's. As if I have not been trying to get there for a decade.

And then Short and Bald are ready for another round, and Han drifts over, asks if they'd like another whisky, attempts to make a recommendation, a favorite of Joe Himself's, and there is a rancid silence, and when I look over they are staring at Han as if he's said a dirty word, as if he's suggested warm vomit and not a nice $20 Highland dram, and the veneer of Han's smile is a little chipped as he turns away and gets them the same whisky as before.

I don't know why I fucking bother, he says when they go. Olsen looks after them. They're always nice to me, he says, and Han says, I fucking bet. Olsen rolls his eyes at me, but I think I know what Han's getting at. I hear Gina in my head, saying, *dudes are bartenders, chicks are waitresses.* Amend it to, *white* dudes are bartenders.

Hayley misses all of this, distracted by her phone, a text from Tyler, her tapping out a feverish reply. I'm telling him to come here, she says, and behind her back I mime gagging, and Han chokes, trying not to laugh. A nonissue, because Tyler refuses to come to Bed-Stuy. I better go, Hayley says, and Han and I try to talk her out of it, but it's clearly a lost cause. Don't worry, she says. I'll be back.

She calls a car and she gets up, leaving a twenty on the bar in spite of Han's protestations. Han, she says, reaching over the bar to take his hands in her own, I love you. Olsen—and he looks over, wary, from the far side of the bar—you hurt Sam again and I will castrate you.

I linger over my drink, feeling the liquor gilding my insides, texting Ben to see if he wants to get dinner, because all I've had today is a croissant and if I keep drinking I will get myself into trouble. Carver shows up while I'm waiting for a reply, looks around, and doesn't even bother clocking in. He sits down to my left, orders a beer, and says, I think we should make some changes to the schedule.

No kidding, Olsen says.

Yeah, I mean clearly you don't need me this early on a Saturday, Carver says, but there's more, he keeps talking, and I feel nauseous, my drinks curdling in my stomach, my whole body gone taut. Closing Mondays, he says, that one's easy, and it means one fewer shift for me but three nights a week is not bad, I can live on that. The real bad news comes after. Carver says, There's no point in having two people on weeknights anymore. None of us are making enough money.

We're not going to have enough shifts for all of us, Han says. I'm not getting another job, Carver.

I will, Olsen says, which I think surprises everybody. What? he says. I know people. And I miss that Manhattan money.

And so Carver draws it up, the new schedule; my Sunday goes to the newly part-time Olsen, my Thursday to Han, although Carver is kind enough to give me his own shift on Saturday. Still, look how quiet Saturdays are. How am I going to stay afloat on two shifts a week? How am I going to learn anything without my Thursdays with Han?

And why do I feel so heartbroken?

Olsen doesn't even want the Sunday, I tell Carver.

He rubs his temples. He's retreated into the office again, crunching numbers or whatever on the ancient bar laptop, and I lean against the door, look down at him. I hear Gina's words again, and I wonder if perhaps I am a pawn in some game between the two of them, if Carver is taking out his anger at Gina on me.

I was a barback for two years before I ever got my own shift, Carver says.

And I bet you hated that.

I did, he admits, meeting my eyes at last. He looks exhausted. But you're not ready.

How am I going to get ready if all I'm doing is waitressing on the weekend?

I'm not trying to fuck you over, Sam, he says, but I am not sure I believe him. I want to bartend, I tell him, and yeah, okay, I've had a couple drinks and I'm getting a little worked up, and I say, If I were a dude you wouldn't put me on the floor all the time.

Carver looks genuinely hurt by this. It's not because you're a girl, he says. It's because you're a good server.

This is patently absurd, and I tell him so. I'm a terrible server.

Au contraire, he says, and he pulls out his phone. We've had a three point nine on Yelp forever, he says, opening the app. Every bad review this bar has gotten has been about service. Every single one. Some of those, I will admit, were complaints about me. But then there was Dave, who didn't know nearly enough about drinks, and then there was Becky, who knew a lot but got overwhelmed, and then Olsen hates being on the floor, people can just smell it on him.

He shows me our Yelp page. Four point three, he says, and he brings up our most recent review, five stars, great drinks, beautiful space, our server was accommodating and friendly and generally made our night.

That could have been Han, I say, and Carver shakes his head. What about Joe Himself? he says. I've never seen him open up like that. You bring something special to this place, and I want that on the floor on a Friday night.

So I just never get to bartend, I say, and Carver inhales deeply, but before he can speak, we are interrupted by Han's unexpected appearance, rescued by his simple demand:

I want her on Thursdays.

We both turn to look at him, standing there just behind me. They get hectic sometimes, he says. And when they're not, she can help me with the Instagram, and then I'll train her up and send her home early.

Carver looks from one of us to the other. If you don't mind sharing your tips, he says, I guess it's fine. But you know what that means, Sam.

I better be learning, I say, and he nods. And you have to put a drink on the menu.

Sure, I say, okay.

And no more bitching about me to Gina, he says, and I start to stammer out an excuse, or at least an explanation, but Han grabs my hand and drags me up the stairs before I can finish.

OLD-FASHIONED

2 1/4 ounces rye whiskey
Sugar cube
Angostura bitters

Soak the sugar cube in Angostura bitters and muddle
it in a mixing glass. Add the whiskey and stir with ice,
then strain into a rocks glass over ice and garnish with an
orange twist.

I spend the next week obsessing over my lost shifts. I look for office jobs on Craigslist, Glassdoor, LinkedIn. I apply to a few places, even, but my heart's not in it, and most days I find myself staring up at my flash cards instead, flipping through a book borrowed from Joe's, waiting for one of these old recipes to leap out and grab me, to say, *All right, Sam, let's get weird.*

Not happening. It's Wednesday evening and I'm in a foul mood, dragging myself away from my flash cards to go meet Ben, Ben who keeps saying wholly unhelpful things like, You could always get another bar job. I didn't want the bar job I already have; I have no interest in finding another.

So, Wednesday evening, me walking over to meet him at his apartment and finding myself in unwilling conversation with his mother. Until now, I have successfully avoided running into her, but tonight she's standing out front when I arrive, talking over the fence to a neighbor, just enjoying the mild night—it's the tail end of September and our warm days are numbered. She is nearly as tall as Ben, twice as imposing, and she looks down on me with dark eyes and an unreadable expression as she shakes my hand and introduces herself.

Is this the California girl? the neighbor asks, and I want to melt into the ground. Why does this woman know where I'm from? What has Ben been saying about me?

California, Mrs. Jackson says. Why on earth would you leave?

I force out something about liking New York, but that feels insufficient, so then I admit to having gone to school in the city. NYU? Mrs. Jackson asks.

Columbia.

She raises her eyebrows. Ben said you were a bartender, she says.

Just for now, I say, quickly. My phone buzzes in my pocket; probably Ben asking where I am. I don't dare look. I tell Mrs. Jackson that I'm going to go to law school, though I don't say when, I keep this information deliberately aspirational with her, as I have carefully kept it with her son. Law school as an inevitability, but a vague one: no mention of the admission I have already secured, the deposit I have already paid.

Anyway, it works—something in her softens. She tells me it's nice to finally meet me, says Ben and I should come up for dinner sometime, smiles at me with Ben's smile. Something in my stomach twists painfully, but then, maybe I'm just hungry. I'd love to, I say, and then Ben appears, finally, and I say my awkward goodbyes and descend into the safety of his apartment.

You told your mother about me, I say, and he gives me a sort of sheepish grin, a broad-shouldered shrug. No secrets when your parents are your neighbors, he says, but there's that twist in my stomach again. I didn't tell my father about Greg until I was already following him to San Francisco. Which I'll admit was too late, but isn't this too early? Isn't this too serious, too soon?

Ben has the good sense to kiss me then, and I'm distracted enough to let the matter drop.

.   .   .

And then it's Thursday afternoon and I'm finishing up an easy open, sitting down at the bar for a minute with yet another cocktail book in front of me, wanting to pull out my hair as I glower down at the recipes. *Let's get weird.* But I don't get weird. I keep it as simple as it gets: the old-fashioned. The original cocktail, as you may remember: liquor, sugar, bitters, and water. Back in the nineteenth century, as the definition of the word *cocktail* began to expand, as this sacred ur-cocktail became adulterated with liqueur and fruit and vermouth and various other stuff and nonsense, well, there were some disappointed purists. Some snobby, fun-hating proto-hipsters who could not believe all of these drinks that dared defile the good name of *cocktail* began ordering *old-fashioned cocktails*. Cocktails like granddad used to make. Straightforward, to the point, timeless.

The Dans are very serious about their old-fashioneds, or at least, Carver is, and Han and Olsen humor him. There is a whole ritual, an exact procedure to be followed. First: place a square beverage napkin over the top of the fancy mixing glass, and put a sugar cube in the middle of it. Soak the cube with bitters, wearing down its sharp white edges with the purple-black of the Angostura. You can throw in a dash of orange bitters here if you like, too. When you have saturated the sugar, slip the napkin away, like a magician with a tablecloth, drop the cube into the glass, and muddle. *Muddle*: bartender for "crush." From *muddler*, a sort of thick stick made out of steel or plastic or in this case, at Joe's, wood, with a flat round end to press sugar or fruit or whatever else against the bottom of a glass. You could use a wooden spoon instead, if you needed to, but a real muddler is a nice tool to have.

Muddle muddle muddle muddle. Muddle until you hate the person you're making the drink for. Add your whiskey and your ice, stir to mix and dilute, and then pour it all into a rocks glass over ice. Garnish with an orange peel.

At Joe's we make it with rye whiskey, not bourbon—never bourbon, Carver says; see, *snobby, fun-hating proto-hipster*—but this is not actually a rule. You can make an old-fashioned with anything; it is a style of drink as much as a recipe. And so I am thinking about rum. I've seen

Han make a rum old-fashioned before, brown sugar and dark rum and Angostura bitters, and I want to do that but with the addition of coffee, which I know goes well with rum, and orange, which is the traditional garnish for the old-fashioned.

So there I am, chatting to my first guest—Joe Himself—and trying some things out. The simplest execution of my idea would be to substitute coffee liqueur for sugar, and I try that, and then I add some Grand Marnier, and that doesn't work, so I throw it out and try with coffee liqueur and Campari instead, and it's better like that, but too sweet. I like sweet, Himself says, and grudgingly I hand it over for him to taste.

That's interesting, he says, and I can see him looking for something nice to say, and this is terrible, Joe Himself feeling sorry for me, and I snatch the drink back and I dump it out. He chuckles. Don't worry on my account, he says. You know I don't drink cocktails.

Han tries to help, of course, when he gets in at eight. I like rum and coffee, he says. And coffee and Campari play well together, so there's definitely something there.

What if we infused the rum? he asks. Get a nice affordable dark rum, throw some coffee beans in there, and then work from that?

This is a fairly typical strategy of Han's. Now that I have a better foundation in my bartending, I have begun to notice a certain baroqueness in Han's drinks, a tendency toward complexity. Why use three ingredients when you could use seven? Why not infuse your gin with dill, your bourbon with chamomile, your tequila with peanut butter? Why not add herbs and spices to your simple syrup, fruit to your ice cubes, absinthe to your Angostura?

(It's exhausting, Olsen says, but what I have learned in my time at Joe's is that nobody listens to Olsen.)

A bar lesson. There are a few different ways to infuse a spirit, and coffee calls for a simple one: take a bottle of rum, and a bunch of coffee beans, and let them sit. Han digs up a mortar and pestle from somewhere and has me gently crush the coffee; you don't want it ground, but you want it broken up a little. This goes into a clean quart container, followed by as much rum as will fit. Put the lid on, shake, and leave it to do its thing.

Coffee is a slow infusion: a week, Han says, at least, for full flavor. Which is fine, but it means I don't have anything else to do for now, can make no further progress tonight. I try not to seem disappointed, but Han catches it. You can always start on another one, he says. There's no rule that you're only allowed to put one drink on.

What are *you* working on? I ask, and as expected, he is eager to show me, takes over the bar station and starts throwing a drink together, stirs it with his quick, silent stir and strains it into a coupe and passes it to me. It's bitter, booze-forward, sweet. Is it too bitter? he asks, but I don't think so. I offer it to Joe Himself, but he shakes his head; he's settled up already, has to be going, can't drink anything more tonight. Han pretends not to mind, though I can tell he's a little offended.

What's in it? I ask, and Han lists the ingredients for me—rye whiskey, rum, crème de cacao, Zucca.

Zucca? Han pours me a little to try, dark and honeyed and earthy. An amaro, something I don't know much about, but that's what Han is for. *Amaro*: a bitter, sweet, herbaceous liqueur. Italian in origin, but the Italians are rather more laid-back about their spirits than our friends the French, and so the category is nebulous, a sort of know-it-when-you-taste-it classification.

Liqueur, while we're at it: any alcohol mixed with plant matter and sweetener. We have a great library of these at Joe's, and half a dozen in the speed racks for use in popular cocktails. I have drunk my fair share of the more mainstream liqueurs in my younger years, Hayley and me pilfering them from her parents' liquor cabinet the year I went there for Thanksgiving, the two of us giggling over alien green Midori Sours, White Russians, Blue Curaçao with vodka. Neither of us had a taste for real booze yet, and the sugar helped it go down easy.

A sea change in my palate by the time I started really drinking cocktails, and in San Francisco I would always order my drinks *not too sweet* until one day my Martini Soul Mate gently explained that sugar is a vital component in a cocktail, almost always, the one exception being a very, *very* dry martini, which is not a cocktail at all, *just gin in a cup*. That the human body is designed to crave sugar and while we have all convinced

ourselves that avoiding it is some kind of moral choice, this is all ultimately nonsense. And that furthermore, unless I was ordering, say, an
Amaretto Sour, which is effectively just a vessel for sugar, he was not
going to make me something *too sweet*. It's like asking a chef not to make
you anything *too salty*. They fucking know.

But back to the bar lesson. Every amaro is a liqueur and every liqueur can be a modifier, but not every modifier is a liqueur. *Modifier*:
exactly what it sounds like, something used in a cocktail to modify the
base ingredient. Liqueurs and fortified wine—vermouths, americanos,
sherries—and *nonpotable bitters*, which are not in fact toxic as their
name implies but simply not designed to be drunk by themselves, meant
to be used in very small amounts to tie a drink together, a difficult idea
to explain but try an old-fashioned without the Angostura sometime and
see how disappointed you are.

I take another sip. Vanilla. Clove. Burnt caramel. It's a little intense, I say.
Viscous, almost. Maybe try it on the rocks?

Han does this, and tastes it, and grins. Nailed it, he says, passing the
new glass to me.

I drink and agree. That's really good, I say.

I look down into the glass, the crystalline sheen of the big ice cubes,
the dark garnet of the drink itself, and I wonder, Where did this drink
come from? What cocktail was stretched and altered to become it? How
could I possibly be expected to put something on the same menu as *this*?

But I do not have time to dwell on it, because we have guests, bartender
guests, the sort who work in recognizable establishments and are known
for free-pouring and hard-partying (Han's words, after their departure),
and they order, of course, daiquiris. They know Han but they don't
bother to introduce themselves to me, and so let's call them Beardy,
Cheekbones, and Baseball Cap. Beardy and Cheekbones I have in fact
encountered before, albeit briefly, albeit without exchanging names, albeit without leaving enough of an impression for either of them to remember me. I leave Han to chat. I make the daiquiris.

A bar lesson: when you're shaking two drinks at once you want to hold the shakers at their middles, where the two tins meet, and you have to really make sure they're sealed. Sometimes you have to stop and bang the shakers hard against the bar to reseal, if they're leaking, if booze and juice are flying out with every movement of your arm, which even when you think you have a good shake down will sometimes continue to happen.

I make one daiquiri in one tin and two in the other and I straw-test and then I pour them out. When you're doubling up drinks you have to be careful here; there's nothing more embarrassing than pouring one drink higher than the other and having to even them out with the use of a straw, drop by drop. Best to fill each halfway to start, and then to go back and forth between your glasses, doling the liquid out bit by bit. Not too slowly, or things will start to get watery, but evenly.

I remember Cheekbones and Beardy because they were rude to me. Not mean, mind you, just rude. Just *cold*. They work at a bar in Prospect Heights, and I was meeting Ben there, fifteen minutes early as I so often am, and so I was sitting alone at the bar, the place quiet, early on the Tuesday before last, two men behind the bar, Beardy beefy and hirsute, Cheekbones tall and almost unbearably handsome. Neither of them acknowledged me when I sat down, busy talking, because the world is small, about Han, laughing about some past shenanigans of his, Han running around the East Village at four o'clock in the morning, carrying leftover pizza from some event, trying to give it away to understandably wary drunk people, charging down side streets in the pursuit, yelling out, I'm not dangerous, I just want to feed you!

Beardy went off then, still chuckling to himself, to serve a new arrival at the other end of the bar, and Cheekbones finally turned to me. Are you talking about Dan Han? I asked, although I knew that they were.

Cheekbones smiled, not with his eyes, and nodded. He asked no follow-up questions, just put down a menu and a glass of water for me and walked away, and me there wondering what I'd done wrong, and feeling the familiar whole-body horror that I get when people don't like me, that same chill I so often feel around Carver.

There is an inherent vulnerability to going to a bar or a restaurant by yourself, when you feel like everyone is looking at you, wondering what has gone horribly awry in your life to lead you here, alone, friendless, hopeless, miserable. Even when you are just waiting for someone, or even when you are just there to visit the bartender, or even when you are just tired of talking to people and want to sit and read a book in peace. When, in short, you are alone on purpose. Still. I am sure there are people out there, people like Han, who feel no anxiety whatsoever waltzing into any unfamiliar space solo, but I am willing to bet that on the spectrum most people feel at least a little nervous about it, and accordingly, the best gauge of an establishment's service, to me, will always be how it treats its solo customers.

Because, right, you're unprotected. Exposed. You might have the sort of defenses I carry around with me: a book, a copy of *The New Yorker*. One of Scott the Scot's favorite regulars used to crochet at her barstool as she drank her filthy shaken martinis. You might have the sort of excuse I had then, the knowledge that my solitude was temporary. And still, if you are alone, and you get bad service—rude, disinterested, forgetful— you will begin to feel like you are not a person. Like you are worthless. Like you are, perhaps, invisible, or like you wish you could be, like you wish you could disappear into yourself, into the barstool, into the ether, because if this bartender, who is being paid to look after you, will not look after you, then what kind of life are you even living?

Maybe it's not that intense for you. Or maybe you've just never gotten shitty service while flying solo.

You don't like him because you're used to getting special treatment, Ben said, and he treated you like anybody else. Us walking back to his place, the evening autumnal, me with my arms crossed for warmth, although I realized that I probably looked like a caricature of annoyance, and I uncrossed them, although I was still annoyed. I didn't think that was fair. I thought I was perfectly happy being treated just like anybody else, gen- erally speaking, as long as anybody else was getting decent service, too.

But they weren't, that was Ben's point. Pretty white girl treatment *is* special treatment, he said. You would not believe the service I get some- times. Walking into a bar as a Black guy is a great way to feel invisible. Invisible *at best*. He didn't have to name the alternatives; to list the ways in which vast swaths of this city treat him with fear and suspicion. To remind me that he grew up during the years of *stop and frisk* and that we are still in the enduring years of white supremacy, even in theoretically liberal meccas like New York City, even in theoretically Black meccas like Brooklyn.

I'm sorry, I said; I wasn't thinking. And now I felt like a dick for not thinking. Ben waved my apology away. It's fine at Joe's, obviously, he said. But a lot of these new places—he sighed. This was not something we talked about, not really, and I could feel how carefully he was choosing his words. There are ways in which this part of town has changed for the better, he said. But a lot of those changes have come at the expense of the Black folks who have been here forever. He said, The big secret is that segregation isn't really over. And most of these new, upscale cocktail bars are white spaces.

And Ben was right, of course he was right, and I'm not an asshole, I won't complain any more about that petty grievance, and yet the reality remains that Cheekbones is a dick, and the other two don't seem any better, and I'm stuck standing here, wondering what to do with my hands now that there are no daiquiris to be shaken, wondering, *What do people talk about?* Wishing Himself were still here. Wondering what on earth I am going to put on the menu.

Baseball Cap glances at me, I feel it rather than see it, and he asks Han, Who was the other girl that used to work here? That blond chick?

Becky, Han says. God, that was ages ago. I think she's in Philly now.

Becky, Baseball Cap echoes, nodding. Right.

This is the second time I've heard the name *Becky*, and I guess I'm curious, and I guess it's because I'm getting the impression that there's only ever been one other girl working at this bar, and that seems very weird to me. Especially considering that Gina owns the place, and none of the Dans are sexist or creepy or anything else that might deter a woman from taking a job with them. Maybe the bartender before me was the problem. Or maybe after Gina, Carver was just traumatized. *Don't screw the crew.* I guess it's easier to stick to if you hire exclusively straight dudes.

The bartenders want another round and Han takes care of it, makes them the drink he's working on, which they praise, I think, excessively. This is a goddamn modern classic, Cheekbones says, and Han glows, and I feel envy all the way down to the bedrock.

And then the bartenders are ready to go, off to see some other mutual friend at some other establishment. Han brings them their bill, adjusted with the expected upper-echelon industry discount, one free drink per person, plus shots for the road, Fernet-Branca, sticky and black, mouthwash for discerning alcoholics. The bartender's handshake. I'm out on the floor checking on some guests when I hear Baseball Cap call, Becky, and I look to the door, expecting this mysterious ex-bartender, but there's no one.

Becky, he says again, and I turn to look at him and Han gives me an unreadable look and holds up a shot glass, and I don't correct Baseball Cap because I understand that he is doing this on purpose. I take the shot with them, smile out of habit. If you learn nothing else from working in the service industry, you will most certainly learn to smile when people are rude to you. Your face will begin to default to it, a bland contentment will become your new baseline expression, even if you still have resting bitchface on the subway, which I recommend, because that is the only way people will leave you alone, if they do leave you alone, which, maybe or maybe not.

Cheers, I say, and I drink my Fernet and I return to my table, and the bartenders go.

What a pack of raging assholes, Han says when the door shuts behind them. *Becky*. Jesus. I wish I'd charged them full price.

The bartender's handshake: shots of Fernet-Branca as a traditional hello or goodbye between bartenders or industry folks or particularly beloved regulars. You may have encountered it before. We have San Francisco to blame for that; Fernet was legal there all through Prohibition, and the city has a famed love for it. My Martini Soul Mate's bar used to have the stuff on tap. I have never liked it myself, and fortunately it's gone a little out of fashion. Although I do like the idea of doing shots of amaro, and I think maybe I should make the switch, let the Dans drink tequila while I sit back on, I don't know, let's say Cynar—that's the one with the artichoke on the bottle, not nearly so striking in a glass as Fernet but wonderfully complex, earthy, and bittersweet. It doesn't taste like artichokes, but there are artichokes used in its manufacture, and its name reflects this, Cynar, as in, *Cynara scolymus*, the scientific name for artichoke. Cynar is only 16.5 percent ABV (*alcohol by volume*), less than half of what you'll find in a whiskey or tequila or rum or even Fernet; it could help me keep myself out of trouble, although I think about saying the words out loud, Han asking, Whiskey or tequila, and me saying, Actually, I'd like some Cynar, and I know I will never say it, not a fucking chance.

What would it be like, not caring what people thought of me?

I'm angrier than I would like to admit when they leave, these cocktail bros, these people who would never think of themselves as sexist, who probably have the word *feminist* in their Tinder profiles, and yet who will always see me as less than, despite themselves. These people who are going to talk down to me for the rest of my life. And Han understands; being the one Asian guy has its own difficulties. See, Short and Bald. See, the way guests will stand at the bar and wait for Carver's attention when Han is standing right there, eager to serve. They don't even realize they're doing it, he says. Not that that's an excuse.

Another bar lesson, then: When you work in the service industry, you see the full spectrum of humanity. People will be mean to you. People will snap their fingers at you like you're a dog, shove their cards at you like you're an ATM. People will forget to say things like *please* or *thank you* or *may I*, will order while carrying on a conversation on their phone or without taking out their earbuds, will lose the manners they would employ, you'd hope, in any other environment. They will treat you like you're stupid. They will treat you like you're a thing and not a person, a human person who has flaws and who has good days and bad days and who does her best, most likely, most of the time.

Men will *really* treat you like a thing. They will say suggestive things to you, will touch you if they think they can get away with it, will ask you for your number because they've mistaken your professional friendliness for mutual attraction, and you will have to smile and deflect because your tips depend on your smiling and deflecting. And then in almost the same breath they will send back a drink because they think it's *too girly*, will say this casually to your face as if you were not also *girly*, as if the adjective referred to something foreign and disgusting. *Girly*, god. It makes my teeth hurt. Men who won't drink out of coupe glasses because their masculinity is so fragile that holding a dainty glass threatens it. James Bond drinks out of those glasses! Humphrey Bogart! Who the hell do you think you are?

Everyone in the industry has a coping mechanism. Some people are bitches right back. Some cry, or do shots of tequila, or take long moments deep breathing in the walk-in. I like to kill them with kindness, speak in tones so dulcet you feel sick, and repeat silently the mantra, *you are a miserable asshole and you're going to die alone.* And though even in the worst of my server days I never did anything to someone's food, I do always wonder—don't these people understand that I *could*? Haven't they seen *Fight Club*?

Or if you are Han, you poison them. You take your orders politely, with your customary charm, and then you choose your weapons. A cocktail is a weighty thing at the best of times; a standard drink can contain easily three ounces of liquor. If you are unkind, Han will make sure those ounces are strong. Overproof rum, cask-strength whiskey, generous pours.

I can be nice to anyone, he says. But if you're an asshole to me, I'm going to fuck up your whole night. You're trying to get work done tomorrow? Good fucking luck. You're on a date? You're gonna go home and do nothing but sleep.

That's not very responsible bartending, I tell him, and he shrugs. No, he says, not really.

HEMINGWAY DAIQUIRI

2 ounces light rum
3/4 ounce maraschino liqueur
1/2 ounce lime juice
1/2 ounce grapefruit juice

Shake or blend with ice and strain into a chilled coupe.
Garnish with a cherry.

Han texts me, early the next week: *I know how to inspire you.* It sounds vaguely dirty, euphemistic, but I have set aside my fear of anything happening between Han and me. I trust him; I trust Meg; I am beginning to trust myself.

What he means is, he knows what bar to take me to. The best bar, he says. An institution. Their book is sitting on the shelf at Joe's, one of my favorites. And so we go to the East Village and he introduces me to the doorman, a smiling, round-faced white guy who shakes our hands and walks us back to the only free seats in the house. The bar is dark as a cave, the sort of place a stylish vampire might enjoy, with hip-hop on the speakers and the conversation loud around us, two men behind the bar in shirts and ties and waistcoats, a barback all in black, two beautiful women on the floor, pouring waters, carrying trays of glittering drinks. Bar-top gleaming marble, glasses of water on branded coasters, and a thick black book of a menu between them. The taller of the two men sets Snaiquiris down in front of us, grinning through a thin-trimmed beard, his smile dazzling as anything else here, me already a little in love.

Do I have a bartender fetish? Is that what this is?

We down our perfectly balanced shots and Han makes introductions—Sam, Timothy, Timothy, Sam—and they begin catching up and I open the menu. I peruse the offerings, pleased when I can recognize or at least guess at a drink's genealogy, lightly annoyed when I have to ask Han about an ingredient. Meanwhile Timothy has taken another order, and gotten to work. He is so quick, unimaginably quick, chatting away with us easily as he builds the round, the economy of movement and grace beautiful to watch, almost like dancing. Me more in love by the second, although I notice that Timothy has a ring on *that* finger; a mercy, really, because while I am a little in love with him, I am not afraid to speak to him, like I might be otherwise. He is unattainable; the stakes are low. I am not interested in wrecking homes that aren't my own.

So yes, he is talented and graceful and handsome, but the other thing about Timothy is, Timothy is kind. Generous, even. With us, of course, but we're industry and he and Han are friends and that's easy. But Timothy is lovely to everyone; to the too-loud Long Islanders drinking vodka next to us; to the older couple down the bar who must be handheld through the entire menu, Timothy explaining every other ingredient to them with a smile and no trace of impatience; to the Parisian bartender alone in the corner, such an unbearable blowhard that I would have given up on him immediately.

And I'll say something to this effect when the bartender goes, and Timothy will answer with an elegant shrug. He was just excited, he'll say. He won't say that this bar is sacred, that people come from all over the world to visit, that he encounters pilgrims every night of the week—although later I will learn that it is, and they do, and he does. He will say, This might be the only time he ever gets to come here. And, For me it's just another day of work, but for him it should be really special.

I'll feel something, then, a longing not for Timothy himself but for what he has, for what he is. That sense of purpose and pride even when you're just bartending. When was the last time I felt that way about anything?

·   ·   ·

But first, our drinks. My natural inclination is toward a Gibson, but I go for something deliberately weird instead, aquavit and tequila and vermouth and something called Kümmel, and Han asks for dealer's choice. I have learned about this at Joe's, *dealer's choice*, about the questions I should ask when someone wants us to choose a cocktail for them. Stirred and spiritous or shaken and citrusy? Any particular spirits you like or dislike? Any particular flavors? Any allergies or dietary restrictions we should know about? Every palate is different, and just because I like something doesn't mean you will. This is why asking a bartender what they would drink is not actually a good way to make a decision. Han, for example, is one of the best bartenders I know, but his tastes run sweeter than mine; I, for example, drink onion martinis like an old English spinster.

But Timothy knows Han, and he asks no follow-up questions. He goes to take the menu but I hold on to it. Do you mind? I ask. I'd like to keep looking. He smiles and withdraws; he does not mind. He makes our drinks, so quickly, and Han and I touch glasses, and we drink.

This is insane, I say. I could never think of something like this.

Sure you could, Han says. I mean, maybe not now, not on this menu. But give it a few years. Timothy's been working here for seven years, Han says, and bartending for over a decade. You have a good palate, he says. You're already learning.

Nice of him, but I can't help but hear Carver's voice again, *I was a barback for two years.* Maybe I'm doing this all wrong, getting ahead of myself. Maybe Carver's right.

Han thinks this is ridiculous. I love Carver, he says, but I think he's being too hard on you.

He's just stressed, I say, and I shouldn't say anything else, I should keep Carver's secret with the same fastidious care with which I keep these various secrets of my own, but I tell Han about the conversation I heard the day of the meeting, the one about the lease.

Well shit, Han says. Yeah, I guess that would explain it.

Why the long faces? Timothy asks, and Han and I look at each other, and Han says, How do you save a bar?

What's wrong with Joe's?

Joe's is great, Han says. However, it has been brought to my attention that people don't know we exist.

Timothy frowns. Hey, Elliott, he says, and the other bartender comes over. What do you know about Joe's Apothecary?

The name rings a bell, he says. Isn't that in Queens?

Not an auspicious start, we can all agree. The barback is even worse, asks if there's any relation to Joe's Pizza, and Han looks like he wants to throttle him. Well, Timothy says. I will be bringing those guys out to visit. He leans against the backbar, considering. We're lucky here, he says. We were early to the scene, and we had a lot of press when we first opened, and then we put out that book.

But how do you get people to start talking about a place that has already existed for almost five years? In an outer borough? We're not going to put out a book, not soon enough to make a difference. There are various best bar lists and awards—Timothy's bar has been on several of these over the years, though not, he says, with a hint of chagrin, recently. But these are hard to control, and unlikely to help in time, either. What do you do in the short term?

Events and marketing, Timothy says. We have a full-time social media guy promoting this bar, which I guess must be doing something or he wouldn't still have a job. And then we charge like ten grand for a full buyout. Anything to get people through the door.

But, of course, if anyone knew the magic formula to save a bar, no one would ever go out of business.

Timothy returns to his Long Islanders, who are closing out, and Han and I look at each other. What would you do? I ask him. If we closed?

Han sighs, heavy and long, and looks down into his drink. I love this industry, he says, but god, some stability would be nice. He lifts his glass, swallows, sets it down again. It's different somewhere like this, he says, gesturing; it's fairly corporate, with a second location in LA and talks of a third, with a bestselling cocktail book and merch available online, with paid vacation and benefits. With enough money that Han could work just three days a week if he wanted, and spend the rest of his nights with Meg.

Meg and I are going to start trying, he tells me, and it takes me a second to figure out what he means, trying *what*, but I get it, and maybe it's the aquavit but I tear up a little. Han would be the world's greatest dad.

Don't tell anyone, he says, and I mime zipping my mouth shut, but I can't stop smiling.

He smiles back, and then he swallows it, changes the subject. What would *you* do? he asks.

I'd be fine, I say, too quickly. But I can't tell him why I'd be fine—have no desire to bring up my divided loyalties, certainly not now, certainly not here—and I can tell he doesn't believe me.

We have another round. I go weird again, something with gin and sherry and carrots, and Han asks for a classic, something called a Hemingway Daiquiri. I wonder, for a moment, if this counts as the Daiquiri Test, but Timothy, of course, doesn't mind, because Timothy, of course, has nothing to prove.

Once upon a time, Han tells me, back when Havana was Vegas, Hemingway used to drink at a bar called El Floridita. I mean, Hemingway—every bar in Havana will tell you he used to drink there, and he wasn't exactly picky. But El Floridita, they're serious about it. They have a bronze statue of him sitting at the bar now.

Somewhere along the line, Hemingway develops a fear of diabetes. He's not in great health, the older he gets, and he knows all these daiquiris he likes so much aren't helping. So he goes to his barman—one of his many barmen—and says, Can you make me one without any sugar? The barman thinks about this, and he figures, all right, I'll sweeten it with just maraschino instead. Decides to throw some grapefruit juice in, too: maybe he thinks it'll go better, maybe he just wants to change things up a little. Shakes it up—well, no, this is Cuba, they don't shake their daiquiris—blends it up and pours it out for Papa H, who loves it.

It's not a story that holds up under close interrogation. There's plenty of sugar in maraschino, and rum is made of sugar, and technically there's sugar in fruit juice, too, although in a more complicated form. You have to figure Hemingway would have known better. Although, maybe not.

Although, it's not important. This is how stories about Hemingway are. This is how stories about cocktails are. False, but with a nice, literary falseness. They may not have happened, but they're *honest*.

After one final round—dealer's choice again for Han, an impeccable Gibson for me—it is time to return to Brooklyn, where we will be meeting Meg and Carver, who I guess are friends, because everyone in Brooklyn is friends with Carver except for me. We seal the evening off with another round of shots, sherry, an unusual choice, but it's what Timothy likes to shoot. Low ABV, he explains. If I were doing shots of full-strength liquor I'd never make it through the night. The sherry goes down nutty and dry and I think this is another good option for me, like the Cynar. Or, let's be honest, it's another thing I will be too nervous to ask for.

Always a pleasure, Timothy says, and Han says, Never a chore, and everybody shakes everybody's hand, and by the time we make it to Casey's all those cocktails have caught up with me and I don't remember anything after walking through the door.

I wake up with a foul taste in my mouth and a deep-set headache and—well, you know what a hangover feels like. Stomach churning as I try and fail to piece the end of the night together. But it's impossible. Blackout is not forgetting; blackout is your brain not making new memories at all.

I am in a bed that is not my own and my first thought is Greg and my second thought is Ben, who really should have been thought number one, but the bed I am in is Han's. Han's and Meg's, and me sandwiched between them like a kid with a nightmare. I'm afraid to move, afraid that I will wake them and they will throw me out in disgust, when despite myself I feel warm and safe and beloved.

When I do get up, reluctant but desperate to pee, I go quickly and carefully, waking no one, padding through an unfamiliar new-build apartment, into a bathroom with a fancy shower but no bathtub. My jeans are gone but I'm still in my T-shirt, my bra digging into my ribs underneath, and I flush and I wash my hands and I start shoveling water into my mouth from the tap. I look like shit. I wash my face, clean up the twin smears of black makeup under my eyes, and then I shrug at myself in the mirror and go back out and that's when I see Carver, curled up on the couch, a blanket sort of half on top of him, his shoes on the floor, his jeans, too, and I freeze by the bathroom door, feeling incredibly exposed, my legs pale and a little hairy, my underwear perhaps not as modest as it could be.

In the service industry it's easy to lose sight of traditional professional rules and boundaries. The work seals you together, boxes you up tight, until you have no secrets from one another, until even skin feels permeable. You know the things that close friends know—sex lives, family histories, financial situations—but even more than this, you are intimately familiar with eating habits, hormonal fluctuations, bodily functions. You know that, say, Han gets hangry every night around eleven and becomes totally insufferable until he can sit down and have a snack, or that Olsen can't drink a cup of coffee without immediately having to take a shit.

What I'm trying to say is, it is not odd that I should work with a man whom I have seen in a state of undress: see, Olsen. I am not even worried about waking up next to Han, and have every intention of getting back into bed with him and his wife. It is, however, odd that I should be half-naked with my manager in the cold light of morning. Because he is my manager, for one, and because he does not particularly like me, because we are not friends.

I keep my eyes pointed down and I make a run for it. At the bedroom door I have an impulse to check to make sure Carver's still asleep. I don't.

Meg blinks up at me as I get back in bed, and I hesitate, but she smiles and makes room. It's far too early for me to get up, even just to go home. How's the head? she asks, her voice low and thick with sleep.

On a scale of one to Janis Joplin, I say, how wasted would you say I was last night?

Lindsay Lohan, she says after an alarmingly short consideration. In *Mean Girls*, she clarifies. Not in real life.

Oh, god.

She laughs. It's all right, she says. It was all very contained. You threw up in the bathroom and then you were pretty much fine. You just apologized a lot and told everyone how much you loved them.

Don't tell me any more, I say, I don't want to know, and she laughs again and acquiesces.

And so I'm lying there in the middle of this bed with the taste of my insides lingering on my tongue, with the familiar rough burn at the back of my throat, and I'm quietly devastated. Until last night, I had not thrown up since San Francisco. I have spent most of this year not throwing up. Learning how not to throw up.

Bulimia nervosa: an eating disorder characterized by cycles of bingeing and purging. How did this happen? I never worried about my body in high school, the years in which everybody else seemed to be worrying about their bodies, and so naively I thought I had dodged that particular bullet, eating disorders being, I thought, the purview of children, something outgrown at the age of eighteen and never a threat again. And then there I was, twenty-three, discovering that suddenly I was worried about my body. It did not look the way it had in college, when I was too broke to overeat and had not yet discovered that food could be delicious. It did not look the way Hayley's did, larger than mine but perfectly proportioned, whereas I was developing a gut; or the way my mother's had when she died, thirty-eight and so, so beautiful; or the way Vanessa Garfield's did, with her flat stomach and her tiny round ass. Nobody called me *large*, but I became *curvy*, which everyone knows is a euphemism for large. Went up a jeans size, two at most, but I felt as if I had become unmoored, as if I were drifting out to sea, and I did not know what I might look like at the end of the journey. For my entire life, I had been praised for being smart and skinny. I did not feel smart in Silicon Valley: between my coworkers and Greg and Greg's coworkers and the cleverer of the Girlfriends, there was always someone smarter. And now I had ceased to be skinny. What did that leave me with?

I attempted diets, but I didn't actually believe in diets, because diets don't actually *work*. I counted calories for a while, but then I'd get drunk and eat all the snack food in the apartment and ruin the whole experiment. And then one night I looked in a mirror in a single-occupancy restaurant bathroom and stuck a finger down my throat, just to see. I had to dig around in there for a minute, had to endure some dry, ineffective gagging and a nameless fear, and then something caught, like a stove click-

clickclicking until all at once the gas ignites in a great burst of blue. I only just made it to the toilet. I cleaned myself out four, five, six times until I felt dry and fresh like a wrung-out sponge. I flushed and rinsed my mouth out, washed my hands three times, and my life with bulimia began.

But here is the big secret about bulimia nervosa: it doesn't actually work, either. Not consistently. The problem is that your body is too well designed: it starts absorbing calories the minute that sweet, sweet junk food hits your tongue, and so even if you empty out your entire stomach, you're still usually taking in as much as half of what you've eaten. So sure, you're skipping out on a little bit of the sugar and the fat, but mostly you're just wrecking your teeth, and your stomach lining, and your heart, and your esophagus, and your impulse control, and your metabolism, and your interpersonal relationships, and your self-esteem, and if you're really lucky and you combine it with a couple other particularly egregious bad habits, you can follow the stilettoed footsteps of that great bulimic queen Amy Winehouse right into sad girl heaven.

And then suddenly your life is falling apart around you, and you find yourself at a rehabilitation center in the Arizona desert, your father trying not to cry when he checks you in, the bony anorexics regarding you with open scorn, the other bulimics recognizing one of their own in your puffy face and your ugly belly and your red eyes. Your world reduced to white walls and group therapy, too much TV and supervised meals, and you sitting there with your shiny new offer of admission from your forever dream school, deferring, for your *health*.

The tightness of that world its own form of relief.

I have fallen back into an uneasy sleep, and when I wake up again, properly, Meg and Han are gone and I can hear voices coming from the kitchen. The second sleep is my secret weapon against a hangover, and sure enough I feel almost like a human, ready to push my old disorder back down and face whatever's out there. I put my jeans on this time, and I walk out.

.   .   .

I walk out and Carver greets me with a smile and a Red Snapper, which is a Bloody Mary but with gin instead of vodka, because of the bartender snobbery thing, and I must look surprised because Meg laughs and says not to worry, that there's coffee coming, too. But I get the whole Red Snapper thing, the hair-of-the-dog thing, the one-drink-to-get-back-to-neutral thing. The old cocktail books are full of drinks for this purpose: eye-openers, morning glories, pick-me-ups, anti-fogmatics. The history of drinking in America is a history of hangovers. Back in the day they drank a lot more than we do—hard as that is to believe when you look around New York, land of the bottomless brunch, the drink and draw, the drunk yoga, the three-martini lunch, the wine-drenched gallery opening, etc. etc. etc. Still, we didn't invent drunkenness, and our mimosas and Bloody Marys are positively tame compared to some of these old drinks.

So yes, I get it. I am just surprised to have it here, from Carver's hands, immediately upon waking, and when he knows I'm working later. I like to take a three-pronged attack with a hangover, Carver says. Coffee, grease, and alcohol.

Han and Meg's apartment is small but nice, hardwood floors, framed prints on the walls, a fancy stereo system and a shelf heavy with Han's enormous record collection. Han in the tiny kitchen, Meg working from home on the couch, Carver and me at the wooden dining table, which Carver has also been using as a bar. I take a tentative sip from my drink. I take a bigger one. This is incredible, I say, and Carver performs an awkward little bow.

Coffee appears, steaming and fragrant, Han choking his with sugar and milk but the rest of us drinking it black, and then there are eggs, eggs and bacon and bread thick with butter, and surely I have told Han that I don't eat meat, we have ordered enough takeout together that surely he knows, but there is bacon on my plate and for an awful moment I consider just eating it, that it will be easier to just eat it, that maybe I don't have to be a vegetarian anymore. In light of the end of the world, I may as well enjoy every last epicurean delight. In light of the end of the world, none of my reasons for abstaining hold up: the respective ships have sailed on carbon emissions, world hunger, deforestation. The animals are suffering, but soon enough the animals will no longer be suffering. Those bred into weakness will die, the strong will survive, soon the most highly evolved pigs will be reclaiming the towns and cities, clopping along abandoned roads, eating our corpses.

I take a cautious bite of egg; it is unsurprisingly delicious, it is exactly what my body wants right now. I chew it until it's dissolved into nothing, trying to pace myself. I hear Carver laugh. For a bartender, he says, you are a hell of a slow eater. A valid point: eating on shift is a necessarily hasty affair, a few seconds snatched between waves of guests, half a sandwich eaten standing up in the prep kitchen or sitting just out of sight on the stairs, an apple inhaled just before starting. I shrug and I take another bite, carefully steering clear of the meat on my plate, still not knowing what to do about it, and I can feel Carver watching me, staring like it's nothing, when to me it's like being naked.

Once upon a time, a young bulimic was sentenced to group therapy. It was an integral part of rehab, and occasionally genuinely useful, although never our bulimic's favorite form of counseling. The group met in a room designated for the purpose, circled up like attendants of a sad, old summer camp. There were arts and crafts, show-and-tell. Mostly tell. They would sit in a baggy loop, an amoeboid shape on a carpet like schoolchildren, and the counselor would sit with them and ask questions, encourage them to share. Many of the campers were eager; begging to be seen even as they attempted to disappear themselves. The bulimic was a poor student of the art, compared to these people, the serious anorexics, these vanishing women. She had done no lasting damage to her health, not even to her teeth. Like many bulimics, she was not even underweight. She would sit in silence, taking the stories as cautionary tales, telling herself, *This is not sustainable, this will kill me.*

Sometimes the group had picnics. The counselor would sit them at a table heavy with foods that are sold in supermarkets with seductive, judgmental words like *indulgent, decadent, sinful.* Doughnuts, cookies, cake, muffins, bagels, potato chips, curly fries, pizza. The idea being that the disappearing women would eat *a little*, only a little. The idea being that they would neither binge nor abstain, that they would sample and sate and not go overboard. The idea being that it was possible to walk a line between starvation and gluttony. Sometimes one of the anorexics would throw herself on the ground like a toddler throwing a temper tantrum. There were always tears. It was always, universally, excruciating.

If you are an alcoholic, you stop drinking. If you are a drug addict, you stop taking drugs. I'm not saying these things are easy. I'm saying these things are possible. Moderation is harder than abstinence, but abstinence is part of the trouble, and moderation is the only solution.

Oh, Carver says, and he reaches for my plate, and he scrapes the bacon off of it and onto his own.

NEGRONI SBAGLIATO

1 ounce Campari
1 ounce sweet vermouth
sparkling wine

Build in a flute (or in a rocks glass over ice, if you prefer).
Top with sparkling wine and garnish with an orange peel.

Once upon a time, there was a young Italian, the tenth son of a Lombard farmer. The farmer's son took a serving job, for the same reason so many do: because he needed the work, and that was what was available. Found, like so many have, that this sort of work suited him, so he began working on a creation of his own, a bitter liqueur, sixty different ingredients, its recipe guarded so jealously that even today, nearly two centuries later, it is still a close-kept secret.

He mixed this elixir, first, with sweet vermouth—it was Italy in the mid-1800s, this is what you did—and the blend became a Milano-Torino. He added some seltzer; it became an Americano. And then our dear old friend Count Camillo came along and threw gin into the mix, and everything burst out from there.

Campari, I'm talking about Campari. It's Thursday afternoon and we're finalizing the new menu on Monday—later than Carver initially intended, and you can bet he's annoyed about it, but I'm grateful for the delay. Between the length of my coffee rum's infusion time and a busy couple Thursday nights, I haven't had a chance to really get to work on my drink. So I have my rum, strained through a coffee filter back into its original bottle, where it looks rich, seductive, almost black, and now I just have to put that together with some Campari and turn these ingredients into something greater than themselves. I will not bore you with a full catalog of my failed attempts. I will only say that by the time Joe Himself arrives I am eager to put my experiment aside.

There has been a change in Himself, over the past month; something within him has opened up, not just with me, but with the Dans, too, even with some of the other regulars. He still brings his book with him, still spends much of his time at the bar in silence, but when he does talk he talks freely. Last time he was in he told Carver and me about his daughters, which none of us knew existed; spent a good quarter hour on their various talents and accomplishments, the younger one's athleticism, the older's scholarship. Joe, Carver said. I had no idea you had kids.

They live with their mother, he said, and we didn't push him on that, but you could tell this was a source of sorrow, a deep root of Joe Himself's loneliness.

All of which is to say it's nice to see him, Joe Himself, and nice to step away from my drink, to pour him a glass of rye, a small taste for myself. Black pepper, peach, something nutty on the finish. We're talking about baseball, of all things; the World Series starts next week and Himself is apologizing in advance for abandoning Joe's for a sports bar on Nostrand. Awful whiskey, he says, as if to reassure me.

You're allowed to go to other bars, Joe, I say, and he says, Don't let Carver hear you talk like that.

At any rate, baseball. I don't follow it but I have a good foundation, which is useful for a bartender, because so much of the job is small talk, and sports are an easy subject. Growing up I used to actually care about it, baseball I mean; used to go to games in San Francisco with my father, with Hayley's family, but then with Greg it became another thing I had to compete against for his attention, and even before the breakup I began to take a spiteful pleasure when the Giants lost. Now I lean on the bar and listen to Himself complain about the Mets—So close, he's saying, but they can never quite get it together to make the Series.

The door swings open and it's Olsen, guitar in tow, on his way to band practice. How have you already found a band? But he just shrugs. Apparently there's a dearth of lead singers who can also actually play an instrument. Apparently his reputation precedes him. Apparently timing is everything.

I pour Olsen a beer and a shot of whiskey and I go to check on the group of schoolteachers at their usual table, topping up waters and wines, asking how they are, asking how are the future leaders of America. Oh, honey, one of them says, if these are the future leaders of America we really are in trouble. When I get back, Himself has returned to his book, and Olsen is on his phone, and so I am left with no choice but to return to my drink. Tinker with different liqueurs and bitters—chocolate, vanilla, black walnut. A splash of cinnamon syrup, blackstrap rum, absinthe.

You're stressing me out, Olsen says. He's put his phone down and picked up his beer, and he's looking at me with something like pity and something like exasperation. It doesn't have to be the best drink ever invented, he says.

But it's different for him. He's been doing this for longer. Plus he's a straight, conventionally attractive white man, and he can get away with mediocrity. When I attempt—politely—to articulate this, he frowns into his beer and then he asks, Do you ever feel like your feminist anger is getting in the way of your ability to live your life?

I blink at him. I do not know how to begin to answer his question. Although I guess it's rhetorical. Still. I am torn between twin desires to laugh and to slap him across the face. Um, I say.

The stakes are higher, Himself says. Olsen and I look at him, both, I think, surprised. But then I suppose this is something he's had to think about, with the daughters. I nod. This is what I was trying to say. This is what I was always failing to get through to Greg. Like how the only way a woman survives in STEM is by being silent or perfect or both. Like how the only way a woman survives as a chef is by having the thickest skin and the filthiest mouth, or by being so good no one can step to her. I can count on one hand the number of female cocktail bartenders I've met; I have to assume this is a related issue. Sometimes it feels like the whole world is a boys' club.

Also, I say, I find my feminist anger really satisfying.

Himself laughs, a deep, hearty chuckle, and Olsen says nothing, just drinks up and leaves a five on the bar-top and heads out to catch his bus. Ten minutes later he texts me: *Someone has a crush on youuuuuu*

And I glance at Joe Himself, who has dipped back into his book, and I feel that feminist anger welling up again. I am not stupid, I am not *that* naive: I know that some of what I bring to Joe's Apothecary is my gender and my surface-level appearance, fitted denim, mascara, perfume. But it's not just that. I refuse to believe that it's just that. I pour Himself another whiskey, and I don't text Olsen back.

Maybe it's just not an old-fashioned anymore, Han says. We've had a good afterwork rush, busy straight through 'til ten, and now I'm messing around with the drink again.

I don't want to start over.

I'm not saying start over, he says, and he's giving me this look like he's trying to coax something out of me, like there is a right answer and if I can just think a little harder, I will find it.

Once upon a time there was an American sportswriter, although he was known (and beloved) for having only a cursory knowledge of sports and highly questionable writing ability. It was Paris between the wars; things were different then. He was notably petite, friendly, and ancient. Indeed, when he died at the age of eighty-three, aspersions were widely cast that eighty-three was a considerable understatement. At any rate, our sportswriter used to call everybody in his life, from dearest friend to newest acquaintance, *old pal.*

One of the sportswriter's old pals was one Harry MacElhone, of the great, enduring Parisian establishment called Harry's New York Bar. MacElhone published two cocktail guides in his lifetime, and in each there is a recipe for the Old Pal cocktail—credited, naturally, to the sportswriter. Unfortunately, these recipes are different. Both are isometric constructions—*isometric,* having equal parts, a scientific term that I am, admittedly, slightly bastardizing, and yet I like the sound of it, and yet the word pops into my head every time I read a recipe that calls for equal amounts of each ingredient—isometric constructions of rye whiskey, Campari, and vermouth. The first recipe calls for French vermouth, which in the lexicon of the day meant dry. The second calls for Italian, or sweet. Two completely different and equally delicious variations on the Negroni theme.

However! There is another drink, also in one of MacElhone's books, called a Boulevardier, which consists of whiskey—bourbon this time, but still—Campari, and sweet vermouth. *Boulevardier*: the French equivalent of a man-about-town, which I guess isn't really a phrase we use anymore, but I think you probably understand what it means. A socialite, I guess, although this has elitist and gendered connotations that I don't think "boulevardier" does. At any rate, it was the name of a magazine published by another pal of MacElhone's, Erskine Gwynne, who may or may not have come up with the recipe.

All of this is to say, both combinations of whiskey, Campari, and vermouth are natural enough leaps from the Negroni, and any number of bartenders or drinkers might have come up with them, and in the interest of clarity, the Old Pal uses dry vermouth and the Boulevardier uses sweet and they are both delicious. All of which is to say, I take my coffee rum, and my Campari, and I add some sweet vermouth, and the drink pretty much instantly comes together.

And then it's Friday morning, and it's my birthday. How did we get to my birthday already? Leaves fallen from the trees, radiator in my apartment clunking at all hours of the night and day, houses all over Bed-Stuy decked out with spiderwebs and jack-o'-lanterns and animatronic skeletons. My father calls me in the morning, my father and his wife, Diane. My father is concerned when I tell him I'm working on my birthday, but the truth is it's a relief. What else would I do? *Have a party?* It would just be me and Hayley, and Ben, and everyone else in my life would be at work. Plus I can't stop thinking about my birthday last year, undeniably terrible, and I'm looking forward to being too busy to dwell on it.

Besides, Friday nights at Joe's are actually pretty fun.

We wish we could celebrate with you, Diane says, and I know she means it. Diane is a nice lady, genuinely; I have opinions about how soon she and my father started dating after my mother's death—just over three years, which I guess is not *so* soon, but which when I was a miserable high school junior seemed downright offensive—but still, she's no evil stepmother. She is, if we are all honest with ourselves, much more pleasant than my real mother ever was; I am sure she's much easier to be married to.

When are we seeing you next? she asks. What are you doing for Thanksgiving?

Working, I tell her; not quite true, we won't be open on the day itself, but I'm certainly not taking the time off to go to Arizona. Same with Christmas. Getting holidays off work like a normal person: another thing that will be much easier when I am a lawyer.

Not that I am in any hurry to go back to Arizona anyway. Obviously. Two months living with my father and Diane was more than enough. My father and I, as I've mentioned, have not been close since I was a kid, and his attention in Arizona felt forced at best, performative, if not wholly artificial. Diane attempting to mother me out of some sense of moral obligation or Christian charity or just habit. I'd rather be alone.

So I go into Joe's at six and we're busy and I say nothing about my birthday but then Hayley outs me, comes in at quarter to eleven with a box of cupcakes and a gift, and the Dans all look at each other and Han says, Why didn't you tell me?

I'm telling you now, I say, and he quite reasonably points out that no, *Hayley* is telling him. It's not a big deal, I say, and he asks how old I am, and I tell him.

Twenty-*five*? He flails a little behind the bar, knocks a cocktail tin into the ice well. That's a big one, he says, retrieving it. You're a grown-up.

This is scientifically accurate. When you're twenty-five, your prefrontal cortex finishes developing. Your brain is fully cooked, you become more rational and more sure of yourself and, theoretically, wiser. But it's a bad thing, too, because you are at your peak, and it's all downhill from there.

But I'm the youngest person here, and I know better than to say any of this out loud.

Take off your apron, Carver says. You're done. And I do as I'm told, and I sit next to Hayley, and Han makes me a cocktail: yet another Negroni variation, but this one with champagne, because it's my birthday, and on your birthday, Han says, you drink champagne. *Negroni Sbagliato*: the fucked-up Negroni.

Once upon a time there was an Italian bartender at a Milanese bar, making Negronis. The bartender could make a Negroni in his sleep, even back then, in the days before the cocktail renaissance. Almost literally in his sleep. But one of the bartender's coworkers had accidentally switched some bottles around behind the bar, and when the bartender went to make the aforementioned mind-numbingly familiar cocktail, he reached for the bottle of gin and found himself pouring champagne instead. This is where all that *mise en place* stuff we've been talking about is so important. Not to worry, the bartender's patron said. Let's give it a go. And he tasted it, and approved, and now the fucked-up Negroni is a modern classic.

I say *champagne*, but I don't necessarily mean champagne. Bubbly wine; sparkling fermented grape juice that in many cases attempts to imitate champagne, but made by Americans, by Spaniards, by Italians. *Champagne* being another appellation, a specific style; the French, you'll recall, have a lot of rules. An absurd number of rules, it's pedantic, really, but then you have a real champagne sometimes, a good one, and you think, all right, you French bastards. I suppose if it's going to be this delightful I will allow you to be snobs about it. Which of course is the whole French thing. Which of course is the whole mixology thing. Which of course is what sophistication and so-called high culture are all about.

I sit next to Hayley and she hugs me and presses a cupcake into my hands. Rich chocolate cake and thick chocolate icing, pretty and delicious—Hayley's an excellent baker. I bite into it and I tell myself not to feel guilty, because junk food is not a moral failing. Because chocolate is delicious. Because it's fine, because being on the floor all night has definitely burned off this small indulgence.

If you'd told me back in high school that the only thing I would use all those years of mathematics for would be controlling the size of my body, I would have been devastated.

She nudges the gift toward me, too. From me and Tyler, she says, and I'm not sure what look I give her but it makes her laugh. From me, she says.

Where is Tyler? I ask. And she shrugs with a nonchalance that might convince me if I hadn't known her so long. Vegas, she says. A bachelor party.

Isn't that kind of a cliché?

Right? And she laughs, but her eyes flit to her phone. I know those eyes. She's waiting to hear from him. She's worried.

Excuse me, bartender, I say, and all the Dans turn to look. My friend needs another drink.

Don't try this at home, but there is a way to open a bottle of sparkling wine with a knife—a saber, if you have one handy—and it is marvelous. It is marvelous to watch; I would never have the courage to do it myself. I'm not comfortable around knives, get nervous in the kitchen, anxious chopping vegetables, sawing into bread, although in the latter instance it's true that I tend to be more nervous around the carbohydrates than the blade. Regardless. I am not comfortable around knives. I am also uncomfortable around champagne. Opening a bottle, I feel as if I am cradling a live grenade. I have a phobia of having it explode in my hands, of hitting a friend, or god forbid a customer, with the cork. I understand the principle: hold the bottle at a forty-five-degree angle, to allow for more air contact; keep your hand over the cork and untwist the metal coil that holds the cage on; keep your hand over the cork and turn the bottle gently, gently, gently. Wait for the pop.

Alternatively: take a saber, or failing that, do as Carver does now and take the dull side of a large kitchen knife. Hold the cork side of the bottle away from yourself. I hope that goes without saying. Hold it away from anything or anyone breakable. Take off the foil, the aforementioned cage, hope and pray that the cork does not go flying off on its own accord. Locate the seam on the side of the bottle, follow it up the neck. You are aiming for the intersection of this seam and the lip of the bottle. Keep your fingers out of the way. Ready. Aim. Fire.

But aren't there shards of glass in it? you might well ask. No, Carver says. It's science, Han says, and I start thinking about pressure and about gases and liquids and potential energy but it's all muddy, it's all gone, what little might be lingering in the dusty corners of my mind has been washed away by champagne, or bubbly wine, or fake bar stories, or the pleasant warmth of my bar and my friends and my birthday, a good birthday, an auspicious start to the year.

And Hayley doesn't put her phone away but she does turn it facedown on the bar-top, accepts her share of the sparkling wine, clinks glasses with everyone, even Olsen, and then Ben is there, I guess Carver must have texted him, and I'm happy to see him, although I am also nervous, nervous when he kisses me hello, in Joe's, in front of everyone, our relationship brought abruptly from *open secret* to just plain *open*, not that anyone seems to mind or even notice. Nervous again as I introduce him to Hayley, like a girl in an eighteenth-century novel introducing her suitor to her father. Her suitor with whom she'd already been quietly sleeping for the past two months. Her father who was actually something more like a sister.

It's not a perfect analogy.

It doesn't matter, they are fast friends, find instant common ground in the great New Yorker pastime of bitching about the subway system, which is both an indisputable marvel of modern engineering and an unspeakable shit show. I swear to god, Ben's saying, I got on the Five in Crown Heights and ended up in Forest Hills three hours later. Didn't even stop in Manhattan. And Hayley's laughing, talking about all the ambient panic about the L—on the one hand obviously you want them to do the repairs, nobody wants to die in a subway car, but on the other hand nobody wants to have to take miserable MTA shuttle buses forever.

Meanwhile, the Dans are talking about astrology. Of all things. Olsen saying, Of course you're a Scorpio. I should have known.

People always say that to me, and I don't know what it means. Well, all right, I know a little about it—I know that as a Scorpio, I am stubborn, and intense, and that I require a great deal of sex to function. I suspect that there are good qualities as well, there have to be, but I don't know what they are, how they might be excavated from my mess of a personality.

Carver says, I have a long history with Scorpio women. They're the best. They're the best right up until that tail comes out of nowhere and—here he makes a motion with his hand, a stinging motion, the fatal consequence of hanging around with someone like me.

Jesus, Ben says, turning away from Hayley. Should I be worried about that?

No, no, no. I pat his shoulder. No, Ben, you have nothing to worry about. I am not going to sting you. I'm a *nice* scorpion. And he puts his arm around me, and it feels right.

The chefs arrive then, and Hayley distributes the remaining cupcakes, and Paula punches me in the bicep, says, You should have told me it was your birthday, and I shrug and press my face into Ben's shoulder. Everything is a fucking secret with this one, he says, more or less fondly.

Hayley picks up her phone again. He's still not texting me, she says.

He's probably just drunk, I say. He's at a party. He's fine. Don't smother him.

Is that what Greg did wrong? she asks. I can tell all the booze is starting to hit, there is a gleam in her eye and a slight slipperiness in her speech. I can feel it working its magic on me, too. She asks, Did he smother you? And I think she's being mean at first, but I look in her eyes and I can tell she's really asking. No, Hayley. Pretty much the opposite. Tyler isn't me, I tell her, and she says, Thank god for that.

Here is another part of the story I have not been telling you. I know, I know, everything is a fucking secret with me, but I wanted us to get to know each other better. I wanted you to be able to forgive me.

Imagine: my twenty-fourth birthday, San Francisco, shortly before the end, although I didn't know that then. I still thought I could turn it around. I thought, in fact, that I *had* turned it around. Sure, there had been months now of not having sex and not keeping down what I ate, there had been loud fights and louder silences, and yet. And yet I had just had my interview with Harvard, a quick half-hour conversation with a nice lady in a pantsuit, and it had gone well, and my acceptance seemed imminent, which meant, presumably, that my life would imminently begin to fall into place. This was not as absurd an assumption as it may sound. Greg had genuinely brightened when I told him about the interview, had kissed me without it seeming like an obligation, had told me he was proud and seemed to really mean it. Clever girl, he said, and he put an arm around me, and for perhaps a week things were good again.

And then it was my birthday, and I came home early from work and I took a long bath and I did a face mask and I got all dressed up and I looked great, I'd been living off kale and black coffee for the past week to fit in this dress, and I looked at myself in the mirror and I thought that Greg would have to be made of stone not to want to have sex with me tonight.

But Greg was late, of course he was, just because we were having a good week didn't mean he'd changed all his ways, and at eight o'clock I went to see my Martini Soul Mate alone, and he was the first person to wish me happy birthday, and he made me a champagne cocktail, and he told me I looked beautiful in a tone that was more serious than usual and it hit me right in the clitoris. And eventually Greg met me, and we ordered all the vegetarian options on my Martini Soul Mate's food menu, and I had been so good all week but now I was ravenous, I ate until I was sick, I ate everything, I was losing her, the Sam Greg wanted, the Sam I wanted to be, and when we got home I threw everything up and Greg said we have to talk about this, this throwing-everything-up thing, and I didn't disagree but it was my birthday and it was not the time for serious conversations, it was the time for birthday presents and birthday sex and birthday sleep, but when I kissed him he pulled away and told me I tasted like vomit, and when I'd finished brushing my teeth again he was asleep, or pretending to be, and I sat on the edge of the bed for what felt like forever and then I put my jacket back on and I went back to the bar.

My Martini Soul Mate was closing up, but he poured me a glass of champagne and I sipped on it as the chefs and the servers clocked out and drank and left and then it was just us, and I drank up, I didn't want to overstay my welcome, but he topped up my glass and poured one for himself and when he kissed me I was not surprised, and it was no trouble to repurpose my desire for Greg into desire for him, and it was no trouble to let him run his broad calloused hands over my body, and it was a joy and a relief when he hiked up my dress and bent me over the bar and fucked me until I couldn't breathe.

James, his name was James. He ruined me.

I like her, Ben says. We have said our good nights and put Hayley in a Lyft and stepped out into the witching hour, and we're walking back to his, hand in hand, me with a bit of a sway in my step, him steady as ever.

She's the best, I say.

We come to a stop at a corner, waiting for the light to change, the traffic is light at this hour but this is Brooklyn and there is still traffic. Why didn't you tell me it was your birthday? he asks.

I didn't tell the Dans, either.

I'm not the Dans, he says.

The light changes and we don't move, we stand there as a group of drunk people travels past us into the crosswalk, and I would like to join with them, to drift downstream on their current. Ben is looking down at me with such earnestness and I feel newly, brutally sober.

Ben says my name. I like you a lot, he says.

Something twists hard in my chest. My heart hurts. I like you, too, I say, and I do mean it. And when he says he's not seeing anybody else, well, neither am I. And then he just stares at me, and I guess it must be my turn to speak, but I don't know what to say.

He is, I know, looking for permission to call me his girlfriend, to kiss me in public, to put his arm around my waist in Casey's bar and in Joe's. To bring me to dinner with his parents. I know that granting him this is no sacrifice on my part, will most likely make me happy, too. I know and I know and I know and meanwhile I have given up on the flow of the other walking people and have the irrational urge to step out in the other direction instead, into the oncoming cars.

There is so much he doesn't know, still. There are depths to me that I have kept carefully concealed, facets that I have kept from the light.

Arizona. My mother. My ex-boyfriend. *Harvard*. He has only just met Hayley. Isn't it too soon to be having this conversation?

But no, count backward. Two months. Two and a half, really. Two and a half months of good conversations and great dates and fantastic sex. Two and a half months of kindness, of patience, of exploration. Two and a half months of Ben's high, easy laugh, of watching movies in his apartment, of eating together and not throwing up after.

Han saying, *a square*.

Hayley saying, You deserve someone nice, after Greg.

I could do worse, I know. The trick, really, would be somehow doing *better*.

Okay, I say, and we hash out the rest of it, the exclusivity clause, the applicability of the words "boyfriend" and "girlfriend," the abandonment of secrecy, and then I am tired of talking about it and I do what anyone else would do, I throw my arms around him and I pull him close again. His lips on mine, my tongue in his mouth, his hands shifting to press the small of my back, to brush a hip bone, to twist in my hair. This is the easy part: the alignment of form, the gentle pressure, the simple knowledge of what comes next, the understanding that we will hurry home to his apartment, that he will be inside me before I have finished taking off my clothes.

When I was growing up I was afraid of sex, because everyone loves to tell young girls how much of themselves they will be giving up in the act. But that isn't always true. Sometimes sex is the opposite of intimacy.

RAMOS GIN FIZZ

2 ounces gin
1/2 ounce lemon juice
1/2 ounce lime juice
1/2 ounce simple syrup
3 dashes orange flower water
1 ounce heavy cream
1 egg white
Seltzer

Shake everything but the seltzer over ice for as long as
you possibly can. Strain and dry shake, strain again into a
Collins glass over ice. Top with seltzer.

We have our bar meeting on Monday, the Dans and me,
no Gina this time, which disappoints me a little, just the four of us in an
empty bar, all the lights on, Wilco on the speakers, and we make all of
our cocktails, snapping photos for the bar's Instagram, fine-tuning the
specs and the names. Carver goes first, with his gin tiki drink, strange and
delicious, then with a potent brandy cocktail, and then something in the
family of a martini, which is obviously my favorite. Han suggests a couple
of tweaks, a little more lemon in the tiki drink, a dash of orange bitters for
the martini, and Olsen is a silent observer, and I am a silent photographer.

Next is Olsen, and he steps behind the bar to make the two drinks
he's apparently been working on, one with whiskey, one with mezcal.
The mezcal is fruity and spiced, and even Han has only nice things to say
about it. The whiskey is a sort of bitter variation on a traditional sour:
lemon, simple, Aperol, and an egg white.

And yes, it's a raw egg white, and yes, plenty of people balk at this, all of us brainwashed by our parents about salmonella, as if that ever stopped anybody from eating raw cookie dough. Anyway, in a cocktail the alcohol should take care of most of that bacteria. And you don't taste it, either: there's a hint of *something*, I guess, but if the drink's been shaken properly, the egg's contribution is mainly textural.

A bar lesson: you have to *really* shake it to get it right. The Dans swear by something called a *reverse double shake*: combine ingredients in a tin, shake over ice, strain from the large half of the shaker into the smaller, discard the ice, shake again until the ice chips have gone and the shake has become silent, then strain. Most bars will do a double shake instead, which as you can probably figure out for yourself is the same thing the other way around: dry shake (without ice) first, then add ice for the second shake. And you can do that, if you want, but the Joe's way is better.

There is only one egg cocktail in my flash cards, a famous one that I am curious about but have never dared to order, because I understand that ordering it is a great way to get a bartender to hate you. The Ramos Gin Fizz. It's not that it's particularly obscure or esoteric or whatever; it's just that it's a legendary pain in the ass to make. Gin, citrus, sugar, orange blossom water—straightforward enough—but then there's the egg white, which complicates things as we've already established, and then there's a full ounce of heavy cream, and between the two, you have to shake the ever-living shit out of this cocktail to get the right texture.

Once upon a time in New Orleans, according to Han, Mr. Ramos himself had thirty-one designated shakers for this drink. Thirty-one! They'd do it assembly-line style, shake as long as they could bear and then pass it along until eventually it was ready to pour.

But this is only a sour, and Olsen pours it into a coupe, paints the top with a few dashes of Peychaud's bitters—grapefruit, anise, caramel—and then the glass is in Han's hand and Han takes a sip and chews on it. He passes the glass to Carver. Olsen is looking away, cleaning the shakers— the eggy ones always need extra attention, a rinse in cold water first, should really probably go through the glasswasher between uses—but I know he's waiting for the verdict.

Han says, Hmm. He gestures to Carver, who hands it back, and he takes another sip. I feel like it's missing something, he says, and he passes it to me. It's good, he says. But it's just, like, a sour.

What about some vermouth? Carver suggests. Like a Clover Club. But Olsen says he tried that already. It was too weird with the whiskey, he says.

What about Cynar? Han suggests, and Olsen scowls but he tries it, shakes up another version, sets it down for us to compare. Now it's too bitter, he says, passing it to Carver. Carver drinks and says nothing. Han drinks and says, Oh, no, I love that.

He passes it to me and I love it, too. And so this is the version that is chosen, the specs that Carver writes down. Name? Carver asks, looking up.

Why don't you let Han come up with one, Olsen spits.

Don't be a dick, Olsen, Han says. I'm just trying to make the drink better.

The drink was fucking fine, Olsen says, and Han reaches for the half-drunk first version to make a point, but what that point is none of us gets to hear because he knocks it over, sending cocktail spreading out over the bar-top, neatly breaking the stem of the coupe.

Once we have cleaned up and thrown out the glass, Carver wisely moves us along. Sam, he says. Why don't you show us what you've been working on.

I pass the camera to Han and go around to the business side of the bar. Okay, I say, smiling. My palms are sweating, my chest tight. I hear Blue's voice in my head, *just breathe through it,* the yoga instructor's answer for everything. I do my best.

The Dans call the space behind the bar *the fishbowl,* because being there is like being encased in glass, on display. The downside being that there is nowhere to hide, the upside being power. Something about standing behind the bar makes you sexier and more charming and more trustworthy and more respectable and just generally *more.*

Like Scott the Scot, who was not an unattractive guy but who had

women throwing themselves at him in a way that felt nonetheless dispro-
portionate. Phone numbers on receipts, on at least two occasions a key
card to a hotel room. I had always assumed it was the accent, but maybe
it was more than that. Or, of course, Olsen; certainly his position as bartender had been part of his appeal. Or, of course, James, but thinking
about him is too painful.

My fishbowl self smiles, sets the fancy mixing glass on the bar.
Reaches for the vermouth. My hands feel strangely disconnected from
my body, but they hold steady. *Meniscus*, I say to myself, *meniscus*. Pour
my three ingredients in, a scoop of ice. Crack a couple of cubes with the
tap-icer, which I have learned, at last, to use. Stir in something in the
family of silence, not for long because the drink is going on the rocks.
Strain. Garnish. Stand there behind the bar awaiting judgment.

Well you know I think it's great, Han says, passing the drink to Olsen. I
could get into trouble on these.

You could get into trouble on Diet Coke, Olsen says, and Han flips
him off. It's good, Sam, Olsen says. Totally worth spending an entire
afternoon on.

Carver lifts it to his lips, and I have to remind myself, again, to
breathe. He sets it down on the bar, looks down into the glass like there's
something to be read in there. What are your specs? he asks, and I tell
him. Quarter ounce more rum, he says, and I do it, and he tries it, and
he rewards me with a smile. Nicely done, he says, and I skip out of the
fishbowl before anyone can change their mind.

We get through Han's contributions quickly—the bittersweet one I've already tried, a hot toddy with ginger and applejack, and a flip, which uses
a whole egg and has to be shaken like crazy, which comes out creamy and
entirely too easy to drink—and then we are finished and Carver has gone
downstairs and the rest of us are drinking the remnants of the various
cocktails, and the conversation returns to names. This is something I will
struggle with forever. Do you name the drink something descriptive? Do
you name it for the drink it's based on? A movie reference? A song lyric?
An inside joke? Whatever works, is the answer.

Han has helped me name my drink—Breakfast of Champions, because of the coffee, and because of Kurt Vonnegut—and now he has returned to Olsen's, but of course Olsen does not want his help. Anyone else would know to let it drop, would see Olsen's hackles rising and back away, but it's Han, single-minded and stubborn, well intentioned always but right now being ridiculous, not to mention we've all had a fair bit to drink.

I really don't care what we call it, Olsen says. He's gone behind the bar to clean up, because Joe's is closed tonight and there are sinks to clean, juice to put away, bottles to wipe and cover.

You should care, Han says. You'd be a really good bartender if you cared a little more.

Olsen slams down the bottle he's holding, so hard I half expect more broken glass, but it stays intact. Fuck *off*, Han, he says. Could you just shut up for once in your fucking life?

There is a long, excruciating silence. Olsen turns away, the tips of his ears and the back of his neck going red, and he busies himself over by the glasswasher. Han looks at me, and I look back, but I can't find any words to give to either of them, and just when I'm getting ready to start screaming or crying or something, anything to break this horrible silence, just when I'm wondering if anyone will ever speak in this bar ever again, Han says, Fine, and he gets up, and he goes.

I go out after him. It takes me a minute, a minute of Olsen saying, Fucking Han, I can't believe him, can you believe him? And I say No, and then I say I'll be right back, and he gives me a look of utmost exasperation, but I don't care, and I go out into the street, windy and cool but still sunny, and I call Han's name, and he turns back, he's at the corner, and I jog over, and Han has a cigarette in his hand and he pulls on it hard, and when I get to him I say, Olsen was out of line.

Han rolls his eyes. Blows out a long stream of smoke. Says, At this point I'm just waiting for him to fucking quit already.

My heart is beating hard in my chest, I feel a little light-headed and I have the horrible impossible urge to fix this, to make Han and Olsen make up, to preserve the version of Joe's to which I have grown accustomed. I tell Han, He's just sensitive, that's all.

He's just an asshole, Han says. Another drag. Look, he says. This is my career. This is my *life*. I know I get a little silly sometimes but I do take it seriously. If Olsen isn't going to, he can fuck off and leave the rest of us to do the job right. He taps the side of his cigarette, ash drifting in the breeze, and he says, Joe's is too small a bar to have someone working there who isn't all in.

I absorb these words like a punch to the gut. I want to tell him the truth, that I am in the service industry on a temporary visa, that I have one foot out the door, that I am not the girl he thinks I am. I want to tell him and I want to make sure he never finds out. Silence settles between us, the same poisonous silence that I left behind in the bar, and I'm grasping desperately for a way to break it and finally I say, I just don't want to see my dads fight, and Han laughs a real laugh and says, Sam, you know your dads are me and Carver.

Olsen's on his way out by the time I get back, talking to Carver as he pulls on his jacket. Sam, Carver says. We were just talking about you.

Uh-oh.

All good things, he says, glancing at Olsen.

I want to give you my Sunday, Olsen says, and I feel my mouth open, but nothing comes out. I look from one Dan to the other. Seriously?

Carver shrugs. I think you're ready.

Olsen, as promised, has gotten another job; some dive bar in the Lower East Side, Sunday and Monday but it's Manhattan money, which is almost always better than Brooklyn money, and anyway it's easy, just cracking Coors Lights and mixing vodka-Redbulls like it's 2009, my nightmare, but perfect for Olsen, because it will give him the funds and the free time to prioritize his new band.

The cliché of New York service workers is that they are all actors or musicians or writers or whatever else, artists of some description, just working until they get their big break. Bars and restaurants are good for this: the hours are flexible, and you're less likely to have to take work home with you. There is space, physical and emotional space for whatever the real priority is. For the side dream.

It's been way too long, Olsen says; I haven't played a show in years.

I don't know what to say to that. I will live my entire life without playing a show. Music is a language that was spoken to me in my child-hood, but that I never fully learned: I understand it when I hear it, but I can't answer. Certainly my voice has never been any good. I played violin when I was a kid, but I never really got the swing of it, and I keep carrying a guitar of my own around, a little acoustic that I do play from time to time, but I'm not great at it. You're gifted in other ways, my father told me once when I complained. My father, who *is* great, who has a rich deep voice and can learn any song on the radio, who used to tease and delight me with goofy renditions of Backstreet Boys songs or whatever, back when he was fun. And my mother, not a musician, her voice even worse than mine, could never carry a tune, but of course she was an artist, too, and of course I was never a good visual artist, either.

In fact the most artistic thing I do now is *this*. Which is not nothing: there is a lot of creativity involved with bartending, from the obvious matter of inventing and assembling cocktails—*mixology,* to use the word Carver loves to hate—to the storytelling, the weaving and passing on of myths and histories. Or then creating in the way a parent does: home-building, carving a safe space out of an unwelcoming world.

We launch the new menu the next day, flood social media with photos of the new drinks, the promise of novelty, and it's a tough week, none of us quite as quick or as comfortable as we usually are, not to mention the fact that Han and Olsen are not, presently, on speaking terms. But the important thing is that people are happy. The important thing is that peo-ple order my drink and seem to enjoy it. There's one guy on Friday night who goes through three of them, one after the other, and it takes all of my self-control not to grab him by the shoulders and say, That's mine, I came up with that.

Also, maybe slow down, because there's a hefty dose of caffeine in those and it's eleven o'clock already.

And then it's Sunday, and I'm brewing coffee in the prep kitchen as I start my open. I have grown comfortable doing the open by now; I have come to enjoy the solitude of it, the soothing monotony. It was a good thorough close last night and my work is easy, I have the place set up well before three, and I sit down for a minute, drink my coffee, eat the granola bar I've brought for breakfast, and then I lower the lights and turn on the music and my first solo shift begins.

It's not hard. I'm worried it will be hard, but it's Sunday, and my guests are by and large languid and relaxed, and there are not too many of them, and most of them aren't even drinking cocktails. I could work by myself any night of the week if all I had to do was pour wine and make gin and tonics. There's a group of parents in the back room as always, Kay on their laptop at the window. Joe Himself, briefly. The Mayor, even more briefly.

There is a regular who is a couples therapist, and there is a running joke that the Dans and I should go in to see her, that we'd get some kind of friends-and-family discount, if not a free session, considering all the wine she's been comped over the years. Teresa. She brings in dates sometimes, men whom she complains about after—Ridiculous, she says, being a couples therapist with a shitty love life—but most often she comes in alone and she sits at the bar with a glass of pinot noir, an expensive one and slow seller but one that Carver refuses, for Teresa's sake, to take off the menu. She sits there with her wine and she reads her little e-reader and she takes pin after pin out of her gray and black hair, amassing a huge pile of them on the bar-top, until finally her thick tight curls are free to breathe and halo around her face and she starts to actually look relaxed.

She's not enormously shy, Teresa; not a Joe Himself type. She's quite friendly, really, when she feels like it; I have seen her fall into spirited conversation with Han and Meg on several occasions; she has even been known to coax a smile out of Carver. She just spends all day talking to people, and she likes having some downtime. Tonight is no different— she's spent the weekend upstate visiting friends, and she's here, now, for the quiet, and I am happy to deliver.

Later in the evening Paula comes by, Gina and Meg in tow. My baby's all grown up, Gina says, and she orders my drink, and they pass it around and say nice things about it, and I blush extravagantly and stammer out my thanks.

It pains me to say it, Gina says, but Carver's really been turning this place around.

And it's true, Joe's is getting busier. Whether it's the new menu or the better reviews or the more consistent use of social media or, hell, just the time of year, Joe's is getting busier. My shifts stretching out to eight or even ten hours, me earning as much as I did in San Francisco, even just working three days a week.

This fucking bar, though—and I think she means Joe's as a whole, but she means specifically literally the bar-top itself. Remember when it was new? she asks, and Meg nods, and Gina pulls out her phone and starts digging for a photo, finds an old piece in one of the many trendy New York publications, and there at the top, a picture of a woman behind a blinding bright bar.

All it needs is a good round of Brasso, Gina says, but you know how the Dans are, they're never going to do it.

Boys, Paula says. It's like working with children.

I look closer at the photo. Gina, is that *you*?

Gina takes the phone back. Christ, I look awful, she says, laughing. And I laugh, too, but I wouldn't have said *awful*. I would have said *thin*.

So did Olsen finally quit then?

It's eleven already, a small contingent of chefs joining Paula and Gina at the bar, Meg gone home to her husband (nursing a hangover, she explains, but he sends his regards). A small contingent of chefs, Negronis all around, everyone surprised but, I think—I hope—pleased to see me behind the bar for a change. I shake my head—no, he hasn't quit—and I tell them about the second job, about the band, about the side dream.

Chefs, for their part, are not expected to have side dreams. Perhaps this has to do with the money, money for chefs being notoriously bad, or the hours, hours for chefs being notoriously long. It is not, perhaps, the sort of work that allows space for anything else. And yet in many ways our jobs are not so different. We are all acolytes of flavor, students of the human palate, mad scientists attempting to take the same ingredients that have always existed and transform them into something greater than themselves.

To be a chef, Mikey says, you just have to last. If you can make it through a decade or two of working your ass off for minimum wage, you can eventually break through and make some money, you can build a life out of it. A life that does not require living in borderline poverty, toiling in hot kitchens to make food you yourself could not afford.

Mikey is the most egregiously, obviously chefly of our regulars, and you sense that he knows what he's talking about. He is if nothing else the most tattooed of the bunch, botanicals in clean black ink on his neck and hands, a choice, he says, because he needed to commit to the life. He had to be forced to last, had to mark himself unfit for any other occupation. Looking like he looks you could never, say, get a job in a lawyer's office, line up an interview with a hedge fund. Especially, he points out, as a Black guy; people see tattoos on dark skin and assume gang member. You would be stuck in the service industry or the arts or perhaps you could maybe make it as an academic at a very open-minded university, as a sort of diversity hire. One of the therapists in Arizona had sleeves, I remember, although they were still only sleeves, still might have been hidden had he rolled down the cuffs of his shirts, had he wanted them to be hidden.

We have regulars who work in a tattoo shop down the road, too, three men named Owen and Oscar and Oliver and you could put a gun to my head and I would not be able to even hazard a guess as to which one was which, because they only ever come in all three of them together and therefore have never become differentiated. Carver could probably tell you. And then they all drink the same thing, tequila on the rocks, and never too much of it, never enough to start the next day with a hangover, consummate professionals that they are.

At any rate they don't look alike, except inasmuch as they, too, are so tattooed as to be unfit for other employment, except, I guess, that they could be chefs or bartenders. There's the oldest one, who looks like an actual Viking, enormously tall with a long graying blond beard and long graying blond hair and an octopus on his left wrist, its tentacles creeping over the back of his hand. There is the youngest one, skinny and always smiling, head shaved to show geometric designs all over his scalp. And in the middle is the handsome one, with sailor tats and shaggy hair and holes plugged in his earlobes big and round as quarters. Carver says they are the best in the borough. Says if I ever want work done I should go there, that we have given them enough free liquor over the years that I will get a good price. A good price for what, Carver? What, in this hypothetical, am I getting tattooed on my body?

Paula, too, sports a plethora of tats, although her approach has been less methodical than Mikey's, her arms covered scattershot, each image— roses, sparrows, women—the bright and various work of friends. My first girlfriend had a gun, she says, so I got to be practice. She says this without regret, in a way that suggests that both the girlfriend and the tattoos had been good choices, even if the girlfriend had long since moved on, even if that early ink was uneven and faded in places. She shows us a mermaid on her right bicep, says, Can you see how the scales are fucked up? But you don't notice it unless you're looking for it, and we tell her so, and she lets the sleeve of her T-shirt fall, reaches for her drink, says, Right, I know.

And Gina, of course, has colorful ink of her own, and in fact I am the only one here who doesn't have anything, virgin skin, and it's not that I'm opposed, in theory; and it's not even a matter of work prospects, because as long as I don't go the Mikey route a little ink is not going to close too many doors for me; it's just that my ideas are bad, and my mind is changeable, and every time I have thought I should get a tattoo, my next thought has been, after the next five pounds, then I will be ready, then my skin and the flesh beneath it will be the appropriate shape and size to be illustrated. But I have learned not to say things like that out loud.

But back to this side dream business for one final minute. To clarify: I am not saying that chefs don't have other dreams. Anthony Bourdain being the famous example, writing novels even before *Kitchen Confidential*, before he was Anthony Bourdain. It's not as if there's some rule about who is allowed to have secret aspirations toward art or fame or whatever exactly it is they are aspiring toward. My point is that as a bartender, or a server, you are expected to have something else going on. Carver hates that people assume this about him, that he is doing something else, that this is just a holdover. When people ask him what else he does, or if he's just a bartender—and people do ask—I have seen him snap back: This is my bar, or, Running a bar is a full-time job, or simply, *Yes*. And it's an unfair expectation, just as condescending as asking him if he wants a real job, based on a similar assumption: that no one would choose to do this for a living, that bartending is a form of failure.

Though of course Carver is an artist, and though I am afraid to ask him, I assume that he would like to be making art.

I, too, dread the question. I read extensively, I watch movies, I go to the occasional museum—I am a consumer of the art of others, but as we have already established, I have always found the creation part of the equation essentially horrible. This was not such an issue back when I thought I was going to be some kind of physicist or engineer or whatever, which even after the NASA dream died was still my plan when I first started at Columbia: scientists and mathematicians are also not expected to have side dreams. My therapist says this is unfair. She says, Isn't it enough to love what you do, to simply search for happiness on the side? To balance your job with the simple joy of being alive, the great gift of living in this city, in this country, in this century?

Well, *no*. But then I suppose it will all be different when I am a lawyer. And so maybe that is my side dream, practicing law, although that sounds absurd.

Maybe it's the other way around. Maybe bartending is my side dream.

HARVARD

2 ounces cognac
3/4 ounce sweet vermouth
2 dashes Angostura bitters

Stir over ice and strain into a chilled coupe. Top with
seltzer, if you must, and serve without a garnish.

I have a quiet Thanksgiving in Brooklyn, a warm, mellow dinner with Paula and Gina and a few of their friends, our apartment temporarily transformed, sparkling clean and smelling of rosemary and garlic. The musicians join us, somewhat unexpectedly; descend from their sex den with several conspicuously nice bottles of wine from somebody's work, with bread from the bougie bakery down the street. Orphans' Thanksgiving, Paula calls it, and while none of us are really orphans, not in the traditional sense, we all have our reasons for being here.

And then we are plunged into December. December is always a strange month for a bar; starts with the dead quiet of Thanksgiving and ends with the dead quiet of January, but in the middle there are office holiday happy hours, regulars stopping in on their way home from Christmas shopping, schoolteachers drinking their way through the end of the semester. Cold apartments to be escaped, the inevitable stress of the arrangements and the family obligations and the expense driving people to booze. Carver has wrangled a few buyouts, too, boozy and intimate nights with catered charcuterie and limited drink options, easy and lucrative. One of them for Meg's work, at her suggestion: a raucous affair with what felt like half the staff of the museum milling around the bar, drinking wine and beer until the still–mostly sober Meg had to put a couple of the higher-ups in cabs, at which point things began to die down.

I'm working five days most weeks, and often as not getting called in to help if things get out of hand. Forever bailing on Ben to run off to Joe's, him muttering about healthy boundaries, me telling him to take it up with Carver. My roommates and I are ships in the night and I don't see Hayley at all, except for one Friday night visit that ends abruptly when she and Tyler get into some indecipherable fight and go seething back to Williamsburg.

Ben's brother Theo comes to visit and they come into Joe's, Ben and the brother and the brother's wife, fresh in from LA. Theo looks like a lanky version of Ben, taller and narrower but with the same bright smile, and in the manner of very tall men he has married a very small woman, a light-skinned actress named Shae. I like them both immediately.

They sit at one of the high-tops and I go over to greet them, shaking hands, exchanging pleasantries, blushing when Theo says he's heard so much about me. Saying the same back, even though it isn't true. Making my excuses for not joining them for Christmas—family obligations, I say. I don't say: it's too much. It's too soon. I summon my best fishbowl self, the version of Sam who can make conversation with anybody, who is self-confident and a little flirtatious, who teases and makes jokes and can talk to you about Scotch whisky and fine wine; or about politics, local, national, or global; or about indie rock 'n' roll circa 2009; or about Kanye and Kim; or about this year's Pulitzer Prize nominees. I have been cultivating this Sam, carefully, over the past months; constructing her through conversations with strangers and regulars alike. She is the reason Joe's Apothecary has been getting better reviews. She is the reason I am having such a good time here: I have begun, slowly but surely, to absorb her into myself.

So Fishbowl Sam and I chat with Theo and Shae about their flight, about their plans in New York, and we join in with Theo when he starts teasing Ben about his gym habit, and we make plans to do a yoga class with Shae, and it's all going great until one of us makes one quip too many. LA, I say, I'm so sorry. A beautiful town with a rotten center.

I grew up there, Shae says, and there is an edge to her voice, and I backpedal, of course there are many good things about LA, too: the weather, the tacos, the music scene. Oh, god, she thinks I'm an asshole. A snotty white girl looking down on where she's from, no better than any of the unfriendly gentrifiers ruining this neighborhood, no better than the rich kids at Columbia who were always talking about Harlem like it was some kind of war zone.

Oh, god, I am an asshole.

Don't mind her, Ben says; she's from San Francisco. She can't help it.

Shae bursts out laughing. San Francisco, she echoes. You want to talk about rotten centers. And I am quick to agree. That's why I'm here, I tell her, and then I hurry off to get them drinks before I make any more mistakes.

Hayley's parents come out, too: a week and change of Christmastime in Manhattan, bright lights and big wreaths and chestnuts roasting on street corners, Christmas music pumping out of every storefront, throngs of rosy-cheeked tourists. The Kanes darting from museums to restaurants to Broadway shows, and me a last-minute plus-one whenever I'm not working, because Tyler has fucked off to Connecticut.

We didn't break up, Hayley insists. He's just taking some time. And I know better than to argue, but I can't help giving her a look, like, *Don't bullshit a bullshitter.* Like, *I know what it's like, limping toward the end.*

Shut up, Sam, she says, even though I haven't spoken. Anyway, all his shit's still in the apartment, so one way or another he's coming back.

And I think about Greg, early this year, giving me two weeks to get out of what was still, then, *our* apartment. Sleeping in a coworker's guest room to give me some time. A mercy, because where would I have gone? To James? I had stopped seeing him, stopped going to the bar, stopped going out entirely. I spent my two weeks looking at apartments I didn't want, the whole city tarnished by my unhappiness. I guess on some level I knew I was leaving. A functional adult would have quit her job and made arrangements, or else found a sublet to buy time to quit her job and make arrangements, or at least admitted to herself that there might be arrangements to be made. I did none of this. I fell into a deep funk, and this was the peak of my journey through disordered eating. I told myself that I was sad, that it was okay to eat a burrito the size of my head or a whole box of Annie's mac and cheese or half a pizza, that it was okay to eat ice cream straight out of the pint container, that the rules were different while you dealt with heartache. I told myself nothing about the purges after; these had become simply a part of life.

Greg came back for something, I don't remember, and he found the apartment in its sorry state, and me in my sorry state, on the couch watching *Friends*, nothing packed, the garbage can in the kitchen over-flowing, all of the signs pointing toward a woman in need of help but the most glaring one when he saw my face, the hideous shock of it. I had burst a blood vessel in one of my eyes, which is a thing that will happen to you when you're throwing up all the time, yet another point against the enterprise. My right eye a horror show, blood all around the iris, and me saying, It looks worse than it feels, which was true, and him saying, Sam, you have to stop. And this after he had told me, during one of the final fights, that I was a terrible person and he never wanted to see me again, and he didn't apologize now or take it back and he was still worried, which is when it sank in that it was bad but also when my stupid heartbroken brain thought, maybe if I let him nurse me back to health, he will take me back, and so for once I was honest. I don't think I can, I said, and he called my father and a week later I was in Arizona, at the facility full of other people who couldn't stop, either.

But Hayley knows all this already, and I don't remind her. What would be the point? And besides, selfishly, I'm happy to be included. Expensive lunches in SoHo, walking the Highline, *Wicked* on Broadway on my one night off. Me feeling like a child on vacation with her parents, trailing along with the Kanes and wondering why I am only just now going to, say, the Met Breuer; why I have not been to a single musical since moving back; why, in short, I am living in my expensive shoe box in this expensive city if I am not taking advantage of any of this, any of the reasons for which New York is expensive. What is the point of being here if I am not actually *here*? We all love to bitch about tourists, and yet, are we on some level maybe jealous? Do we envy the dedication of the visitor to taking all of it in? Do we wish that we could just unabashedly soak in the city? Apparently I do.

I'm nervous at first, because I haven't seen Jackie Kane since my largely unexplained departure from San Francisco last February, my sudden absence from Jackie's firm, which cannot have reflected well upon her, Jackie, who got me the job, a girl fresh out of college with no relevant experience, basically nepotism. Hayley's been making my excuses, I know: a bad breakup, a moment of personal crisis, Arizona to *regroup*. I am no great fan of euphemisms, under normal circumstances, but better to say *regroup* than *go to rehab*.

All of which is to say, it would be extremely reasonable for Jackie to be resentful, and I'm worried, but there's no need. Jackie hugs Hayley first, and then me, and I breathe in the scent of Chanel, and I relax a little. You look great, she tells me when she steps back, which is what polite people say when they want to tell you that you look skinny. I say, So do you.

It was inevitable, I guess, that Jackie and I would become close. Hayley and her sisters had a nanny, always, a woman named Maria whom we all loved, but when Jackie returned from work she pulled all the light. I have mentioned, I think, that my mother admired her, and perhaps this was, at first, what drew me to her, too. My mother who was always on the outside, so different, I understood from an early age, from the mothers of my classmates. She was not an embarrassment as a painter; she never could have made a living at it, but she sold pieces for respectable and occasionally large sums of money, her work hung in galleries in Mountain View, San Jose. Jackie, in fact, owns a couple of her pieces; last time I visited, one of them was hanging in the upstairs hallway, a big, red-heavy abstraction of a woman that made me want to weep.

So it wasn't exactly that people felt sorry for her, like they might have if she were truly a failure. It was just that she didn't have anything in common with the Palo Alto moms, had no traditional career, did not wear pastels or mom jeans or khakis, wore loud lipstick and dyed her hair with henna, didn't shave her legs or armpits. Was not involved in the PTA, did not go to Pilates, did not do brunch.

And then there was Jackie, who was perfect. And she was always kind to me, and to my mother, and when my mother died she stepped in. She invited me over for dinner, me and my father both, and she asked me about my classes, about my friends, about the books I was reading and my plans for the future. She took interest, and she stayed interested.

When the time came, she signed me up with the same college counselor as Hayley, booked us back-to-back appointments, drove us both, sat in on my appointment as if I were her own daughter. My father clearly annoyed by this, but in no position to object: our relationship at the time was in one of its deeper valleys, what with the new appearance of Diane and his indefensible resistance to the idea of me going out east.

The counselor was a middle-aged white woman, frizzy strawberry blond hair, kind eyes, and she looked at my transcripts and she talked me through my options: reaches, targets, safeties. I told her I wanted to go to Harvard, and she said, I can't promise that. But, she said, you have a very real shot. She said, I got a young woman in last year who scored a hundred points lower on the SAT. She stroked my ego, in other words; she set me up for disappointment. We made a list of nine schools and talked a little about my personal statement and then she shook my hand after, and then she shook Jackie's, and said, You must be very proud.

She knew that Jackie wasn't actually my mother; I am not sure what relationship she thought we had. But in that moment, I pretended that we were mother and daughter, that I was part of her family, that this was my life. I am, Jackie said, and she smiled at me like she was pretending the same thing.

My father calls me late Christmas morning, bright and cheerful on his end, two hours behind and just sitting down for breakfast. I can hear voices in the background, music—Diane has the whole family over, he says, and I can imagine it: her three adult sons, whom I've met a handful of times, her siblings, everybody's husbands and wives and children. I am relieved to be skipping it. I wish I were there.

My father asks how I am and I tell him I'm all right. He says, I know the holidays can be hard, and I know he's talking about my mother and my skin tightens up and my stomach hurts and I don't say anything. What would he know about it? He has a new family now.

He says my name and I say, Yes, I'm still here. Yes, the holidays can be hard, but I'm all right. I continue to be all right. There is nothing for him to worry about, nothing I want or expect from him at this late date in our relationship. Hayley's parents are here, I tell him; I'll be spending the holiday with them. I'm not alone, this is important for him to know. He does not say that he is worried about me, but it is clear in every irregular phone call that he is worried about me. This is, in part, why our phone calls have become so irregular. How am I supposed to move on with my new life when my father is always asking me *how I'm doing* with his voice dripping with dark significance?

His turn to pause. Sounds like Jackie, he says. Swooping in to save the day. Say hi for me.

We have Christmas dinner at Paula's restaurant, at her insistence. If I have to work, she says, I at least want to feed people I *like*. And so the Kanes schlepp out to Bed-Stuy, Jackie and Eric trailing their daughter through the subway stations and the gray streets, and I meet them for the second seating, eight forty-five, stepping into the warm, fragrant sphere of Paula's domain. A modest but airy dining room, candles flickering on tables between glasses for wine and water, fake holly and real balsam. There are two servers on the floor, both in dark jeans and clean black tees, waist aprons. I don't know either of them, though I recognize the runner, a stocky Colombian guy named Luis who occasionally accompanies the chefs to Joe's, and the bartender, a slender Black woman named Rochelle.

We sit down and one of the servers comes over, a lifer if I've ever seen one, forty-something and potbellied, talking us through tonight's prix fixe offerings with the confidence and efficiency of the very good fine dining server, and he presents us with a fat encyclopedia of a wine list, and he asks what sort of water we'd like, and when he returns with our water, there is a woman with him, who gives us a red-lipped smile and presents us with glasses of champagne. Compliments of the chef, she says, and the Kanes all look at me.

I guess they like you here, Eric says, and I brush it off, but the evening will prove him right, all the special little extras from the kitchen, the complimentary coffees and amaro at the end. A great service industry perk. Pretty white girl treatment is one thing; insider treatment is another level.

So how did you ever end up bartending? Eric asks. He has the wine list open in front of him, though he's not looking at it. Did you have to take classes for it?

Bartender classes are a scam, I tell him, and it's true. They're good if you just want to, say, make a better martini in the comfort of your kitchen, but they don't do you any favors on a résumé. You have to learn by doing. And you have to work your way up. I tell him my trajectory, an abbreviated history of my time in the service industry. You don't start out as a bartender, I say. I don't say, I am only barely a bartender.

You know I'd be happy to help you find something here, Jackie says.

Jesus, Mom, let her have a year off, Hayley says. She'll be back in the fold before you know it.

But this bothers Jackie, I can tell. Sure, she smiles, and she changes the subject, asks her daughter about her job, Hayley's I mean, the nonprofit she's been working at for the past year and a half, Hayley bright-eyed as she starts talking about some recent initiative to keep girls in STEM, but then the sommelier comes over to help us with the wine, and Eric says, We should let the bartender choose, and Jackie's face darkens, her smile falters. I twist my hands together under the table, but I smile, I keep smiling. Of course, I say.

I have learned a little about wine over the past four months, but not as much as I might like; my foundation is shallow, shaky. Carver has attempted to teach me; we don't do a ton of wine at Joe's, but we do enough. I need a list, I tell him. I need you to write down the characteristics of each grape, of the terroir, I need tasting notes to which I can refer. When he says things like, You can tell Malbec by its disco purple wash line, that is helpful. When he says that cabernet sauvignon tastes of green peppers. The river stone minerality of Riesling, the cat's piss acidity of sauvignon blanc. These are things that I understand. *Malolactic fermentation*: creamy, buttery smoothness. Maturation in different types of oak: notes of vanilla from French oak, dill and coconut from American, hazelnut from Hungarian.

And then there is the question: Do you pair like with like, or do opposites attract? To quote Carver: yes. Rich red wine, rich dark chocolate. A crisp light white with fatty, earthy cheese. Fruity wine with spicy food, spicy wine with heavy all-American cuisine. Is it all guesswork? I ask, and he gives me his disappointed dad face, like, maybe she can't be taught after all.

Paula's somm is a pro, though, and we talk through it together. A white to start, we decide; something with some body to it. Some oak, but not one of those California chardonnays that wants to punch your lights out. We land on a midlist white Burgundy, and she has me taste it, pours a splash into one of those massive globe wineglasses, and I fake my way through, swirl it around, suck it through my teeth like I've seen Carver do. Peach, honeysuckle, something like brioche on the finish. Beautiful, I say, and she fills our glasses and retreats.

The food is beautiful, too. *Amuse bouche*: amusement of the mouth. The starter before the starter, a small sign of affection from the kitchen, a single piece of arancini on a bright stripe of some sort of red pepper sauce. Then there is ribollita for me, some sort of paté for the Kanes, mozzarella burrata for the table. Warm white bread, a pot of fragrant olive oil beside it. Pasta all around, the somm sweeping in with a bottle of Nebbiolo (round and rich, cherry and tobacco) to replace the Burgundy that seems to have evaporated. The way a good meal can consume you, the world stopping as you give yourself over to epicurean delight and pleasurable company.

Mains, as if any of us were still hungry: beef cheeks, branzino, delicata squash. All of us slowing down, but still going, because everything is so good.

I can't, Jackie says at last, laying her fork and knife neatly on her plate. Where do you *put* it? she asks Eric, shaking her head. I'm so sorry, Hayley, she says; I wish you'd gotten your father's metabolism.

Hayley looks at me and makes a big show of rolling her eyes. They're holiday calories, Mom, she says. They're not real.

I look at my own plate, nearly empty now as well, and I set my own silverware down. Put my hands on my stomach, which is pressing against the seams of my dress, and it's not like I'm in any danger of tearing anything, but now that I've started noticing the tightness I can't stop noticing. This is a familiar warning sign, a drop in pressure, earthquake weather. The way the sensation of food in your belly gets tangled up in anxiety, a roiling in your stomach that becomes a tightness in your chest, that will not subside until the fullness does. I reach for my wine, take a fortifying sip. Take slow, careful breaths through my nose. It's only food, I tell myself. And it's *Christmas*. And by the time our server has taken my plate away, the danger has passed.

Well, nearly. Paula sends us dessert, of course: tiramisu, olive oil cake, pannacotta. Italian espresso, bitter and burnt; small elegant glasses of Amaro Noveis, bitter and sweet. *Digestif*: an alcoholic substance designed to aid in digestion. Does it work? Well, it doesn't *hurt*.

The restaurant has emptied out; we're not the last table there, but we are in the final throes of the night, I can see Rochelle beginning to shut down her bar, the servers polishing silverware in the service station. Paula comes out, resplendent and sweaty in her chef's whites, and she kisses me on the top of the head and introduces herself to the Kanes, asks how everything was, asks how they're enjoying the city. New York at Christmas is the best, she says, and she clearly means it, even though I know she's been pulling sixty-plus-hour weeks all month and has not really gotten a holiday of her own.

We thank her profusely for our meal, and she waves it all away. I made Sam promise to bring you here, she says; I had to make it worthwhile. She lays a hand on my shoulder. I'll be done in twenty, she says, meet you at Casey's? And I'm surprised to hear that Casey's is open, but I say yes.

.   .   .

Hayley and I say our goodbyes to the Kanes, and I hug them both, Eric a little awkwardly, Jackie tightly. I'm just so proud of you, she says. I hope you know that.

This is the wine talking, but it's still nice to hear.

She steps back and pulls a gift bag out of her purse, and I flush, because of course I haven't gotten the Kanes anything, and they've already paid for this extravagant meal, and I don't deserve anything else, but then it's in my hand, and the Kanes are getting into a car, and we're all wishing each other merry Christmas, and then Hayley loops her arm through mine and we walk to Casey's bar, which is indeed open, an old Christmas episode of *Doctor Who* on the screen in the back with the sound off, Casey in a fantastically ugly Christmas sweater behind the bar, although as she explains to us, she's Jewish, herself.

What did you bring me? she asks, nodding to the present, and I start to stammer out an explanation but she's joking, of course she's joking. We sit down and she makes us gin and tonics, pours us big glasses of water, and I reach into the bag and I pull out a sweatshirt, soft and dark in the flickering candlelight, but I know what it is, I know what this deep shade of red means, and I unfold it, and sure enough, there it is, white letters across the chest spelling out my destiny.

There is actually a cocktail called a Harvard. This is not on my flash cards; no one will ever order it from me, and I will never order it from anybody else. But I was curious, and I looked it up online, and yes, there is a cocktail called a Harvard. It's an old one, too, making its first appearance before the start of the twentieth century, although beyond that it's hard to glean anything else about it. The recipe is for a drink that is effectively a cognac Manhattan topped with seltzer, and at the risk of sounding like a total boozehound, it's quite good so long as you omit the seltzer. Look, I'm not opposed to the stuff, but when you put it in a coupe glass, it goes flat so quickly and then you're just drinking a watery cognac Manhattan with a subtle hint of baking soda. I don't think that's what you want. This is why coupes are rarely used for champagne anymore: flutes keep the bubbles sprightly for much longer.

·   ·   ·

My impulse is to shove the sweatshirt back in the bag, but Hayley's taking it from me, It's so soft, she's saying, and then Casey's looking over, saying, I thought you went to Columbia, and Hayley says yeah but she's going to Harvard next year, and Casey says *smahht gahl* in the worst Boston accent I've ever heard, and I force a laugh, and my heart is thudding hard in my chest and I'm being ridiculous, I know, it's just a sweatshirt, it's a nice gesture from a woman who cares about me and is excited about my future, and if I'm going to have any feelings about it, they should be feelings of joy and gratitude and the good kind of anticipation, but it feels wrong here, out of place in this bar, in this borough. Like some kind of invasive species, cropping up where you least expect it, destroying everything if left unchecked.

Excuse me, I say, and I leave the sweatshirt with Hayley, and I go to the bathroom, which is one of those single-occupancy unisex ones, thank god, and I lock the door and I tie back my hair and I open my mouth as wide as I can and I reach two fingers back to my uvula, and it's so easy, after all this time it's still so easy, I wiggle my fingertips for a moment and my stomach seizes and I vomit neatly into the toilet, taste of wine and stomach acid and pappardelle, again, cheese and tiramisu, again, sweet, salty, bitter, again, acid and water, again, just to see, and then I spit, and I wipe the seat, and I flush, and I wash my hands twice, and I rinse my mouth out, and I wipe the corners of my lips, for obvious reasons, and I check my mascara, because throwing up makes your eyes water, and I rinse my mouth again and I flush again, just in case, and I wash my hands one last time, and I do all of this in a matter of minutes, a normal amount of time for a girl in a bar bathroom with nothing to hide, and I walk out feeling lighter, and brighter, and relaxed.

And then Paula is there, and she's congratulating me, too, and I explain that it's old news, that the acceptance came months before and the matriculation is still months off, but it's no use, and then Ben is there, and he's happy for me, too, even though I should have told him, even though everything is a secret with me, and I'm smiling and blushing and drinking my gin and tonic and my throat hurts, and my stomach hurts, and something, I know, is becoming real, and something else is ending.

SEELBACH

1 ounce bourbon
1/2 ounce Cointreau
5 dashes Angostura bitters
5 dashes Peychaud's bitters
sparkling wine

Build in a champagne flute and top with sparkling wine.
Garnish with an orange twist.

Once upon a time there was a sad high schooler in an idyllic
Californian suburb. She was sad for many reasons, general and specific;
that suburb was only really idyllic for the parents, and in her parents'
case, not even them. There is a horror movie to be made here, something
sinister lurking under the streets of that silicon paradise, clawing at the
fragile and the frightened, the unprotected and the unlucky. It reared up
behind our high schooler, nipping at her heels, another suicide cluster
her junior year, child after bright, hopeless child dead on the tracks.
Nobody she knew; by some inscrutable decree, death had taken only
students from the rival high school across town. Still of course it shook
everyone; still of course it shook her in particular. Imagine her waiting
for the train to San Francisco, backed as far away as possible from the
bright edge of the platform, not because she wanted to jump, or wanted
to die, but because some part of this felt bigger than she was. If every

inch of her life had been circumscribed for her thus far—and it had; that was how things worked in this suburb—then why not this?

But there was a promise of escape, out there on the horizon: Harvard University, those hallowed halls, the sprawling greens. Our high schooler knew that this was the answer, and when she received her rejection, that Thursday afternoon in spring with the sun bright and the caterpillars falling from the trees, she crumpled. She cut class, walked across the street to the mall where the stoners hung out, sat on a bench and wept for an afternoon. She was fine; nothing was as dire as it felt. But she was young, you understand, and she had pinned all her dreams on this.

And so six years later, our high schooler now a college graduate, a newly minted adult, her acceptance into this most vaunted institution felt like the solution to all her problems. Her life would have new meaning; her body would slim and lengthen, her boyfriend would love her again. And for a few weeks, for perhaps as long as a month, she was right.

Harvard, Ben says. I can't believe you're going to leave me for *Harvard*.

We're in his bed, morning light breaking across our bodies, groggy and a little hungover and ravenous in the aftermath of the holiday. There is a half-smile on Ben's face and a half-laugh in his voice, but there's betrayal, too, just underneath. It's not that far, I say. I'll come visit.

I won't, he says, because like every good New Yorker, he thinks Boston is a bullshit excuse for a city, and he doesn't see the point.

Well, technically it's just *outside* of Boston, I say, and Ben bursts out laughing. Jesus, he says, you're already talking like one of them. I swing a pillow at him, and he laughs into it, and then he rolls over and pins me to the mattress. I will miss this, I think, I know, and I am furious with myself.

And I wonder—Will I come visit? Will I really?

When Greg and I talked about it, I was so certain. We had a whole plan. I'd go home to him every break I got, he'd come out to Cambridge and work remotely for a week here and there, we'd meet for long weekends in New York, where Hayley was, or DC, where his high school best friend was, or Chicago, or wherever, it didn't actually matter where, as long as we were together.

With Ben it's different. But is it good different, or bad different? Is it different because New York is closer than California, or is it different because I'm not desperately in love with him?

You play things pretty close to the chest, don't you, Ben says. His eyes deep and gentle as they stare down into mine. I don't know what to say, except, well, *yes*.

By New Year's Eve, everybody knows. *Three men can keep a secret* and all that. Everybody knows, and Han, for his part, is not taking it well. An iciness between us, undeniable when I ask him about his holiday and he answers in monosyllables, and he stays firmly in his section whenever I approach the bar, talks more to Olsen than to me. We do Snaiquiris at eight, same as always, and you can really feel the tension then, the four of us in our little circle with our little shots. The Germans say that if you don't make eye contact during a toast, you will be cursed with seven years of bad sex. Han is the one who told me this, and yet he is the one who won't look at me as he knocks his glass against mine.

And so I keep my distance out on the floor, and Han busies himself with the bar. We have this regular who is both beloved and, quietly, famous. Grace Tomlin. She's a concert pianist, so it's not the kind of famous where everyone is stopping you for your autograph, but it is the kind of famous where one day your friendly neighborhood bartender opens up a copy of her roommate's *New Yorker* and there's a whole write-up about you, right there, at the start of the Music section. Grace is unfathomably kind, and funny, too, and whenever she wins an award or sells out a concert she comes in and buys a bottle of wine, generally of the sparkling variety, and she drinks a couple of glasses and gifts the remainder to whoever happens to be working that night. We would like her regardless, but this has endeared her to everyone forever. Tonight she is in with her mother, who is gray but still bubbly, and the family resemblance is strong, and they are sweet together, sitting very close and showing Han photos of the mother's dog, comparing their fresh matching manicures, taking sips of each other's cocktails. It is just as well that they're in Han's section, in the area of Joe's that is newly forbidden to me. I don't think I could bear it. I find them devastating to watch, even at a distance, because I miss my mother so acutely and because I know that even if she were alive, we would never be like that.

Grace Tomlin and her mother, Teresa and her adult daughter, one of the schoolteachers with what seems like his entire family—that's the sort of night we have, regulars and their loved ones. It never gets crazy, Joe's not being the most party-party of bars, but by quarter to twelve we have a full bar and a full back room, and Han and Carver are pouring out small servings of sparkling wine for everyone in the building, to get ready for the countdown.

You know how this goes. At the last minute you cut the music, and you hold up your glasses, and you start at ten and when you reach zero everybody yells *Happy New Year!* And you all clink glasses and if you're lucky, you kiss someone you like. And it's silly, the way we treat this arbitrary date as something special, the way we celebrate it with parties and resolutions, convinced that something will be different now, that somehow, something is being reset.

And yet, aren't I a hypocrite? Wasn't that the point of all those times in all those bathrooms? Scooping out my insides so that I might start afresh? As if the Sam that came out would be somehow different from the Sam that went in?

And yet, it's nice kissing Ben, who has arrived just in time, snagged the last remaining seat at the bar, in the cramped corner of Han's section, between the register and the door. And once the champagne flutes have been collected and washed and polished, I am released to go join him.

He gives me the barstool in spite of my protestations, stands behind me and a little to the side, and I do appreciate it, being able to sit down after a shift, but also having the heat of him there to counteract the chill coming off of Han. What are you drinking? Han asks me, and to anybody else it might sound perfectly normal, polite, attentive even. But I know Han too well.

I order a flash card cocktail, with the vague hope of impressing him, or at least softening him, or at least prompting him to tell me a story, because the drink I've ordered has a good one behind it. Han just nods, and turns away to take another order, and gets to work.

So I tell the story to Ben instead. Once upon a time in Louisiana, I tell him, a couple of newlyweds were staying at a lovely old hotel called the Seelbach. It's still there, though it's a Hilton now. This was before Prohibition, and the newlyweds were having a grand old time at the bar. He was drinking champagne, she was drinking whiskey cocktails. The bartender went to open a new bottle of champagne, but it had been shaken too much or it was not cold enough or perhaps it was something to do with the bottling, it doesn't matter, the point is, the cork goes flying off, miracle no one lost an eye, and sparkling wine starts overflowing. Our bartender grabs the nearest glass at hand, which happens to be the bride's cocktail, and so he ends up with something that is more or less a Manhattan with champagne in it. He's about to dump it out, but then he thinks, Hell, I'll drink it, and it turns out to be delicious. And so they name it after the hotel and put it on as the house drink for a glorious couple of years before the Volstead Act comes around and ruins everybody's fun.

That's not actually true, Han says. He sets my Seelbach down before me, fragrant and effervescent. Some guy made it up to sell more cocktails. He owned up to it a few years back.

This industry's full of liars.

One o'clock and the bar is still going, though it's clear things are winding down, Carver breaking down his side of the bar, checks down on a couple tables. Ben and I are finishing up, too, nursing a final round of bubbly, Ben's thumb tracing a circle over my hip bone, cash already on the bar, though Han is ignoring it. Is ignoring us. I have been trying to catch his eye for twenty minutes and he has been deeply engrossed in conversation with the schoolteacher, whom I know for a fact he doesn't even like.

I see my chance when he goes for a smoke break, trading his apron for his winter coat, cigarette in his hand before he even gets out the door. I squeeze Ben's shoulder and down the last of my bubbles and I go out after him. There are a couple chefs smoking outside already, and I return their smiles and their greetings, and then I turn on Han, walk over to where he's lighting up by the curb, get as close as I dare, stare up at him until he has to acknowledge me. Say his name. Say, This is too small a bar for us to not be talking to each other.

I'm talking to you now, he says, and I want to scream, I want to slap him across the face, I want to rip the cigarette out of his hand and stomp on it. I stare at him as he takes another drag. I hear congratulations are in order, he says. And then, something breaking: When were you going to tell me?

I haven't bothered to put on my jacket, and I'm freezing out here, and I cross my arms over my chest. It's not 'til September, I say. So presumably in like eight months.

Are you fucking kidding me? There is real venom in his voice, in a way there so rarely is. Han, happy-go-lucky, friends-with-everyone Han, is *furious*. He pulls on the cigarette again, hard. What am I spending all this time teaching you for? he asks. So you can make drinks for all your bougie little lawyer friends at your bougie little parties? Tell them stories from your fucking—bartender gap year?

He flicks the last of the cigarette into the gutter. I thought you were one of us, he says. But you're just a fucking tourist.

He walks inside, and I stare after him, speechless, motionless. Ben comes out with my coat and my bag, and he takes my frozen hand and leads me away. I clench my teeth to keep them from chattering and I don't say anything when Ben asks if I'm all right, I just nod, so quick and curt and thoroughly unconvincing that Ben starts laughing.

He'll get over it, he says, when we have descended into the warmth of his apartment. I don't really understand why he's so upset anyway.

He wanted a mentee, I say. If I'm not in it for the long haul, he has to find someone else.

Ben says nothing to this. He hangs up his coat, bends over to take off his shoes. I'm the one who should be upset, he says. You're my girlfriend.

He called me a tourist.

I mean, Ben says, and I look at him, feeling my jaw drop open, surely he can't *agree*? It's a little harsh, he says, reaching out to squeeze my shoulder in a way that is no doubt intended to soothe. But you can see where he's coming from, can't you?

I sleep badly, and I'm out early, leaving Ben groggy and disappointed and alone, power walking back to my own apartment. There is a gnawing in my gut I take for hunger, and I pad into the kitchen and pour a bowl from the box of off-brand honey nut cereal on top of the fridge. I wash a spoon, steal a splash of somebody's milk, and retreat to the relative safety of my bedroom.

I eat my cereal quickly and set the bowl aside, half a cup or so of sweet milk still at the bottom. The smoke detector beeps again and I throw myself back onto the mattress. *My bartending gap year.* It's actually a pretty good name for it. But just because there's an expiration date on it doesn't mean I'm not serious. I lie back on my mattress and I look up at the flash cards, which I have come to know so well, which I have begun to augment with other drinks from reputable websites and the ever-shifting stack of books beside my bed, some of which, I remember with an unpleasant jolt, I really need to return to Han.

A tourist wouldn't bother. A tourist would do what Olsen's doing, and get a mindless job in a Manhattan dive bar that makes her twice as much money. A tourist wouldn't put a drink on the menu, or fight for her own shift, or break Joe Himself out of his shell.

I get up for more not-Cheerios, and when I finish the second bowl I know that what I took for hunger has turned out to be the other thing, and now that I've started feeding that, stopping is all but impossible. Luckily there's not much left in the box, and when it's gone I feel bloated but not monstrous, and I drop the bowl into the full sink and walk into the bathroom, where I stand in front of the toilet and put my hands on my belly and remind myself in my therapist's words that purging is a tremendous act of violence against my body, and that I love my body. I cannot go back down this road. I take big deep gulps of air. I lift my T-shirt up and poke the tip of my index finger into the shallow, warm indent of my navel. It's okay, I say. I won't do it.

A year ago, in San Francisco, this same internal conversation over and over. Trying to talk myself out of my bad behavior at the supermarket, even as I picked out the junk food that would be easiest to bring back up.

I leave the apartment. I don't even change my clothes, just put my jacket back on and tug a hat down over my bed head and go out. Brooklyn is sleepy and hungover, and the café I like is closed for the day and so is the second place I try and by the time I get myself a coffee I'm in Fort Greene, and the morning is becoming beautiful, clear blue skies and not too cold, and so I keep walking. By Cobble Hill I'm sweating inside my winter coat.

There is a version of my affliction that manifests like this: exercise bulimia. *Orthorexia*: disordered eating dressed up as health and wellness. This is arguably the most common eating disorder these days. The one that people have quietly, people like Ben (not that I would ever dream of asking him about it). In this world in which we conflate wellness with virtue and virtue with weight. In Arizona our exercise was strictly monitored, confined to specific activities and specific times. But this has never been my particular problem; I'm too lazy, for one, and throwing up is a lot less *work*.

All of which is to say, I am not concerned when my walk stretches into its second hour. In another part of the world, with different scenery, you would just call this a hike, and no one would think you were weird. And if I'm walking, I'm not eating, and I'm not throwing up. I am in almost a fugue state by the time I reach the bridge, hardly realizing what I'm doing until I find myself at the first pillar, weaving around a knot of tourists, pausing to take in the view, Manhattan glittering and fantastical across the water, Brooklyn gleaming behind me, looking like home.

I'm listening to The Clash again, *the only band that matters*, their self-titled blaring in my headphones as I down the last of my coffee and look down at the water. The opening track, "Janie Jones," all about hating your boring job. Its sequel on the B side, "Career Opportunities," all about how every job you can get is boring. But these songs are for people with side dreams. Not for me.

The Girlfriends Club were happy for me, when my Harvard news came through. They said they were happy for me, anyway; some of them probably were. Vanessa Garfield, holding my hand across the table at some shiny new hipster beer garden in SoMa, after work on a Wednesday, our usual hump-day happy hour repurposed as a last-minute celebration. My little Elle Woods, Vanessa said.

I'm going to miss you guys so much, I said. I'm going to miss the city.

A couple of the Girlfriends laughed at that, which confused me and kind of offended me until Katie Richardson gathered herself and explained. Katie was the one girl at the table actually drinking beer, because Katie was one of those infuriating skinny people with a crazy metabolism, which we all resented her for, although we comforted ourselves with the fact that she had gone to UC Barbara (embarrassing) and worked, now, as a yoga instructor (unimaginable). I'm sorry, she said. It's just—Sam, you *hate* the city.

And everyone at the table nodded, and it's stupid, I mean in retrospect it was so obvious, but at the time, this was news to me. At the time, I was floored.

There is a cocktail for every borough in New York City except one—sorry, Staten Island, but don't act like you're surprised. The Manhattan is the most famous one, of course, and in fact I've never had a Brooklyn, because it requires an old *aperitif* called Amer Picon, which is impossible to get in the United States. Nearly impossible to get outside of France, in fact, and everyone will tell you that even the version you get there, in France I mean, is but a faded afterimage of what Amer Picon once was, before it disappeared during the cocktail dark ages. Han has a bottle of it in his apartment, the newer version I mean, 21 percent ABV and tasting of burnt orange and gentian, a gift from an old regular, and once upon a time he promised to bring some into Joe's and make me a proper Brooklyn with it, but now that's obviously never going to happen.

I hunch my shoulders against the wind, and I keep moving.

Hayley has suggested that the Brooklyn Bridge is more beautiful than the Golden Gate, and I neither agree nor disagree, although I cannot make this walk without thinking about San Francisco, imagining what it will be like there now, foggy and damp and yet somehow still in drought, the bridge rising up out of the bay brilliant and rust-colored. To keep it looking like that, the painters start at one end and by the time they finish, it is time to start again: endless circles of maintenance to keep it glowing no matter what happens. Job security, Hayley says, but I find the idea horrifying; apeirophobia all over again. I look out at the water and I think about that, the utter horror of forever, the endless march of days ahead, no respite in view, and I wonder if it's thoughts like these that are killing those kids in Palo Alto: the knowledge that while, okay, sure, junior year will not last forever, still there will be a year after that and after that and after that, and there is no guarantee that any of them will be any less unbearable.

There is another kind of jumper, too, and although no one in my circle has ever thrown themselves from a bridge, it is a common enough occurrence, dozens of people a year from the Golden Gate alone, well over a thousand since the bridge was built, enough that there are suicide nets now, enough that there are people whose job it is to patrol the bridge and talk people down, literally and figuratively. And there are the Golden Phones, telephones placed at strategic points along the bridge's span that connect you instantly to a hotline, where hopefully another person whose job it is to keep you alive will be able to help you, will convince you to go home, to give it one more day. When people do jump, which they do, and survive, which they do less often, they report an instantaneous regret, a realization just as they begin to fall that every problem in their life can be solved except for the fact that they have just jumped off a bridge. I wonder if anyone ever jumps just in search of this kind of clarity.

I lean against the railing now, my heart beating faster and harder in my chest. I've never been great with heights. The water gleams below, frigid, filthy, hard as concrete when you hit it from this far up. Imagine knowing exactly how to fix everything in your life, imagine being reborn like that, waking up in a coast guard boat or a hospital bed aching but saturated in gratitude, sick with it, having experienced a flash of such horrifying insight. Paired with the impossible humiliation of having jumped and survived.

.   .   .

I wonder about my mother, who swallowed a bottle full of pills on a Wednesday afternoon, in her studio, pale and silent and alone. Did she get that final moment of unknowable clarity? Or was it all a blur of Xanax and hydrocodone? Or was it like freezing to death, which they say feels just like falling asleep?

I shake myself free of the thought, and I back away from the railing, and I walk the rest of the way a little more quickly, a little farther from the edge.

AVIATION

2 ounces gin
3/4 ounce lemon juice
1/2 ounce maraschino liqueur
1/4 ounce crème de violette
1 dash simple syrup (optional)

Shake with ice and strain into a chilled coupe. Garnish with
a cherry.

January: gray and ugly, the infrequent snowfall turning almost instantly to mud, the sun gone before Joe's even opens in the evenings. Quiet again, maybe bar-closing quiet, although this is another seasonal thing. Although our Fridays stay reasonably busy, and our Saturdays uneven enough that we have to keep three bartenders on the roster just in case. I lose my Thursday night, though, almost immediately. There's no point having two bartenders on right now, Carver says, like I don't know that the real reason is Han. Han, who barely speaks to me now, and who, when he needs my attention, calls me *Law School* as often as he calls me *Sam*.

Switzerland, Meg says, when I try to get her to help me with her husband. I'm just here to drink mocktails and hang out. *Mocktails*: fancy nonalcoholic concoctions for people who are not drinking, whether because they are recovered alcoholics or religious abstainers or taking some time off the sauce or pregnant. Meg says she's just doing Dry January, but I wonder.

And either way it's fair enough, not drinking is fair enough, being Switzerland is fair enough, and I don't push her on either, no matter how desperately I may want to.

Once more, I become terrified of losing my job, what remains of my job, and I fall over myself attempting to prove myself useful. I polish all the bottles on the backbar every Sunday, I sanitize everything I can reach, I scrub out fridges and forgotten corners. I place holds on every single bartending book in the Brooklyn Public Library system, tramp my way over on my days off and sit in the tropical heat of my neighborhood branch with the men from the shelter on Marcus Garvey and the West Indian nannies, finding a corner where I can camp out and take notes.

I run into a regular there one Friday afternoon, Tonya, the older lady who has known Carver and Ben forever. I'm sitting at one of the big wooden tables and she taps my shoulder, smiles down at me. She's still wearing her jacket, one of those long puffy ones, and her arms are full of books, and she says it's nice to see me, and then something about how she's sorry she hasn't come to Joe's lately. Dry January, she says. Trying to give the old liver a bit of a break.

I ask her what she's checking out and she shows me—a fat biography of someone I've never heard of; something by Stephen King; a romance novel she's clearly embarrassed about. She nods at the book in front of me, the notebook beside it. What are you studying for?

I lift the book to show her. It's just for work, I say.

I see why he likes you, she says, and I think she means Ben, but no. She means Carver.

The book in question is another old one, or a reprinting of an old one anyway—*The Savoy Cocktail Book,* by Harry Craddock. The Savoy is a hotel in London, and for over a century it has been home to one of the world's most famous cocktail bars: The American Bar, where Craddock was head bartender. The book begins with the type of foreword I've come to expect, a sort of statement of purpose, an establishment of authority and intent, and then meanders into a frankly bizarre meditation on the origin of the word "cocktail," which, Harry Craddock posits, is a bastardization of the name of an Aztec princess. By the time I get to the recipes I'm smiling to myself, and I spend a pretty pleasant afternoon taking notes and making flash cards, and then I go home and get changed and go into work feeling like things are going to be okay.

It's eight o'clock and cold and clear, me picking my way across patches of ice on the sidewalk, stepping into a bar that is already packed, Carver and Han hard at work, and Olsen should be here, too, but he's not. He says he's sick, Carver reports, but we all know he's just been offered a shift at the Manhattan spot, which is an understandable financial decision, but nonetheless a dick move. A bar lesson: when you work in the service industry, you don't call in sick. There are a couple reasons for this. One is simply pride, resilience—what kind of wimp lets a little illness keep them home? More importantly, you don't, generally, qualify for paid sick days, and if you do, you're just getting paid minimum wage, a significant cut from what you would otherwise earn with tips. But perhaps most importantly, calling in sick if you don't absolutely have to is a dick move, because it means someone else will have to pick up your slack. Someone who thought they'd have some backup behind the bar will have to fly solo, sweating and stressing their way through a night that could have been fun, easy. Or someone who had plans will have to cancel them and come in to cover.

Is Gina coming in? I ask, hopefully, but she's not. Instead, coming through the door just after I do, we have my least favorite regular, whose real name I still don't know and at this point, refuse to learn: Darling.

I have never seen anyone so excited about a shift. He's practically glowing, grinning as wide as Han, his hair perfectly mussed, his T-shirt clean, and when he shrugs into one of the aprons, Carver catches my eye and I'm not sure what face, exactly, I make at him, but he has to duck behind the bar to hide his laughter. Hello, darling, Darling says, shaking my hand.

Darling falls immediately into the barbacking and the glassware, leaving me predictably on the floor, Gina's words bouncing angrily around inside my skull, boys are bartenders, chicks are waitresses. Still it makes me nauseous, literally sick to my stomach, watching him settle in so easily back there with the Dans.

.   .   .

On the bright side, seeing us this busy makes me marginally less concerned about my job. We're slammed until eleven, and then things begin
to slow down and we cut Darling and he sits in Han's section and orders—
say it with me—a daiquiri. He orders a daiquiri and he downs the whole
thing like a shot, and this is where any of the Dans would switch to beer
or straight whiskey; something simple, something you don't have to think
too hard about while you unwind. Darling, it seems, does not want to
unwind, and he looks at the menu and this is where a different bartender
would be polite and order a menu cocktail but he doesn't do this either,
he puts it down on the bar-top and asks Han for an Aviation.

This is not a total cocktail douchebag order, but it is definitely toward the willfully obscure end of the spectrum. It's a classic that, Carver
will tell you, people have been bastardizing for almost a century, starting
with our dear friend Harry Craddock in 1930, who took it upon himself
to take out the crème de violette. It's true that if you put too much violette in there, it tastes like soap. Carver will tell you just to use a barspoon
or a scant quarter ounce, just enough for a hint of flora and a tinge of
blue. You can add a dash of simple syrup, too: Han will, but Carver won't.

Darling sips merrily away and chats to Han and I catch snatches of their
conversation as I do my rounds to and from the bar, and I think about
how much I hate being a waitress and how when I'm done with law
school I will never have to do this ever again. How I will be able to work
relatively normal hours—nine to more-or-less five, Monday through
more-or-less Friday. How I will get health insurance and a 401(k) and
a paycheck that is not determined by things like the weather and how
much makeup I'm wearing and how effectively I've been sucking up to
my tables. How I will be able to wear impractical shoes, to paint my nails,
to wear my hair down.

My bartending gap year.

Meanwhile Darling is lifting the Aviation to his lips like it's the goddamn sacrament. Sipping like it's the elixir of life. Sometimes, he says,
you drink a cocktail and you think, these ingredients were made for one
another, even though logically they weren't, they were made in different

years, countries, by people who would have hated this adulteration, maybe. It's a sort of odd miracle when they fit together this well, something almost eerie about it. How did anyone ever think to put these things together? And what a tragedy if they hadn't.

Carver and I make eye contact over the bar, and I can see how hard he is working not to laugh, and this gives me strength. I do another round on the floor to gather myself, and I return to the bar with a tray full of dirty glasses, and Darling waves me over. Darling, he says. You have to try this.

He is holding the glass out to me, and I know he doesn't mean to be rude or condescending, or at least I don't think he does, and yet it takes every ounce of my self-control not to knock the drink out of his hand, and I do not have any self-control left over to stop me from saying, I know what a fucking Aviation tastes like.

Darling makes a big show of taking the drink back, and when I return to the floor he and Han start talking again, and I am almost certain they are talking about me.

We should give that kid a job, Han says, after Darling has stumbled off into the night. You know, when Olsen inevitably quits on us forever. He says nothing about what will happen when I go.

He has just finished himself, sat down with Mikey and Bob and a couple of the other chefs, accepted a Negroni from Carver. I stay on the opposite end of the bar by the glasswasher, polishing coupes with a lump in my throat. I imagine working with Darling every weekend, he and Han closer and closer, Han's books moving from my apartment to Darling's, me never allowed in the cockpit ever again, nobody even asking if I want to put something on the spring/summer menu, nobody testing me on wines and whiskeys, me just gradually fading away and then, in September, gone.

I don't know, Carver says. Has he bothered to learn Sam's name yet?

He knows Sam's name, Han says, and Carver says, Then why does he keep calling her fucking *darling*?

It's one o'clock in the morning and we're working on our close, me collecting candles and Carver cleaning the ice well, and I come back to the bar with my tray full of spent tea lights and Carver looks at me and says, You and Han need to make nice.

Excuse me?

I've accepted that he and Olsen are never going to be best friends, he says. But I can't have half my team not talking to each other.

He's being unreasonable, I say, and Carver looks up.

Absolutely, he says, and I am a little surprised. I love Han, he says, but he can be a petty motherfucker. Which means fixing this is going to be on you.

Sometimes when you finish a shift you want to collapse into bed and sometimes you are too wired, the energy of the night still pulsing through you, and this is why everyone goes to Casey's for nightcaps after work, and this is why Carver and I go there now, and why when we get there, Olsen is sitting at the bar, sheepish when we walk in, Carver punching him in the bicep and asking him how he's feeling.

Casey's bar is dying down, peopled at this hour with the service in-dustry crowd and a small, mostly drunken contingent of daywalkers. Ben is among these, on the other side of Olsen, a little drunk him-self after a friend's house party. JD's place, he says, which clearly means something to Carver, although the truth is I've only met one of Ben's friends, a beefy Black guy named Troy who came into Joe's one night in December, and whom I didn't have much time to chat to.

Wait, why have I only met one of Ben's friends? Should I be worried about that? I mean, sure, he's only met one of my friends, but I only *have* one friend, so it's not really the same. Is he keeping me out of his life? Or am I keeping him out of mine? I knew all of Greg's friends. I didn't like them, but I knew them. I made sure I knew them. Shouldn't I be doing the same now?

I spot Paula then, on the other side of the bar, and excuse myself to say hi to her. She greets me a little too enthusiastically, because she, too, has had a little too much to drink. I don't mind. Sam, she says. Fuck, marry, kill: Han, Luke, Leia.

Casey says, Anyone who wouldn't kill Luke and marry Leia can get the fuck out of my bar right now. She squeezes my hand over the bar, asks if she can get me anything. Just a whiskey, I tell her.

Fair, Paula says. Even I would fuck Han Solo. No one's *that* gay.

I accept my whiskey, clink my glass against Paula's and Casey's. Okay, Paula says, wiping her mouth. What about, Han, Carver, Olsen.

Oh, no. Oh, no no no. It's no fun when it's real people, I say, but Paula disagrees. It's the *most* fun when it's real people, she says.

Two of them are *here*, Paula. But this doesn't dissuade her, either. I think I'd marry Han, she says. And kill Olsen.

And fuck your girlfriend's ex-boyfriend.

Paula shrugs. She'd get over it, she says. Casey?

I guess I'd kill Olsen, too, she says.

I'm sorry, Olsen says, *what*?

Our conversation has summoned them, I think, or else they were just wondering where I went, but at any rate, here they are, Olsen and Carver and my boyfriend. Casey has the decency to look mildly horrified, but Paula is drunkenly unfazed. Just playing fuck, marry, kill, she says. I wouldn't take it to heart.

I don't love that Casey wants to kill me, Olsen says. Who's she marrying?

Carver, of course, Casey says, and Carver blows her a kiss over the bar.

And fucking Sam?

I wish, Casey says. She wasn't on the menu.

Han, Paula explains.

What did Sam say? Olsen asks.

Oh, no, I say. I'm not answering that. You're all my work husbands and I'm claiming spousal privilege.

Ben takes my hand, squeezes. Good answer, he says, and I lift our linked hands up to my mouth and kiss his knuckles. And that could have been the end of it, should have been the end of it, but Olsen has to go and ruin everything, saying, Well, she's already fucked me.

It's early afternoon and I'm walking to Ben's apartment on leaden feet, steeling myself to apologize. If he were a woman I would bring him flowers, I have seen this in movies, although I have never experienced this myself, because no man has every apologized to me for anything. I pick up whisky instead, Laphroaig, not his favorite but the best Scotch I can find in the immediate vicinity, and I hold up the bottle when he opens the door, still in his pajamas, smiling but not happy to see me. He doesn't kiss me when I walk in and he doesn't take the Scotch and I stand there in his kitchen scrabbling for words.

I tell him I'm sorry, first and foremost. I put the Laphroaig down on the kitchen island, and I tell him that I'm sorry, and that he has nothing to worry about, because there is no longer anything between Olsen and me. It was five years ago, I say.

Ben sighs. I know, he says. Olsen told me, after you ran off last night. He felt bad about it.

Oh. I am minutely less furious with Olsen.

Ben continues. But, Sam, for this to work, he says, you're going to have to occasionally *tell* me things.

This is, I have to admit, a fair point. I think we can all agree that I could be a little more forthcoming, in general. But I don't think it's all on me. I like Ben, I like him so much, but sometimes it feels like all our conversations are stuck on the surface. Sometimes it feels like all we talk about is taste, our shared loves of smoky Scotch and outdated indie-rock and N. K. Jemisin, our mutual fondness for *Community* and black coffee and a really good martini. Sometimes it feels like taste is the only thing keeping us together.

But then, maybe that's not the worst foundation for a relationship.

I want it to work, I say, and he kisses me, finally, and he goes for glasses, and pours us each some Scotch.

I begin with the matter of Dan Olsen. I didn't tell you because it's so embarrassing, I say. I was a drunk, twenty-year-old idiot who'd never gotten to do anything fun in her entire life, and I went a little crazy.

I'm sorry, Ben says, didn't you grow up in *Palo Alto*? They don't have fun there?

Yes and no, I say, and then I have to tell him about Palo Alto, what it does to children. What it did to my mother. We're both quiet for a minute after that. The Laphroaig tastes like pepper and bacon and it smells like gasoline and for some reason people still like it and for some reason I have become one of those people.

We weren't allowed outside, Ben says. Bed-Stuy in the nineties, two little Black boys in the murder capital of the country.

It's hard for me to imagine, I say, and Ben touches my shoulder, and says, It's impossible for you to imagine.

But Ben loves Bed-Stuy in a way I could not possibly love Palo Alto. I could never go back to that town and I would be absolutely fine. Ben's never even *left*.

It's *home*, he says, and I feel a sharp pang of envy. I would like to feel that way about somewhere. Even in the good San Francisco year, I never really put down roots.

I feel bad complaining to you about Palo Alto, I say.

You should. He's smiling, but I can tell he's not really joking. You've had a cushy fucking life, Sam, he says. It sucks about your mom, though. And he kisses me, and I'm annoyed, but I also know he's right.

We get a little drunk, day-drunk, sitting there in his kitchen, and we talk. I tell Ben about my STEM thing, and about my Harvard thing, and, haltingly, about the things that drove me out of San Francisco—Greg, the Girlfriends Club, Jackie's firm. Skirting around the matter of my Martini Soul Mate, around the bulimia. One big terrible secret at a time. He tells me about growing up in his older brother's shadow, about a broken engagement when he was twenty-three, about burying his favorite cousin at twenty-five. About racing through his BA and his MBA only to end up stuck in the same job for years and years.

We talk and we talk and then suddenly it's evening and I remember that I have to go to work, and Ben makes me coffee and feeds me bread in hopes of sobering me up, and it more or less works, I mean I wouldn't drive a car like this but I'll manage at Joe's just fine, and he walks me over, stands with me out front, the sidewalk busy and golden light streaming out through the big windows. Han is inside, but he won't be able to see us, and we linger by the door, and Ben kisses me, and then he hugs me, and I press as close into him as I can. This was good, I say. Right?

I feel like I know you marginally better than I did twenty-four hours ago, he says, and he kisses me again, and squeezes my frozen hands in his inexplicably warm ones, and tells me to have a good shift.

You're not coming in?

And watch you and Han be all weird and mean to each other? Not tonight.

So I go in alone, the bar still quiet, Han behind it talking to Tonya and Lacey, Joe Himself in his usual place with his usual book. Han gives me his fakest smile and I give him one of my own and then I turn my attention to Joe Himself, who knows nothing about the secrets I'm keeping and the secrets I'm failing, increasingly, to keep, who is simply happy to be here, with his Willett neat and his book and his seat at the bar. And me, I think we can agree that he is happy to see me.

Our next guest is Teresa, another easy one, and she comes over, takes the seat next to Joe Himself, and Han swoops in with a water and a glass of pinot, and he sparkles down at her, and I would give anything to have him sparkle like that at me. And then he's gone again, laughing at something Lacey's said, leaving a vacuum in his wake, and I'm standing there with nothing to do, and Teresa takes out her e-reader and Himself opens his book and if I don't say something now I won't ever say anything again, and so I make a frail attempt at a joke, something about the Joe's Apothecary Book Club, and Teresa does me the great kindness of laughing.

Joe Himself looks pleased and embarrassed. I'm sure Teresa has much more sophisticated taste than I do.

Teresa reaches for Himself's current paperback, a detective novel by an author I've never heard of. I've been known to enjoy a mystery from time to time, Teresa says. I can't tell if she's being generous or sincere. She lifts her glass to her lips. When I was little, she says, I read every Agatha Christie book in the Cleveland library.

I love Agatha Christie, Joe Himself says, and they fall into conversation, and I feel like I've done something right.

It is a comfort to me, too, this bar. Even when Han is being a dick to me, even when I'm not making nearly enough money—on a Saturday night, no less—even when I know that Olsen will be here any minute and I would rather die than have to speak to Olsen right now.

But I don't have to speak to him, because when Olsen comes in, he gives me the same tight smile Han does, and he takes over the glass-washer, and I leave Himself and Teresa, and I leave the Dans, and I tend to the floor, and I try not to let it bother me that Han and Olsen are talking and laughing together behind the bar, which they never do, and I try not to let it bother me that we don't have Snaiquiris, and I try not to let it bother me that Han cuts me at ten o'clock, a paltry four hours, and I hang up my apron and I go back to my apartment without even a shot for the road, without even a goodbye, and when I get home I go to the pantry and cook myself a box of mac and cheese, and I eat all of it, and I still feel empty, so I follow it with half a sleeve of Oreos, and I still feel empty, so I eat the rest, and then I feel terrible, and I go to the bathroom, and I bring it all up.

As usual, the relief is followed quickly by regret. Is this a relapse? Am I having a relapse? It has been almost exactly a year since I went to rehab, and maybe that's what this is, the anniversary, the way the body remembers dates even when the mind doesn't, the way every July is heavy with the echo of my mother's death.

A year ago: after the burst blood vessel incident, things moved pretty quickly. Greg called my father, my father called several different rehabilitation centers, each of those centers called me. I had long conversations about my disorder, interviews in which I attempted to portray myself as bad but not that bad. I was ambivalent about the idea of rehab; on the one hand it seemed like something that existed for other people, people with real problems; but at the same time, I knew I needed help. And then there was that inane voice at the back of my head saying that Greg would want me back afterward.

My father and I chose a center, and I flew out to Arizona, and he drove me there, the tensest car ride of all time. I was making absurd attempts at small talk—how's Diane, how's work, are you still liking Tucson? He had no idea what to say to me. He hasn't known what to say to me since my mother died. And he never knew what to say to *her*, either. When he dropped me off, handed me over to a nurse and some sort of administrator, he cried, and I told him I was going to be all right, and I meant it. Your father's very sweet, the nurse said, and I agreed with her, and they gave me a quick tour of the building, the rec room, the dining hall, the various smaller spaces for group and individual therapy. Introduced me to everyone we passed, the staff welcoming me with gentle, pitying smiles, the residents mostly just staring at me. They took me to my shared bedroom, where I dropped what little I had brought with me, and to the shared bathrooms, where the nurse waited just outside the stall as I peed.

And then they took me to the doctor, who weighed me and checked all my vitals and took a blood sample, and to the therapist, who grilled me for over an hour, and then treatment began in earnest.

Two months. Two months of my life in that strange country, what felt like an age, what felt like no time at all. Most girls stayed longer, I told Hayley after I got out, and she laughed, affectionately, and said, Leave it to you to be an overachiever in *rehab*. The truth is I was well suited to that place. I mean, it wasn't fun, it wasn't a vacation, but I liked the structure, liked that I could just eat what I was fed and do what I was told.

And it worked. Most importantly, it worked. I didn't throw up the whole time I was there. I stopped purging the minute I boarded that plane to Arizona, and I told myself that was the end, that I knew better, that I was too smart to do something so stupid to my body, that I had not been put on this earth simply to be as skinny as possible, no matter what bad lessons I'd learned from Julia Roberts or *Vogue* or the Girlfriends Club. I wanted to get better. I wanted to get better and get back to my life and get back, one way or another, to Greg.

Lying in Corpse Pose after yoga as Blue led us on a meditation, led us through each piece of our bodies: send gratitude to your fingertips, to your wrists, to your elbows. Imagine a golden light pulsing through. Send gratitude to your shoulders, to your collarbones, to your solar plexus. One of the anorexics crying quietly on the mat to my right. To your navel, to your pelvis, to your thighs. Me with my eyes closed, trying so hard. To your knees, to your calves, to your ankles. To your toes and the bottoms of your feet.

This is your body, Blue said. This is your only body, and you have to take care of it.

And I promised that I would. And I really thought I meant it.

CHAMPS-ÉLYSÉES

2 ounces cognac
1/2 ounce green Chartreuse
3/4 ounce lemon juice
1/4 ounce simple syrup

Shake with ice and strain into a chilled coupe. Garnish with
a lemon twist.

I think I'm going to start looking for another job, I tell Hayley.
We're on our way to Gina's bar, meeting up at the subway station,
because Hayley is avoiding her apartment, because Tyler is in the process
of moving out. What happened? I ask, and she gives me this look, like,
what kind of a stupid question is that? And I understand, and I should
know better. When people ask what happened with me and Greg—and
they do ask, still, every now and again; Jackie, Hayley's NYU friends, the
occasional Columbia acquaintance—when they ask I want to scream, or
weep, or else smile as wide as I can and say, It ended happily, can't you
see, we're married, shacked up in Park Slope with all the other happy
couples. Kids with names like Mason and Arugula. *What happened?* It
went well until it didn't. *What happened?* He broke my heart, and then
I broke his, and then I left California forever. *What happened?* I am
biologically incapable of experiencing love. I am missing a line of coding

in my DNA, suffer from some mutation that does not allow me to be in a relationship like a normal person.

What happened? When I was twelve years old my mother killed herself, leaving me to grow up in a quiet, bitter house, sad and angry and alone and with no idea how *love* is supposed to work.

Aboveground it is cold and black and beginning to snow. It has hardly snowed all winter—thanks, climate change—but it's thickening by the second, fat wet flakes melting on our noses, clinging to the sleeves of our jackets. The same thing that always happens, Hayley says, I guess. It wasn't working.

But she doesn't want to talk about it, she wants to talk about Joe's, which is at present just shy of totally unbearable. Here is the thing about bartending: it's hard work. Physically, emotionally, mentally. If it weren't also fun, no one would stick with it. Not if you didn't have to, not if you could go do something practical for the same amount of money, if not more. This past Friday at Joe's I tracked ten thousand steps, all in the limited area of the bar, the back room, up and down the stairs into the basement. Ten thousand steps!

You're tracking your steps again?

That's really not the point. Ten thousand steps and smiling until my face hurt and carrying drinks and glasses and remembering orders and being as charming as humanly possible and not having time to eat or drink water or even pee until after midnight. All of that and then having to clean every square inch of the bar at one o'clock, two o'clock in the morning.

All of which is worth it, when it's worth it. When you're introducing someone to their new favorite whiskey, when you're chatting to people who you genuinely like, when you're mixing up cocktails. When you're talking shit and cracking jokes and taking shots with the Dans, these coworkers who have become your closest friends.

Except that now they're not. Han, furious. Olsen, embarrassed. Carver, inscrutable. So now I'm just a waitress at a bar where I don't feel comfortable, and so it's just a job, and it's a job where I'm not making much money.

Maybe I'll call your mom, I say. See if she knows anyone who needs a paralegal for the next six months.

Oh my god, Hayley says. You are such a fucking *quitter*.

Excuse me?

We're turning the corner, leaving the busy avenue, Gina's bar half a block away. Me with my shoulders hunched and my hands shoved as deep into my pockets as they'll go. Hayley walking half a step ahead of me, telling me a story.

Once upon a time there were two little girls in an elementary school music class. In fourth grade they got to choose between strings and winds; they both chose strings, because they were prettier. Got their tiny half-size violins and their tiny horsehair bows and drove their parents to distraction with their screechy practicing. Two years of this and then it was off to middle school, where they muddled their way through school orchestra, graduating to full-size instruments and Tchaikovsky, and then one pubescent autumn, one little girl auditioned for a city-wide youth orchestra, and one little girl took a visual art elective instead and stopped playing entirely.

But that's hardly admissible evidence, because, as I remind Hayley, I was an *awful* violinist.

So was I, she says.

You were in that city orchestra.

I was a *third* violin, she says. The *only* third violin. I had to sit in the corner with the *violas* and play the easiest parts they could give me.

She mounts her case. Violin, first, and then guitar, and then photography, and then cross-country—another thing we had done together, another thing Hayley was always better at than I was—and then my math degree, and then Greg.

I didn't *quit* Greg.

Look, you know I think he's the worst person I've ever met in my entire life, she says. But he's not the one who started fucking somebody else when things went sour.

But that's not fair. He quit me first.

Hayley throws her hands up. Okay, she says. Okay. Not Greg. But you can't say there's not a pattern here.

. . .

We walk into the bar, already half-full with the afterwork crowd, claim a couple of barstools, start taking off our outer layers. So you're saying you don't think I should get an office job.

An *office* job, Gina says. Good god, *why*?

I don't know how to answer. I hear Carver's words in my head, *no more bitching about me to Gina*, and I feel like that applies to all of the Dans, to the entirety of Joe's. It's all right for you, I say, gesturing around at the room. You're doing this.

You could do this, she says, and I laugh and she says, Of course you could. Get a gig at a bar with a name, do that for a couple of years, move up from there. I could introduce you to some people. Carver would put in a good word for you anywhere you wanted to work. And after that it's really just about persistence.

I think about Mikey saying, *to be a chef you just have to last*. An oversimplification then, and an oversimplification now. Persistence and raw natural talent, I say, and she waves her hand and says, Less important.

I'm not a career bartender, I tell her, and she says, Not with that attitude.

Of course I've imagined it, idly, imagined scrapping everything and just doing this forever. Can you do this forever? I have a vision of myself bent and gray behind a bar, and it's true that I have seen old-timers like this, wrinkled and majestic, but they are memorable mostly for their rarity, and you wonder: the body must begin to fail. Already I feel it after a long shift, my legs and my arms and my back, the physicality of the work undeniable, perhaps unsustainable. Where do the old bartenders go? The good ones, I suppose—the lucky ones, the persistent ones—go into the less physical side of things, work for liquor companies, distributors, buyers. Own or manage or consult.

But what jobs do take care of their old? The oldest partners at the firm in San Francisco were always barely hanging on, it seemed, clinging to the ledge, junior partners stomping on their fingers. Derided behind their backs. And certainly everyone Greg worked with was young. The old punk mantra: *don't trust anyone over thirty*.

.   .   .

We ask for dealer's choice, which yields a hot toddy for Hayley and something called a Champs-Élysées for me. Cognac and lemon and green Chartreuse. I had never tried Chartreuse until Joe's, which Han found outrageous, maybe even offensive. A snobby bartender thing, this obsession with Chartreuse, the collecting of vintage bottles, the devotion to this strange, sweet, strong liqueur, spring green and tasting of brown sugar and fennel and pine nuts. A snobby bartender thing that I am not entirely above: it is like absolutely nothing else on the planet.

And, of course, there is a good story behind it. Once upon a time, Han will tell you, if he's speaking to you, a great scholar turned his back on his fame and success and worldly possessions and moved into the Chartreuse Mountains for a life of Christian asceticism. He founded an order of monks that would last for centuries, that to this day is one of the oldest in the world. Many years after our scholar's death, his order received an ancient manuscript containing a recipe for an elixir of alcohol and herbs, a mysterious recipe that would take the monks more than a hundred years to unravel. The first obstacle: they couldn't make any sense of it. When they did, at last, the monks went on to produce this Elixir of Long Life, as it was then known, from their seat at Grande Chartreuse. Its recipe a closely guarded secret, known only to a trusted few.

The liqueur grew popular, first for its medicinal properties and soon after for its recreational ones. A familiar story. Then came the French Revolution (obstacle number two), the monks kicked out of the country, one sole copy of the recipe smuggled out of the Bastille, kept secret and safe by a friend of the order. Sold to a trusted pharmacist. Then the third obstacle when Napoleon called for all secret medicinal recipes, and the pharmacist had to give it up. A lucky break: the recipe was returned to sender, deemed *not secret enough*. And after the pharmacist's death, returned to the monks, who had by then been reinstated and began to produce the liqueur once more.

Not quite happily ever after, not yet. The fourth obstacle: the distillery was seized by the government, nationalized, the monks once more expelled. Until the government-operated distillery went bankrupt and friends of our monks bought it up and reinstated the Carthusians. Back to business as usual. Interrupted by one final obstacle, a devastating landslide, but the distillery's next location has thus far stuck, and we are all blessed with the unique beauty of Chartreuse.

Persistence. Right.

The bar fills up further as the evening deepens; the snow is still falling, all the people with real jobs will have snow days tomorrow, which means they are all out getting drunk. And Gina's good, not to mention basically unflappable, but I can see how the glasses are piling up, the sweat sheen on her forehead. Usually, Wednesdays are pretty chill, but sometimes everybody in the neighborhood wants to go out at exactly the same time. Hayley and I finish our cocktails, but Gina doesn't have time to even look at us. And I hate being here when it's so busy, I feel like I should be working, and after a couple minutes I get up, and I work.

I clear glasses first; this feels like an unobtrusive move, something that Gina cannot protest. I am not saying this is a thing you should do in a busy bar; nine times out of ten, you shouldn't. Ninety-nine times out of one hundred. As thoughtful as it may seem, it is also presumptuous, it also suggests that you think the bartender is not doing a sufficient job. Which, maybe they're not, but you don't have to make them feel *bad* about it. However, I know Gina, and technically I work for Gina, and so I feel okay about this, and when I deliver the dirties she flashes me a grateful grin and I say, Can I help?

She hesitates, and then the door opens again, the bar now standing room only, and she nods. Glasses and ice, she says, and I get on it.

Everyone in Williamsburg is out drinking tonight, and everyone who can fit is in this bar. I promise Hayley that I'll call her, and that I'll take care of her drink, and she blows us kisses and gets out, her seat at the bar taken immediately. There's no hope of table service—it's hard enough to get out to the floor for dirty glasses; it would take a much more graceful waitress than me to get out there with full ones. Instead Gina pounds out round after round from the bar, cocktails and wine and beer. She holds dozens of orders in her magnificent head, she is quick and efficient and yet remains, always, charming. I feed off of her, and find myself becoming quick and efficient and charming, too.

·   ·   ·

Where's Raph? I ask, when it occurs to me to ask, bringing yet another bucket of ice for the dwindling well. Raph, Gina's customary barback, a sweet guy about my age, short and stocky with a winning smile and an even more winning Venezuelan accent. Gina shakes her head. He had a comp tonight, she says.

Cocktail competition: an event pitting various professional bartenders against each other, to be judged on the quality and creativity of the drink or drinks they've submitted. There are hundreds of these every year, sponsored by liquor brands and conglomerates, with distinct rules and requirements; the winners can receive anything from a cash prize to a trip to Europe to a job as a rep. Gina's win netted her the funds to open Joe's, although that level of life-changing success, she explains, almost apologetically, is rare.

I didn't think it would be a problem, she says. Most Wednesdays I end up clocking out by eight and letting him run the place.

Not this Wednesday. I stay until the end. Gina does last call at twelve thirty and I clean the bar as she restocks, and when she is done restocking she pours me a large whiskey and she orders me to sit down as she finishes up. You want to come work here? she asks, grinning at me as she drags the last of the mats toward the door.

Seriously, though, she says. Don't quit. You made it through January, things are going to get better.

It just sucks, I say.

I worked with Carver *while* we were breaking up, she says. You don't have to tell me.

How did you guys not murder each other?

We came close, she says, which I sense is a joke that is not wholly a joke. But at the end of the day, we both wanted Joe's to succeed, and as long as we stayed focused on *that*, and never, ever got drunk together, we made it through.

I want Joe's to succeed.

Don't tell me that, she says. Tell *Han*.

Easier said than done. I go to see him on Thursday, which of course once was our night together. Go early, to catch him before he gets busy. A bar lesson: the kindest thing you, a guest, can do for your bartender, is not show up right when they open. I mean, okay, the kindest thing you can do is tip well, but. Sure, there are bars like Timothy's with big names and long waits, and these places expect you at 6:00 P.M. on the dot, but anywhere else. Give it five or ten minutes. Let the bartender catch their breath after their open, sit down and have a snack maybe, finish up whatever it is they couldn't quite get to in the hour they had to set up the entire bar. There's no rule about this; once the bar's open, the bar's open. But it's *nice*.

So I get there ten minutes after opening time, and I'm still the first guest, and Han turns his enormous fishbowl grin on me for a brief, dazzling second before he realizes who he's smiling at and puts it away and just says, Oh.

Hey, Han. He's in the prep kitchen and I walk over, stand just outside. There's something simmering on the little hot plate we use for making syrups, scent of thyme and blackberries. I don't know what to do with my hands. I'd considered picking up some Scotch on my way here, seeing as that seemed to help with Ben, but I decided against it. I wish I had, now.

What are you making?

Just something for the new menu.

I didn't know we were working on that already, I say.

We're not, he answers. He's watching his syrup with what feels like an undue degree of focus. Carver and I are just starting to toss ideas around.

I'm not gone yet, Han.

He looks up then, and my heart's pounding, and my stomach hurts, and his expression is more tired than angry, and that almost feels worse. He opens his mouth, and I steel myself, and then his eyes flicker to the bar. I've got guests, he says, and I look over, and it's the schoolteachers.

I can watch this for you, I say, but he shakes his head. Turns it off. Can I do something for you, Sam? he asks, and everything I wanted to say to him slips through my fingers.

How do I tell Han how I feel if he won't talk to me? This is the question. I worry it like something stuck between my teeth, pick at it like a scab. I am my most charming self on Friday and Saturday, talk and joke loudly with my tables, sell the more adventurous guests on unusual flash card cocktails to catch Han's attention. Tell Han's stories.

There is this regular we all love to hate, a finance bro with a clean, close haircut and a clean, close shave and a different, equally nice suit every time I see him. Reid. A Patrick Bateman type if I've ever seen one. All he does is go to work in FiDi, go to the gym, and get prodigiously fucked up in his free time. He comes in and talks about trading like any of us at Joe's has two stocks to rub together. He'll bring in the worst kind of New York girls on dates, painfully skinny girls with no opinions on anything, with pancake makeup and strict diets of ice cubes and vodka-sodas. He reminds me of my life in San Francisco, hardly a selling point, but I do understand him, and with the help of Fishbowl Sam I don't mind talking to him, and the other thing is, he's actually a pretty nice guy, underneath everything. He's polite, and patient, knows all our names, asks how we are and really seems to care about the answer. Plus, he's an excellent tipper.

And so as a rule the Dans leave him to me, even when he's sitting at the bar, and tonight he's technically in Han's section but I'm standing there with a tray in my hand talking him up, and I can feel Han listening in. *Bartender ears*: an almost supernatural ability to hear anything that pertains to you, the bartender, even in a crowded room, even when you're deep in conversation with someone else. So I talk Reid into getting the Breakfast of Champions, the one mark I've left on this bar so far, and I'm hoping when he asks Han for it Han will remember, for a moment, that I do care. That I have been trying.

This is a good drink, Reid says, and Han says, Thanks, that's one of mine.

Maybe you *should* just hire Darling, I say. It's Carver and me closing up, my head pounding and my stomach growling because I was too anxious to eat when the Dans ordered takeout, which of course I now regret. Carver gives me a look uncannily similar to the one Hayley gave me on Wednesday, exasperated and mildly annoyed. I'm not going to hire *Darling*, he says. One Han is already more than enough.

This cheers me a little, but not enough. I'm cleaning the bar-top, scrubbing at the spattered bitters and the sticky spots and the general dross of the weekend, of the years. You'll have to hire *someone*, I say. When I go.

September? Carver asks, and I nod. A lot can happen between now and September, he says, and something in his tone makes me pause. He's standing at the POS, counting out the night's takings, and when he's done counting he reaches up for glasses and pours two generous servings of Teresa's pinot. Hands one to me. Rent's going up, he says, and I feel like the bottom's fallen out of me, I feel like something inside of me is caving in.

Fucking gentrification, he says. And this is not directed at me, not exactly, but I am part of the problem and I know it.

I drink too much of the wine. Plum, blackberry, mushroom, lingering, I can understand why Teresa likes it. Carver's counting the drawer now and the silence is spreading like a spilled drink and when I speak my voice sounds strange, wrong, out of place. Fucking New York City landlords, I say, and Carver nods his agreement.

Because the history of New York is the history of scumbag landlords. They have been here as long as the cockroaches and they will last in the same way, not caring that the world would like to stomp them out, self-assured and complacent inside their exoskeletal superiority. Look at my apartment now: three weeks of silence and then a different smoke detector started beeping, and meanwhile we're paying a collective four grand a month for the privilege. Look at Carver himself, with a good steady job and a master's degree, and still he's been priced out of the neighborhood of his birth, rents rising astronomically while our wages stay pretty much stagnant. And then bars and restaurants get it as bad as anybody; maybe worse. Carver, I say, are we going to close?

I really hope not.

We finish the close in silence and then we sit down at the bar with the rest of the pinot, Joe's quiet and clean and too bright, and somehow we've started talking about tattoos, Carver's, I mean, because I still do not have any, because my body is not ready. We've been through this. But you've thought about it, he says, and I say Yeah, I mean of course I have. You'd look good with a sleeve, he says, and he recommends Oliver, one of the tattoo regulars, says he'd take good care of me. How long would something like that take? I ask, and Carver pulls up a shirtsleeve to display the full glory of his left arm and says, This one was maybe fifteen hours total, but it depends on your artist and your design and how long you can sit at once.

Did it hurt? I ask, feeling stupid again, but Carver drops the shirt-sleeve and reaches for his wine and says, Of course it hurt. People with tattoos love to tell you that it doesn't, but it does. It's just . . . it's not bad pain, if that makes sense. And I think it does. And it varies, he says, setting his glass down again. Like, here, he says, touching my bicep, where there's more flesh, it's not so bad. But here—he brushes the bony part of my forearm—this is worse. And here—the nub of my elbow—that's the worst of all. Like, maybe leave that blank when you get your sleeve.

The moment breaks. I guess lawyers probably can't get that much ink, though, he says. He takes his hand away, sips his wine as if I am not still feeling the ghosts of his fingertips electric on my skin, and I think that no tattoo needle could burn like that, and I drink my wine, and I think maybe I would want a tattoo to commemorate this time in my life, to mark myself as not only a lawyer, to link myself cosmically, artistically to Carver forever.

Don't say anything to the guys, he says. We're outside, snow amber and glittering in the light of the streetlamp, my body tingling with something more than the cold. For a moment I don't know what he means, but he's talking about the lease, of course, the lease. I mime zipping my mouth shut. Carver checks his phone. Bus in five, he says. Are you okay to get home?

There is an evil part of me that wants to say *no*, that wants him to put his arm around me and walk with me and come in for a nightcap and—I snap myself out of it. Go catch your bus, I tell him, and he hugs me, which I don't think he's ever done before, and I power walk home with my breath shallow and my body light, and maybe I do have a bartender fetish, and maybe I am missing a line of code in my DNA, and maybe I am a terrible person and a slut, just like Greg said.

And when I get home I make myself ramen, eat it alone in my dark, beeping kitchen, burning my tongue and my throat and not caring, and when I am done with it I go back to the pantry and I eat a bar of chocolate that is not mine and I drink a large glass of bourbon that I do not need and neither of these things makes me feel any better, so I put some more liquor on the wound, and when I wake up in the morning I feel like I have been eating art supplies: newsprint, perhaps; chalk; turpentine.

CORPSE REVIVER #2

3/4 ounce gin
3/4 ounce Cointreau
3/4 ounce Lillet Blanc
3/4 ounce lemon juice
absinthe

Rinse a chilled coupe glass with absinthe. Shake other
ingredients with ice, then strain into the prepared coupe.
Garnish with a cherry.

I don't quit. *A lot can happen between now and September.* I
can ride it out a little longer. I don't say anything to the Dans about the
lease, or to Ben. I don't say anything about the awful gnawing hunger I
feel, now, newly, around Carver, not to anyone, not even to Hayley, not
even to my therapist. I certainly don't say anything about the purges,
the awful slide back into my bad habits, although sometimes I want
to, sometimes the guilt of keeping this from Hayley makes me want to
scream.

I spend my nights at Ben's more often than not instead, trying to
keep myself distracted. He is happy to help. Happy to have me there
straight after my shifts at Joe's, slow-moving in the mornings, lingering
on the weekends until I have to go to work. He clears me out a drawer
in his dresser, makes me a copy of his key. On Valentine's Day he cooks
me a beautiful dinner, cauliflower steaks and roast carrots and a salad,

bread and cheese from the bougie bakery down the road. Greets me at the door with real champagne. The only nice thing Greg ever cooked me was fancy mac and cheese, and he stopped making that when I started getting fat.

You are too nice to me, I tell Ben, and he laughs like I'm joking. And I don't throw up after, I never throw up at Ben's; it is a safe place, same as Joe's.

The first email from Harvard arrives at the beginning of March, a ping on my phone as I'm standing in the kitchen of my apartment waiting for coffee to brew, and I open it with my hands tingling and my stomach tight. There is a part of me that worries they're rescinding my admission. There is a part of me that hopes they are.

But it's nothing like that; it's just about money. I say *just*; tuition at Harvard Law School is over sixty thousand dollars a year. A stomach-turning number. Not that it's news; Greg and I had long conversations about this, when I was first applying, and later, when I was paying my (also not cheap) deposit. Not that Greg ever would have understood, with his trust fund and his perfect credit. Me with my entry-level job and my forty thousand dollars in student debt already.

I pour myself some coffee and stare down at the message. Harvard has shaved a generous fifteen thousand dollars off of my tuition for next year, for which I am obviously grateful, but I'm standing there in the kitchen doing the math, and it's making me feel sick.

The front door opens and Paula comes in, sweaty and flushed from her run. It's a nice day, all things considered, sky clear, bright sun overhead, but it's still winter in Brooklyn, sidewalks unevenly shoveled and salted, patches of ice when you least expect it. I haven't been running since—what—*December*? No wonder I'm getting fat again.

Paula takes off her earmuffs and pours herself a glass of water from the tap. Asks me what's wrong, and I tell her nothing, nothing is wrong, everything is just peachy. Just an email from Harvard, I say, gesturing with my phone, and she puts her glass down. Ooooh, she says, *fancy*.

They're just asking me for money.

What do they need *your* money for? Aren't they, like, richer than the queen?

I laugh, somewhat despite myself. Not really how it works, I say, and Paula says yeah, obviously she knows. She digs through the stack of mail on the kitchen island, comes up with an envelope addressed to her. You see this? she says. This is Sallie Mae asking me for *my* money.

Once upon a time, there was a little Puerto Rican girl living in Long Island. She was a difficult child, by all accounts, though she had her reasons: bullied at school for her soft body and her tomboyishness, the way children can smell the difference on you. An unpleasant divorce when she was ten, she and her older sister sitting at the top of the stairs listening to their parents fight every other night, crying and clinging to their father's legs when he moved out at last. Dead set on education as the way out, the way forward. Off to college for a practical degree—communications, Paula says, and mimes gagging—graduating with a BA and a mountain of student debt, to which she added, after one miserable year working a nine-to-five, by enrolling at the Culinary Institute of America. Happily ever after.

I love being a chef, she says. I'd love it a lot more if I weren't still paying off my goddamn student loans.

This can't be a surprise, Ben says. Another Saturday in the warm cocoon of his apartment, me up too early, by bartender standards, turning Harvard over and over in my mind.

And it's not, obviously it's not. It's just suddenly real, and I'm not feeling what I should be feeling. None of the joy and relief I felt last year, just the heaviness of the real world pressing down on me.

Just *fear*. I am afraid that this is another misstep. That I will follow this path and I will end up just as miserable as I was in San Francisco or I will end up back in that Arizona desert or I will end up just like my mother. When I was a kid I used to read those Choose Your Own Adventure books with my fingers stuck in the pages so I could flip back if one of my choices led me astray. But you can't do that in real life. You just have to move forward.

And I think about Paula, taking on all that debt only to end up in restaurants forever. What if that's me? What if I come out of this and I just want to keep bartending?

Do you?

But I don't know. What do I want? It has always felt like a stupid question. Irrelevant. Because my own goals have been set from birth, unchangeable as my blood type: a good education, a good job, a nice suburban house, a nice suburban family. I thought, when I was younger, that this is what everybody wanted. I am only now having these assumptions shaken.

I don't know what I want, I say, and Ben rubs the back of his neck, and this irks me. You could at least *pretend* to have a little patience for me. And he looks at me with this expression I know well, a blend of bewilderment and frustration, an echo of my ex-boyfriend here in my new boyfriend. Ben saying, I just don't understand what you could possibly be upset about. Me hearing Greg's voice underneath, asking, *What is wrong with you?*

Imagine us at Vanessa Garfield's twenty-fifth birthday party, a vision in millennial pink, cupcakes and rosé and flavored vodka all courtesy of various sponsorships. The Girlfriends Club and their boyfriends all there, plus a dozen other influencer types I didn't know or care to, everyone taking a thousand photos a minute. Me, not photogenic at the best of times; this, far from the best of times. My dress a size too small for me, my face puffy and breaking out, in this room surrounded by sample-size women. Running into Vanessa Garfield herself in the bathroom, midline, straightening up and sniffing hard and asking if I wanted some.

But I didn't do coke, had never done coke, hated even watching the other Girlfriends do it, my sinuses itching and aching in sympathy. Which of course Vanessa knew. Which of course coked-up Vanessa chose to ignore. Come on, Sam, she said, it's a party. It's my *birthday*. Can't you have fun for once in your life? And then she reached out, grabbed the jiggle of fat on my upper arm with her slender fingers, digging into my skin with her long pink nails. It'll burn this right off, she said. It's a win-win.

So I did the line. I did the line and for the better part of an hour I had a great time, I was bright-eyed and cheerful, I was friends with everyone,

I was in all of the photos, I wasn't eating, I wasn't throwing up. Even in high school all the cool girls had done coke, and I understood why, I finally got the appeal.

But as with everything else, having had a taste, I wanted all of it. After the second line I was talking too fast, I could feel myself doing it but I couldn't stop, and after the third I got mean, and then Greg was man-handling me into a cab, and I wasn't too far gone to understand why, to understand that I was a mess, as always. Imagine Greg and me back in our apartment, him telling me I'd embarrassed him, couldn't I just act like a normal person for one fucking night of my life.

I am trying so hard with you, he said, and I looked at him and I could tell he believed what he was saying, and in retrospect I know why. He thought he was trying. He thought he was being helpful, when he came home after nights out without me full of suggestions like, *what if you ate better, what if you drank less, what if you tried Prozac*. As if those would treat anything more than symptoms. You never used to be like this, he said. What *changed*?

But nothing had changed. That's what he didn't understand. All the bad things in me had always been there, it's just that they were only now coming to the surface. And somehow he was surprised. When he said *You never used to be like this*, what he meant was, *I was under the impression that you were fun and bright and quirky but I did not understand that those traits might have other sides, might have shadows that loom from time to time*. When he asked *What changed*, what he meant was, *I am only just realizing that you are a full human being and not a Zooey Deschanel char-acter come to life*. What he meant was, *This is not the girl I signed up for*.

I fucking hate it here, I said, and two days later we were broken up.

I didn't think I was going to get settled, I say. Another bunch of loans felt worth it when the alternative was losing my mind in San Francisco. But I like my life here. I like Bed-Stuy. I like Joe's. I like *you*.

He kisses me, and I am mollified, for the moment. And then he steps back, looks down at me. You could just stay here, he says, as if it were that simple, and I don't know what to say to that, so I press into him again, loop my fingers through his belt loops, kiss him, feel him hardening against me. Back him into his bedroom and start taking off my clothes.

I don't want you to go, Ben says, after. I'm getting dressed, it's five thirty and I have to go to work, and Ben's sitting there in his bed, pouting up at me.

It's a Saturday night, I say. This is what you get for dating a bartender.

To Boston, he says. I don't want you to go to Boston.

I have to, I say, and he sighs, and he says he knows. Maybe I'll go with you, he says. Maybe it's time to get out of New York.

You love New York, I say, and then he tells me he loves me.

What did you *say*?

Sunday, bright and almost warm, me relaying the conversation to Hayley over the phone as I walk to Joe's. I said it back, I tell her. I don't know. I panicked.

Well, do you?

I think of Ben's face, somber and maybe scared. I think of Greg, the first time he said it, the two of us pressed together in a school-issued twin bed, his suite mates' voices loud through the wall, his voice soft but not hesitant, not uncertain. Always so sure of himself, even then. Which of course for me was a selling point. I remember I cried, and then we both started laughing, and then we had sex, and then, I think, I cried again.

I don't know, I tell her.

Then you don't, she says. Hayley, the Sam Whisperer. You said it to be nice, or because you felt obligated, or whatever, but he meant it. She pauses, considering. He did mean it, right?

I'm pretty sure.

I'm pretty sure, too, she says.

Well, shit.

Maybe your feelings will change, she says, but she doesn't believe that, and neither do I.

I think of *ikigai* again. Is there an equivalent for relationships? If I am safe, and happy, and sexually satisfied, is *love* all that important? How far did love ever get me with Greg? How far did it ever get my parents?

When I say this to my therapist, she looks like she's going to cry.

And I'm thinking of Carver, too, that night in the office, the feeling of his body so briefly against mine when we said good night, the ache when he disappeared into the dark. The text in the morning making sure I was okay. A dangerous crush taking root, I recognize it when I see it. But then, you can be in love and have a crush on someone else. That is a thing that happens. Imagine me in those final months in San Francisco, still so in love with Greg, Greg so clearly tired of me, always tired, and I would exacerbate the problem with everything I did to help: cooking him verdant, nutritious meals he didn't want to eat, initiating sex he didn't want to have.

You need a hobby, he told me once, back late from after-work drinks with people I didn't know, finding me halfway through a bottle of wine in front of the TV, the beautiful salad I'd made soggy on the table, dressing congealing at the bottom of the bowl, avocado going brown.

I have a hobby, I said, gesturing to my guitar in the corner of the living room, and Greg looked at me with his beautiful, knowing brown eyes and said, Sam, when was the last time you even took that out of the case?

I play it all the time, I said, while you're out with all your new friends; but it was a lie and we both knew it.

And so, in lieu of a hobby, my Martini Soul Mate. Slouching into his apartment in the early evening on his night off, avoiding eye contact with his roommate, another bartender, going straight to James's bedroom. The sex was fine, but only ever fine. It was just that I had been yearning for Greg so intensely for so long that it had become corrupted, that yearning—directionless, all-consuming. I could only eat and vomit so much of it away. James was another outlet. And like the bulimia, it never really worked.

I'm half an hour early at Joe's, too antsy to stay in my apartment, my nerves jangling and my stomach full of wolves. I've eaten too much today, gorged myself on a late breakfast of cheesy eggs and fried potatoes with Ben, who can eat like that on a Sunday because he's going to be at the gym all afternoon, who, when I attempt to voice my concern, rolls his eyes and says, You have nothing to worry about, as if being told not to worry has ever helped anyone in the history of human civilization. All of that churning and howling and demanding to be released. But I won't. I'm not going to throw up at *Joe's*.

So I walk in and I tell the wolves to settle down in there and I turn on the heat and the lights and the loudest music I can handle and I get the opening duties done quickly, too quickly, and then I stand behind the bar at a loss. It would be all right if I thought I was going to be busy today, if I thought I would have enough work to do to keep my mind clear and my body quiet, but it's a Sunday, and I know better than to hope for that.

I still have Harry Craddock's book out from the library, my third renewal, me curiously unable to return it—thank god no one else has put it on hold—and I start there, start flipping through and find myself face-to-face with one of my flash card cocktails, the Corpse Reviver #2. A Corpse Reviver, back in those days, was a type of morning-after drink, although I can't imagine drinking one with breakfast, no matter how heavy the hangover. The Corpse Reviver #1 is a brandy concoction that sounds more likely to kill you than wake you up. But the #2 is a classic for a reason, another perfect isomer, gin and Cointreau and Lillet Blanc and lemon. Absinthe rinse, cherry garnish.

So I set the book aside, and I step into the cockpit, and I get to work. Bring me back from the dead, Harry Craddock.

My idea is that I want to make a dark version of it, whiskey or cognac instead of gin, which I know is probably more of a winter drink and I should be thinking about spring, but bear with me. Really the heart of the idea is that I want to trade the Lillet Blanc for Lillet Rouge, a bottle of which is currently languishing in the back of one of the lowboys.

Lillet: a French aromatized fortified wine, in the family of vermouth. Well. Like the cousin of vermouth, vermouth being flavored with wormwood, while Lillet is technically a quinquina, that is, flavored with quinine. Lillet Blanc is a reasonably common cocktail ingredient, shows up in a handful of other classics, in one of Joe's house cocktails. Lillet Rouge is its red wine–based, dark sibling, still delicious, but decidedly less popular.

So, Lillet Rouge. I take the bottle out and set it on the bar, but from there I'm uncertain. I try trading the gin for bourbon, for rye. Swapping

Campari in for the Cointreau. I'm just doing one particularly ill-advised take with grapefruit and Cynar when Olsen walks in and I kind of panic and dump the whole thing out.

What are you working on? he asks, and I tell him. It's a stupid idea, I say. I list off all the things I've tried, going red, thinking about how much product I've wasted, but obviously Olsen doesn't care about that. He reaches over the bar for the Lillet, opens it, takes a sniff. There's your problem, he says, passing it back. This has probably been sitting open in the fridge for months.

A bar lesson: fortified wine goes bad. Not as quickly as regular wine, which is really only good for a couple days, but after a month or two, it will lose its flavor, it will go sour and flat and you'll want to dump it out and start fresh.

Olsen takes a seat, sets his guitar down beside him. I pour him a beer and a shot of whiskey and I dump the Lillet down the sink, but when I go downstairs for more there isn't any, and when I go back up the first of the young parents have arrived, and then there's Joe Himself, and by the time I get back to the drink I've run out of steam. And then Olsen's getting up, off to band practice, and he hesitates for a moment, standing there at the bar, and I wonder if he's going to apologize for that night at Casey's. For the new awkwardness between us since. This would be a first, Olsen saying sorry. I doubt he's ever said *sorry* to a woman in his entire life. But the moment passes. Shot for the road? I ask, and he accepts, and I pour one for Himself, too, a little bourbon from the backbar, stone fruit and butterscotch and that distinctive corn whiskey burn on the finish. Always a pleasure, Olsen says, and I say, Never a chore, and he's gone.

The rule at Joe's is, no one who works here pays for drinks, but it's considered good form to tip. Olsen's left a twenty under his empty beer mug, far too much money. I guess that's as good an apology as any.

Meg and Paula and Gina come in as the sun goes down, take their spaces at the bar, order a mocktail for Meg and spritzes for the other two. *Spritz*:

a mix of sparkling water, sparkling wine, and bitters. From the German *spritzen*: to spray, squirt, splash. Once upon a time in Italy, Austrian soldiers reared on Riesling were struggling to adjust to the taste of the local wines. Even less palatable was the prospect of occupying a country while sober, and so some enterprising soldiers started adding a *spritz* of water to said wine. Water became sparkling water, and wine became *aperitivo bitters*, and sparkling water became a mix of sparkling water and sparkling wine, and the drink became not only popular, but also an intrinsic part of Italian life. Bright, bubbly, and not too alcoholic, it's the perfect aperitif cocktail, consumed prodigiously in its home country, and slowly catching on here.

If you buy a bottle of Aperol, you'll notice there's actually a recipe right there on the label for this most famous spritz. The official specs are two parts Aperol, three parts prosecco, one part seltzer. This is a fine way to do it. An excellent way to do it. But, of course, Carver and Han have taken it upon themselves to make the recipe a little more complicated, cutting the seltzer, adding a splash each of lemon and simple. And so I do that, and the drinks are jewel-toned and delicious, and I would like to be drinking one myself, but I'm not sure how Gina will feel about this, so I pour myself a glass of water instead and lean against the bar to talk.

Meg has been away for the weekend, for a friend's gallery opening out in Massachusetts. I have only ever been to Boston, and then only briefly, years ago, visiting colleges with my father, and I remember the dreariness of winter there—my father careful to take me east at the worst possible time of year, so that I would know what I was getting into, he said, as if a little bit of snow might be enough to keep me in sunny California, as if he had paid any attention to my presence over the past four years, as if he weren't already talking about moving away himself. As if a gray sky would convince me not to go to Harvard.

No, Meg says, not Boston. I've made her a virgin mojito, a *fauxjito*, as Han calls it, mint and sugar and lime and seltzer, my go-to mocktail, fresh and delightful and just complex enough, and Meg takes a sip and she tells me about Northampton, about how quiet it is, about how she might like to live there, many years from now. It's like an Elysium for smart lesbians, she says, and I picture it, a town without men, knowing that such a thing is impossible.

Well you know what they say, I tell her. If you can make it here, you can make it anywhere. And Paula laughs and says, That's absurd, nobody says that anymore. We're all in New York because we can't make it anywhere else.

And then Paula wants another spritz, but something different, less sweet, she says, more bitter; and on a busy night I would just swap the Aperol for Campari and call it a day, but I have plenty of time and anyway I said I was going to invent a drink and so help me god I will do it. I'm thinking about the Negroni Sbagliato, sweet vermouth, Campari, prosecco. I grab the Cynar first, for my bitter, and then I go to the vermouth fridge and pull out a Chinato, a decidedly uncommon bitter style of Italian vermouth. Check it first, to make sure it's still good—lesson learned. Soften it with simple and lemon. Paula's eyeing me like she doesn't trust me, or maybe she's just impatient, or maybe just curious. Less sweet, more bitter. I top it with sparkling wine and I give it a taste and it's weird, but I like it, and I push it toward Paula. If you hate it, I'll drink it, I tell her, and she nods. Yes; if she hates it, she will let me know.

She takes a tentative sip and her whole face brightens. Yeah? I say, and she grins and says, Yeah.

Gina gestures for it. What are your specs? she asks, and I tell her, and she nods. How would it taste with Cointreau instead of simple? she asks, and I make it again. Better, she says, but now it's a little heavy on the citrus. She gets a faraway look on her face and sets down this second attempt next to the first, and then she gets up and she comes behind the bar, to the disorganized mess in the middle that we refer to, optimistically, as our Bitters Library. She fishes for a moment and then lets out a triumphant noise and shoves a small black bottle into my hands.

Okay, she says, returning to the other side of the bar. Cut the lemon, just use those. The bottle in my hand says YUZU BITTERS, and I taste them the way Han taught me, a little dropped on the back of my hand. This could work. I make it one final time and Gina nods. She tastes through the trio again, each different version, and she lifts this latest attempt up. That's the one, she says. Now it's perfect. Paula tries it and agrees, and even Meg takes a sip, savoring it with an exaggerated expression of bliss, and something inside me blooms.

What's it called?

Oh, god, I say, and Gina laughs but doesn't push it. This is really good, Sam, she says. Write down those specs. Make it for Carver.

I feel a smile breaking across my face and I try to suppress it, to play it cool, like, this is nothing special, like, of course it's good, of course I'll make it for Carver, of course my inventions are worthy of praise and menu space. When really I want to dance around and make one of these weird bitter spritzes for every single person who walks into Joe's for the rest of the day.

Joe Himself wants to try it, too, and while this drink is nothing I would ever recommend to him, I'm not exactly going to tell him *no*. So I make another one, set it down in front of him feeling weirdly nervous, watch him lift the glass to his lips with my hands clasped together and the color rising in my cheeks.

Tastes like Coca-Cola, he says, and I'm mortified. You don't have to drink it, I say, reaching out, but he snatches the glass away. I didn't say I didn't *like* it, he says, and he takes a big gulp of it to illustrate his point, and maybe he's just being nice, but it means as much as Gina's approval, somehow. Maybe even more.

SAZERAC

2 ounces rye whiskey
sugar cube
Peychaud's bitters
absinthe
lemon peel

Soak the sugar cube in Peychaud's, muddle in a mixing
glass, add the whiskey. Rinse a chilled rocks glass with
absinthe. Stir the whiskey, sugar, and bitters over ice, and
strain into the prepared glass. Garnish with a lemon twist.

Absinthe: a liquor infused with herbs and spices, with the primary flavor coming from green anise, fennel, and our old friend wormwood. *Absinthe* being the French word for "wormwood." Once upon a time there was a French doctor looking for a way to make his patients consume the stuff, wormwood being known for its restorative properties. Naturally, he distilled liquor with it. If you have been paying any attention whatsoever, you can guess what happened next. From medicine to the favorite drink of France, beloved of aristocrats and bohemians alike, brilliant green and unconscionably strong.

Not actually a hallucinogen, in spite of everything you may have gleaned from repeat viewings of *Moulin Rouge* back in your impressionable teenage years. The truth is that all those bohemians were acting like maniacs on absinthe for the same reason they act like maniacs on gin or tequila or beer or whiskey. Ethanol plus placebo effect.

.   .   .

Though, really, you're not using enough absinthe in the Sazerac for it to matter one way or another. Just a little—a quick *spritz* with an atomizer in the empty glass. The Dans call this *micro-dosing*, and the first time I hear Han say it I think of San Francisco, of the small but statistically significant contingent of Greg's friends and coworkers who took a small drop of LSD with their morning Soylent to open up their minds or whatever. Greg and I tried it once, but the stuff he got was a little too strong and we just found ourselves wandering through the city, holding hands and staring around like tourists, everything rose-tinted and hilarious.

I mention all of this because it's just shy of eleven on Friday night and the bar tide is at an ebb and Olsen's clocking out and Han is working on a baroque, absinthe-heavy twist on the Sazerac, something with gin and sweet vermouth, fragrant and potent and, no doubt, delicious, and I keep an eye on him as I do a round cleaning up the floor, and then I put down my tray and I swallow hard and I say, I've been working on a drink for the menu, too.

I am mildly offended by the open surprise on the Dans' faces. Surprise and, I think, skepticism. I made it for Paula, I say. She liked it.

Go on then, Carver says, and Han yields the bar station and I feel all of them watching me, and it is a great challenge to keep my hands steady and my face blank, it's not a test but it feels like a test and I'm careful with how I hold the jiggers, with my meniscus, with my ice. And they watch and watch and then I hand the drink to Carver, and he tastes it, and he looks past me, considering.

I realize that I'm holding my breath, and I let it go. Okay, so maybe it is a test.

Carver hands the glass to Han, who hands it to Olsen. The drink's half-gone and no one's said anything yet, for a moment it's like no one will ever say anything, for a moment I want to snatch the glass away and dump it out and tell everyone to forget it, it was a stupid idea. Carver beckons to Olsen, takes the cocktail back and drinks again. Looks at me, finally. Those bright gray eyes. I love it, he says.

It's weird, Olsen says, but *good* weird.

We all look to Han, and for the first time in what feels like years, he smiles at me. It's a good drink, Sam, he says, and his approval is like an agave high, like a glass of champagne, like the first taste of the best whiskey on the highest shelf.

But there is no time to linger on it; the door opens, the chefs sweep in, the moment disappears into the second act of our Friday. Negronis and beers and shots of well whiskey. We turn off Carver's college coffeehouse music and put on something with a beat, and Carver complains, but he doesn't really mind, or at any rate, he doesn't stop us. Sometimes you have a night like this, when everyone wants to stay out and talk themselves hoarse and drink themselves silly, when Mikey and Luis are dancing in their seats and Meg and Paula are in unexplained hysterics in the corner, when even Olsen is lingering, laughing, having a good time. Carver and Han cut me at midnight and I take the stool next to Ben, and Han makes me the drink he's been working on, and he leans across the bar, raises his voice to be heard over what has become indisputably a party, and he tells me a story.

Once upon a time in Switzerland, there was a farmer. He was a poor man who lived with his wife and two daughters in a state of isolation and unhappiness, and he did what so many like him have done and turned to drink. He started his days with absinthe in water, his own personal Corpse Reviver and not an enormously uncommon one in those times, and he continued throughout the morning and afternoon with the usual stuff you drink during a workday, you know, wine, cognac, crème de menthe. Came home, told his wife to wax his boots, and they had an argument, no doubt related to his inebriated state, and he did the sort of thing angry men have been doing for centuries and shot her in the head. Shot both his daughters, too, and then shot himself, but didn't manage to die.

An ugly business all-around, and no one could believe that a man had done something like this, and so a scapegoat was sought. They might have worried about the brandy; they certainly might have worried about the gun. But they lit upon the absinthe. Within a decade it was illegal all over. And no man has ever murdered his entire family since.

.   .   .

Pretty dark, Han, I say, and he shrugs. It was illegal in the United States until 2007, he says. We had to make our drinks with *Pernod*.

You love Pernod.

It's the principle of the thing, he says, and I get it. I watch him get back to work, the way he can flit between tasks and conversations so seamlessly, the whole spirit of the night taking residence inside of him like some sort of living Dionysus. I think about *ikigai* again, and how clear it is that Han has found his, the way the chefs brighten and relax around him, the way *Carver* brightens and relaxes around him. Maybe it's the gin, but I'm getting teary-eyed at the bar, overcome with gratitude and affection. If Han is Dionysus, I am a disciple, I will sweep the temple and light the candles and pour the wine.

Okay, yes, *that* was the gin.

If I didn't know better I'd be jealous, Ben says, and I laugh, and I consider it, looking at Han with his lean frame and his unbelievable cheekbones, his laughing eyes and his big smile, and obviously I get the appeal, but that's not what this is about. This isn't the old bartender fetish. I don't want to fuck Han. I want to be his friend, or his sister, or his daughter, or maybe in some way I just want to be *him*.

I am sorry, I tell him, later. Sitting at the bar at last call, after last call, the chefs moving along to Casey's, Ben standing by the POS, trying to convince Carver to take some of his money. Just Meg and me at the bar, and Han wiping down bottles on the other side. I should have been more honest, I say.

Han meets my gaze. I'm willing to concede that I may have slightly overreacted, he says, and Meg tries and fails to swallow her laughter. Han ignores her. Sets down the bottle in his hands and tells me another story.

Once upon a time there was a bright young economics student at a name-brand university. He had grown up not in Palo Alto, but in a town with a similar sensibility, one on the East Coast, near another name-brand university, where his mother taught psych. His father was a businessman, commuting into the city, home only on weekends, and it was understood that the economics student would follow one of these paths, or one similar enough not to raise any eyebrows: if not academia, then publishing or law; if not business, then medicine or engineering.

The econ student did well enough in school not to trouble anybody, but his true passion began to emerge despite himself. One day at an upperclassman's party, one of those painfully earnest college parties that's trying to be classy by eschewing Popov and Kool-Aid for recognizable labels of gin and whiskey, bottles of Schweppes and real fruit juice, the econ student began mixing what could be called, if not quite cocktails, then at least respectable highballs. He did this first out of boredom, not being overly fond of his fellow partygoers, but soon enough found himself mixing drinks for the whole party, to universal praise.

This was before the cocktail renaissance really picked up speed—certainly before it had reached his sleepy collegiate town—and he was on his own to learn about his craft, limited to the mediocre and dusty offerings of the local liquor store, but between his own curiosity and some early-adopting forums on the internet, he learned. By the time he turned twenty-one he was effectively running a bar out of his dorm room. That summer he took a bus into the city and sweet-talked his way into a barbacking job at a name-brand bar, and that fall he didn't go back to school. A year later he was bartending in his own right, and his timing was perfect: when the craft movement really got going, he was ready to catch that wave and ride it in to shore.

But my parents still don't get it, Han says. They'll never get it. My dad sends me job listings all the time, my mom sends me brochures from the university. And my siblings act like I'm this embarrassment, this family joke. The holidays were a nightmare, he says, and Meg nods her vigorous agreement. Doesn't help that he married a Black lady, she says, and Han covers his face with his hands, shakes his head. Yeah, no, they *hated* that.

I'm not fucking stupid, Sam, he says, looking at me again, and I tell him I know. I'm good at this, he says. And I love it. And I'm so much happier than any of those elitist assholes.

I know, I say again, and he reaches over the bar and squeezes my shoulder, and then he pours shots neither of us need, and I knock my

glass against his and then against Meg's shot glass full of water, a solidar-
ity shot, she calls it, and the tequila washes something away, relaxes some
muscle I didn't know I was tensing, and things don't go back to how they
were before, of course they don't, but they're so much better.

And I should call it a night then, and Ben is ready to go, the impatience
radiating off of him, this boy who loves me, oh god, how did this happen?
He wasn't supposed to get attached. I wasn't supposed to get attached.
Don't you want to come home with me? he asks, his voice low, his hand
on the small of my back, and there is a part of me that does, but there is
a louder and bossier part of me that wants to drink all of the liquor on
the planet first. Han and Carver are closing up, but they are not kicking
us out, and Han is finally talking to me, and Meg is still here, and I don't
want to miss whatever might happen here for what I know will happen at
Ben's, which is sex, of course, but also mostly sleep, which is the brother
of death, or the cousin of death, or at any rate not exactly life.

I'll see you tomorrow? I say, and Ben rubs the back of his neck again,
and sighs, and the sober part of me knows I should go, and the self-
preserving part of me is repeating *you love him* over and over like a
mantra, and the drunk part of me lets him go, says that his expression
and the brusqueness of his lips on my cheek are nothing to worry about.

The night is slippery after that. Carver and Han finish closing up, and
they sit down with me and Meg for one more drink, and then Carver's
disappearing, his stupid bus, in spite of our offers of couches to sleep
on, and then Han is locking up Joe's, and Han and Meg are walking me
home, and walking me inside, and putting me to bed, all of it grainy and
unclear in my browned-out memory in my gritty hungover morning. I
text the two of them first, to say thank you and I'm sorry, and Han texts
back a string of emojis that I take to mean, *let he who has never gotten
a little too fucked-up at work and had to be put to bed cast the first stone,*
and Meg texts just a single red heart. And then I text Ben, *I'm sorry, I
was drunk, I should have gone home with you.* And he doesn't text back.

I'm just getting ready to go into work when my phone finally buzzes in
my back pocket. For a moment I'm relieved, and I start telling myself a

story, like, Ben must have slept in, he must have been with his parents, he must have been at the gym, there are so many reasons he might not have answered my text right away, and now he's getting to it, and everything's fine. But it's not Ben. It's Greg.

I feel like I'm having a heart attack. I haven't heard from him in nearly a year; my phone shows text after unanswered text from me to him, frequent at first, though I am surprised and relieved to see that I haven't messaged him since last summer, since Ben, since Joe's. Good job, Sam; you've achieved the bare minimum of self-respect.

Anyway, yes, I feel like I'm having a heart attack, but it's a text about nothing, cold and short and businesslike. *Mail for you,* it says. *Address?*

And before I can answer, a photo: that distinctive crimson *H*, because of course I never thought to change my mailing address for Harvard, and of course they're sending me mail. I make three passes at a reply, agonize over emojis and punctuation marks, and I picture Greg staring down at the three blinking dots, growing increasingly impatient, and I panic, and I call him.

He picks up on the second ring, his voice strange and familiar both, clear and even across all those miles, after all those months. Hey, Sam, he says, and I have to sit down. Arizona treating you well?

I'm back in New York, I tell him. I feel dizzy and sick and turned-on all at once, I feel everything I am supposed to feel for Ben. And I want to scream at him—acting like he has no idea what I've been up to, like he hasn't stalked me on the internet, like he's some mythical good ex, capable of emotional maturity and clean breaks.

But then, maybe he is.

I tell him I'm sorry. About how things ended, I say. I don't get into the gory details, nobody wants that, but I think a blanket apology is in order. Greg says it's okay, it was a long time ago; that he understands, now, that I was going through something bigger than him, something more difficult, something that ultimately required outside help and a dissolution of our relationship.

This, I can tell, is the story he's been telling himself for the past year, the story he has repeated to his friends, that he has had repeated back to him. The story that my fucking around and my time in rehab has solidified—he had nothing to do with what happened, there was nothing he could have done.

But that's not fair. You hurt me, I tell him. Saying this out loud feels like scooping out my own intestines, and the words hang there, and we are both shocked into silence.

It is pathological for you to act like any of this was my fault.

I loved you so much, I say, and it's true, I did, and I still do.

Do you have an address or what?

Don't fucking strain yourself, I say. I tell him to throw everything with my name on it away, that I'll go update my contact info, that it's 2019 and I'm sure I can find everything I need online.

He's quiet again, and I get up, I'm due at Joe's in fifteen minutes and I have to get going, and I'm holding the phone to my ear and neither of us is saying anything, not for a long minute, so long I am almost concerned that I've lost him, that he's hung up. Finally he says my name. I wish you well, he says. And I hope we never see each other again.

Joe's is busy, thank god, and I go through the night on autopilot, watching Fishbowl Sam as if from a distance as she smiles and laughs and works the floor. Han a little worse for wear himself when he comes in at eight, drinking seltzer heavily spiked with gin and bitters, Carver unaffected. I'm done at eleven, take a shot for the road with the Dans and step out. My stomach is finally grumbling, the hungover nausea only just now subsiding enough to consider food, and I go to the bodega on the corner and I get a sandwich and I pick up a pint of ice cream too, because I haven't eaten all day and I'm in an absolutely miserable mood and I deserve some ice cream, and I'm going to go home but I see the sign for Casey's out on the sidewalk, and I go there instead. Sit at the bar and accept a whiskey. Stare down at Ben's name in my phone with no idea what to write.

Casey's bar doesn't serve food, and so she doesn't mind you bringing in your own, as long as you clean up after yourself. And so I take out the sandwich right there at the bar, and when I am done with that I feel almost human again, I feel better for a minute or two, and then my

stomach is churning again, swollen against the waist of my jeans, and I
am disgusted with myself, and Ben still hasn't texted me back, which at
this point is actually a dick move on *his* part, and I open up my messages
with Greg, see that red *H* again, which is supposed to be the solution to
all of my problems, but which, in this moment, makes me feel worse.

The bathroom at Casey's bar is cleaner than you'd expect, even on a
Saturday night, for which I am immensely grateful. Bread is an absolute
nightmare to purge, gets all gummy and clotted in your stomach, but I
have been drinking water steadily all night, which is one of the old bulimia tricks, and it takes me less than five minutes to empty my stomach
out into the toilet, and I feel better. The horrible thing about this is that
in the first moments after, I always feel better.

I flush and I clean up and I walk out and Gina is there, and I try to
surreptitiously inhale, to see if I've left an odor, but the sad fact is I am
all too comfortable with the smell of my insides, and I honestly might
not notice. You okay? she asks, and I don't know how to answer. Paula's at
the bar, she says, and so I still don't go home, I sit with Paula and I have
another whiskey, and I keep checking my phone.

Ben, Gina says. I just don't get the appeal.

Oh, I like Ben, Paula says. He's nice.

Sure, Gina allows. I just think if the first thing you say about someone
is *nice*, you've got a problem.

Spoken like a real bitch, Paula says, and Gina takes this as a compliment.

I just don't feel like there's a ton going on under the surface, Gina
says. And that's why he's always dating these Manic Pixie Dream Girl
types, because otherwise he'd be bored to death.

I hear Han's voice in my head, *a square*. But I don't say anything.

Still, when they are ready to go home I cannot be dissuaded from going
to Ben's instead. Picture me standing out there in front of his family
home like a character in a rom-com, my body full of liquor, the black
plastic bag from the bodega still hanging from my wrist. It's three o'clock
in the morning and all the lights are off, and he doesn't pick up when I

call him, and I turn to go home, and the next thing I know I'm halfway to Clinton Hill, snapping out of a blackout with a rush of adrenaline and cold sweat. My phone is dead in my pocket and I desperately need to pee and I know where I am, more or less, because I've been here on my runs, back when I went for runs, but I am a long way from home.

I walk back, because there is nothing else to be done. Stop a few blocks in to crouch between two parked cars and pee into the gutter like the disgusting animal I am. Keep walking, keep walking. In spite of everything I've heard over the years and in spite of everything Ben's told me about the Bed-Stuy of his childhood, I do not feel unsafe. The people I pass are uninterested in me, quiet couples or half-cut bartenders on their ways home, knots of men smoking pot on their stoops, a few night owls walking their dogs. They are uninterested in me, and yet I feel protected by them. Palo Alto at night was always deserted, frightening in its quietness in a way New York has never been.

I walk and I walk and I walk and when I get home I am halfway to sober and it is halfway to daylight. The ice cream is gloopy and soft in its pint, although it's cold enough outside that it hasn't yet begun to leak. I take a spoon to it there in the kitchen. I don't skimp on my indulgences, have spent seven whole dollars on this melted pint of calories, and it is delicious. The human palate is designed to crave sugar, fat, and salt, and this is what I taste, plus the cool feels nice against the dry heat of the apartment, plus the creamy, thick mouthfeel. Sugar, fat, and salt. We can train ourselves to enjoy bitter flavors, sour flavors, but we are built to survive, which is to say, we are built to gain weight. We are built to store up calories for the lean times.

I don't quite finish the pint, but it's close, and the only reason I don't is that I throw it away before I can, and then I pour dish soap on it, just in case. I have never dug food out of the garbage, but there is a first time for everything.

After that I can breathe a little easier, the danger of the ice cream thoroughly dispatched, and I don't feel sick yet, though I will, and I drink a big glass of water and I sit on the couch for a few minutes, exhausted, and the smoke alarm beeps at me and I get up and I go to the bathroom to erase my most recent indulgence in several rushes of cold sweet bile.

REMEMBER THE MAINE

2 ounces rye whiskey
3/4 ounce sweet vermouth
1/4 ounce Cherry Heering
Absinthe

Stir over ice and strain into an absinthe-rinsed coupe.
Garnish with a cherry.

Are you seriously ghosting me right now?

This is what gets Ben to respond, finally, on Wednesday afternoon, although even then it takes him six hours, and when he does answer, it's some bullshit excuse about being *busy*. No one's that busy, Hayley says, and I'm inclined to agree with her. And so I'm already in a bad mood when I get to his apartment, him fresh home from work and looking, to be fair, exhausted. This softens me, a little, and so I do what I promised myself I wouldn't do, and I apologize again.

I had an interview yesterday, he says.

That's great, I say, and it is. I still feel like you could have texted me.

He sits down on the couch, and I follow him, and we sit there as far apart as two people on a love seat can be, and he looks me in the eye and he says, The job's in Boston.

Oh.

I didn't want to say anything about it until I got the offer, he says.

And did you?

Sam, I can't follow you to Boston if you can't even come home with me when I ask you to.

Jesus, Ben, it was a party.

It was your fucking *work*, he says. There he goes, grabbing the back of his neck again, rubbing at some knot of tension that I have done nothing to ease. My weight on his shoulders, on top of everything else. I'm all in, Sam, he says. What about you?

In one of the branching paths of my life, I say yes. I say yes, and I kiss him, and probably there is some crying and definitely there is some sex, and the rest of my time in Brooklyn is a happy blur and then we're moving into an apartment in Boston, a nice one because the rent there is cheaper, and I start school in the fall and it's hard work but I love it, I've found it, finally, my purpose, my *ikigai*, and Ben proposes just before graduation, and there's a party, his mother and his father and Theo and Shae welcoming me into the family, and we talk about moving back to Brooklyn but we've settled in Massachusetts despite ourselves, and Ben loves his job, and we stay, and we buy a house and we have two adorable children and Ben is the best father, and I am not so bad a mother, all things considered.

And then when I'm thirty-eight, I look around and I say, *This is not my beautiful life*, and I burn it all down.

I'm at my worst this weekend, forever on the verge of tears, short-term memory shot, slow and clumsy like I was when I first started. The Dans are nice about it, a small mercy; everyone knows about me and Ben, and they treat me like something alien and breakable, and I hate it, and I am so grateful. Han offers to take my Sunday shift, and I'm tempted to say yes, but the only thing worse than having to work would be having to be alone with my thoughts.

And so I trudge through cold rain to Joe's on Sunday, and I get the bar set up, and I feel empty, directionless, standing there with my arms by my sides and nothing to do. It's nearly April and we'll be finalizing the spring menu soon, but I can't focus, I look at the books behind the bar and they mean nothing to me, I just keep seeing Ben's face and feeling sick and stupid and cruel.

So I get to cleaning instead. I take to the bar-top itself today, fill Joe's with the diesel stench of brass cleaner, follow the instructions on the back of the bottle to the letter: soap and water, Brasso on, Brasso off. Thinking of that old picture of Gina, Joe's new and gleaming around her. It's hard work, fumes and elbow grease, and I lose myself in it. A relief. I start on the end nearest the door, burnish until my arm hurts, switch arms, burnish some more. Move my careful, steady way across the bar. Sundays start slow, most weeks; we open at three, but it's not uncommon for the bar to stay empty until four, five o'clock. This is annoying, often; having nothing to do makes me sluggish, and it's hard to get myself in gear when guests finally arrive. Today, though, it's ideal, because I can put all my time and energy into this.

On a scale from one to Ozzy Osbourne, Paula says, how high are you right now?

I jump a little; I have been so absorbed that I didn't hear the door. So much for bartender ears. It's the usual trio, Paula and Gina and Meg, peeling off their jackets and approaching the stinking bar-top with understandable caution. Like a Willie Nelson, I say, although I don't feel high at all, and Paula laughs, and I wash my hands, and I put down coasters before I pour them any water.

It's looking good, Gina says. They're sitting in the section I've finished, and she's right. Some Brasso and some serious elbow grease and the muddied gold of the bar has lightened and brightened and begun to shine. She says, I haven't seen it like this in years.

Fuck, marry, kill, Paula says. Willie Nelson, Bruce Springsteen, Bob Dylan.

You're disgusting, Meg says. And obviously I would fuck Bruce Springsteen.

The usual young parents come in then, push their strollers to the back room, order their wine and their gin and tonics and settle in. Teresa arrives just after, with her e-reader, sitting down at the bar and rubbing the bright gleam of it with a finger. I didn't recognize the place, she says, and I smile and resist the urge to tell her to get her greasy fingers off my bar-top.

Kay comes in next, no laptop today, their boyfriend with them, Roy, a lanky, light-skinned Black guy with a shaved head and big, beautiful eyes, the two of them dressed up, waistcoats and ties, it's their anniversary. Seven years, Roy says, like he can't believe his luck, and I pour them the good bubbly on the house, watch them settle in at the window with affection and no small helping of envy. *Seven years*. I can't imagine.

Joe Himself a few minutes after, making a big show of reeling from the fumes. It smells like a gas station in here, he says, taking the seat beside Teresa. I'm almost done, I promise, and I am, just one small patch left to finish, on the end of the bar nearest the glasswasher. Still, he's not wrong. I pour Himself a whiskey and I light some palo santo for the smell, leave it smoking on the back bar, and then before anyone can ask me for anything else I get back to it. I can't explain how satisfying it is, wiping away the green and brown and black, the old spills and the watermarks and the fingerprints. Putting my weight into the work and watching it pay off, the bar-top shining with the light of a small, cool sun.

And then, Monday morning, a rare text from Carver, so early there is a distinct possibility he hasn't been to sleep: *Hey guys, team meeting tomorrow, 2 P.M. Need everyone to be there.* No further information offered, which makes me nervous, and I wonder if this is about the lease, but I tell myself we're just going to be talking about the new menu. I tell myself we're just overdue for a bar meeting. I tell myself not to worry, and then I worry my way through the next twenty-four hours and by the time Tuesday afternoon arrives I am almost zen about the whole thing, I have almost passed through to the other side of fear, where nothing can touch me.

I'm the last to arrive and I sit down next to Han, who is not nervous at all, who is talking at Olsen about the new menu, saying, If I fucking miss rhubarb season again this year I'm going to lose it. Olsen rolling his eyes and saying nothing.

After a couple of minutes Carver comes up from the office, and Gina follows him, and the sight of her heightens my anxiety still further, I am almost dizzy with it, and she sits down on my other side and Carver goes to stand behind the bar, shifting his weight from one foot to another, jaw tight, visibly exhausted. He talks for a minute about how far Joe's has come since he opened it, about how much our help has meant to him. How proud he is of the team, of the drinks, of how much he's learned, of the community that we've built. The way he goes on I guess we all sort of know what's coming, *I know* I know what's coming, and still when he says it I feel like I have lost several organs and probably some bones and all I am is a horrible furious mass of pumping blood.

Our lease is up at the end of the month, he says, and we have decided not to renew.

For a while nobody says anything. We sit at the bar that is an important structural component of each of our lives—a rib maybe, a femur, at worst a spine—with the sunlight coming in around the edges of the curtains, and Carver's words permeate the room like smoke, pungent and inescapable, settling on our skin, into our clothes. We are all carefully not looking at each other. There is a smudge on my bright bar-top, and I rub at it with my fingertip, half listening as Gina says she's sorry, that she's heartbroken, that she wanted so badly to make it work, but she just can't. She says she'll do anything she can to help us find new jobs, and her voice is thick with tears and none of the Dans will make eye contact with her and I am not quite brave enough to do it either, though I reach out and take her hand, hold it tight.

She falls silent, and Han raises his head and says, Shots?

Carver laughs, shocked and mostly humorless, and he's already lining up glasses, and we drink fancy tequila, butter brown and mellow, too nice to shoot but here we are, all of us looking tired, looking lost, looking like abandoned children in a large, bright supermarket, no one coming to claim us.

Carver says he'll announce the news officially that weekend, but that it's no secret; he says he's kept it a secret for as long as he can, he says the secret has been eating him up inside, doing more damage than the alcohol or the sleep deprivation or the greasy food or the loneliness. I mean, it's implied. He says he's hardly slept all week. He chokes, and the boys look away, and I go around the bar and I do the girl's job, I hug him close, I allow him to feel what he needs to feel. I'm sorry, he says into my shoulder, and I dig deep and I make my voice as bright as I can and I say, What, have you been running around inflating real estate in Brooklyn again? And this gets him to spit out another one of those bitter, surprised laughs. It's better than nothing.

I say *the girl's job* but it is really the bartender's job, isn't it? Aren't we conduits for human emotion, less a therapist than a sponge? There to witness a guest's pain, acknowledge it, pull it into ourselves so that they can leave feeling a little lighter?

Carver shakes himself free, sighs, rubs his eyes. Gina stands up and retreats to the office, and Carver goes after her, and I stand there heavy with his sadness, with my own.

Come on, Han says to Olsen and me. Let's go get a drink.

There is a long and glorious history of drinking in a crisis. In one of Han's old books, a once-famous writer named Charles H. Baker waxes nostalgic about drinking cocktails in Havana during the Cuban Revolution, sipping his Remember the Maine (rye, cherry, vermouth, hint of absinthe) as the bombs went off and the bullets flew, drinking in a crisis taken to its logical extreme. Some might say it is the perfect time for a drink, although there is a solid counterargument to be made that you might be better able to handle said crisis if you were sober.

It's not yet three, early for a bar, and so we go to a Mexican restaurant a few blocks over, sit down at a table, order a pitcher of margaritas and a huge plate of chips and salsa and guacamole, and we clink our glasses together grimly and I sit there with my Californian disdain for East Coast Mexican food at war with my innate desire to eat my feelings, and Han and Olsen start bitching about Gina.

What kind of fucking idiot do you have to be to close a place like Joe's? Han says. It's the perfect bar. We have great regulars, a great team, great drinks—I mean, her Williamsburg place is fine, but it's not *Joe's*.

I don't disagree, though I feel a certain loyalty to Gina. Though on the other hand, I've seen her twice in the past week and she didn't say anything about this, just hung out in my apartment like everything was cool.

Could have given us some fucking notice, too, Olsen says, refilling his glass for the third time already.

Oh, come on, Olsen, Han says. You were going to quit anyway.

What about you? he says. Out there sucking Timothy's dick trying to go corporate.

Come on, guys, I say. Everybody's allowed to be sad.

Says the girl going to Harvard, Han says.

But that's not fair. This is not the fucking sadness Olympics, no room on the podium for me, languishing down here in fourth or fifth place. We are all allowed to be upset. I drink the rest of my margarita, and then I get up. I'm going to go check on Carver, I say.

Olsen makes a vulgar, sexual gesture, and Han swats at his hands in a tiny but not unappreciated gesture of condemnation. I am going red as always, I can feel it, I hate the way my body betrays me like this. I try to metabolize my embarrassment into anger. Something you'd like to say to me, Olsen?

Oh, come on, he says, we all know you have a thing for Carver.

Do we? I look at Han. He puts his hands up like, I am not getting involved in whatever is happening here. Olsen says, It's your whole groupie thing. You got the job because of me, you kept it because of him.

He's drunk. I know he's drunk. He's drunk and he's wrong and I'm not a groupie and I don't have a bartender fetish, I don't, I just like this job. The voice in the back of my head asking, *Do you? Is he?*

I tell Olsen to shut up. Carver's my friend, I tell him. I thought you were, too.

Still Olsen's words are ringing in my ears when I walk in, and I feel so nervous around Carver, and so awkward, and I sit next to him at the bar where he is drinking a glass of wine alone, Gina gone off to Williamsburg already. He says, I have to get out of this city.

I feel sick, although maybe that's because all I've had to eat today is tortilla chips and tequila, and I ask him, Get out and go where?

He laughs. Spoken like a true New Yorker. He gets up, gets a second glass, pours me some cabernet sauvignon, savory and heavy, black currant and green pepper and something like smoke. Philly, maybe, he says. Denver. Detroit. Somewhere a bar like this can still afford to exist.

What about Boston? I ask innocently, and he says, Sure, Sam, maybe Boston, but I know he doesn't mean it.

We sip our wine in silence and I do feel like a groupie, and I wonder if that's such a bad thing, this being, after all, not my *ikigai* but only my gap year, and I wonder if it would be so awful if I slept with Carver, especially considering the fact that this is all nearly over and we will all be going our separate ways and I am not naive enough to think that Carver and I are going to stay in touch. Ben comes to mind; I push the thought of him away. Lay my hand on Carver's arm, leave it there. I'm so sad, Carver, I say, and he says, Fucking same, and then the door opens and I withdraw my hand like I've touched a hot stove and it's Han, obviously tipsy, coming back because he's forgotten his wallet.

I go home and I get straight back in bed, lie there in the windowless dark, staring at the ceiling. I knew this was coming, I tell myself. I was ready. But I guess I wasn't.

Sometime late in the day I sit up, I shake myself, and I start to take the flash cards off my wall, all these drinks whose contents I now know, even if I have not yet made all of them, tasted all of them. I pile these cards up, an inch, two, three, four, and when I am done my walls are the clean, bright white of a psych ward. The clean, bright white of my walls in rehab, because I was always so sure it was nearly over, and I never bothered to put anything up.

I go into the kitchen, surprised to find the apartment still light, it's only six. I go to the fridge and pull out a Tupperware container full of pasta, leftovers from the big batch I made last night, three servings probably, well over a thousand calories, and I take this into my cave and I go to work on it, cold, straight from the container. Alternating bites with sips of water.

When I have finished eating I wash the container out and I have another long swallow of water and I'm enormous and sober and sick, not only to my stomach but all over, head to toes, bones to skin. The musicians are going at it, of course they are, a low, escalating *yes* coming from their doorless room, and I retreat into the bathroom and it comes up easy, once, twice, three times, cold water and warm wine and big chunks of pasta—am I a child? Can I not even chew my goddamn food properly?

Again and again until it's just liquid, and then it's dry, and then there's a sensation in my head like a capacitor, that whine and burst, and then nothing.

I'm not out for long, I don't think, although everything that happens after has the ethereal sheen of a dream, my body and mind not quite my own, and certainly not quite in concert. Coming to in the living room, Paula and Gina standing over me, looking terrified. An argument in which I have no voice about the relative merits of different Brooklyn hospitals. The three of us in an Uber, icy silence in the back seat while the driver is blissfully ignorant, bopping along to the radio. Bright lights, nice people in colorful scrubs, the smell of pain and disinfectant. Gina and Paula hovering as I am poked and prodded and assessed: blood pressure and pulse measured, temperature taken, blood drawn.

The whole time I'm trying to tell Gina and Paula that I'm okay, really, I'm fine, and they are not listening to me. I'm not being heroic, or stupid, or dishonest. I don't feel great, obviously, but I do feel okay. My throat is sore and I have a deep throbbing headache and my mouth tastes like something has holed up in it and died, but going to the emergency room feels like overkill to me. I thought you were dead, Paula snaps, and that shuts me up.

Dehydration, for the record. That's what we land on, the doctor and the nurses and me. Low blood pressure, electrolyte imbalance, slight fever, headache. Food poisoning, my doctor posits. She is not much older than me, really, I don't think, and I feel a ridiculous stab of envy, this young brilliant doctor, the shape of her life so well defined, her worth obvious, her vocation clear. Food poisoning, Gina echoes, her eyebrows raised all the way up, but the pretty blond doctor either doesn't register the cynicism or chooses to ignore it.

Yes, I say; that sounds right.

The doctor goes and a nurse replaces her and he plugs a bag full of water into my arm and tells me that I have to stay until the water is all gone, but then most likely I will be good to go. Most likely I will be fine as long as I rest a couple of days and drink Gatorade or coconut water or Pedialyte or whatever. I nod and nod and nod, and then the nurse leaves, and then Hayley appears, and she and Gina and Paula go and talk out of earshot, out of sight, and I lie there alone in my little curtained cell, cold water dripping into my dried-out body, trying to listen in but all I can hear is the mother and son in the cell next to me, her moaning, him comforting her, all in Spanish, and my stupid perfectionist brain is pleased that I remember enough from high school to understand, *me duele, me duele, me duele; estoy aquí, no te preocupes, estoy aquí.*

Hayley returns, alone, and she sits down in the chair next to my bed, and I start crying immediately. She holds my hand, stroking little circles with her thumb, she tells me it's okay, and when I have gathered myself together she stops telling me it's okay and becomes stern. I called your dad, she says. He's flying out first thing tomorrow.

I open my mouth to protest; she raises her hand to stop me. You told me you were better, she says. You told me I didn't have to worry. I will be here for you, but I can't be the only person who's here for you. And I guess that's fair enough. I guess if our roles were reversed, I would call her parents, too.

I didn't say anything to the doctor, Hayley says. I didn't know what they'd do, if they'd move you to the psych ward or whatever, if they'd put you back in rehab.

I don't know either, and I don't want to find out.

I am not sorry that I went to rehab—all evidence to the contrary, I think it did me good—but also, I have no desire to ever go through something like that ever again. The weigh-ins and supervised meals, the bargaining chip of phone and internet privileges, the utter lack of privacy or autonomy. The constant work of it. Sure, I slept a lot, watched way too much TV, spent long afternoons in mute despondence lying in the sun in the garden. Still. We were all there to break ourselves into pieces, to excise the rotten, damaged parts and learn how to be a person again. I am not ready to repeat it. I am still just putting myself back together.

I had a roommate, for a time, who was a repeat visitor; a woman in her forties, an anorexic, skin stretched so tight over her bones she looked breakable. Christina. The staff all knew her, and liked her, and I liked her, too. A lot of the anorexics were flat-out mean to me—as a bulimic, I was either (a) not actually in need of help or (b) hideously fat or (c) both. Christina was sweet, caring, an advocate of wellness, body positivity. A great believer in the system.

 And yet, she kept coming back. I know better, she said, when I asked her about it. I just forget sometimes, out there.

But that's not me. That can't be me.

You're killing yourself with this, Sam, Hayley says, even more quietly. I try to tell her the thing I have told every therapist I have ever met, which is that even when things are at their worst, when the world seems dark and hopeless, even then, I will never, ever kill myself, because I have seen too many times the ugly aftermath, because I could not possibly do this to my father, because I could not possibly do this to Hayley, because unlike those poor sick hopeless children throwing themselves in front of trains back in Palo Alto, I know deeply and incontrovertibly that I can and must go on.

Hayley lets out a sigh, one of those long, heavy ones that seems to hold all the pain and exhaustion in the world. She says, Just because you're doing it slowly doesn't mean you're not doing it.

COSMOPOLITAN

1 1/2 ounces citron vodka
3/4 ounce Cointreau
1 ounce cranberry juice
1/2 ounce lime juice

Shake with ice and strain into a chilled coupe. Garnish with
a twist of orange or lime.

We reach a compromise: Hayley will not have me commit-
ted, and in return, I will stop being a filthy bulimic. That's it; it's that
simple.

I mean, obviously it's not that simple. If I learned anything from
Christina. If I've learned anything in the past year. Still. Hayley doesn't
say anything to the doctor and I am simply kept until I'm pronounced
reasonably hydrated and otherwise more or less okay. Outside it's early
morning, the daylight blinding, and everything in my body hurts, and
I made the mistake of looking in a mirror before we left and I'm self-
conscious, with my sickly pale skin and the pattern of red spots around
my eyes, not as overtly hideous as the bloody eyeball back in San Francisco, but I certainly don't look *well*. But this is New York, and nobody
cares.

Hayley takes me back to her apartment and puts me in her bed and

I'm asleep immediately, and when I wake up it's three and she's still there, she's taken the day off work, and I feel guilty for this, but she waves my protestations aside and she sits down next to me and outlines a plan, a plan that includes outpatient care at a clinic in the city, self-help books, a body-positive yoga studio. A plan that includes meals and very gentle exercise with her, Hayley.

You don't have to do this with me, I say, and she says, You don't have to do it alone.

And then my father and Diane arrive, landing at JFK and staying in one of those fancy-ish but uninspired chain hotels in Midtown. Midtown! A nightmare. I meet them there, sore and tired, my damaged skin barely masked by concealer, my voice scratchy and faint. Hayley comes with me for moral support, and we have a strained, small-talky dinner in the mediocre hotel restaurant—and what an utter waste is a bad meal in New York City, where there is more good food to be had than I will ever in my life be able to get through—and everyone is watching me eat but pretending not to. And then before you can blink, Diane is sweeping Hayley away with her to Times Square, because, she says, she wants a tour guide. Hayley flashes me an apologetic smile, but it's all right. Perhaps it is best to talk to my father alone.

So how can I help? he asks. We are still sitting at our table, drinking coffee, and he sounds as tired as I feel, and he looks older than I remember, he looks like I have aged him. Hairline receding, remaining hair flecked liberally with white, skin just beginning to sag. And I look at him and I think about Hayley's words, *you're killing yourself*, and I wonder if this is what he's thinking, if he sees my mother when he looks at me, and I feel horrible, I am seized by the ridiculous urge to comfort him. This poor old man. It's not his fault all the women in his family turned out to be crazy.

But I'm angry, too. I am reverting, unwillingly, to my resentful, petulant teenage self, only worse, because I am no longer a teenager, and I no longer need my father's concern like I did then. You don't get credit for being a good dad if you only start *after* your kid's all grown up.

I don't need your help, I tell him.

Our server walks over to check on us and wisely backs away. My father says, We came all the way here.

Congratulations, I say; you've cleared the lowest possible bar of being a decent parent.

But I can't keep this going. I am not good at anger. Especially not when my father's sitting there just letting it wash over him. When I could kick him to death right here and he wouldn't lift a finger to stop me. I drink my coffee and I keep quiet, and after an excruciating minute or two, my father asks if I want to come back to Arizona for a while, except he doesn't say Arizona, he says, *home.*

It's not my home, I tell him, and he goes quiet again, and our server refills our water glasses, opens his mouth, thinks better of it. Poor guy. Just the check, I tell him, and he's visibly relieved.

To my father I say, I'm going to be all right.

And he sighs, and he says, What about law school?

What about it?

Are you sure it's a good idea to go now? Do you think you might want to defer another year?

I've thought about this myself—Hayley and I talked about it last night—but I don't tell him that. I can't defer *again*, I say, and this clearly does nothing to convince him, and this annoys me further. Mom would want me to go, I say, and then I regret it immediately. My father says, Would she?

I am surprised by his surprise. Surely we talked about this during the era of college applications. Surely I made clear the vital importance of going to that most name-brand of name-brand schools. Didn't I? That was her dream, I say.

My father picks up his coffee, lifts it up, puts it down again without drinking. He swallows, his Adam's apple bobbing. Your mother was so wholly her own person, he says. The problem was that she thought her own person wasn't good enough. Spent a decade trying to fit a square peg into a round hole, an eccentric artist into a conventional Palo Alto life. She wanted you to fit in better than she did, my father says. Shave down the edges and make yourself round. When really she would have been better off finding a square hole that fit her comfortably.

I'm sorry, he says, raising his cup again. I never had your way with words.

But I do understand him. He wants me to stay a square peg. I'm actually kind of moved.

I go home with Hayley again, sleep in her bed, wake up when she goes to work, fall back asleep, wake up again, and go back into Manhattan. Gina's covering my shifts tonight, tomorrow; she offered to take the whole weekend for me, but with so little time left at Joe's, I didn't want to let her. My father has work to do in the morning, and I have promised to keep Diane company, which I suspect is more about Diane keeping an eye on me, which I guess is fair. And anyway I don't mind, not really; her sheer elation at just being here is a balm for the heaviness of the past week, plus it's spring in New York, everyone beaming and light on their feet under the intoxicating influence of the sunshine. Plus then Diane loves to walk, and we have this in common. We go through Central Park first, cut a large, meandering loop, me still half asleep, and then we stop for coffee and pastries at one of the truly opulent hotels on Lexington, and then the next thing I know we're window shopping our way through Barneys, Bergdorf, Bloomingdale's.

All the classics, Diane says; you know, from *Sex and the City*.

Sex and the City. This is her New York cultural touchstone, and I am both pleased and a little perturbed to learn that we have a love of this most risqué of shows in common. I used to watch it with all my girlfriends when it first came out, she tells me. We were obsessed. They were so sassy, and independent, and glamorous.

All those shoes, I say, and Diane agrees. And those pretty pink drinks, she says.

Cosmos, I say, and she nods. Do you make many of those?

They've gone a little out of fashion, I tell her.

This is something of an understatement. The Cosmopolitan has of late fallen victim to some very gendered and silly denigration. I won't defend the Cosmo all that hard, in large part because of its vodka base, but I will say that it's secretly a pretty good drink, if you make it right, and that people shouldn't be such dicks about it, and that we wouldn't make nearly so much fun of it if, say, James Bond drank it instead of Carrie Bradshaw.

Although the truth is that the origin of the Cosmo *is* gendered and silly, and yet is also a lesson in how you should drink what you want to drink, and how a bartender's job is to help you find what that is. Once upon a time in Miami, a lady bartender noticed a rising trend of women ordering martinis simply because of how they looked in the glass. They didn't seem to like the taste much, left the half-drunk cocktails lying around, a liquid accessory rather than something to be enjoyed. How, the bartender wondered, could I make the martini more palatable? What could I put in that glass that would be pretty but also more to the taste of this particular breed of customer?

Around the same time, a midlevel vodka brand introduced the first of its soon-to-be wildly popular series of flavored vodkas. This one was *citron*: lemon with a hint of lime. Our bartender threw this in a shaker with some lime cordial, a splash of triple sec, and some cranberry juice, mostly for the color. The result was a lovely blush pink and just fruity enough to be accessible. From there, everybody started drinking them.

At Saks Fifth Avenue we finally cave and start trying things on, and I do enjoy myself, despite myself. If this were a movie there would be a montage now, a big middle-aged woman and a skinny young one together in a department store changing room, parading up and down along the stalls in outfits that run the gleeful gamut from absurd to beautiful, all set to something poppy and quasi-feminist. In reality it is quieter and slower and less fun, and my skin looks awful in the dressing room mirror and I keep picking at a zit on my chin, which at the start of our montage is barely visible and at the end is big and red and angry, which is no worse than I deserve. Regardless. We try things on, and in the end Diane insists on buying each of us a dress, in spite of my protestations, that it's too expensive, that I was just trying it on for fun.

It's your daddy's money anyway, she says, like *that's* going to make me feel better, like he has not already spent a fortune on my private college education and my months of rehab, like I have not, in short, cost my father more than enough already.

Oh, but he likes it, Diane says. It brings him joy. We're in the shoe section now, Diane wandering from one display to another. You know, it was hearing your father talk about you that really made me fall for him.

I did not know. I have carefully avoided learning things about the relationship between my father and Diane; I have especially avoided learning about its foundation, which came as I have said already only three years after my mother's death, too soon I thought, plus then I was fifteen at the time, maybe sixteen, and the very idea of my father having a dating life was repulsive.

She says, He used to talk about you all the time in the group, and I ask her what group and she gives me this look and says, The support group.

My dad was in a support group?

My therapist has suggested support groups for me, for my problem, but I have, thus far, declined to go down this road. Whenever she mentions it, I think about the support groups in *Fight Club*, and about the AA meetings I have seen in TV shows, and I would never take those away from the people who need them, but I am not one of those people. I would feel like an imposter. Like the guy in *Fight Club*. And so I'm imagining Diane and my father in some tragic church basement surrounded by gray people with name tags and Styrofoam cups full of weak coffee. It seems impossible.

For people who had lost spouses, Diane says, and I remember with a horrible jolt that, of course, she lost someone, too. I think of her always as a divorcée, but in fact her husband died—a heart attack, if I remember right. Diane is already continuing, she's saying, I won't repeat everything he said, it's private, but you should know he was really there to figure out how to help you. And I was going through a bit of the same thing with my boys, though they're older than you, and then I had the church, which helped an awful lot. Still. Hard enough to lose a parent—there's never a good time for something like that to happen—but right as puberty's hitting? You don't stand a chance.

I stay in Hayley's apartment again, and I tell myself that this is a matter of convenience, while my father is here, the subway ride into Manhattan being much shorter from Williamsburg than from Bed-Stuy, but of course it's not only that. It's Hayley's soothing presence, the knowledge that she will have the fridge stocked for me with vegetables and full-fat yogurt and coconut water, and it's my own reluctance to return to my real life, to have to see Gina and Paula and my apartment and the Dans.

And so it is with some reservation that I return to Bed-Stuy on Saturday, straight from the subway to my shift at Joe's, slipping through the door at six o'clock with those wolves in my stomach again and an awkward, compulsive smile on my lips.

The rule in the service industry is, leave your shit at the door. Emotionally, I mean. You walk in, you become your bartender self, your fishbowl self, and not your self-self. This is not to say you can't be honest; if a favorite regular asks how you are, you are allowed to answer with something besides *fine*; you can, at least in a place like Joe's, have a life and personality that shines through; you can allow, as I have, your self-self and your fishbowl self to blend and merge, but you also have to buck up and put your best personality forward.

And so being back at Joe's it is as if nothing has happened. Here I am on a Friday night like any other Friday night, Han greeting me with a smile and a high five over the bar, me shrugging into my apron and getting to work.

Well, no. It is not as if *nothing* has happened. The word about Joe's has spread quickly, the whole universe knows already, regulars who haven't shown face in months appearing to pay their respects. Grieving. There is something a little horrible about this; a cosmic joke; like, now that you are going out of business, here is the custom that might have prevented this. We're slammed already, the room a loud tangle of regulars and first-timers both, Han and Olsen deep in the weeds when I get there and barely any better when Carver shows up at eight. But still I'm happy to be back.

The Dans give me the early finish, which I tell them is unnecessary, which *is* unnecessary, but which is nevertheless appreciated, because I am still quite some distance away from feeling like myself. It's twelve o'clock and the bar is still full, and I am exhausted and a little light-headed and when the Dans ask me what I want to drink I say I'm just going to head home, and when they offer me a shot for the road I shake my head, and they look at me like I'm insane.

Jesus, Sam, Olsen says. What happened to you?

And I'm mildly offended; the way they're acting it's like I'm some kind of dipsomaniac, although I suppose if we're all honest with ourselves, I have been going pretty hard lately. I repeat the official story—food poisoning, dehydration—and if the Dans have any thoughts about the veracity of this claim, they keep those thoughts to themselves. I'm trying to be responsible, I say, and Meg, listening from the other side of a fauxjito, defends me, tells the Dans to stop bullying me. There's nothing wrong with taking a night off, she says, and Carver shrugs, gives up, but Han pulls a cartoon sad face and says, But how do we tell her we love her if we can't give her whiskey?

I step into the darkness of my apartment with no little apprehension; it's been less than a week since I was last here but it feels like an age. I find the place unchanged, of course; the same messy kitchen, the same chirping smoke detector, the same sad, white-walled shoe box bedroom. The bathroom alone feels different—pristine and smelling of cleaning products and sage, and I feel guilt heavy in my stomach, imagining Paula cleaning up after me, whatever mess I might have, must have, made. I notice, too, that the scale has been removed from its usual place under the sink, and this, in my fragile, tired state, brings me almost to tears.

In the morning Paula and Gina are there, and we sit down together over coffee, and I feel like I'm being interrogated. You scared the shit out of me, Paula says, and Gina nods, and I say I'm sorry, and I am. I can imagine how they must have felt, finding me like that, a toilet bowl full of vomit and me collapsed on top of it, reeking of sweat and bile, pale and unresponsive.

Feeling, I realize with a shock, how my father must have felt, finding my mother with a stomach full of pills slumped in her studio, the phone lying off the hook like perhaps she'd changed her mind and wanted to call for help, like perhaps she'd wanted to call and say goodbye. I imagine Paula lifting me up, searching for a pulse. Calling to Gina for help, the two of them dragging me out to the couch, lifting my legs, checking my breathing, waiting in tense anticipation until I woke up.

Food poisoning, Gina says. And she says it in this knowing tone, not mad but disappointed, and it all comes pouring out of me. I tell them what really happened and I tell them that I thought I had it under control but it's back, it's never gone away, and then I tell them about Palo Alto and Greg and my mother and square pegs and round holes and even I am not entirely sure how all of this fits together, but I know that somehow it is all connected.

They let me talk and talk and then when I peter out, Gina says, Did Carver ever tell you about my coke problem? Which obviously he did not, and I sit there blinking at her, and she and Paula share a look, and Paula gets up to make breakfast, and Gina leans in close and tells me a story.

Once upon a time there was a baby bartender from a small inland town. Showed up in New York the traditional way, with nothing, and took jobs serving and barbacking, but serving and barbacking at places with reputations, with names. She worked six or seven nights a week and knew three different cocktail menus by heart. She lived in a room-share in the East Village and survived on a diet of dollar pizza, tequila, and cocaine. Still, she was good at what she did, and she got promoted, and then poached, and then soon enough she could afford her own bedroom and soon after, her own apartment. She fell in love with a young art student and began cutting down on her work, if not on the substance abuse. And then she entered a competition, a big one, and she won, and so when she was ready to open her own place, finding investors was not difficult. She hired the art student to do the design, and poured tens of thousands of dollars into the work, tens of thousands of dollars and every scrap of herself. She didn't get a full night's sleep for a year, worked unimaginable hours making everything perfect.

After two years, the bar was better than ever and the baby bartender was no longer a baby. Her younger sister came to visit, newly twenty-one, first time in the city, and the bartender took her out, got monumentally drunk with her, and the two stumbled back to the bartender's apartment at five o'clock in the morning, passed out together on the couch. The bartender woke up to someone shaking her roughly and yelling her name, woke up to see her sister crying hysterically, found herself groggy and covered in blood. Just a bloody nose, she told her sister, the apartment's so dry, and she cleaned herself up but her sister still looked horrified, and that horror crept into the bartender's bones, into her blood, into her septum, and two days later she flushed the last of her cocaine down the toilet.

Things fell apart with Carver pretty much right after that, she says. I'd just opened the Williamsburg spot, so I was busy with that, plus I gained a lot of weight once I stopped doing all that cocaine, which is one of those things guys like Carver say they don't care about but absolutely they do.

You still look great, I say, and Gina rolls her eyes at me and says, Yeah, Sam, I fucking know.

She says, I haven't used in years, and it's awesome, and if I so much as think about it for too long I start getting heart palpitations. If I see someone do a line—even on TV—I break out into sweats. It's crazy.

She says, People talk about these problems like you fix them once and they go away forever. But nothing is ever over that easily.

Jesus, thanks a lot, Gina.

I'm not saying it's always going to be as hard as it is right now, she says. I'm saying, you shouldn't feel bad that you're still figuring it out.

She says, I think you should come work with me.

Excuse me? I've just told her everything that is wrong with me, deeply wrong, actively wrong, and she wants to give me a job?

Look, she says, I know you want to go to law school, but I think you have a lot of potential, and I think you should give this a go first.

I don't want to go to law school, I say, and I hear Paula laugh, and Gina is visibly taken aback, and I feel like I should clarify, like no one wants to go to law school, it's a means to an end, a necessary evil even, but instead I let the statement hang in the air between us. Oh, Gina says. Then you should *really* give this a go first.

She says, I think working with me would be good for you. I drink less than the Dans, for one. And I'd make sure you had time to sit down and eat on shift.

Why are you being so nice about all this? I ask, and she says, Because I wish someone had done this for me.

Just think about it, Gina says, and I promise that I will.

· · ·

I have lunch in Manhattan, sit with my father and Diane in a cramped café near Union Square. They'll be leaving tomorrow morning, and they want me to follow them. Not right away, my father says, of course; I've told them about Joe's imminent closure, and he understands that I want to be here for that. But after.

There are solid arguments in his favor, I'll admit. A summer living rent-free would not be the worst thing for me just before I plunge myself deeper into debt at Harvard. But I don't want to leave Brooklyn. I am already dreading my inevitable departure in September. I see no reason to hurry that along.

Let me get through this last week first, I say, and everyone agrees that this is reasonable. And our lunches arrive and they watch me eat, and I take small, even bites and I drink a ton of water, not to make throwing up easier, but because I am still slightly dehydrated from the big purge, and because it's water, and it's good for you. Han's voice in my head, saying, *Hydrate or die, kiddo; hydrate or die.*

My second-to-last Sunday, exactly a week before the end, Carver packing things up and, later in the evening, jumping behind the bar to help out. Han and Meg sitting at the bar from nine o'clock on, guests coming in wave after wave after wave. Every night until we close will be at least this busy, I know, and it's exhausting, and it's perfect. No space in my brain or my body for anything but work. The send-off this place deserves. The afternoon and evening streak past, I couldn't tell you what happens or when, until suddenly it's ten o'clock and the door swings open and it's my father and Diane and I am so surprised I almost drop my tray, and I laugh at myself and I hug them both and I squeeze them in at the bar and pour them waters, and tell Carver to take extra good care of them.

My father and Carver hit it off immediately. Carver's playing his customary dad music, despite my many attempts tonight to get him to play something a little more upbeat—It's my shift, I say, and he says, It's my *bar*—and my father is telling him a story about meeting Tom Waits back in the 1970s, a story I've never heard before, in which my father is working tech or whatever at the campus theater where Tom Waits is performing, and the musician in question sends him, my father, out for a pack of cigarettes, which he, Tom Waits, proceeds to furiously smoke, one after another, standing in the middle of the stage.

You'd think someone could have gotten the guy a fog machine, my father says, and Carver laughs a real laugh, not a fishbowl, worried-about-tips laugh. So that's why his voice sounds like that, he says, and my father says yes.

That can't be true, Han says, which is rich, coming from the bar's resident bullshitter. And really, what does it matter? What does it matter if any of these stories are true or not?

I see my father and Diane off just before midnight, my father decidedly tipsy, hugging me harder than he usually does, a hug I feel in my bones, and then he lets me go and he tells me he's proud of me. Proud of what? I ask him, unable to help myself.

He gestures at the bar. This is great, he says. Your coworkers are great. You're great at what you do. You seem like you're at home here.

I watch them climb into their taxi and then I go back inside, and I look around at Joe's, dark and lovely, the flickering candlelight on the high-tops, the room's reflection in the dark front window, the shelves heavy and shining with bottles. Waxahatchee on the speakers, the steady buzz of conversation, the loud laughter of the chefs at the bar. Han and Carver arguing about something, affectionately. What I realize is, I am at home here. What I realize is, I don't want to leave. Not now, not in September, maybe never.

What I realize is, in all my care not to build my life around a boy, I have built my life around a bar.

LAST WORD

3/4 ounce gin
3/4 ounce green Chartreuse
3/4 ounce maraschino liqueur
3/4 ounce lime juice

Shake with ice and strain into a chilled coupe. Garnish with
a cherry.

Joe's final week of business brings awful, gorgeous weather,
and I go for a long run first thing Monday morning, slow and steady
all the way out to the river, and then I walk along the promenade, light
playing over the water, my music blaring in my headphones. There is a
Ramones song called "It's Not My Place in the 9-to-5 World" and they
were always more Greg's thing than mine but I'm listening to it today
on a loop.

I stare out at the Manhattan skyline, the city's gleaming spires, and I
imagine my mother here. I think she would have liked it. No one would
have looked twice at her hippie dresses or her paint-spattered jeans; no
one would have thought she was weird, because there are so many people in this city who are weirder. I imagine her paintings hanging in some
Brooklyn coffee shop. I imagine her befriending punks in the Village,

hanging out in the legendary Chelsea Hotel, going to poetry readings at St. Mark's. I imagine her happy.

I know that New York City is not perfect. It's a disaster, if we're all honest with ourselves. But it's *open*.

It is a strange, mournful, hectic week. My own troubles all but forgotten, swept away in the great tragedy of Joe's Apothecary. The nights long and wild and sad, two bartenders every night, standing room only. My body aching, my head aching, my heart swollen and painful in my chest, my smiles nevertheless real.

I am most concerned about Joe Himself. He comes in every day now, even more regular than usual, getting drunker than usual, although the blame for that should probably fall on us, his bartenders. *How will he know we love him if we don't give him whiskey?* Sometimes he doesn't bring his book at all, just stares at the backbar and talks—to the Dans and me, but to the other regulars, too. Where will he go come April? Plenty of our regulars will follow Han or Olsen or, depending where he ends up, Carver, or go to Casey's instead, or find some new bar to replace Joe's, but Himself strikes me as much more seriously attached to this particular place. And I understand. We have built a little community in the jungle that is New York City, we have cleared away the poisonous plants and the deadly snakes and spiders, have made a safe haven for a weary adventurer, one where you can have a nice drink (maybe a gin and tonic, to continue the metaphor, with quinine to ward off the malaria), but more importantly one where you can find patience and good conversation, gentleness and quiet, a real community, real affection. Who will look after Himself, after us? I couldn't possibly bear the answer. I just give him as much of my time as I can spare, and I help Han get him as liquored up as we can in good conscience allow, and we send him out into the night with the eternal exchange, Always a pleasure, Never a chore.

I have still not given Gina an answer, and she hasn't asked again, but I feel the pressure nonetheless. I talk to Carver about it on Friday, on our last-ever Friday. What happens is I ask him if he's decided where he's leaving me for, and he says, LA, and I am unable to disguise my horror.

LA? That's absurd. I cannot imagine Carver in Southern California. All that sun and surf and green tea and good tacos and goodwill and, okay, yes, I see the appeal, but no matter how little I liked San Francisco in the end, I am a NorCal girl forever.

Whatever, Boston, he says.

But Boston is feeling a lot less certain, all of a sudden. Gina offered me a job, I tell him.

I thought she might, he says, which surprises me. You should take it, he says, which surprises me more. She's a good bartender. You'd learn a lot from her.

How are you guys so nice to each other? I ask. After everything?

What everything? he asks. It didn't work out. Sometimes I think we weren't ever in love with each other. We were just in love with the bar.

And I wonder if maybe that's all my unexplored feelings for Carver are, too: a natural side effect of my feelings for Joe's. I would like to believe that.

It's a great bar, I say.

He sighs and says, The best.

It's Ben's fault, for the record. This LA nonsense. I run into him on my way into Joe's on Saturday, the two of us making awkward small talk by the door, polite and desperately uncomfortable. My brother's out there, he reminds me. He'll put us up while we figure things out.

Us? But you love Brooklyn.

Brooklyn's great, he says. But I don't think I'm here for the right reasons anymore. I think it's just *easy*. I feel like I'm settling.

Plus I'm sick of these goddamn winters, he says, cracking a heartbreaking smile, and he moves like he's going to hug me but thinks the better of it, touches my shoulder lightly, says he'll see me around.

And I go inside, feeling decidedly off-balance, and as I'm putting my apron on it occurs to me that in a bizarre twist, I might actually be settling for Harvard.

And so I say no. I pull out my phone and I text Gina, yes, I want to work for you. And I should wait for a response, I should wait until I've talked to my therapist or I've talked to my father or I've talked to Hayley, I should at least wait until tomorrow, but I know in my bones what I have to do, and I know that I have to do it now, and I stand there in the prep kitchen and I tell Harvard to release my spot, that they can keep my deposit if they must but I have changed my mind, I will not be attending in the fall, not this year, not ever, *thanks but no thanks*.

This done, I write an email to Greg. I tell him I'm sorry. I tell him I'm grateful—for the parts of our relationship that were good, yes, but perhaps most of all for the bad parts, the parts that ripped me open so that I could put myself back together again. And for Arizona. Without him, I might never have gone. I might have hated myself to death.

I don't send it. I sit there and I read it through again, and I think about Carver and Gina, *I'm not sure we were ever actually in love with each other*. It's not the same; I was in love with Greg, and I am pretty sure that he was in love with me. But maybe that's not enough.

Gina texts me a string of emojis—hearts and smiley faces and champagne. So I guess I have a job.

The final night at Joe's Apothecary begins a blur and ends a blur. The bar packed almost from the moment we open, all regulars, and Carver comping everything, just an outrageous pool of cash tips growing larger and larger in the jar next to the register. Bowls of nuts and olives along the bar, cheese and charcuterie. Bacchanalia. The final days of Rome, the last supper, gorging ourselves as the ship goes down. I'm being dramatic, I know, but I won't apologize. The mood in the room is like this, a distillate of sorrow and gratitude and preemptive nostalgia. It's like a New Orleans jazz funeral, Han says, and I wouldn't know but it sounds right: loud and raucous and determinedly joyous, yet tinged undeniably with loss.

Ben comes in early, greets me with a nod, sits at the bar, only talks to Carver. Timothy visits, his coworkers in tow, and Han has me serve them, watches me shake up daiquiris with an unmistakable expression of pride. Grace the concert pianist has a bottle of champagne that she's sharing with Kay and Roy at one end of the bar; Joe Himself is drinking top-shelf Scotch at the other, no book in sight, Teresa leaning into him in a way that has Han and Carver and me losing our minds. Paula has taken the night off work and she's in at eight and she doesn't move, nursing Negronis, Meg at her side drinking for the first time in months—Fuck it, she says, I'm not pregnant yet—Gina hovering behind them, flitting away now and again to clear glasses, to get us more ice. Even Hayley makes an appearance, looking nervous and out of place but falling in naturally enough with Paula and Meg and Gina, and I think, this could work. This could be my New York family.

We are so busy that it takes us 'til almost nine to realize that Olsen hasn't shown up. This is what we in the industry call a *no-call-no-show*, and it is not an unforgivable offense but it is only barely, rarely forgivable. On the last night? Unthinkable. And Han starts going off about how we should have known this would happen, how we *did* know this would happen, and Carver is trying to be slightly more forgiving, like maybe something came up, it's not like Olsen not to at least call, and I have nothing to say. I go back to the floor with a fresh bottle of water and fill up the glasses and I know with an impossible certainty that I will never see Olsen again.

The remaining Dans and I are drinking Last Words, small ones, split up like Snaiquiris, because Han insists and cannot be dissuaded, not that I would want to. This is another perfect isometric cocktail, as I've come to recognize as my own preference. Elegant simplicity. A cocktail at its best: the ingredients varied and incongruous and blending into something ambrosial. This one invented a century ago in Detroit, still perfect today in Brooklyn, and forever in my life when I taste it I will think of this night. I will be brought back forcibly but not unpleasantly to this place, this time, these people. I will taste it and see Carver's face, hear Han's laugh, close my eyes and imagine Joe's just as it is now, as I am carefully searing it into my memory.

.   .   .

Look at all these people. Where do they go now? Joe's is irreplaceable. It's not without its flaws, like the second well isn't big enough and I always feel like I'm going to kill myself on the stairs down to the office and the liquor storage area is never organized properly and Han is forever leaving the bitters out when he closes and Olsen is always in a goddamn mood and now is not even here, and Carver is, well, Carver. But these are small things, really, and at any rate they are all under the surface. The visible part is smoothly gliding, regal and beautiful and inimitable and heartbreakingly perfect.

Too much thinking, Han says, handing me my share of the latest Last Word. Not enough drinking.

You're a bad influence, I tell him, and he pretends to be shocked and offended.

And at the end of it there are only the three of us, Han, Carver, and me, with the doors locked, all of us drunk and exhausted and crying or close to it or just after it. Carver is pouring champagne, the whole bar stinking of liquor and emotion. It is very, very late, the threat of dawn peeking in around the curtains. Gina is downstairs, has tactfully left us to our grief as she packs leftover alcohol into boxes, whatever we have not pillaged or given away, as she works at emptying the place out for the next guy.

To you, Carver says, raising his glass to each of us in turn. It has truly been an honor.

Love you both, Han says, and Carver surprises me by saying it back, and I am left with no choice but to do the same, and my chest aches with the sense of an ending, the knowledge that this is never to be repeated.

And I will see Han again, I know it. Carver, though, Carver may be lost to me forever. And so this moment, too, I will sear into my memory, the final quiet beauty of the end of Joe's, that brief, bright flash in my life that will color everything to come.

THE DRINKS

Americano

1 1/2 ounces Campari
1 1/2 ounces sweet vermouth
Seltzer

Build in a Collins glass over ice. Top with seltzer and garnish with an orange slice.

Aperol Spritz (Joe's specs)

2 ounces Aperol
1 dash lemon juice
1 dash simple syrup (optional; Han's addition)
Sparkling wine

Build in a wineglass or Collins glass over ice. Top with sparkling wine and garnish with a slice of orange or lemon and an olive.

Aviation

2 ounces gin
3/4 ounce lemon juice
1/2 ounce maraschino liqueur
1/4 ounce crème de violette
1 dash simple syrup (optional)

Shake with ice and strain into a chilled coupe. Garnish with a cherry.

Boulevardier

1 1/4 ounces rye whiskey
1 ounce Campari
1 ounce sweet vermouth

Stir over ice and strain into a rocks glass. Garnish with an orange twist.

Brandy Crusta

2 ounces brandy
1/2 ounce Cointreau
1/2 ounce lemon juice
1 dash simple syrup
1 dash Angostura bitters

Rim the edge of a port glass with sugar. Peel a long strip of lemon and set it inside the glass. Shake the first five ingredients with ice and strain into the prepared glass.

Brooklyn

2 ounces rye whiskey
3/4 ounce dry vermouth
1/4 ounce maraschino liqueur
1/4 ounce Amer Picon

Stir over ice and strain into a chilled coupe. Garnish with a cherry.

Champs-Élysées

2 ounces cognac
1/2 ounce green Chartreuse
3/4 ounce lemon juice
1/4 ounce simple syrup

Shake with ice and strain into a chilled coupe. Garnish with a lemon twist.

Clover Club

1 1/2 ounces gin
1/2 ounce dry vermouth
1/2 ounce lemon juice
1/2 ounce raspberry syrup
1 egg white

Reverse double shake and strain into a coupe. Garnish with a raspberry or paint some bitters across the white frothy top.

Corpse Reviver #1

1 1/2 ounces cognac
3/4 ounce Calvados
3/4 ounce sweet vermouth

Stir over ice and strain into a chilled coupe. Garnish with an orange twist.

Corpse Reviver #2

3/4 ounce gin
3/4 ounce Cointreau
3/4 ounce Lillet Blanc
3/4 ounce lemon juice
Absinthe

Rinse a chilled coupe glass with absinthe. Shake other ingredients with ice, then strain into the prepared coupe. Garnish with a cherry.

Cosmopolitan

1 1/2 ounces citron vodka
3/4 ounce Cointreau
1 ounce cranberry juice
1/2 ounce lime juice

Shake with ice and strain into a chilled coupe. Garnish with a twist of orange or lime.

Daiquiri

2 ounces light rum
1 ounce lime juice
3/4 ounce simple syrup

Shake with ice and strain into a chilled coupe, or into four large shot glasses.

El Diablo

2 ounces tequila
1/2 ounce crème de Mûre
1/2 ounce lime juice
Ginger beer

Build in a Collins glass over ice. Top with ginger beer and garnish with a lime wheel or a blackberry.

French 75

1 ounce gin
3/4 ounce lemon juice
3/4 ounce simple syrup
Sparkling wine

Short shake the first three ingredients with ice. Strain into a champagne flute and top with sparkling wine.

Gibson

2 ounces gin
3/4 ounce blanc vermouth
Onion brine to taste (1/4–1/2 ounce)

Stir over ice and strain into a well-chilled coupe. Garnish with a pickled onion.

Gimlet

1 1/2 ounces overproof gin
3/4 ounce lime juice
3/4 ounce simple syrup

Shake with ice and strain into a chilled coupe. No garnish.

Harvard

2 ounces cognac
3/4 ounce sweet vermouth
2 dashes Angostura bitters

Stir over ice and strain into a chilled coupe. Top with seltzer, if you must, and serve without a garnish.

Hemingway Daiquiri

2 ounces light rum
3/4 ounce maraschino liqueur
1/2 ounce lime juice
1/2 ounce grapefruit juice

Shake or blend with ice and strain into a chilled coupe. Garnish with a cherry.

Last Word

3/4 ounce gin
3/4 ounce green Chartreuse
3/4 ounce maraschino liqueur
3/4 ounce lime juice

Shake with ice and strain into a chilled coupe. Garnish with a cherry.

Manhattan

2 ounces rye whiskey
3/4 ounce sweet vermouth
2 dashes Angostura bitters

Stir over ice and strain into a coupe. Garnish with a cherry or an orange twist.

Margarita

2 ounces tequila
1 ounce lime juice
3/4 ounce Cointreau
1 dash simple syrup

Shake with ice and strain into a chilled coupe, or into a rocks glass over ice. Garnish with a lime slice and an optional salt rim.

Martini

2 ounces gin
3/4 ounce dry vermouth
Optional: olive brine, orange bitters, etc.

Stir over ice and strain into a chilled coupe or a martini glass. Garnish according to preference—generally with olives or a twist of lemon.

Mojito

2 ounces light rum
1 ounce lime juice
3/4 ounce simple syrup
Mint

Very gently muddle a handful of mint with the simple syrup at the bottom of a Collins glass. Add the lime juice and rum and fill with crushed ice, pausing a couple times as you go to stir. Garnish with a sprig of mint.

Negroni (Joe's specs)

1 1/4 ounces gin
1 ounce Campari
1 ounce sweet vermouth

Stir in a mixing glass over ice. Strain into a rocks glass over ice; garnish with an orange twist.

Negroni Sbagliato

1 ounce Campari
1 ounce sweet vermouth
Sparkling wine

Build in a flute (or in a rocks glass over ice, if you prefer). Top with sparkling wine and garnish with an orange peel.

Old-Fashioned

2 1/4 ounces rye whiskey
1 sugar cube
Angostura bitters

Soak the sugar cube in Angostura bitters and muddle it in a mixing glass. Add the whiskey and stir with ice, then strain into a rocks glass over ice and garnish with an orange twist.

Old Pal

1 1/2 ounces rye whiskey
3/4 ounce Campari
3/4 ounce dry vermouth

Stir over ice and strain into a chilled coupe. Garnish with a lemon twist.

Paloma (Joe's specs)

2 ounces tequila (blanco)
1/2 ounce Aperol

1 ounce grapefruit juice
1/4 ounce lime juice
1/4 ounce simple syrup
Seltzer

Build in a Collins glass with ice, top with seltzer, and garnish with a lime wheel.

Piña Colada

2 ounces aged Spanish-style rum
1 1/2 ounce coconut cream (Coco Lopez, traditionally)
1 1/2 ounce pineapple juice

Shake with ice and strain over crushed ice, or blend with ice. Garnish with a pineapple wedge or a sprig of mint, maybe a little umbrella if you have one.

Ramos Gin Fizz

2 ounces gin
1/2 ounce lemon juice
1/2 ounce lime juice
1/2 ounce simple syrup
3 dashes orange flower water
1 ounce heavy cream
1 egg white
Seltzer

Shake everything but the seltzer over ice for as long as you possibly can. Strain and dry shake, strain again into a Collins glass over ice. Top with seltzer.

Red Snapper

2 ounces gin
Tomato juice
Worcestershire sauce
Lemon juice
Hot sauce
Salt

Pepper
Optional: pickle juice, red wine, smoked paprika, lime juice, horseradish, celery salt, etc. etc. etc.

Build to taste in a Collins glass or a large tumbler over ice, or gently toss over ice from one tin to the other and pour into your glass. Garnish with whatever you want. For a Bloody Mary, replace the gin with vodka. This is, as you can see, more of a rough guideline than an actual recipe.

Remember the Maine

2 ounces rye whiskey
3/4 ounce sweet vermouth
1/4 ounce Cherry Heering
Absinthe

Stir over ice and strain into an absinthe-rinsed coupe. Garnish with a cherry.

Sazerac

2 1/4 ounces rye whiskey
1 sugar cube
Peychaud's bitters
Absinthe

Soak the sugar cube in Peychaud's, muddle in a mixing glass, add the whiskey. Rinse a chilled rocks glass with absinthe. Stir the whiskey, sugar, and bitters over ice, and strain into the prepared glass. Garnish with a lemon twist.

Seelbach

1 ounce bourbon
1/2 ounce Cointreau
5 dashes Angostura bitters
5 dashes Peychaud's bitters
Sparkling wine

Build in a champagne flute and top with sparkling wine. Garnish with an orange twist.

Sidecar

2 ounces cognac
3/4 ounce Cointreau
1 ounce lemon juice
1 dash simple syrup

Shake with ice and strain into a chilled coupe (with an optional sugar rim). No garnish.

Southside

2 ounces gin
1 ounce lime juice
3/4 ounce simple syrup
Mint

Shake gin, lime juice, simple syrup, and a generous handful of mint with ice and strain into a chilled coupe. Garnish with a mint leaf.

Tom Collins

2 ounces gin (ideally Old Tom)
1 ounce lemon juice
3/4 ounce simple syrup
Seltzer

Short shake the first three ingredients, then strain into a Collins glass over ice and add seltzer to top. Garnish with a lemon wheel.

Vieux Carré

1 ounce cognac
1 ounce rye whiskey
1 ounce sweet vermouth
1/4 ounce Bénédictine
2 dashes Angostura bitters
2 dashes Peychaud's bitters

Stir over ice and strain into a rocks glass over one large cube. Garnish with an orange peel.

Whiskey Sour

2 ounces whiskey (Scotch, bourbon, rye, Irish whiskey, etc.)
1 ounce lemon juice
3/4 ounce simple syrup
1 egg white
Angostura bitters

Reverse double shake everything but the bitters. Serve up or on the rocks, and paint the top with bitters.

ACKNOWLEDGMENTS

Thank you, first, to my incredible agent, Rebecca Gradinger, for finding me, and for making me write so many drafts. Thank you to my editor, Caroline Bleeke, for your passion and clear, incisive editorial vision. Thank you, Elizabeth Resnick and Sydney Jeon, for helping keep us all organized and for your astute comments on earlier drafts of this project, and to Kelly Karczewski, Megan Lynch, Malati Chavali, Bob Miller, Christopher Smith, Katherine Turro, Keith Hayes, Kelly Gatesman, Donna Noetzel, Jeremy Pink, Vincent Stanley, Shelly Perron, Sara Thwaite, and the rest of the fantastic teams at Fletcher & Co. and Flatiron Books.

Much of the bar mythology in this book is just that—lore and lies handed down by coworkers and friends over the years—but a lot of research went into this book, too. I relied particularly heavily on *Death & Co* by David Kaplan, Alex Day, and Nick Fauchald; *Imbibe!* by David Wondrich; and *Vintage Sprits and Forgotten Cocktails* by Ted Haigh; as well as on classic guides by Charles H. Baker Jr., Harry Craddock, Harry MacElhone, Jerry Thomas, and Trader Vic. Thanks also to *PUNCH* for serving as my go-to online bar encyclopedia.

Enormous love and gratitude to my family: Mom and Dad, for instilling me with a love of reading from such an early age, and Jack and Jean, for those three months I spent on your couch in 2016, and for still hanging out with me after. To all the friends who made my own Palo Alto childhood a happy one, and especially to the crew that went on the pandemic publication journey with me over Zoom—Joanna Bell, Kasper Kimura, Noa Kornbluh, Jasmine Mark, and Sereena Ojakian—I am so lucky to have you.

Thank you to my dear friend and first, harshest, and best reader, Max Suechting. To my cheerleaders Nicole Kanev and Daniel Bamba, for your early and unceasing enthusiasm. To Nadia Pinder, for your support and insight. To everyone in the Brooklyn College MFA program: this novel would not have been possible without the guidance and boundless energy of Joshua Henkin; the enthusiasm and warmth of Madeleine Thien from the very first pages; and the generosity and wisdom of Julie Orringer, Ernesto Mestre, and Ted Thompson. Thank you also to my peers, especially Emily Neuberger, Jill Winsby-Fein, Chelsea Baumgarten, Jivin Misra, Drew Pham, Cherry Lou Sy, and Ricki Schecter; and, of course, Sameet Dhillon, my writing buddy and my rock.

Before I wrote this, I wrote a lot of other stuff of wildly variable quality. Thank you to my teachers at Amherst College: Judy Frank, for taking a chance on me at an awkward, inconvenient time; and Daniel Hall, for teaching me to think like a poet; I don't know how I would have gotten here without the two of you. To my extended Zü family, for your faith. To Rebecca Kim Wells—look at us now! And to Dr. Frederic Roth and Greg Kimura, who loved my writing so early and so strongly: I wish you were here to read this.

Finally, thank you to the coworkers and communities that have made my bartending career so wonderful and given me so many stories to draw from. The Foxglove family, who taught me how to mix drinks, pull pints, and Brasso the hell out of a bar-top; the Joe Taylor crew, who bullied me into creating my first-ever original cocktails; the beautiful people of BKW, for an amazing introduction to life in New York; and everyone at the New York Distilling Company, for giving me my home base. And a big, heartfelt thank you to all the regulars who have taken care of me over the years, especially Lisa Finn, Colyn Lowrey, and Dan LeFranc.

And, of course, thank you to my favorite regular of all, Damien Yambo, for coming with me through all of this; I love you.

ABOUT THE AUTHOR

Wesley Straton is a writer and bartender based in Brooklyn. She writes fiction about found families, alienation, and how where we live shapes who we are. She studied fiction at Brooklyn College, where she received the Himan Brown Creative Writing Award and served as an editor for the *Brooklyn Review*. Her fiction has appeared in *Glimmer Train* and has been short-listed for the Disquiet Literary Prize, and she has written about international bar culture for *Roads & Kingdoms, GQ,* and *Difford's Guide. The Bartender's Cure* is her debut.

Recommend

The Bartender's Cure

for your next book club!

Reading Group Guide available at

flatironbooks.com/reading-group-guides

Additional recipes and bonus content available

at wesleystraton.com/bartenders-guide